THE CROW LORD

Other Books by J. M. Failde

A Krampus Story

For Teen Readers

Where Did the Wind Go?

THE CROW LORD

J. M. FAILDE

B

BOOKLOGIX®

Alpharetta, Georgia

ISBN: 978-1-6653-0780-2 - Paperback
ISBN: 978-1-6653-0781-9 - Hardcover
eISBN: 978-1-6653-0782-6 - eBook

Library of Congress Control Number: 2023918434

⊗This paper meets the requirements of ANSI/NISO Z39.48-1992 (Permanence of Paper)

Illustrations, cover, and layout design by Anto Marr.

092623

To Anto, Brandi, and my mom.
Thank you for always favoring
the blood-sucking hotties.
This spicy tomato juice is for you.

CONTENT WARNING

This book contains dark and mature language, themes, and content that may not be suitable for all readers, including violence, blood, abuse, attempted sexual assault, and explicit sex. Reader discretion is advised.

The Maggot Mansion

The Crow Court

The Viper Morada

The Arachnid Estate

MALVANIA

T he forest was silent, the birds were asleep, and the layer of snow on the ground sat undisturbed, but the peace was quickly broken as Lila ran for her life. She wasn't particularly fast, nor was she athletic. In fact, the girl was rather weak, and her short, narrow legs often collided with one another as she walked. She begged her legs not to fail her now.

For Lila would die if they did.

She could almost feel the claws *woosh* through her long lilac hair, could almost feel the fangs digging deep into her ivory neck. After all, this was just a game to them. They were faster, stronger, and smarter—everything Lila was not. They were the predators, and she was their prey.

The vampires of the Viper Morada, the Reinicks, enjoyed toying with their food, and this was just one of the many games they liked to play with her. It made their meals "interesting" and gave them a thrill. Most nights, the vampire household would just send someone to the small room she shared with her younger brother, Marcus, to take turns drinking from them until they passed out.

Most nights, they quivered when they heard the key click in their lock. Being bitten and sucked to exhaustion was one thing, but what really made them terrified was this — their game of mouse and snake.

"Mousey, Mousey," Hektor cooed. He was the second son of Lord and Lady Reinick of the Viper Morada and thoroughly enjoyed tormenting the girl. "You must run faster if you're hoping to get away." Hektor had the most painful bite. Lila assumed it was because he was so eager to satisfy himself.

He lunged at her, slashing her forearm just as she banked hard to the left, cutting behind a tree.

Not good, Lila thought to herself as fresh blood oozed from her wound. Now they'll really be after her, sent into a frenzy from the scent of her wound. She only had a little farther until . . .

"Don't spoil all the fun," Rebekkah said. She was the youngest of the Reinicks and the only daughter. Lila still had a puncture mark on her cheek from the last time Rebekkah fed on her in a fit of unusual violence. She said it would show the human some "respect for those more beautiful."

But neither of the younger snakes compared to the Horned Viper of the Viper Morada, their oldest brother, Ciro. Ciro was cold, collected, and sadistic, wearing a horned crown on his head. He rarely bothered with her and her brother, but she feared him more than anything. If Lord and Lady Reinick ever passed, he would be the head of the family, and the thought sent violent shivers down her spine.

And right now, she knew he was the biggest threat. He slid in front of her, so close she almost ran into him, before he bore his fangs at her. His normally golden eyes were tinged in red as he tried to grab her.

Before she could blink, Lila's wrist was in his mouth and his fangs were piercing her skin. Her cry echoed between the trees, spurring Ciro on as his eyes shone brighter. He loved hurting her and she could see it in the slightest changes in his otherwise stoic expression.

But Lila, though overall weak, still had more fight in her—which only made her the perfect target for the Reinicks.

Lila thrust her palm out, striking Ciro's nose, causing his bite on her arm to loosen. The moment he let go, she dashed again, begging her feet to keep going. She wouldn't stop now—she couldn't. Not when the unfamiliar looming manor was in view.

Lila knew it was a bad idea the moment it came to her. She knew running from one predator to another may not have been the best option, but right then, that dark manor looked like a haven. She could sneak in, stay the night, and leave by morning. The only problem was the iron scent of the thick, warm ooze dripping from her arm and the heavy breath that raked her body. Of course, there was also the problem of actually *sneaking into* a vampire's lair. But, as the Reinick siblings gained on her, she didn't have time to think of just how stupid she was being. All she could think of was how once she was past the manor's doors, the Reinicks couldn't enter, and she would be safe from their chase.

She just needed to get past the door.

"Lila, where do you think you're going?" Rebekkah cackled.

"We just want a little bite, we won't hurt ya," Hektor teased.

Ciro remained silent.

Almost there, almost! Lila dashed past a tall, iron gate, throwing it open. She thanked the heavens it was unlocked and then realized it probably didn't need to be.

Other vampires couldn't enter without permission and other humans wouldn't be stupid enough to trespass. But Lila knew her shortcomings.

Before her were a number of stone steps. The marble was cool to the touch under Lila's bare, battered feet. She ran up, pulling her torn skirts away so as to not trip in her final moment of escape. The door's magnificent knob was in her reach as a crow squawked overhead.

Please be open, she begged. Her fingers grazed the cool gold of the handle. She thrust all her weight into her feet, ready to leap inside.

"Oh no you don't, pet," Ciro grabbed a fist full of her hair at her scalp, pulling her back toward him. He was grabbing so hard, she could feel his pointed nails digging into her head.

"Let me go!" Lila urged. She squirmed and fought with all her remaining strength. She was so close, she just needed to get through this door. Ciro pulled her to him, her body slamming against his. It was like crashing into stone. He wrapped his corded arm tightly around her waist as she used the little momentum she had to kick the door open. It was only a small gap, but it was right there.

With renewed hope, Lila lashed out again, jerking her body against his, kicking and screaming, but all he did was laugh. She heard the siblings inch up the steps to either side of their older brother. They were like serpents finally ready to constrict their prey. Fangs flashed as Ciro leaned his head down and she felt the icy tip pierce into her.

But he didn't expect Lila to bite back. She ground her teeth on Ciro's hand. Human teeth may not be as sharp as vampire fangs, but what they lacked in piercing power, they made up for in blunt force.

"Fuck," Ciro cursed, loosening his grip once again. She

used the moment of hesitation she had to push off him and spring through the open door.

Lila landed hard in the cold dark room and turned to face her assailants.

Ciro stood tall in the middle, clutching his bruised hand. His eyes were cold, distant. But she could see the sparks of seething fire threatening to ignite her. His tall, lean body was taut, his jaw clenched, knuckles stark white against their normal olive complexion, and his black hair swooped into his eyes as he swiftly turned. Hektor and Rebekkah stood behind him, their disappointment more outright.

"Fuckin' bitch," Hektor spat at Lila. The rage in his expression reminded her of the last time he was like this. She couldn't open her left eye for two weeks.

Hektor had curly dark brown hair and the same golden eyes as his brother. In fact, all the Reinicks did. Shorter and broader than Ciro, Lila imagined he could crush all the bones in her body with a simple squeeze. He dressed in form-fitting clothes, flaunting his muscular physique to the ladies and gentlemen of the house. And he always got what he wanted.

Almost, Lila smirked.

Next to Hektor, Rebekkah glowered at the human girl below her. Though she was also petite, Rebekkah carried herself in such a way as to look down on everyone, making them feel small. Lila always found the daughter of vipers to be unearthly beautiful, with long, dark auburn curls, pale olive skin, and a curvy figure. But her most impressive power lay within her eyes. Her recognizable Reinick-gold orbs glowed with a vibrant, slightly disturbing crimson. Marcus once commented in the vampire's presence that it felt like Rebekkah was always hungry, as the others' eyes only had that hue while feeding. That mistake earned him a lashing.

Rebekkah stood, her face blanched. Lila knew from years of experience that the girl was about to have a tantrum.

"You rat! Get out here, right now!" Her whole face scowled, but Lila didn't move. She didn't have to. Their demands didn't work now that she was in another vampire's manor. She was . . . safe.

And what was better, the night was almost over. The siblings would have to make their way back to their manor before sunup or risk severe damage. The vampires realized this as well, she noticed, as they looked over their shoulders into the changing dawn.

"Don't think that because we can't get to you, you're safe, murine," Hektor said in a sing-song voice as he crouched down to be at eye level with Lila. "If Draven doesn't eat you alive, we'll be back tonight. And then you'll *really* be punished." He smiled, and she could only imagine what they'd do to her.

"If you come with us now, however," Rebekkah cut in, "we'll forgive you. And we won't drink from you for the rest of the week." The vampire's smile was stiff and artificial, teeth gleaming from the dim light of the manor. Lila knew better than to trust them.

"No," and before she could think twice, Lila nudged the door closed with her foot, encasing herself inside.

She finally gasped for air, her breath returning in ragged heaves. Her entire body felt sore as she flopped onto the ground, her chest rising and falling. The cool stone floor felt nice against her hot skin, and she desperately wished to rub her entire body against it. But she knew she was equally as unsafe here as she had been outside. Only now, her monsters were unknown.

6

Lila sat up and turned to face the dim-lit room she was in.

It was enormous. The foyer alone was the grandest thing she had ever seen. The floor reminded Lila of a marble chess board, black and off-white squares that sat under a plush rug of wine and onyx. Oil lamps, turned low now, were lined against the walls, leading to a grander room that split in three directions. On the left and right walls were sets of dark wooden doors, and directly in front of her was a carpeted staircase.

Lila squinted into the darkness and immediately froze. A pair of eyes were watching her. Was this the lord of the manor? She had heard of him in stories and in passing from the Reinicks . . . the Monster of Malvania.

The Crow Court was the closest to the Viper Morada, and the Reinicks seemed to hate him more than any of the other vampire lords. As children, she and Marcus were terrified he would eat them in their sleep.

"What do we have here?" said a voice that could only belong to the eyes. It was . . . softer than she had anticipated, its smooth cadence echoing in the darkness. But Lady Cassandra Reinick had proved to Lila that looks and sounds could be more than deceiving.

"I-I'm sorry for trespassing—" Lila began as the figure stepped out from the shadows. An older man, with gray hair and a matching mustache stepped into view. But it wasn't another vampire lord as she had expected, it was a human. The crow's feet around his eyes smiled at Lila.

"A child?" the man questioned as he neared. Lila was twenty-two and hadn't been a child in years, especially after the life she'd lived. But she didn't correct the man, only watched, still wary. "What are you doing here, at this hour?"

"I-I . . . got lost," Lila lied. "It was dark and cold and this was the only place I had seen for miles."

For a moment, the man just looked at her, his blue eyes unmoving. Then his mustache twitched. "I ask again, girl. What are you doing here at this hour?"

He stepped toward her, and Lila immediately shrunk away, crawling back until she was pressed against the door.

For a moment, all was still. The man didn't move, and Lila didn't breathe. And then, the most melodic voice Lila had ever heard—a voice that made her think of liquid gold and thorns on a flower, a voice that made her toes curl— said, "Now, now, Kazimir. Is that any way to treat our guest?"

2

thump, thump, thump. As he descended the stairs, Lila knew *this* was the lord of the manor. *This* was Ambrose Draven, the vampire Lord of the Crow Court, and he was coming—toward *her.*

Lila had heard a number of rumors about the vampire lord. His reputation painted him as more ruthless than anyone at the Viper Morada. He was a monster, inside and out, with the wings of a bat and claws that reached the floor. Lila felt her heart jolt and her breath grew shallow. She was shaking, knees knocking together, lip quivering.

This was a mistake. I'm such a fool to think it was safer here than with the Vipers! Lila cursed herself.

But . . . as the lord of the manor stepped into the dim light of the room, she realized he was the same kind of monster as the siblings. Not of claws and wings, but of sharp angles and beauty. In fact, Lila quite thought the man before her had to be the most gorgeous thing she had ever seen.

He sauntered into the light and Lila immediately noticed his long, wavy stark-white hair and his dark complexion.

For a moment, she almost thought the Lord of the Crow Court had charcoal-colored skin, but the closer he stepped toward her, she saw he was just a very ashen brown. Lord Draven's black eyes focused on Lila, sending a chill down her spine.

As he approached, his lips gave her a lazy smile. He had a narrow face and eyes as black as the shadows of her room at the Viper Morada.

The rumors of him being a giant beast were true. The vampire towered over her, making her truly feel like nothing but a tiny mouse. He was muscular as well, with shoulders that took up the whole doorway.

He was a hauntingly gorgeous monster.

"What do we have here? A mouse from the Vipers' Den?" As he spoke, she saw two sharp fangs glisten where his lateral incisors should be.

It wasn't till the servant, Kazimir, coughed that Lila realized she should have responded.

"Ye-yes," she squeaked, once again noticing how mouse-like she truly was. "Yes. I apologize for barging into your home, my lord." Lila folded herself forward. She figured it was better to be face to face with the floor than stare into his hypnotic eyes. If one looked deeply into the eyes of a vampire, they could be enthralled to do *whatever* the creature of the night bid of them. It didn't help that something about him reminded her of falling into an endless pit.

She heard . . . well, she heard nothing. Ambrose Draven remained motionless. She felt heat trace along her spine and knew he was staring at her. Waiting for a better response. A vampire's gaze drove some mad with want and desire, but Lila knew better. Lila knew the heat that radiated from a vampire's stare wasn't the heat of lust or passion, but the hunger for a new toy. A trick to ease their prey into ideas of burning passion, when really they were just tightening the noose. She had experienced it a number of times from each of the Viper siblings and quickly learned to run from that heat-filled stare whenever she felt it.

Draven remained silent. Should she confess the truth? Would he throw her out? It didn't really matter, she couldn't stay here, and traveling by day was far safer than traveling at night.

But what if he decided to take her as his own meal? Away from the Reinicks, yes, but perhaps in an even worse kind of hell? What if he didn't even wait till she finished her story, and just drank her dry right there?

Lila stayed close to the floor, feeling the cool air rise off the marble and prickle her face.

"I'm running for my life. I'm from the Viper Morada, I'm one of their . . ." Lila hated referring to herself or Marcus as *murine*, but that's what the Morada called their human blood-bags. "I'm looking for my brother. They said he ran away last night . . . I snuck out to look for him, but they caught me and decided to make a game out of it," she took a deep breath. "I ran here from their manor. I knew that once I got in, they wouldn't be able to enter. After all, a vampire can't go where they are not welcomed."

Lila looked up, hoping to see the slightest amount of pity on his face. She wasn't proud enough to not accept pity. Pity was good.

But there was none in his expression, only amusement.

"So, their little pet got out of her cage and ran all the way here?" the vampire almost hummed. "Those snakes always did like to play with their food." He looked at her now, his eyes raking over her body, till each bit of her skin prickled with heat.

The vampire's eyes rose back to hers, lingering on her hair. Lila knew it was an odd color, not many could say they had lilac hair naturally. In fact, she had never met anyone else with the same as her namesake color.

"Do you know who I am?" he asked, eyes still following the strands of light purple framing her face and cascading over her shoulders and back.

Lila gulped. "Ambrose Draven. Lord of the Crow Court—" She knew there were more titles, titles long forgotten. The last thing she needed was to offend him.

"And what should I call you? Unless you like being called Mouse."

"Lila," she sputtered. "Lila Bran. And my missing brother is Marcus. May I ask, has another human passed through your land?"

Ambrose raised one of his elegant, thick eyebrows and turned toward Kazimir.

"No, madam. I do not believe so. No other new human not already a part of the Crow Court and its surrounding territory has been through here." The older man looked down. Lila didn't see any puncture wounds on his neck. She wondered . . .

Kazimir turned to the vampire. "Shall we get the lady a blanket and some tea? Clearly, she's freezing." Lila almost gasped, for a human to speak so boldly to their master was unheard of in the Viper Morada, they'd have their tongues ripped out on the spot. But Kazimir didn't even flinch, nor did Ambrose. In fact, the vampire nodded.

Tearing his gaze from her, Ambrose turned to the door behind him. "Do as you wish. Clean her wounds. And then"—the vampire lord looked over his shoulder, flashing his pearly white fangs at the girl still on her knees—"toss her back into the viper pit."

3

B ut, sir," Kazimir argued.

Lila's heart dropped. For the briefest moment she allowed herself to believe this stranger—no, this *monster*, she reminded herself—would help her! Why was she always so filled with damned hope?

"Wait! Please, let me stay, just the night. I'll do anything. My blood! I'll become one of your murine."

Without taking a moment to consider it, Ambrose responded, "There is nothing you can offer me that I cannot simply take."

He wasn't wrong.

Ambrose went through one of the doors into another room, closing the door on the conversation as well. Kazimir hesitated a moment before he scurried off, presumably to grab the supplies to bandage her arm. But Lila didn't want to wait around and accept the fate this impertinent vampire forced on her. Against her better judgment, Lila let her frustration and stubbornness rule her.

She stood up, brushed off her skirts, and stalked toward the room Lord Draven disappeared into. She shoved the door open and burst inside. "Would you please allow me to stay until morning?! The sun is almost up. I'll stay in the foyer if I have to. Outside, even!" she begged.

There came no response. Lila thought she had shouted at Ambrose, only to find that she was alone. She glanced around, looking for the Crow Lord.

The room was a small study of sorts. An ornate, dark-wood desk sat in the center, a lush red velvet high-backed chair behind it, and the walls were packed with stocked bookshelves. Under her was a rug so lush, her feet felt better than they had in years just standing on it. Behind the desk and chair was a narrow window.

Lila took a step forward, realizing the window had been open as she felt the cool night air send shivers along her arms. She hadn't fully warmed from her run through the woods moments ago, and already the goose flesh on her skin rose.

Could he have left through here? she wondered. As she stood before the window, trying to imagine the vampire's large shoulders fitting through it, she felt a rush of wind behind her.

Lila quickly turned around, standing face to face with Lord Draven. She yelped as she took in his large form — feet anchored at the ceiling . . . upside down. He stalked closer to her, causing her to step back toward the window.

He studied her then, but there was no heat in his stare as before. Though, she admitted, in this one instance, it would've been appreciated. She was freezing.

"What will you give me?" His voice was like melted gold. Like a whisper in the bedroom. A demand more than a question.

Lila felt her knees buckle.

His gaze roamed everywhere but her eyes, and like a shark hunting prey, Ambrose began to circle her.

The warmth from his stare burned her, and became a welcoming threat, even as it roamed over her body, the curve of her breasts, the low neckline of her dress, the shape of her hips.

When his eyes landed on the bite from Ciro on her arm, Ambrose stopped his movement. She felt his demanding presence behind her, but the air between them was eerily still.

"Anything," she breathed out, attempting to collect herself again. "I just need to find my brother. I can't do that if the Vipers kill me."

Silence.

Lila felt her heart race. *Thump, thump, thump.* She waited for him to say something, anything. She almost turned to face him, but he beat her to it. Once again he was face to face with her, standing upright, and towering over her. His white hair fell around him, reminding her of an angel.

"Five favors. They will all be within your power. But once asked, they must be done. And I want access to the Viper Morada."

Five favors? Lila wanted to believe it was that easy. But making a deal with a devil always had strings attached. "Can't you just *make* me do favors for you?"

"Yes. But it's so much more fun this way. Decide now or I'll just kill you myself." Ambrose stepped closer, grabbing her by the waist and pulling her against him. He tugged her hair to the side, jerking her head to reveal her neck. Lila felt his hard body against her. He was like stone, like the very marble she felt on the foyer floor.

"Five favors," she choked. "Five favors and entrance to the Reinicks's manor."

Ambrose's grip loosened as he pulled away, his hands still possessively holding her body and hair.

"Excellent. I'll retrieve you when you're needed." He smirked down as his grip finally released her hair, traveling down her spine. She stiffened. His fingers were soft, delicate, but his nails were sharp like talons. She knew he could rip her spinal cord from her body with little effort.

As his hand traveled down her back, Lila felt a new tingling sensation on her skin in the wake of his path. She pushed against him on instinct, but it was like fighting a tree trunk.

"What are you doing?" she demanded.

"Marking my property," his finger had reached the halfway point on her back when Lila felt the sudden burn, as though a million tiny needles injected into her skin. She wanted to scream, but before she could, Ambrose spoke. "Thank you for your business, Little Mouse."

It wasn't until the words were whispered that Lila noticed the warmth of the rising sun on her back, the peaks of natural light igniting the room. She had already made it till morning. She was already safe.

So why had she just made a deal with the devil?

"You tricked me," she realized. If she had stalled for just another moment, surely she wouldn't have had to make this bargain at all.

Ambrose pulled his hand from her waist, and the other from her back. "Did I?"

He smirked at her as he took a step farther into the shadows and pushed her out the window as the sun finally rose.

That egocentric, preposterous swine! Lila thought of a whole line of slurs that she could call the wicked vampire, but the wind had been knocked out of her on impact.

She hadn't fallen far, in fact, she fell from a first-floor window, only passing the basement or cellar or dungeon—whatever it was—on the way down. On top of that, she landed on a bed of soft snow. Had he known?

Still, he pushed her from a window, and knocked the wind right out of her! Though truthfully, she hadn't really been breathing since the moment he wrapped his arm around her waist.

Just then, the window she was pushed from slammed shut, and the curtains were drawn tight.

"Urgh!" Lila groaned. She stood up, shook the snow from her tattered gown and hair, and attempted to figure out her next steps.

Before she could decide on anything, she heard what sounded like a heavy door open and close, and a pair of feet scuttle in her direction.

"Miss!" cried Kazimir as he ran to her. "Don't mind the master. He's a bit . . . prickly in the mornings."

"Prickly? Try sadistic, evil, conniving—" Lila scoffed. And to her surprise, Kazimir smiled.

"That is a bit more accurate, yes. Here," he said, handing her the softest coat she had ever touched and a scarf big enough to be a small blanket. "The master—um—*parted with you* before I had the chance to give you these. You must be freezing!"

Lila was the type of person who was never truly freezing. Cold, yes. But she had spent a number of nights without so much as a sheet and been perfectly fine while Marcus nearly got hypothermia a number of times during their time in the dungeons of the Viper Morada.

"Thank you," was all Lila could say as she began to shrug the coat on.

"Ah-ah-ah. Not before I at least clean those wounds." Kazimir gently pushed the thick coat from her shoulders and raised her arm with Ciro's bite. It had turned a nasty shade of red in the short time since and Kazimir immediately began to dab it with a stinging solution he brought outside with him.

Lila squeezed her eyes shut but didn't jerk away. All her life of living with vampires taught her to never flinch. It only made it more fun for them, and more painful for her.

"Pardon me if this is nosy, but . . . Are you not one of Lord Draven's murine?" Lila was curious, but mostly trying to distract herself from the pain.

Kazimir laughed. "Dear lords, no. Believe it or not, the master doesn't own any murine. Human servants, yes. But they're all paid, and most don't reside in the manor like myself."

A vampire who doesn't own murine?

"Don't be too shocked," Kazimir said, reading the expression on Lila's face. "The master just doesn't see humans as . . . vermin—like the vipers do."

Lila thought of what it would be like to live somewhere where she wasn't treated like a toy or someone's next meal. To be treated like a *person*. She was a bit jealous of Kazimir at that moment.

"Do you know which way the nearest town is?" she asked, reminding herself why she was out here—to find Marcus. She still couldn't believe he had left her behind. Part of her hoped he got so far away, the Vipers wouldn't be able to find him, even if that meant she'd never find him either.

"Just through there," he said, pointing toward the trees that encompassed the large manor. Lila knew she was only seeing a portion of it, the front door, a front room, and the grounds before it. *He probably even has a rose garden. That's why he's such a prick.*

She assumed her brother needed to travel through at least a bit of Draven's land to run from the Reinicks.

Lila looked back at Kazimir. "Thank you for your hospitality." She shrugged on the coat. Kazimir hesitated before giving her a sad smile and let her walk away.

"Be careful," he called. "I would not wish to see you back here with fresh wounds like these again."

Lila walked through the forest. The light layer of snow from the night before was already melting under the warm Fall sun. She wasn't exactly cold, but Lila knew her body wouldn't be able to take a full day and night of this. She hoped she'd find at least a trace of Marcus before nightfall.

As she walked, she considered her next steps, after finding her brother. They would have nothing, nowhere to go. No money, no food, and definitely no help.

Their parents had passed away when she was still young, her mother in childbirth with Marcus, and her father just a few years later. The people from her village told her it was an accident, but Lila always knew her father had died the moment their mother did, and that he only stuck around long enough to make sure Marcus and her would survive. She didn't blame him. She didn't blame either of them. That was just life. You live, you love, you die. If anything, Lila thought it was romantic.

She trudged through the trees, feeling her stomach rumble and growl. Lila had grown accustomed to the feeling from her time in the Vipers' den. She could live with it—even though she would do anything for just a bite of cheese.

Lila could already smell the neighboring town and hear the bustle of people. The towns in the Vipers' land were far starker. Small villages were just trying to survive, as their inhabitants waited to become the next murine. They cooked and provided for themselves until they were needed, at which time they would be taken to the Vampire Morada to "donate" themselves.

Unlike Lila and Marcus, most murine were used for a week at a time before being sent back home. They were summoned back once a year to serve as the main food supply for the hungry vampires. Sometimes, they weren't summoned at all, but caught during a hunt through the city—those murine often didn't make it back. Lila assumed this was how most of the manors operated. A select amount of in-house murine—usually their favorites based on taste, looks, or anything else that piqued their interest—and the rest in rotation all came from the wide region of the Viper Morada the vampires reigned over, especially the villages closer to the manor itself.

However, upon approaching this town, she wondered if the Crow Court operated in the same way, or if any of the others did as well. Growing up confined in the Viper Morada didn't allow her to learn much about the other manors. All she knew of them were from the stories she'd been told.

But she was quickly learning that stories weren't fact as she gaped at the town before her. The entire town's disposition was drastically different from anything she'd heard of the Crow Court territory. Lila saw children running and playing, women huddled together gossiping, men working with one another. And all around she saw *life*. Smiling faces, warm embraces . . . and heaps of gloriously smelling food.

This wasn't like the villages nearest the Vipers' den at all. This was . . . pleasant. Lila *wished* she could call a place like this home. She saw no fear in the eyes of the villagers, and they all had meat on their bones—they weren't starved like the people of the Viper Morada.

Lila's eyes grew wide as she drank it all in.

This is what her life had been missing. This is what she craved more than anything.

As she heard the children shriek with laughter, the sun clear and bright, Lila felt a spark ignite in her chest. She didn't even know what to call it, peace? Joy? It didn't matter, she wanted *this*.

Lila stepped forward, breaking the barrier between living a life with no other purpose than to survive and now finding something to fight for. She walked into the town.

Lila wondered if this was an average morning here. Bakers were baking, butchers were butchering, shop owners were selling, and people everywhere were mixed in the hustle and bustle of everyday life. The houses and shops were quaint as they all stood atop each other on the cobblestone path. Lila realized it should have looked over-crowded to her, but all she felt was the odd feeling of familiarity. Not that she was familiar with this town, but everyone seemed like family to one another. She watched as people on the streets helped each other carry large items up sets of stairs, shop owners slid extra items into shoppers' bags, and all-in-all comradery.

She was overwhelmed.

She was out of place.

With her tattered dress, violet-hued hair, and definitely worse-for-wear appearance, Lila felt like she didn't belong. She was sure at any moment someone would point at her and scream "Trespasser!" before escorting her out of the village.

But no one really seemed to notice her.

She walked up to a stall filled with fresh fruit and vege-tables. The scent of bright apples, vibrant oranges, and crisp lettuce wafted toward her, reminding her, yet again, how hungry she was. Behind the stall was a portly woman, with dark brown hair and matching wide eyes. Her cheeks were rosy and warm. The woman reminded Lila of a sweet peach in the spring.

"Excuse me?" Lila called, trying to get the woman's attention.

"Oh, hello. I haven't seen you 'round here. What inter-esting hair, it's such a gorgeous color."

Lila's cheeks turned pink. "Ah, thank you! By any chance, have you seen a young boy pass through here within the last few days? He has brown hair and eyes, is skinny as a stick, and probably looks like a right mess."

"Dearie, you just described half the boys in this village. Is there anything else of note about him?" The woman raised her eyebrow.

"He's my brother, Marcus. He went missing about two nights ago. He's just fourteen, and still truly hasn't had his growth spurt so he's rather small, and . . ." she hesitated.

"And what?"

"And he probably has a few bite marks along his neck and arms."

"Vampire bites?" The woman took the smallest step back, barely noticeable, as her eyes grew wider.

Lila nodded.

"Well, I haven't seen anyone like that around," she seemed to consider her next words. "Where are you from? Surely, the vampire who bit your brother wasn't Lord Draven?"

"No, no. It was the Reinicks."

Immediately, the woman cringed. "And . . . that is where you're from? One of their villages?"

"N—" Lila had the sudden thought, *Don't say you're the Vipers' murine.* "Yes. That's where we're from."

"How on earth did you make it here?"

"I ran."

The woman's jaw fell. "And your brother?"

"I suppose he ran as well." *What an odd question,* Lila thought. How else would she have made it to the Crow Court?

"And you're sure he ran away? I hear those Vipers steal women and children from their beds all the time. Are you sure he wasn't taken?" The woman looked concerned, for Lila or her brother or both, she didn't know.

"I'm sure." At least, Lila hoped she was. Why would they kidnap him when he was already in their manor? They'd been summoned all over the castle, at all times of the night, to be available whenever the Vipers wanted. They were like the glass of water always available on a bedside table. There was no reason to kidnap him. No, no. Surely he ran away. He made it out. Lila just wanted to know he was safe.

"Well, I haven't seen him. I'm sorry, dear. Have you tried going to Lord Draven's manor? They could probably help you better than anyone here."

Lila sighed. "I did but thank you." She wandered away from the shop owner, asking a handful of others but everyone seemed to have the same reaction.

"Haven't seen him."

"You're from the Viper Morada?"

"Have you seen Lord Draven about this?"

And so on, and so on. She got the impression that the people here actually liked the vampire prick. That they looked up to him rather than feared him.

She wandered the town until early afternoon when exhaustion was finally setting in. She had not slept much the day before, and after the night she had, her body felt the need for rest. Lila sat on a wooden bench in the middle of the town square. Kids were laughing as moms called to them. The sun was so warm, bathing her in warmth she hadn't felt in what seemed like years. She had been stuck inside the walls of the Viper Morada, abiding by their schedule rather than that of a human. She slept during the day and woke at nightfall.

Lila closed her eyes, just for a moment—the sounds were like a melody. Laughter and love, mixed with the blanket of the sunlight, it was all . . . so . . . peaceful . . .

A scream startled Lila awake. The mothers were grabbing their crying children and running into the nearest buildings. Screaming, wailing, and darkness consumed her.

That was when Lila noticed the once-sunny day was now dark. The wind picked up, blowing harshly through the lanes of shops and villagers. It looked as though it was about to storm so roughly, it would swallow the village whole.

Dusk had come.

Lila heard a shriek of laughter, but as she turned to find the source, she realized it wasn't from the children as it had been before. The shrieks of laughter were coming from the skies.

The vipers had found her.

L ila pushed herself up from the bench, darting into the madness. The screeches of the vampires, the thunderous sound of their flapping wings, she realized these were sounds this lovely town had probably seldom heard. Lila dashed between stalls and vendors as people shoved her, desperately running and hiding. But Lila had nowhere to go.

And the worst part, she knew this was her fault. She had ruined the beautiful peace of this town all because she wandered in. She wanted to preserve this place, the peace she felt.

She dashed toward the forest she came from. If she could just make it out of the village, surely the Vipers would follow her and leave the innocent people be.

But she didn't make it.

As soon as she turned the corner around a jewelry vendor, a monstrous creature landed before her. Ciro now stood about seven feet tall, his skin had faded from the warm brown to an ashy white. His body was corded with muscles and fleshy wings, like that of a bat, sprouted from his back. His dark hair had grown over his face, pushed back behind long pointed ears. His teeth and nails also elongated, sharpening into fine points, and his eyes were an illuminated vibrant yellow. This grotesque figure was that of a vampire in its true form.

Before she could react, Lila heard two more sets of wings flap behind her as massive figures landed. Hektor was slightly smaller than his brother, but bulkier, like his humanoid form. Rebekkah, on the other hand, was even more slender than she normally was, and her deep burgundy hair fell across her pale shoulders, reminding Lila of blood on the snowy ground.

"Found you, pet," Hektor snickered. "And here, of all places? I'm betting Ambrose took one whiff of you and threw you out, didn't he? He has a much more . . . refined taste than yours truly." Hektor smiled a fangy grin. "You know I like my food a little dirty." He took a threatening step forward and Lila instinctively backed up, right into Ciro.

He threw his arms around her, nearly crushing her ribs as he pulled her against him. For a moment, she couldn't breathe.

"Let's go home, we've been here long enough." Ciro's voice was gruff, and she feared what he might do once they did arrive "home."

And Marcus . . .

"You weren't even going to say hello to the lord of this land before so rudely leaving?" The voice like liquid gold interrupted her panicked thoughts.

Ambrose smoothly landed atop the jewelry vendor's stall, the owner long since gone—as were most of the people in the village. Lila saw glimpses of limbs and heard the hushed sound of voices. They were hiding and based on the glares from the Reinicks toward the arrival of the Crow

Lord, Lila hoped this meant the village people would be safe.

She wouldn't be able to live with herself if anyone was harmed because of her.

"What are you doing here?" Ambrose demanded. He stood up on powerful legs, towering over them. Like the Vipers, Ambrose was also in his full-vampire form, his dark skin now a charcoal gray, illuminating his red eyes under his thick, white mane that fell well past his shoulders. Lila couldn't tell if it was because he already stood atop a wooden hut, but she felt like he towered over them, even Ciro. Ambrose was bigger, broader, and scarier. His claws were sharper, his teeth longer, his wings wider. She had the strange sensation he was . . . ancient—at least compared to the Viper siblings.

"A-Ambrose Draven," Rebekkah stuttered. "We're sorry for—"

"I ask again," the vampire lord cut off, his bloodthirsty gaze bore directly at Ciro. "What made you think you were allowed on my land?"

Lila saw Ciro's jaw work above her, but it was Hektor who spoke up. "There was a human at your border. We . . . *convinced* him to tell us where the nearest town was, as we assumed you would've had enough of our murine and thrown her out."

Convinced was a kind word for what he probably did to that man.

Anger flashed across Ambrose's face. "You *enthralled* one of *my* people?"

The vampire lord jumped down to the ground between the siblings. Lila had been right; he was larger than the rest of them. Intimidatingly so. He could hold her entire head in the grip of his hand if he tried, his palms alone were larger than her face.

Ciro's arms were still wrapped around Lila, if not, she felt like her feet would've run of their own accord, deep into the forest. As it was, she felt her knees knock together in fear. She had run right into this *monster's* den, not knowing any better . . . the Monster of Malvania. He could've killed her so easily. And she made a bargain with him.

How could she be so stupid?

Ambrose took a step forward, any closer and she would have become squished in a bat-sandwich as Ciro and Ambrose stared each other down as if in a war of wills.

Ciro lost.

He turned his gaze down. "I'm sorry, Draven. We shouldn't have. We only came to collect what is ours." His grip tightened on Lila's arms, causing her to squirm as her feet now dangled above the ground.

She felt Ambrose's hot gaze fall on her, and she felt herself shrink back, though she wanted to scowl.

"This Little Mouse seems to get into all sorts of trouble, doesn't she?" He placed one long, sharpened claw under Lila's chin, immediately causing Ciro to stiffen. Her gaze met his for the first time since he arrived in this form. Two blood-red rubies stared at her, searching her features.

Are you all right?

Lila jolted at the sudden voice like velvet. It sounded like the vampire Lord of Crows was speaking . . . in her mind.

"What?" she whispered.

Our bargain—it struck a connection. There is a mind link between us now, a Concord. We can speak freely without listening ears. Now answer, are you all right?

Shocked and confused, Lila thought through the Concord, *Yes. I think so. Please don't make me go back with them.*

Ambrose clenched his jaw and removed his finger from her chin—his nail softly grazing her skin—and looked back at Ciro. That was the only warning she got.

"Then take her and leave. I will not have you disturb my people again. They are not rats available for slaughter like this one."

Lila's mind was reeling. For the briefest moment, she hoped someone would actually be compassionate enough to save her. She hoped she'd be *safe*, that she wouldn't have to go back with the Vipers.

But all hope was yet again lost.

"Of course, thank you," Ciro gritted out, slightly bowing his head.

"Until next time, Draven," Rebekkah croaked.

Hektor snickered and reached to grab Lila's arm when Ambrose caught his wrist.

"Oh, I almost forgot. This Little Mouse and I have struck a bargain. You *will* respect this, of course. When I come for her, you will hand her over, no questions asked." His eyes bore into Hektor now, as the young vampire scowled.

"Why should we? She's our property."

"Not anymore. If memory serves me correctly, since she made it into *my* manor last night, she actually belongs to me. The mark on her back proves so."

After a moment's hesitation, Hektor ripped Lila from Ciro's grasp and pulled the coat from her shoulders, revealing the mysterious mark along Lila's spine and shoulder blades. This must've been the mark she felt him leave on her when they struck their bargain.

He had claimed her.

"Fuckin—" Hektor swore. Rebekkah blanched. But Ciro's eyes were a fathomless pit of hate.

"You know the laws of bargains, Reinick. She breaks it,

she dies. And, for some reason, I have a hard time believing you'd be okay with that. So, I will give her to you now in exchange for leaving my territory and never returning. I don't know why a *murine* would be worth this much to you, but these are my terms."

Lila noticed how emphatically he used the term murine as if it were a nasty taste on his tongue. His words stung, but she felt even more spiteful he was just throwing her away again.

Lila felt the bloodlust emanating from her captors. They were furious. Humiliated. They *lost*. But Lila had the sinking suspicion that even three-on-one, they wouldn't win against Ambrose.

"This will be the final time I repeat myself. *Get off of my fucking land.*" Ambrose's wings flared open, and together they were larger than the width of the stall and the one next to it.

Hektor tensed. Lila knew he wanted to fight back. It was his way of trying to show he was the alpha male in a situation—even though he very evidently was not, and everyone knew it.

"Of course," Ciro spoke, his voice curt. Before Lila could take a breath, the vampire launched into the sky, with her in his grip, Rebekkah and Hektor right behind them.

Lila caught Ambrose's eyes one final time and almost thought she heard, *I'm Sorry*, in her mind through the rush of wind and flaps of wings.

6

All Lila could hear beyond the wind sailing past them was Hektor's incessant cackle. Even Rebekkah seemed to know to shut up when it was good for her. And Ciro was as stiff as a board behind Lila. She could feel how, even though he held her, he kept distance between their bodies, as though he didn't want to touch her by any means. She knew it had to do with the mark the Crow Lord had left on her.

Good.

Lila could still feel the mark on her back pulsing—not in pain, but almost as if it was reminding her it was there, like a heartbeat or a pulse. Even though she was high in the air, the mark made her feel grounded, reminded her that *eventually*, Ambrose would come for her, even if he took her for just a bit, even if being under his care was worse. At least it would be a break. And from what Lila could tell, Ambrose didn't treat the humans on his land like the vipers' treated their murine. The town was too cheerful and Kazimir was too kind. No one with that much warmth could be found in the Viper Morada—no one but

Lila and Marcus, and even what little light they had left was being stomped away.

She hoped her brother would be happy now. Hoped he got as far away from here as possible, hoped he would just forget his first fourteen years and start new. Even if that meant forgetting her. At least then he'd have a chance.

"I claim the first bite when we return home," Hektor cooed.

Once again, Ciro stiffened behind her. "No." His voice was flat, plain.

Hektor grimaced and tried to argue, "But I—" Before he could continue his protest, Ciro stopped in midair.

Lila glanced around, afraid he would suddenly unclasp his arms and let her fall the rest of the way till she *splat* on the ground and became nothing more than a puddle.

But what he did was worse.

He held her closer.

And then he dug his teeth deep into her neck.

Rebekkah's mouth fell open, and Hektor growled territorially. They all got like this when they feasted near each other. Like animals fighting for scraps.

Lila heard herself scream before she felt her throat constrict as she squirmed in Ciro's grip. She now preferred the *splat* ending the ground would've granted her over this. She squeezed her eyes shut, hoping he would just let go.

His fangs were massive in this form, biting into her neck and shoulder. As he bit deeper, his tongue roamed across her skin, licking every drop it could get. His arms squeezed tighter as his claws punctured into the flesh on her arms, drawing small droplets of blood.

Lila heard each lick and swallow as he drank from her. She felt the fight leaving her body as the blood drained from her veins and the animalistic hunger in the other two

Reinicks only grew more and more feverish. They would keep their distance unless allowed if they knew what was good for them.

Ciro was territorial and right now *she* was his territory.

Just before his bite became hard enough to snap bone, Ciro released his grip on her shoulder. Her blood coated his mouth and ran down his bat-like muzzle.

Lila felt her head swimming and knew Ciro had taken too much, too quickly. She would pass out and be left totally vulnerable once they returned to the Viper Morada. She wouldn't be able to even attempt a last-minute escape.

Her vision started to blur.

"When we return home, dear brother, the murine won't be any fun to play with." Lila would never get used to his voice, how cold and far away it always sounded. "At least, not until later."

The last thing Lila remembered before everything went black was her blood dripping from Ciro's chin as he watched her bleeding form.

Lila woke with a start, not quite remembering where she was. She glanced around the dark room; the stone floor was filthy and cold, and in the corner sat a bed of straw with a thin blanket. In another corner sat a wash basin and a small trunk.

This was the room she shared with Marcus. Her mouse cage.

Only now it felt so much lonelier without her brother there. She gulped. *Good, I'm glad he's out. At least one of us is.*

Lila pushed herself off the ground. The coat Kazimir had given her was gone and she was left in the same simple dress she had been in before. Except now it was even more tattered and disgusting. Her dried blood coated the neckline and ran all the way down the front to her hips. She gingerly touched where Ciro had bitten her, causing a stinging pain to strike down her body like lightning.

He'd certainly done a number on her.

"Ah, the mouse is finally awake!" came Rebekkah's voice from the dark. Lila looked around but saw no trace of the woman.

Something slithered by her foot. It wrapped itself around her ankle before making its way up her calf. Lila looked down to see a black and red viper curling around her.

Rebekkah.

The snake flashed her teeth at Lila, who fought hard not to kick her off or run away. This was one of Rebekkah's favorite games, and Lila knew the moment she showed fear, Rebekkah would strike and bite down.

"Lila, dear, for being such a good pet and coming back home, my brothers and I have put together a little present for you."

Oh no. Whatever it was, Lila knew it couldn't be good. Her heart raced as Rebekkah curved herself around Lila's waist, moving up her stomach, and between her breasts until she was finally coiled around her neck.

"The door is open. Walk," Rebekkah commanded, and Lila obeyed.

She walked, barefoot, through the lower interior of the Viper Morada, the murine quarters. For a while now, Lila and her brother had been the only two murine in the manor. She didn't know what happened to the rest, but she hoped it wouldn't happen to her. *Or maybe,* she thought, *whatever it is, it can't be all that bad if it means they're not* here.

"Hektor's room," Rebekkah ordered. Lila ascended a dark set of stairs, pushed open an old, squeaky door, and found herself in a familiar yet haunting hallway. Lila had walked these halls a number of times, in life and in her nightmares. Each time, she was summoned to another room to be tormented and tortured within. Traveling these hallways always meant pain.

If she could find a glimmer of a silver lining in any of this, it was that Marcus was now free from here.

"Hurry up, we don't have all night," Rebekkah hissed, reminding Lila just how miserable of a situation she was in. She quickened her step. Lila had been unconscious for hours after Ciro bit her. She hoped he was done, she didn't think she could take another blood draining yet. But Rebekkah flicked her tongue against the wound as she slithered around her neck, both tickling Lila and causing panic to increase her pace.

The manor was huge, and she was sure she still hadn't seen it all. The halls of the manor were dark yet regal. The walls were all made of dark gray stone, with red and gold drapes covering the windows. Large banisters hung with three snakes coiled around one another, and between each, sconces of viper heads breathing vibrant flames covered the walls. Even with all the fire, Lila couldn't help but always feel a little cold in these halls.

They almost always cleaned and prepped Lila before they feasted on her, so she hoped this time would be no different. After all, she was filthy—caked in mud and sweat, and covered in the scent of another vampire. No matter how much she hated him already, Lila couldn't argue that the man smelled divine, and it didn't help that he was probably the most attractive thing she'd ever seen. Instantly, Rebekkah's grip on her neck tightened a smidge.

"You better stop your fantasizing or Ciro and Hektor will have their own fun with it," Rebekkah hissed, but Lila appreciated the warning nonetheless.

Lila shook her head, trying not to think of the other lord—or anything for that matter. *Keep your mind blank, Lila.* It was something she had told herself a number of times. She pretended she was in an empty void, far from her body.

As she neared Hektor's room, Lila stiffened. Her worst memories came from behind that door, and she knew whatever was behind it now would be equally as bad.

Rebekkah slithered across her shoulders and shifted behind her. Lila felt the girl's cold hands rest on her shoulder as she whispered in Lila's ear, "Such a good pet. I can't wait to see your face. Oh, you'll be so happy."

With her hands guiding Lila, Rebekkah led her into the room.

Lila saw Hektor and Ciro. The former smirked broadly at her, something like heat and mischief flashing in his eyes as he ogled at her. Ciro had a cold and calculating stare, her blood cleaned from his lips. Both were now in their humanoid forms, but no less terrifying. Something— or rather, someone—stood behind them.

The two men stepped aside, revealing a third younger man with his back to Lila.

This boy had dark brown hair that curled at the ends around his elf-like ears. His skin was pale, and he was skinny as a stick. Lila knew those slumped shoulders, scrawny legs, and long arms anywhere.

As her brother slowly turned, Lila immediately noticed something was off. His light brown freckles still speckled across his nose, but his light brown eyes were now devoid of emotion and . . . something new. They had a red hue, making the usual honey color a hungry burnt maroon. A bite mark on his neck, not angry or red or swollen, but already appearing like a scar.

Marcus looked into her eyes, spreading his lips wide into a savage expression, revealing sharp fangs.

Lila's heart dropped from her chest, maybe even from the universe, she wasn't sure. Her breath hitched and she felt the instant need to run away—as far as she could—while simultaneously wanting to run right to him, to make sure he was okay, to see if he was still . . . him. Panic engulfed her and her entire body shook. She thought she might faint again.

"Marcus . . ." she breathed. "What have they done to you?"

L ila's brother hadn't run away from the Morada. And if he had, he didn't make it very far. All of her searching and hoping, risking her life, and this *damned* deal she made with another vampire—it had all been for nothing. But beyond even that, all the times she sacrificed herself to be dinner for the vampires so her brother could rest, all the bites and drainings she took so he wouldn't have to, *all of it* was for nothing.

Lila's legs gave out. She slid to the floor; her eyes locked on her brother's face. Lila had only ever known vampires once they were already changed. She didn't know how it worked when a human became one. Would he still be himself? Or a ruthless monster like the rest of them? Would he . . . try to kill her?

As if they could hear her thoughts, Rebekkah and Hektor smiled.

"He's still your brother," Hektor said, now circling Marcus. "But he's in sort of a . . . frenzy right now. He's just *dying* to drink you up."

Lila inched back, but with Rebekkah right behind her, there wasn't anywhere to go.

Ciro took a step forward. "He'll be like this at the beginning. Then, he'll be just like your brother again." His words sounded comforting, but his tone was harsh, almost disgusted as he said Marcus would return to normal.

"Well, *almost* like your brother. He'll still have a taste for blood—yours included—and he might not be so keen to wander away from the manor. Especially in the daytime."

Rebekkah lifted Lila from under her arms in a swift motion and pushed her toward Marcus. He immediately lunged, baring his teeth ready to bite her head off, but Ciro stopped him.

He wrapped a palm around Marcus's forehead and pulled him back. Marcus continued to fight against the viper's grip, snapping his teeth like a rabid dog.

Lila's eyes grew and her eyebrows knitted together. He would've killed her just now. His own sister . . .

"Please," Lila whimpered. "Please change him back."

Hektor's smirk turned sinister. "No can do, Mouse. It's too late."

"Please," she begged, as though she didn't hear him. A tear slipped from her eyes, running down her face. And once one gave way, the rest followed suit.

Fury flashed across Hektor's features. He didn't like to go unheard. He stepped forward and grabbed a fistful of Lila's hair, pulling her to him. But before he could speak, Ciro placed his hand on his brother's wrist, stopping him.

Lila didn't care. She grabbed the wrist holding her hair tightly and sobbed.

"Please!" she croaked. "Change him back, take me instead, please, pleasepleasepleaseplease," Lila begged through tears. She knew she was pathetic. She knew it was too late. She even knew the Reinicks could do nothing about it.

She wasn't begging them.

She was begging to *anyone*. Gods, goddesses, spirits, the universe, Ambrose—*anyone, please save my brother. Take me instead.*

But it seemed like no one was listening.

Marcus still squirmed behind the Hektor and Ciro, snapping and clawing at Lila. Rebekkah laughed, finding the whole situation humorous. Hektor held Lila with something like hunger growing in his eyes as his grip on her tightened—his skin felt hot to the touch where her palms gripped his wrist.

"Not tonight," Ciro commanded. There would be no arguing with him. Hektor nearly growled at his brother, but Lila saw the expression disappear before he did. He nodded instead. "Take the murine back to her room. Even rats need rest."

Hektor loosened his grip on her hair, and Rebekkah immediately pulled Lila to her feet and out of the room.

"Marcus, Marcus!" she called, but he didn't react any differently. It was like he didn't even know his own name.

Lila paced, trying to come up with something, anything she could do to save her brother. But nothing came to her. She had never heard of a vampire being changed back into a human, and she had never met a vampire who wasn't a ruthless monster.

Maybe, once he was calmer, she would be able to leave

here with him. She could feed him her blood, and the two would just make do with their situation.

What if his urges were too strong? What if, despite returning to some semblance of himself, it wasn't enough? What if even with her help, he'd still kill someone, or her?

The soles of her feet were already raw from the night before, walking back and forth on the cold, damp stone only made the blisters hurt more. Lila flopped onto her straw mattress, utterly defeated.

What am I going to do? She kept thinking of the look on her brother's face, the look that signified all his humanity was gone. She couldn't believe the Reinicks would do this to him, it never even crossed her mind that they would *consider* making a murine into a vampire.

Maybe . . .

Maybe they could make me into a vampire?

Lila shot up.

Then I could be with Marcus, and I won't be treated like a rat. Then, we could leave here and live night by night. She thought of what it would be like to never feel the warmth of the sun again. She thought of how it would feel to only survive through another's blood. *A life for a life,* she realized. *That's what it is to be a vampire.*

That was how Marcus would live from here on out.

She didn't *want* to be a vampire. In fact, it was the last thing she wanted, she'd rather die a lonely, gruesome death. But she knew Marcus needed her. She knew she would grow old, and he would not. She knew that, whenever they were in a room together, Marcus would be trying his best to not kill her.

He was a predator now, and she was still just prey.

Lila shook her head and flopped back down again. Her mind was reeling in shock. Her breath was still hollow, and her limbs hadn't stopped shaking since Hektor's room. She wrapped herself snuggly in the worn blanket. She was still cold; she was still shaking.

At some point in the night, another servant had stopped by, dropping a piece of toast on the cold, dirty floor outside of her open doorway. The servants were all vampires as well—and very unlike Kazimir. And, for some reason, they were all forced to see to her, to keep her alive. Very rarely would they get the reward of sucking her blood.

She crept out of bed, grabbed the slice of bread, and ate it in the corner of her room, as she didn't know when the next time she'd be given food.

The night was ultimately quiet. For hours, no one entered her hallway, so Lila figured it was as safe a time as any to sleep.

Lila didn't own much in terms of clothing, but she changed out of the rags her simple dress had become and slipped on a thin, white nightgown. It had a tear up the side from where Hektor had grabbed at her once, some old blood stains dribbled along the neckline from when Ciro had bitten her in her sleep, and the sleeves were missing from the time Rebekkah tore them off. But all in all, it was the cleanest thing she owned.

She nestled into her small bed, brought her knees to her chest, and covered her entire body with the blanket. She was far from warm, but the longer she lay there, the warmer she became. It began in her chest and spread through her body down to her toes. Every night, this was how she survived. This was how Marcus survived. They'd hold each other and be okay. Lila couldn't explain it, she just knew it was unique and something the vampires of the Viper Morada gravitated toward.

Are you all right? said a silver-tongued voice dripping with gold. The noise encompassed her, flowing into her body and warming her from the inside out.

What? Lila thought.

Are you all right? the voice repeated. Lila struggled to see where she was. Her eyes were open but all she could see was darkness. And . . . and it felt like she was floating. Or was she flying?

Below her was the softest thing she'd ever felt. It was comfortable, like a bed, but as soft as a feather. She rubbed her face against it.

Little Mouse, the voice called.

Huh?

Lila was dreaming. She knew she was dreaming. So why was this voice so insistent?

Suddenly, the bed beneath her shifted to the side, and she slipped off. The sensation of falling hit her as she tumbled down, down into the dark. She was starting to panic, until strong, warm arms wrapped around her waist.

Answer me, damn it!

I'm fine!

The voice scoffed. *No, you're not.* How did it know? *What's happened to your brother?*

Her brother . . .

The Reinicks, they got to him before I could find him. I don't know if he ever even made it out, or if they lied about that from the beginning. He's . . . Lila's words caught on a sob. Her face felt wet. When did she start crying?

He what? the voice demanded. The grip around her tightened, but not in a painful way. If anything, Lila found it comforting.

He's a vampire. They turned him into one of them.

The arms disappeared, and again she was met with the soft, feather-like bed below her.

I don't know what to do . . . she admitted to the voice after a tense beat of silence. The wind blew through her hair as the thing below her flew through the darkness beyond them.

Don't do anything. Not until I'm there. We might be able to—

What if I were to change? I could be a vampire; I could be with him.

No.

But—

No. You can't be changed. The voice was stern, commanding. It made Lila want to argue, but in truth, it just reassured her. She really didn't want to change either, and now her mind was telling her the same.

Don't do anything. Not until I'm there, the voice repeated. *Do you hear me?*

Lila was drifting. Light was reaching her mind, her vision. Something was shaking her . . . something was . . .

Little Mouse, answer me.

I'll wait, Lila said to the voice. *I'll wait.*

She just didn't know what she was waiting for.

Ambrose? Lila jolted awake, instantly realizing that the voice she'd heard was the Crow Lord's. Only . . . it was a dream?

Did Lord Draven really just communicate with her in a dream? Had it really been him communicating through their Concord?

Or did Marcus's change finally break her mind? Was she just delusional enough now to think a vampire lord cared enough to save her and her brother? The same man who pushed her out of a window, forced her into a bargain, marked her, *and* gave her back to the Reinicks.

She really was losing it.

Something kicked the straw bed below her. She jolted upright and saw Rebekkah, arms crossed, looking down at her. She wore a long, silken nightgown and robe set in all black.

"Get up. I'm hungry."

Impatiently, Rebekkah turned from Lila and stalked out of the room. She knew the vampire wouldn't wait up, and any delay would surely cause a tantrum. Lila scurried up and grabbed the nearest robe she had. Like her own nightgown, it was tattered and had yellow stains from how old it was. But it didn't matter. Anything to cover her up would do at this point.

She followed Rebekkah out of the hall, up a number of staircases, and down many other hallways. Lila assumed they were going to her bedroom, which was in one of the spires of the manor.

J. M. FAILDE

Rebekkah had once said she was a proper lady, and proper ladies get the tower bedroom. Part of Lila thought Rebekkah confused "proper ladies" for princesses in towers from storybooks. She wondered, if Rebekkah was the princess, then who would her dragon captor be?

A number of winding staircases later, Lila finally entered Rebekkah's quarters. It was a large room, accented like the rest of the house, with golds, reds, and blacks. Only, Rebekkah also seemed to favor dark green, the color of the forest. Random bits of decoration in her room were covered with the color including her bedding and the sofas in her sitting room.

Which was where they went.

"Sit," the vampire commanded. And so, Lila did.

Time got confusing while inside the manor walls. Lila never knew if it was night or day, and only had a loose semblance of the time of year. She knew when it was winter because her room got colder, and she knew when it was autumn because of the large banquet the manors would hold in honor of Sanktus Pernox, a holiday in which the vampires reveled in all their ghoulish glory. She believed they were nearing the holiday, maybe a few weeks out.

Rebekkah sat across from her in a dark green lounge chair with a high back. Between them was a small, circular table made of dark cherry wood. Rebekkah clapped once, and out came two servants with a plate of food in one hand and a goblet in the other. Lila recognized the goblet. It was Rebekkah's favorite. However, Lila startled when they placed the food in front of her.

As soon as the two servants left, and the women were alone again, Rebekkah spoke. "I don't like when you taste like stale bread. Eat, and then I'll drink." Rebekkah was cruel, rude, and completely spoiled, but she wasn't *evil*. Not

47

like her brothers. She was just raised wicked, but Lila always felt, in different circumstances, maybe she wouldn't be so vile. There was a certain softness to her at times that wasn't present with the brothers.

Lila sat for a moment, afraid the vampire would change her mind. Everything was a game. A calculated test. And Lila couldn't let her guard down.

"Hurry up, Mouse," Rebekkah demanded.

Lila could hear the growing frustration in her voice and knew Rebekkah was being genuine.

Though her reasonings were skewed, Lila was grateful nonetheless.

She picked up the food and quickly scarfed it down— meats, eggs, cakes—it was an odd mix, not quite breakfast, but Lila's famished stomach and watering mouth didn't care. She savored all of it.

After only a few moments, Rebekkah clapped her hands again. "All right, that's enough. You truly are ravenous, aren't you?" She raised an eyebrow, glaring at Lila's mouth. She must've been eating like an animal—she was sure she had grease spots all over her chin.

Lila quickly wiped her mouth, and the same two servants came in and cleared off the table, leaving only Rebekkah's goblet and a new, silver dagger. Lila knew what it meant.

Rebekkah held out her hand expectantly, resting her elbow on the wooden circle table. Lila hesitated for a moment but placed her wrist within the other girl's palm. In a swift motion, Rebekkah slashed Lila's forearm with the blade. The wound burned as crimson droplets began to form and spill into the goblet below.

The vampire licked her lips as she stared. She had a bit more control than her brothers and liked to wait till her blood was in her glass rather than on the murine she was feasting from.

Drip, drip, drip. Rebekkah squeezed causing Lila to wince.

"Oh, hush, this is nothing."

Lila knew she was right. This was nothing compared to what it could've been. The cut was only a flesh wound, not deep enough to cause any lasting damage. It probably wouldn't even scar.

Just before the goblet overfilled, Rebekkah tossed Lila's bleeding arm back at her and began to take long drinks. She truly was thirsty.

Lila watched in fascination. She would never get over the . . . *lust* a vampire displayed when drinking blood. It wasn't anything like how humans ate food. It was more insatiable. Food may be a need for humans, and a desire for most who enjoy the taste. But blood was the sole purpose of life for a vampire. They enacted all of the seven deadly sins when consuming it.

Gluttony, for they could drink it endlessly.

Lust, as it seemed to be an aphrodisiac.

Pride, for they were the winners. When they drank blood, they were unstoppable.

Wrath, they would kill for it, becoming savage if they had to.

Envy, as they were envious of others who had it when they did not.

Sloth, most vampires didn't care how they got their blood, as long as they got it.

And finally, Greed, for they only wanted more and more, they would stop at nothing to get what they desired.

Now, Rebekkah was ravenously chugging and seemed like she couldn't stop as blood trickled down her chin dripping from the sides of the glass. Lila knew it was time for her to leave. Vampires never seemed to know when to stop once they started, and if she were still in that seat across from Rebekkah when she finished, her arm would likely be bitten apart.

Lila eased up from her chair, trying to make as little noise as possible. Her eyes caught on the silver blade coated in her blood. So far, Rebekkah hadn't seemed to notice Lila moved, and if she had, then she didn't care. Her hand shot out for the blade, and she hid it behind her back. Her heartbeat only grew louder as she nervously inched toward the door. She held her breath, refusing to make more noise than needed. She eased open the bedroom door and slipped out, closing the door behind her.

After taking a huge breath, Lila shrugged off her tattered robe and wrapped it around her arm, and then tucked the blade inside as a makeshift holster.

The scent of blood would definitely be more noticeable than her bare shoulders, and she knew it was unlikely she'd go unnoticed throughout the castle. Not with her fresh blood now permeating the halls.

Once I'm in my room, I can clean this up, she thought to herself. Lila didn't know what she planned to use the weapon for, but if it could buy her a moment, she would use it. She hurried now, down staircases and hallways, through a number of doors. The building was a labyrinth, and she was so thankful to have mapped it all out in her mind. She remembered the first year here, how lost she constantly was, always wandering directly into other vampires hungry for blood.

Marcus had made me a map . . . She felt her eyes well up with tears. Her heart felt like it was shattering each time she thought of him.

Don't do anything. Not until I'm there, the memory of the

voice from last night, Ambrose's voice, trickled through her mind. Should she really do *nothing*? Should she put her faith in a foolhearted dream? Surely she was alone in this nightmare—much like she was in everything.

She had to do something. She would go confront Ciro. If anyone could undo this, it would be the vampire who turned him, couldn't it?

Lila walked with new resolve toward the famed Horned Viper's room. She didn't care she was bleeding, she'd use it to her advantage. She didn't care she was only in a nightgown; he'd seen it all anyway at some point or another. When they were hungry, the vipers cared little for others' privacy.

She marched toward Ciro's room and banged on the door.

Ciro opened, covered in a black tar-like substance.

Vampire blood.

He eyed her, his gaze shooting directly to her wounded arm.

"What?" he hissed.

Lila was frozen. His mouth was coated in the stuff, his shirt had been torn open, revealing tanned abs covered in the black gore. She didn't really expect him to open the door. She didn't know what she was doing there, all re-solve had immediately left her body.

"I-I—" But before Lila could gather her words, Ciro's gaze darted behind her, and he pulled her inside.

He slammed the door behind her. His dark room seemed perfectly in order. The bed was made, the desk had only a book atop it. But as Lila's gaze continued to survey her new surroundings. She saw it—*them*. At her feet lay the decaying skeletal figures of the Lord and Lady of the Vampire Morada.

Ciro had murdered his parents.

9

Lila wanted to scream at the gruesome sight before her. In fact, she might've if Ciro hadn't clamped his hand around her mouth.

"Make a single noise and I'll rip your throat out."

She knew he meant it. His eyes were glowing that vibrant shade of a sickly yellow, like that of snake venom.

"Nod if you'll stay silent," he demanded.

Lila gulped but did as she was told.

Ciro slowly removed his hand and stepped around her. "Not a word of this to anyone. Not yet. Got it?"

Lila nodded.

"What are you doing here?"

Lila didn't respond, afraid to utter even a sound. Ciro rolled his eyes and stepped forward, pointing to the blood-soaked robe. "Rebekkah?"

Lila nodded again. She felt like she couldn't speak even if she wanted to. The smell of death was rancid, it made her want to vomit—which only made her bite her lips harder. If she threw up now, on the bodies of Lord and Lady Reinick, would Ciro even care?

His parents!

Ciro eyed Lila before taking a step back, shifting his attention from her to his parents and then to his own gory appearance. He effortlessly removed his shirt and used it to wipe down his face, which only smeared the licorice blood more.

"What are you doing *here*?"

When Lila didn't answer again, he turned to her and leaned against one of the posts of his bed. Ciro crossed his arms, his biceps bulging as he did so. His golden eyes bore into her, illuminating. He was . . . beautiful. She felt the heat of his gaze wander over her, over her legs, arms, and nightgown.

"I said, *what are you doing here*?"

"Change my brother back." Lila's mouth spoke before she even realized she was speaking, her lips moving on their own accord. Her heart thundered in her chest as she began to panic.

He was enthralling her, and she felt her mind slipping into a familiar haze. Her eyes focused on Ciro and . . . she would do anything he asked. She was trapped.

"I can't. You know that."

"Please," she begged foolishly.

"*Kneel*," he uttered.

She dropped with no hesitation. She would—she would do anything for him.

He uncrossed his arms and slowly sauntered over to her. Just as he got close, he scoffed. "What would you do to change your brother back? Will you do whatever I say?"

"Yes."

He cupped her face with his warm, dirty hand, smearing his parents' black gore across her face. Lila wanted to flinch back, but the thrall made her sway forward.

Lila, stop! she tried to tell herself, but it didn't work.

Ciro rubbed his thumb across Lila's bottom lip, parting them ever so slightly.

"Would you stay with me?"

No.

"Yes."

"Would you *be* with me?" He smirked. He knew what he was doing.

No!

"Yes!"

Lila's body shot up, wrapping her arms around his neck. Internally, Lila fought her actions, but her body did as he commanded. Whatever *he* wanted, *she* would do.

And she would do anything to please him.

They were face to face now, and she knew they both must've looked like monsters, covered in blood—human and vampire—and surrounded by bodies.

Ciro wrapped his corded arms around her waist, lifting her with ease as her feet dangled above the floor. He inched closer, and she could feel the heat of his wandering gaze on her lips.

Lila, please! she begged herself.

But her body begged for the opposite. Her lips parted, welcoming his touch. She was painfully aware of their bodies pressed against each other, only separated by the thin fabric of her gown. She could feel the rapid rise and fall of her chest against the perfect stillness of his. Lila's gaze drifted up from his lips, she saw the hunger in his eyes for the first time—not for blood but for *her*. It was lust, not hunger, she realized.

He wanted her.

And she wanted him, didn't she?

She should give in.

"*Kiss me.*" Ciro's voice was as quiet as a breath and so filled with need.

She *wanted* to kiss him, would do *anything* to kiss him.

No, she would rather do anything *but* kiss him.

Her mind fought itself in turmoil.

Lila leaned forward, so close she could almost feel him on her. Her eyes fluttered shut.

A velvet whisper drifted through her mind, *Do not kiss him.*

Immediately, the haze broke.

She felt herself on Ciro, each place her body touched him felt like she was on cold marble. Lila became incredibly uncomfortable, desiring nothing more than to retreat into her own skin.

Do not kiss him.

It wasn't her own voice in her head. It was the one from the dream.

The Concord.

Lila's eyes shot open.

Ciro was studying her. The lust was gone, replaced with something else she couldn't quite place.

"I said, *kiss me.*"

Lila loosened her grip on his shoulders.

She wasn't going to kiss him, he was the monster who changed her brother. He was the monster who kept her here, who hurt her every chance he got. Why would she *kiss* him?

Lila's skin crawled at the thought.

Ciro's jaw tightened, and his eyes lost the venom-yellow glow they held, turning dark and wicked.

His grip on her waist tightened, fingernails digging into the flesh at her hips.

"It seems like there's an unexpected guest in *my* land,"

he said, his voice strained. His gaze was boring into Lila's eyes, but she felt like he was looking *through* them rather than into them.

As he spoke, Ciro's clawed hand drifted along her back. It felt eerily similar to the motion of Ambrose's caress just the morning before. Only now, Ciro's nails felt like they were out for blood. As they trailed along her spine, he began to apply more and more pressure the closer to the mark on Lila's back he got. She froze, unblinking, not even breathing.

Ciro could rip her heart out through her back right now if he wanted to. He could tear into her jugular with his fangs, and she felt so small, so weak. She felt like prey that just wandered into its predator's mouth before it snapped shut.

"Ambrose," Ciro said. "This is *my* murine. *Get out.*"

As he spoke, he tore his claws down her back, and the pain rippled through Lila's body like she was being torn from the inside out. She didn't even register she was screaming until her throat felt like it was about to rip.

Her back was on fire, burning, but it was also so cold like ice. It ached and it welled and it oozed. She was sure her back was cut into long, ruby ribbons.

The mark from Ambrose scorched against Lila's skin as Ciro finally released his grip. She dropped to the floor, her knees smacking into the wood hard.

Lila couldn't tell if the shaking was from fear or pain, but she knew she couldn't move, even if she wanted to. On the floor, hunched over her knees, her eyes darted around, searching for an escape route.

She needed to run. She needed to get out of there. She needed to find Marcus.

But her eyes only found the barren eyes of Lord Reinick,

devoid of life, and surrounded by skin that had turned to ash.

Ciro *murdered* his own parents, and she would be next. She wouldn't save Marcus—she couldn't even save herself.

The door to his room burst open.

"What hap—" Hektor's voice boomed into the room before falling silent. Had he seen his parents?

"Brother," Ciro called. His voice cool, calculated.

"You did it? You actually did it?" Lila expected to hear shock, sorrow, maybe even confusion in Hektor's voice. His own brother had committed parricide.

But all she heard was the wistful sound of pride.

"You're looking at the new Lord Reinick of the Viper Morada."

She could hear the smile on Ciro's lips as her eyes were still fixed on the fallen bodies. Bile rose in her throat.

Hektor shifted, moving to his brother. She heard them clap each other on the back as the younger congratulated Ciro.

And then she felt Hektor's fiery gaze shift to her. The heat rolled along her spine, lingering only for a moment on her torn back before moving farther down. He stared at her backside, and she could feel the heat of his gaze so scalding, it felt as though he were devouring her.

"And her?" his voice was strained. He cleared his throat. "What is she doing here?"

"Wrong place, wrong time," Ciro said simply. "I thought I'd have some fun with her, Rebekkah already seems to have gotten her share for the day." Now she felt the heat of both of their gazes. "But that damned crow. He broke my thrall."

"Ah," Hektor gulped. "Well . . . Can I have a turn? I like playing with her."

Lila shivered at the thought. Her body reacted before she realized what she was doing. She leaped up and kicked off the ground toward the door. Fight or flight had finally kicked in and, like the rat she was, she ran.

But the predators were far superior to her.

Hektor simply reached a hand out and caught her by her lilac hair.

"Let me go!" She tugged at his grip unsuccessfully.

"Ah, she speaks," Hektor cooed.

Ciro simply smirked and raised an eyebrow.

"You realize he is your new lord, correct? The lord of the manor?" Hektor pulled her in close. Lila fought— fought with all her might—but she couldn't get free from his grasp.

As he pulled her in, he swiftly twisted her and pressed her back flush against his chest. She yelped at the sudden touch against her flayed skin.

But worse, she heard Hektor breathe deeply, inhaling the scent.

"Lords, she is *delicious,* isn't she?"

Lila fidgeted and squirmed to no avail. It was like she was but a tiny bug under their claws. She was *nothing.*

"Quite."

"Are you . . . done with her?" Hektor hesitated. It was only around Ciro did anything remotely similar to fear or doubt entered his voice. She knew Ciro was territorial of her, so she often used it to her advantage.

But today, Ambrose's interference had royally pissed him off.

"She's tainted. Take her. See about having that mark fully removed from her back. I don't care if you have to tear the flesh away, I don't want the reminder that filthy crow touched what's ours." Ciro's voice was filled with disgust.

"Oh, I'll have it removed." He pressed his cheek against Lila's. "And we'll have some fun along the way, isn't that right, pet?"

"Let me go!" Lila threw her head back, smashing it against Hektor's nose — hard.

His grip on her loosened and she took the opportunity to bolt out of his arms. She ran over the decrepit bodies of the old Lord and Lady Reinick, but she couldn't stop, she couldn't feel bad. She just had to keep going.

Lila threw the door of the room open and dashed into the hallway.

She heard laughing coming from the room behind her and she knew she was now playing Hektor's favorite game. His predator instincts were up, and he was ready for the hunt. He *thrived* on it. He loved it when she ran and fought, it only made it more fun for him.

But it was also the only chance she had to get away.

Lila heard the flapping of wings in the hallway and was sure the vampire had turned into his monstrous form. He laughed and hollered as it bounced off the walls. She didn't know how close he was to her, but she didn't dare look back.

She dashed left, then right, avoiding winding staircases that would take her much longer to descend than him. Her feet beat against the cold stone floors, and she could feel the chill that haunted the manor bite at her cheeks and arms.

Lila had to get out before it was too late. She'd come back for Marcus, it wasn't like there was much she could do for him now anyway.

"Oh, Lilaaaa," Hektor called in a sing-song voice. "Look who I have here."

Lila didn't want to stop, she knew it was a trap, she

knew it would ruin her. But she also knew if she didn't, Hektor would have no qualms about hurting her brother. She glanced over her shoulder, begging, praying, but knowing that Marcus would be there.

And as if Hektor had read her thoughts, he beckoned over a dazed Marcus. His fangs were large and sharp, the mark she saw on his neck yesterday already healed. He dragged himself over to Hektor. The two men stared at Lila, one hungry, ravenous, lustful gaze, and one empty and devoid of all humanity.

"Marcus . . ." she whispered.

Hektor clamped a hand on Marcus's shoulder. "Did you really think Ciro turned him? It was my idea. I grabbed him one night and came up with the lie that he ran away. That he left you behind. I knew you'd run after him. And, Lila dear, you are so predictable. I thought it'd be a fun little game of cat and mouse. What wasn't expected was you making a deal with that filthy crow, Draven," he seethed speaking his name. "But that's all right. I decided to give you a little gift in return. I changed him, just before you woke up yesterday."

He had just been turned? Because of me? Lila reeled. She blinked furiously, starting to speak several times, with nothing to say.

This was her fault.

"We still haven't fed young Marcus here. He's probably just *starving*. Won't you be a good sister, Lila? Won't you feed your brother? He needs it to survive."

This was all her fault.

Lila's feet were cold on the stone below her. Her hands shook, and sweat coated her skin from running. Her breath was ragged but she didn't know if it was from her exertion or the realization that this was all because of her.

Hektor smiled at her—a wicked, evil sort of smile—and his grip on Marcus's shoulder released.

In the blink of an eye, her brother was on top of her, snapping and clawing. They both fell to the floor, shooting pain along the tear on her back, as she tried with all her might to fend him off. His nails cut across her cheek, her arms, her neck, her chest. He was so much stronger than before, and she didn't think she could hold him off much longer.

"Marcus, please. Marcus, listen to me!" She begged and begged, but he couldn't hear her.

Suddenly, something grabbed him and threw him off her. Lila was relieved, but only for a moment.

Hektor bore down on her. She screamed as he climbed on top of her, holding her wrists in one hand. Lila bucked and fought to no avail. He took a deep breath, inhaling her scent, her blood. His pupils dilated and his expression changed from hungry to ravenous. She tried to lift her knees, but his weight was too much, especially in this huge, monstrous form. Hektor dragged his free hand along her body, up her thighs and stomach, pawing at her breast, before he gripped her jaw and angled it up, revealing the long line of her neck. He bore his fangs, but instead of biting her as she expected, he dragged his tongue across her flesh.

Lila cringed below him, bucking again.

"Get off!" she yelled at him and shook with all her might, but nothing made him budge. After licking her, Hektor breathed along Lila's ear and slowly inched down. He grabbed the hem of her dress and pushed it up. She kicked with all her might, kneeing his abdomen, but none of it even phased the monster. Hektor grabbed Lila's thigh, pushing her nightgown up dangerously high, and got eerily close to the apex of her thighs.

"Get off of me!" she yelled. "Marcus, help me!" But Marcus didn't move. It was like he was frozen.

"It's my turn for some fun, Lila. Bek got her turn, Ciro had his. Now, it's time for me." Hektor bore his fangs and sunk his teeth deep into her inner thigh. Instantly, she grew woozy. She felt him lick and suck at her inner thigh, draining the blood from her. She felt the heat of embarrassment cross her features. It was too much, too close. The heat would melt her, the pain would devour her. She had lost way too much blood in just the last few minutes between Rebekkah, Ciro, Marcus, and now Hektor, and she was sure she still hadn't recovered from yesterday.

Hektor removed his hand binding her wrists and placed it flat on her stomach, holding her down. But with her newly freed hands, Lila fought. She punched and clawed, before removing the stolen dagger from her robe, and plunged it into Hektor's shoulder.

But he didn't so much as flinch. She stabbed over and over, but as Hektor drank from her, licking and kissing her thigh as the sharp pinch of teeth sunk in deeper, Lila's vision began to go hazy, and her limbs grew heavy. Clouds of darkness swarmed her view of the manor's ceiling.

Is this how I die? she thought. Covered in her own blood, embarrassed from being bitten like so in front of her brother—who just tried to eat her as well and had no semblance of self to try to stop Hektor.

She couldn't help it. She laughed. Her life was horrible. A messy, disastrous, horrible thing. And she could feel it being drained away. She could feel her back still oozing hot blood, the wound on her arm reopened and drenched the robe, covering it. Lila was so surrounded by her own gore, she forgot about the black blood still coating her face from Ciro's killings.

Still holding the blade, her arm fell to her side. She no longer had the energy to fight him.

Let me in. The faintest voice in her head whispered.

Lila could hear each gulp of her blood Hektor swallowed. Could feel each laceration from her fight with her brother sting her skin.

She was dying. A horrible, most miserable death, to match her horrible, most miserable life.

Let me in, said the same voice, just a little bit louder. She felt a tug along her back, a tug on her very soul. The same tug that came every time she spoke through the Concord.

Okay, she thought.

"I believe the lady told you to get off." The voice.

Liquid gold, with a silver tongue.

Ambrose's voice.

With a loud *thud*, Hektor's fangs were torn from Lila's thigh, before the monster was thrown back, crashing into the nearest wall. Stones broke, bricks fell over him, and warm, strong hands encased Lila carefully. She was pressed against a strong, warm chest.

"I'm here to collect on my debt," Ambrose said. His white hair fell forward, cascading down over his shoulders and tickling her cheek. "This Little Mouse belongs to me."

10

ila was floating. Or maybe she was flying? All she knew was that she loved the sensation of it. The wind freely blew her hair back behind her, the gusts pulled under her limbs, the warmth seeping to her from below.

Lila's eyes snapped open. She was in the air, but *she* wasn't flying. The massive form below her was doing that. She yelped as she scrambled to grab onto its snowy hair. It was so soft and blinding, Lila almost thought the color might consume her.

"Not so rough, Little Mouse. Save that for the bedroom."

"Ambrose?" Lila called out. She rubbed her eyes.

Still flying.

She pinched herself. "What's . . ." She hesitated. She didn't know what was going on, but she knew she rode on Ambrose's huge back as he flew through the night sky in his monstrous form.

"You're not dreaming, darling. I came to collect on my first favor. You just happened to be in a . . . compromising situation."

Her head was still swimming from losing so much blood, but she could breathe again.

"You saved me?" Lila asked in disbelief.

"No, no. Don't get the wrong idea. I needed you, so I took you. What was happening in that hallway had nothing to do with it. You could've been riding him—in the middle of screaming his name—and I still would have plucked you from that manor."

Lila was silent for a minute. Something ugly twisted inside of her, but it made sense. Of course he wouldn't be there to save her. A human who forced her way into his home and into a deal. She shook her head. *I just have to be thankful he was in the right place at the right time,* she thought.

"What's your favor?"

"All in due time."

"Where are we going?"

"You'll see."

Lila sighed. "Can't you answer anything?"

"Yes."

She pulled his hair tighter in frustration as she huffed.

The damned vampire flipped in the air, causing Lila to slip from his back, freefalling right to the ground. Her stomach was left behind as she screamed at the top of her lungs.

Just before she reached the tree line, Ambrose swooped down and caught her. He was so huge from this position. Easily triple her size. And she fit into his arms like a little doll. His white hair was draped down his back. His hands had shifted into long claws and his feet formed talons. His skin somehow felt like smooth stone but was warm to the touch rather than cold.

He held her in his arms, one under her knees and the other carefully holding her lower back. Her head still felt so heavy, she knew she could fall asleep laying against him at that moment and wished for nothing more than to have a blanket or pillow made from Ambrose's hair.

"Stop it," he spoke, watching her with eyes as dark as the night. His face was still human but had a larger jaw and the tip of his nose was pointed a bit more up, his ashen skin had gone an even darker shade, like charcoal, and now all of his teeth seemed to be filed to an edge rather than just his fangs. His hair fell around his face, accentuating his high and sharp cheekbones. His jawline was strong, leading into a long neck that drifted to wide shoulders and a broad chest.

Lila, staring, saw his jaw tick just before he pinched her on her thigh where his hand rested.

"I said stop it."

"Stop what?"

"Staring."

Immediately, Lila blushed. Blood rushed to her head, and she suddenly remembered she was in nothing but a nightgown—torn and incredibly shredded apart—and based on the look on his face, he was just noticing it too. That he was holding her, high in the air and could drop her at any moment, and that she owed him a favor and that this *favor* could be anything because she didn't set any rules before agreeing to such a ridiculous thing and—

"*Lila,*" Ambrose said, breaking her away from her spiraling thoughts. "You are hurt, and your blood is rather enticing. Please try to smell less...human. Just until we make it back to the manor." He smirked, and said in a teasing tone, "Don't think about all the ways you'd like to ravage me—"

"I would *never*—" Lila flushed in anger. *This pompous, vain vampire!*

"Don't argue. Don't think about your brother. And, for lords' sake, don't move so much or your wounds will reopen, and blood will get all over me and then I really won't be able to stop myself." Ambrose's wings flapped, reminding Lila that he was a monster, just like the others. "You're going to want to hold on, Little Mouse."

Lila cautiously put her arms around his neck, noticing his nose twitch as her wounded arm circled him.

"Sh-should I move it?"

"No, it's fine. You ready?" he asked, tightening his grip around her.

"For wh—"

But Lila didn't get a chance to finish. With a mighty flap that sounded like a boom of thunder, Ambrose thrust his wings downward, shooting him and Lila across the sky.

She yelled as her stomach did somersaults, her head slamming against his chest. They flew across trees and valleys, mapping out the same run she had done nights before as she escaped the Reinicks manor. The wind made it hard to keep her eyes open and the zooming view made her head spin.

Close your eyes. It'll help, Ambrose spoke through the Concord.

Lila was growing tired of being told what to do by all these vampires. She promised herself this would be the last time. She closed her eyes.

But it didn't help. Each sensation only grew tenfold. Her stomach was dipping and whirling with the movement of Ambrose's flight. But more so, she felt everywhere her skin rested on his. His strong arms beneath her were just so warm. She always thought vampires were cold, since they lacked life. But Ambrose was radiating right now.

Or maybe it was her.

But it was a cool night out, and she wasn't even in a coat. Hell, she was practically naked in her destroyed nightgown.

Which only made her flush more.

Please let us be there soon.

Lila peeked her eyes open and was so happy to see Ambrose's manor in sight. His property was huge, massive. He had a large garden to the right of the building, a gorgeous yard leading into a lake in the backyard, full of gazebos and paper lanterns. The manor must've been about five floors tall and was far wider than the Reinicks'. In fact, it was far more beautiful as well. By the light of the moon, Lila could see the building was made from a luminous white stone, with polished silver accents. A dome resting at the tallest spire was plated and reflected the moon and stars.

"It's incredible," she whispered, not realizing she said it out loud.

Ambrose hesitated a moment before mumbling, "Thank you." He dipped down, and softly landed on the ground, tucking his wings in behind him. Lila unclasped her hands from around his neck, ready to be lowered to the ground, but the vampire continued to carry her. In fact, he carried her up the front steps, through the door, and held her as he called out, "Kaz!"

Upon entering, he shifted back to his humanoid form. Still tall, still corded with muscles with gorgeous dark skin, eyes, and hair as white as snow. It fell over his eyes as he shook it out, making the mane a bit messy as it rested on his chest. Lila felt the urge to bury her face in it.

"You can put me down, you know," Lila reminded him.

"And get your filthy human blood all over my manor? Of course not."

The old man with a friendly face shuffled into the room, and Lila immediately brightened.

"Back so soon, m'lady? I thought I told you I would not like to see you wounded again." He smirked, causing his mustache to hitch up comically.

"It seems like our Little Mouse doesn't listen. Where would you like her, Kaz?"

"The dining table is fine."

The smile faded from Lila's face. Were they planning to have *her* for dinner? It wouldn't be the first time.

As if he read her mind—*Is he reading my mind?*—Ambrose looked at her and smirked. "Don't worry, Little Mouse. I won't be making a meal out of you . . . yet." His eyes dipped to hers, a smirk spread across his lips, and she immediately understood his meaning. Lila gaped at him.

"I'll clean it before supper," Kaz finished, clearing his throat. Lila still didn't swallow.

She tensed as Ambrose sauntered her across the grand entrance. She hadn't before, but now she saw the beautiful room in all its glory. Marble flooring, a chandelier with tear-shaped jewels, and a dark wooden staircase that led to a second-floor landing. She saw paintings and sculptures, all of which she silently promised to fawn over later. Ambrose carried her across the room and then through an open doorway that led into the dining room.

Before her was a large table, she guessed it could easily fit twenty, maybe even thirty people. It was decorated with candelabras and a runner that looked as though it were threaded in gold. At both ends of the tables sat two gorgeously ornate chairs. She could easily imagine Ambrose sitting in one of these, making it known *he* was the head of the table, house, land—head of the world. The table was parallel to a long wall covered in stained glass windows filled with images of birds and hearts, and Lila knew it must be conveying a story but couldn't figure out what it was.

Behind one of the larger chairs, a huge fireplace—the size of Ambrose—dominated the wall. It turned on as soon as Ambrose glanced at it, making the room wonderfully toasty.

He got to the side of the table nearest the fireplace and kicked the chair back far enough for him to stand between it and the table. Delicately, he lowered her down, sitting her on the edge of the table. Her feet dangled from it, and for a moment, the vampire stood there, between her thighs. Lila stared at his position, refusing to look up. She felt his gaze on her, looking—no, *studying* her. They wandered over her head, following the cascade of her hair onto her shoulders, then down to where he was positioned between her. Heat flared in that spot. The same spot Hektor had bitten her what felt like only moments ago. Was it the blood coating her torn skin he desired?

Instinctively, Lila pulled the dagger once again from the bloodied robe on her arm, not thinking of how it got there again, and went to drive it through the vampire.

Ambrose's hand shot up and caught her wrist just as the tip of the blade pierced the flesh above his heart. Black blood trickled onto the blade and down his chest.

His black eyes caught hers, and . . . something like admiration coated his features. She blanched, realizing what she had done, but there was no anger or confusion in his eyes. Only . . . respect.

"I saw this in your hand at the Viper Morada. I figured you may have wanted to keep it."

Lila could hear her heart beating. She just tried to stab the vampire that saved her. Was she even in her right mind?

Ambrose took a step back, releasing her wrist.

"I've gathered the supplies," Kazimir appeared through a near-hidden door next to the fireplace. Lila scurried to hide the blade again in her dress, all the while Ambrose's eyes studied her, his head slightly tilted. He flopped back into the chair behind him and rested his chin on his fist.

Clearly, Kazimir didn't see their interaction, as he continued nonchalantly, "Though she should really take a proper bath before we put any ointment on her or wrap the wounds." The older man stood next to the vampire and looked down at him, tossing a clean linen shirt onto his lap, which Ambrose quickly put on. "Shall I fetch Constance?"

"Stop the bleeding first. Make sure none of her wounds need stitches. As for Constance . . . you know that girl isn't as restrained when it comes to blood yet."

"Nonsense. The girl is perfectly capable of keeping her cravings in check." But Kazamir did as he was told.

He prompted Lila to turn a bit and cut the back of the nightgown to better see the damage. He gasped at the sight and Lila could tell her back truly was torn to ribbons, and in a pain so fierce, she nearly fainted when Kazimir inspected it with delicate hands. "After she washes," Kaz demanded, "I can properly assess it after."

Ambrose nodded.

"I'll go get Constance." Kaz's face was pale as he left the room.

"That bad?" Lila mumbled.

Ambrose watched her for a moment before swinging his long body up and off the chair. "Let me see." He twirled a long finger with well-manicured, sharp nails that reminded Lila more of claws, ushering her to turn. She lifted a leg onto the table and bore her back to him. With her dress cut, she could feel Ambrose study the shapes and curves of her skin, her spine, as his gaze traveled along the wound. It felt nice, the warmth—like adding a warm towel. She released a breath that sounded like a mix of a sigh and a moan. *What a horrible few nights it's been.*

"I have something. An ointment. I haven't used it in decades . . . but it might help."

"Do I have to make another bargain for it?"

He huffed a laugh. "No, pet," she heard the smile in his voice. "Not this time. I need you pretty and healthy for my first favor."

Lila gulped. She still didn't know what he wanted her for. And at this point, she didn't care. She was just happy his timing was so perfect.

"What do I call you?" Lila asked, turning back to him.

"Hmm? You mean 'master,' 'lord,' and 'my greatest desire' don't work for you?"

"No," she hissed. "I mean, Lord Draven, the Crow Lord is a bit of a mouthful—"

"Darling, I'm a lot more than a mouthful."

"Ignoring that. Kazimir seems to call you Lord Draven. The Reinicks referred to you as the Crow. I've heard others call you Lord Ambrose. Is that what you prefer? Clearly, I'm indebted to you. As a murine, I didn't address the Reinicks by their first names."

"You are *not* my murine." Ambrose bristled. She could almost see his hair flair up like that of a bird when antagonized. He took a breath before calming. "But I see. You want to know what name to scream out as you touch yourself at night." He smirked again with light in those black eyes.

Lila's jaw dropped. She jumped from the table, ready to storm out. "You are perverse!"

"Ambrose," he replied calmly. "You may just call me Ambrose."

He towered over her, not even batting an eye, though they studied her again.

Now it was her turn to say it. "Stop it."

"Stop what?"

"Staring."

"Why?"

Her eyebrows pinched together. She was about to argue back but he interrupted her.

"Your hair . . . it's like the lilacs in the Crow Court countryside." He curled a lock around his slender fingers. "It reminds me of the wisteria tree in my garden. I've never seen hair like this before." Lila's breath hitched. *Close. Too close.* And she felt herself grab for the blade again, before Ambrose released.

Taking a deep breath, she said, "My father thought it a mystery as well. Claimed my mother must've had a secret affair with a pixie." She laughed awkwardly, stepping back. She needed as much space from this wicked man as possible.

Just as she did so, the door opened, startling her yet again. Kazimir walked in, holding the door open for a small woman behind him. Not a woman . . . a girl. Large, doe eyes a shade so blue, Lila could only imagine it was the color of the ocean staring back at her. Blond fringe covered her forehead, clearly cut by the child herself.

"Hello," the girl said with a smile.

And that was when Lila noticed her fangs. This young girl was a vampire.

"He-Hello," Lila lifted her hand to wave, rethought it, and scratched behind her ear instead. "I'm Lila."

"Constance," she paused, studying her. "I can feel the questions burning on your tongue. Yes, I'm still a child. Well, technically, I am a teenager now, thirteen as of this year. I turned into a vampire just five years ago, and I am Uncle Kaz's niece."

Lila bit her lip, embarrassed that every thought was so clearly laid out on her face.

"Constance was bitten by a member of another house. So, I took her in. Showed her how to properly feed," Ambrose explained, placing his hands into the pockets of dark pants ripped and torn around his thighs. *They must've torn when he changed into that monstrous form,* Lila realized. She had seen the Reinicks shift before, but never took note of what happened to their clothes.

Lila nodded. *How frightened the young girl must've been, bitten and changed by a monster. Just like Marcus.*

But Constance had Ambrose and Kazimir.

Marcus had no one . . . because Lila left him behind.

She felt a sharp pain in her chest.

"Constance will show you to a bed chamber, it should be equipped with a bathing room and there will be clothing for you in the dresser," Ambrose took a step toward her. She felt his gaze on her again and, without thinking, looked at him.

His expression was hard, all playfulness from before, gone. *Right, down to business I suppose.* She hurriedly looked down again.

"And when you are done, I will properly clean your wounds," Kazimir smiled.

Constance placed her tiny, cold hand within Lila's free hand — the other still gripping the blade under her dress — and before Lila could say goodbye, Ambrose turned and stalked away and out of the room.

"This way, Lilac," the young girl said, tugging her arm.

Lila smiled at Kazimir a final time and then followed Constance.

"It's Lila," she corrected.

Constance said matter-of-factly, "I know. But your hair is lilac. And you're like a flower."

"Because I'm pretty?" Lila coyly smiled.

"No. Because you're delicate."

Lila let the quickest burst of laughter slip out before covering her mouth, causing Constance to stop and stare at her. "I'm sorry, I've just never heard something truer in my life."

Now Constance smiled too. "Well, delicate lilac, you stink. Let me show you your room."

Together the two girls traveled up the magnificent staircase and bore to the right. "There are five floors in the manor," she explained, "as you saw, the first is where we all gather. The dining room, kitchen, library, two sitting rooms, and Lord Draven's personal office. The basement contains the food pantry, wine cellar, and our seldom-used dungeon," she giggled. "On this floor are the servant quarters. This first room," she said, pointing at a large oak door as they passed, "is Uncle Kaz's room. You'll find a mix of vampires and humans employed on the manor grounds."

"And the murine?"

"Lord Draven has no murine. He doesn't believe in treating humans like rats or prey or whatever those other houses do."

"Does he still feed on humans then? Do you?" she hesitated.

"Of course. But those we eat are willing participants. And we always tend to them after—and we pay them."

"You . . . pay them? That's how the town near here was so lovely." she realized.

"Precisely. They feed us, we feed them. It's a give and take."

Something in Lila's chest lightened. It sounded idealistic in Malvania. Vampires and humans have coexisted for hundreds of years, with vampires leading civilization in every way. The four ruling manors controlled their territories how they pleased, leaving humans to just survive. At least, that was what Lila had come to believe in the Viper Morada. Lord and Lady Reinick took murine as their tax. Humans were given the option to be food for the vampires or die. Before she came to the Crow Court nights ago, she believed all four manors to be the same.

But the Crow Lord's ruling made her curious. If he didn't take in human slaves, where did that leave her in this bargain?

The two wandered up another spiral staircase. "My room is on this floor. You're welcome whenever you'd like!"

Lila felt herself smile. "Thank you. Am I on this floor as well?"

"Yes, but farther down, at the end. This floor is for guests, and the final floor is Lord Draven's suite."

I have my own room?

To Lila, the room resembled more of a palace. It was massive. In the front was a sitting room with the coziest-looking couches and a fireplace with flames already dancing within. Beyond that were the bedchamber and bathing room. The bed was huge with the thickest, plushest blanket. Lila desired nothing more than to jump under the covers immediately, but she dared not soil them with her blood, dirt, and sweat.

There was a second fireplace in the bedroom, near the bed, and she felt the sudden urge to dance across the room. She had never been so excited to sleep. She hoped she would have the best night's rest of her life.

But first, she needed to wash. She slipped the dagger

from her dress and quickly tucked it under the top blanket on the bed, before following Constance into the bathing chamber. Upon entering, Lila couldn't hold back her gasp. The tub was massive, almost like a pool. She imagined it could easily hold at least three people. It stood over the floor, with golden-clawed feet. Water was already steaming inside, ready for her to use. Next to it, against the wall, was a matching golden shelf with a bunch of colorful bottles of varying sizes that reminded Lila of a witch's potions. On the far side of the bathroom sat a beautiful, golden vanity with a small stool and a mirror so ornate, it looked like something found in a treasure chest. The mirror had two golden birds flying across each other at the bottom. For a moment, Lila believed them to be golden eagles, but as she looked closer she saw they were crows.

Constance followed Lila's gaze. "Ah, yes. Our lord of the manor loves himself a little too much. He puts the emblem everywhere he can. You also may find actual crows flying around the manor. Don't be alarmed, they're friendly and they do whatever Draven commands." Now that the girl mentioned it, Lila had noticed a number of crow-themed objects around the house. Mostly in the paintings and sculptures, but she had yet to see any flying birds within the building.

"Anyway," Constance continued. "Get in. I've already grabbed you a towel and robe."

The young girl rolled up her dress's black sleeves and helped Lila discard the disgusting nightgown and robe tied at her arm. As soon as they were on the floor, Lila gave the pile a small kick. She planned on burning them as soon as she was finished bathing, never to wear that nightgown again.

As Lila eased into the warm water, she winced. The

wound on her back still singed and she was sure it had to now be infected.

"This looks absolutely grotesque," Constance cringed, looking at the wound. "I'll be careful when washing."

It definitely hurt the most, but Lila also couldn't get over the shooting pain coming from her thigh, neck, and arms. All the places she had been bitten over the last few days. Her feet were swollen from all the running, the cuts and scratches from her brother were angry, and the slice down her forearm from Rebekkah had flared red.

She was absolutely grotesque, she realized. And that wasn't even counting the countless bruises coating her skin. Her knees looked like swollen blueberries. Lila breathed a heavy sigh and eased farther down into the water. It hurt, yes, but it also felt divine. She let herself slide far down enough to wet her hair before Constance leaned against the edge of the tub with a washcloth and soap.

Together, the two girls scrubbed away the mess that was Lila's life. They washed her hair and used liquids that smelled absolutely wonderful: lavender, honey, crisp air. *It really must be a witch's potion.*

And all of it left Lila's hair feeling softer and brighter than it had felt in what she could only assume was a decade. Even her skin felt softer.

The best feeling was all of her muscles relaxing. She had been wound tight for so long, constantly ready to run or fight at any moment's notice. Even in sleep, she kept her body clenched. But now, in this steaming water, her body finally relaxed. She took a deep breath, the first in so long.

"Constance, I could sleep for an eternity in here," she mused.

"As lovely as that sounds, don't. Uncle Kaz needs to take a look at your back still. And you'll have to get Ambrose to help you with these bites from the vipers."

Lila found herself tensing again at the name alone. "Why? Is something wrong?"

"Well, he'll explain it better. But from what I understand, every vampire that is part of one of the four manors has a different kind of bite. The vipers, like their namesake, have a kind of venom. Only another vampire lord can remove it."

Lila rested her hand on her bitten neck. "Venom? But . . . I've been bitten by them for as long as I can remember."

"The only way to remove the scars is to pull that venom from your body."

Lila's eyes wandered over the young girl. "Did he do that for you?" She didn't want to ask any direct questions. Not yet. But she figured any information would be helpful for this situation.

"Yes. I was turned by someone in the Arachnid Estate — someone who had recently turned themselves and was still in their frenzy. Lord Darius Maronai was furious. But by the time he found me, the damage was done."

"The Lord of the Spiders?" Lila had only heard his name in passing. She knew there were four great lords. Ambrose Draven, Lorent Reinick — now Ciro, she guessed — Darius Maronai, and Gustov Nostro. The latter two were farther away so she rarely heard much of them. They were the Lord of Spiders and the Lord of Maggots, respectfully.

"You can imagine like that of a viper, a spider's venom is quite impressive. Their teeth are coated with a paralyzing venom. As soon as they bite you, it's like you are coated in sap. You can't move, scream — you can hardly breathe — and then they drink from you," horror spread across Constance's face at what Lila assumed was the flash of memory. "Even after Lord Maronai and Lord Draven found me, I was paralyzed for a good while."

Suddenly, the water in Lila's bath turned icy cold. She wanted to hug the young girl, so similar in age to her brother. She hated the world this child was thrust into. She hated the vampires. She gripped the side of the tub until her knuckles turned white.

"Anyway, Lord Draven removed the spider's venom. I still have their powers, and technically am under the Arachnid Estate, but the Crow Lord did what he did best. He made a bargain."

Lila gulped as she was increasingly aware of the now-marred mark on her back. She hadn't even seen it in a mirror, she had no idea what it looked like. "Does he make those often?"

"Surprisingly, no. He's rather selective about who and what he bargains for." She eyed the mark on Lila's back again. "I'm not sure what deal you've made with him, but you should count yourself lucky."

It made sense she'd say that, a bargain saved her life. Lila was simply tricked into one—though, she had to admit, making one with him has helped her a number of times since. If she hadn't heard his voice when Ciro enthralled her, who knows what she would've done, what he would've asked of her. She shuddered at the thought.

"Anyway, the sooner you get all of this venom out of you, the faster the scars and wounds will heal. Let's dry you up and get you to Uncle Kaz. He'll fix up the wounds he can first and then Lord Draven will have to take over."

Lila nodded with the plan and as Constance left the room, she rose from the tub. The towel was warm and so soft against her skin as she dried herself before placing the terrycloth robe around her.

"Lord Draven sent these up for you," Constance explained as Lila walked into the bedroom, lifting a small stack of folded clothes from the bed.

Upon lifting them up to her, Lila couldn't help but squeal. *Pants!* Soft pink pants with ruffles lining the bottom hem, and a pale pink matching top with big, long sleeves. The back of the top was tied together with ribbons of the same shade. Lila couldn't even remember the last time she'd worn pants; she hadn't worn anything else other than that disgusting dress and nightgown for years.

She quickly dressed and moaned as she pulled the top over her head and pants onto her body. *Everything in this house is so soft.* She dashed to a full-body mirror, with the same ornate, golden crows from the vanity, and saw herself for the first time.

True, her body was torn apart, her eyes looked like she hadn't slept in weeks, and she was definitely malnourished, but the clothes were adorable, and they complimented the shade of her hair wonderfully.

She twirled and noticed that the slit in the back was perfect. After undoing a few ribbons, it would allow her to remain clothed as Kazimir worked on her back. *Hmm,* she thought. *That's . . . rather thoughtful of the vampire.*

Not wanting to overthink it, Lila inched closer to the mirror to inspect the mark he planted on her. Underneath a number of large gashes, it looked as though Lila had an upper back tattoo. A murder of crows flying in the direction from just below her left shoulder blade, to her right shoulder. The birds had little detail, but they were all in flight. She actually liked the mark. The flying birds looked so free . . . something she was starting to feel now too.

"Can I dry your hair a bit?" Constance stood next to her, but her reflection didn't appear in the mirror. Lila never knew why, but she had grown accustomed to being unable to see their reflections.

"Of course!" Lila was truly being pampered.

They moved back to the lavish vanity and Lila sat in the small stool before it. Constance squeezed the ends of Lila's thick hair out in a towel and then used a brush that, like everything else Lila had seen thus far, was just beautiful. Its bristles were a shimmering silver, and the handle seemed to be a matching gold to the rest of the bathroom. Constance brushed her hair, removing all remaining knots. Again, Lila felt the urge to fall asleep, it was so nice to be treated so well.

With her hair now mostly dry, the pair left Lila's bed chambers. The hall was lit with torches in sconces of ebony crows, their wings splayed with the flames coming from their backs. The rug on the floor was a deep shade of burgundy and covered up the dark wood. Again, the wood rug was so soft under Lila's feet, making the walk on blistered feet bearable.

Whereas the entirety of the Viper Morada felt like a damp, cold dungeon, the Crow Court held the feeling of a warm—and wonderfully lavish—countryside cottage.

She loved it, but a small part of her fought to not get too attached, not too comfortable. Who knew when she'd be forced to return to the Morada . . . living in comfort might even make her hellish life all the more agonizing.

They descended the spiral staircase, each step its own kind of agony as the wounds all over her screamed in pain, onto the second floor, where the hall was much the same but even brighter. In the middle, the landing for the second floor illuminated both sides of the hall due to the chandelier hanging above the first-floor foyer.

Lila and Constance walked up to Kazimir's door and knocked.

As the man opened, a wide smile spread across his face. "You look like a whole new person, miss." Kazimir's eyes twinkled.

"Please, call me Lila," she smiled. She liked this man and his niece. They were the first kind people she'd met in so long.

"Only if you call me Kaz,"

Lila smiled, "Deal."

The three crowded his room as he began to work on Lila's wounds.

"Luckily you don't need stitches for most of these. And I believe Master Ambrose has found an ointment he received from a witch years ago."

"The ointment was from a witch?" Lila gasped.

It was Constance who snickered. "Yes, another of the Crow Lord's bargains. Don't worry though. She was more of a nursemaid than a witch. She was a Charmist, she specialized in herbs. The ointment is more of a lotion meant to heal wounds and scars. He's used it a bunch, especially on those we drank from but now we just use needles to extract the blood so there's been no need."

Kaz nodded. "It may work a bit differently on the bites from the Reinicks—"

"I explained their venom," Constance interrupted.

"Ah, so you already know. The master should be able to remove it from your system, but the ointment will take longer to heal those wounds than the rest. I do think your back may need a few stitches, but the rest will be fine once we properly clean them." Kaz started to pull out different materials: a needle, thread, some kind of orange liquid, and a bottle of clear liquid with a towel. He held up the orange liquid. "This is a topical numbing serum. Everything will sting a bit, but you'll feel so much better afterward," he paused, looking her over. "Are you ready?"

Lila had suffered so much pain over the years, she wasn't afraid of it anymore.

She nodded.

11

K azimir was right. It did hurt. Each dab of the clear
liquid stung, and Lila cursed and shouted relent-
lessly. Constance, being the thirteen-year-old she
was, laughed at Lila's colorful word choice. The orange
substance did little to help with the pain of stitching the
wound and she bit her lip so hard, she thought she'd bitten
right through.

Lila didn't know what to expect from the removal of
the Vipers' venom, she just hoped the worst part was over
already.

Once Kaz was completely finished, he and Constance
walked Lila back to her room. "The master said he'd join
you in here to remove the venom and apply the ointment.
I hope I didn't hurt you too badly?" His scruffy eyebrows
scrunched together.

"No—well, yes, but I don't blame you. There wouldn't
be any wounds to mend if it weren't for the Reinicks." Lila
shrugged and then winced as she realized she probably
shouldn't be moving her shoulder blades yet.

"I've heard such horrible things about them. Is it true what they say?" Constance asked, reaching for Lila's hand.

"What is it they say?"

"I don't know if we should—" Kaz began, but Constance quickly jumped in.

"They say they're ruthless, worse than starving animals. And that the oldest brother is out for his father's head."

Lila remembered Lord Reinick's corpse on the floor.

"And the middle one supposedly has att—"

"That's probably enough. Based on the wounds we found on Lila, we can only assume the rumors are true, dear." Kaz was firm, but kind, looking deep into Constance's eyes.

Lila realized then that Constance didn't necessarily act her age, but rather like a small adult. It was the same for Marcus. Once again, a flame in her gut ignited. Lila knew what it was like to have her childhood ripped from her. She was mad for Constance, for Marcus. For herself. This world was cruel, and Lila would like to see it burn if she could.

Lila thought for a moment and realized the word she had been searching for. The desire of her flame. It wasn't necessarily anger—it was revenge. She wanted revenge on the Reinicks. Revenge on the vampires who thought nothing of their short human lives, who abused their power over the humans they treated like vermin.

"Miss, are you all right?" Kaz placed a gentle hand on her shoulder. Lila turned to him and truly saw him again. He was just a man, probably in his fifties or sixties, with gray hair she wondered was more from stress than age. He wore a dark suit with a crow emblem on his chest. His hair was cropped close to his head and his mustache was of the same shade. He looked like Constance a bit. They had the same eyes, the same face shape. But Constance was young and blond, in pretty and poofy dresses, a bit thin, and had bags under her eyes. She wondered when the last time the girl ate was. She wondered *who* the last person the girl ate was.

Lila cleared her throat. "I'm fine, just a bit tired from the day—*days*, I suppose."

"Yes, it has been quite a week for you, hasn't it?"

This man didn't know Lila's life. And she didn't know his . . . but the look in his eyes told Lila he understood her. Both of them had their family changed into monsters. Both lived in this hierarchy of the vampire lords.

But that was where the similarities ended. They were two sides of the same coin, and Lila wasn't the winning face.

"You could say that. I think I'd like to sleep for a whole week if I could," she said, smiling as they passed Constance's bedroom door.

"You can't do that! You just got here! I haven't even given you a proper tour," Constance whined. Clearly, the young girl was happy to finally have some company.

"I promise tomorrow, at sundown, you can show me everything," Lila held up her pinky. "Deal?"

Constance looked at it for a moment, before knotting her own pinky with Lila's. "Deal. Oh, you'll just love it! Lord Draven will treat you much better than those pesky snakes—"

"Oh, I'm not so sure about that." *Liquid gold.*

Lila swiftly turned to find Ambrose leaning against her door frame, dressed in the same white linen from earlier and untorn, form-fitting black pants. The top was left untied, revealing something that caught her attention. She saw black ink, similar to that on her back. Across Ambrose's chest, she could see a crow, its wings spread from collarbone to collarbone. She only saw its head and the top of its body above the deep *v*-shape of his top. He had his sleeves rolled up to his elbows, crossed over his abdomen. It reminded her of men she'd seen on Rebekkah's romance novels of dashing pirates stealing maidens away.

"He's joking, Lila. The master likes to pretend he's more of a monster than he is," Kaz harrumphed.

"And Kaz likes to think he sees the good in people. But, darling, don't be fooled—there's no good in me."

Lila caught the briefest sight of Constance rolling her eyes.

"Anyway, are we to stand around all night? The sun is nearly up." Ambrose flicked his wrist and a small tub appeared in his palm. He tipped his head, beckoning Lila inside, before turning from them and disappearing into her room.

"Good morning, Master Ambrose," called Kaz, before turning to Lila. "Good morning, Lila. If you should need anything at all throughout the day, please do not hesitate to knock on my door—"

"Or mine!" Constance interrupted and Kaz gave a low, rumbling laugh.

"Yes, right, right. Either of us would be more than pleased to help you. We want you to be comfortable."

Lila felt a warmth spread in her chest. With an almost teary expression, she reached for both Kaz and Constance's hands. "Thank you both so much. I know I am just here for a bargain, but you have truly made this experience—no matter how temporary—perfect. I hope to see you before I go," she beamed.

"Go? Go where?" Constance asked, puzzled.

"Back to the Reinicks, I assume? Surely this stay is only temporary as long as he needs me for whatever this deal is?"

Kaz gently squeezed Lila's hand. "Lila, I don't think—"

"Hurry up already," the impatient vampire called from inside.

"Sleep well!" Lila swiftly let go of their hands and gave them a final smile before entering her room and closing the door behind her.

Suddenly, the room blazed. The fire pit was too hot, the neck of her top too tight. She was in a room—a *bed*room— alone with Ambrose, the most gorgeous, infuriating monster she had ever seen.

And she hated him. He was a vampire just like the rest of them. He was cruel and sadistic and perverse. He struck a bargain with her, nothing more. A bargain she didn't even know the conditions of. He brought her here, to his manor, and she still had no clue as to why.

But he also saved her three times now. Maybe even more than that. And he gave her a massive bed chamber when he could've made her sleep outside. She hated to admit it, but she had been treated like royalty since her arrival.

Yet . . . she still didn't trust him. Couldn't—no matter how much her heart was trying to sway her, her mind stood firm.

Don't trust a vampire lord.

Lila walked deeper into the room. She couldn't find him in her sitting area, so she went into the bedroom.

Of course.

The vampire was sprawled in the middle of her bed, arms crossed behind his head, long legs crossed over each other.

"There you are." He didn't get up, didn't move. So, Lila awkwardly stood by. "Constance has already told you about the different manors' venom, yes?"

Lila nodded.

"Great. Take off your clothes."

Lila startled, crossing her arms over herself instinctually. "What?!"

"Your clothes. I need to be able to see the most recent bites from each Viper." Ambrose pushed up on his elbows and studied her with an arched eyebrow and a sly smile. In a seamless move, Ambrose rose from her bed and stood before her, looking down at her. "Are you afraid?"

There was a look in his eyes, a look of . . .

She didn't see Ambrose, not anymore. She saw Ciro and Hektor. She saw Ciro just before he enthralled her, Hektor as he pinned her to the ground.

Lila leaped from her position and pulled the dagger from under her blankets.

"Little Mouse—" But she didn't hear Ambrose's voice. She turned and drove the blade into Ciro's heart, into Hektor's chest cavity.

She would kill them.

"Lila." Liquid gold filled her ears, as a warm hand wrapped around her fist.

Lila blinked rapidly; her breath hitched.

"You're safe. You're in the Crow Court."

More blinking. She was . . . she wasn't in the Viper Morada. She wasn't in Ciro's room nor the cold, dark halls of that cursed manor.

She was warm.

Her eyes raced around her surroundings. Plush bed, crackling fire, black blood, Ambrose's dark eyes watching her.

She gasped and went to remove her hand from the hilt of the dagger, but Ambrose's hand still held it in place.

She had *stabbed* him . . . through the heart. The blade was plunged to the hilt and black gore spilled from the wound onto their conjoined fingers.

"I—I'm so sorry," she blanched. Her mouth was dry, too dry, but she couldn't swallow, it felt like she had rolls and rolls of cotton stuffed in her throat. It was blocking her lungs, her airways had been cut off, she couldn't breathe—

"Lila, look at me." He tipped her chin up with his free hand, forcing their eyes to lock, and then reached for her other hand. He laid it flat against her stomach, and Lila couldn't help but notice how warm his palms were over hers, how rough his calluses were against her skin, how much larger his hands were as they splayed entirely over her stomach.

"Breathe," he commanded. He mimed inhaling and exhaling, forcing her to do the same. Together, they took three deep breaths, Lila feeling the rise and fall of each of them from her palm. "I will not pretend to know what you have been through, but if this"—he squeezed her hand— "is what it takes to make you feel safe here, then stab me as much as you please. It won't kill me."

His hands gripping hers loosened. She gently released the hilt, letting her hand fall to her side. He pulled the blade from his chest, wiped the blood off on his shirt, and then tossed it back onto the bed. As Lila watched, the wound healed itself, skin stitched back together—the only indication of stabbing him was the black stain on his white shirt. His black eyes, as dark as the stain, studied her.

"I'm still sorry. I—I don't know what came over me," she stuttered.

"Nothing *came over you*. Those fucking snakes are the cause of this." In a breath, his eyes flicked from her own to the wound on her neck. The blood had been cleaned, and it no longer looked a raging red. But the bite still showed each tooth stuck into her by the monstrous Ciro. His jaw was so wide, it traced her neck and shoulder.

90

"This one first. Who caused the bite?"

"Ciro, the oldest."

Ambrose nodded. He lifted his hands and tentatively cupped Lila's face. She flinched, her eyes grew in shock as she looked at him, his expression blank. He left his left hand cupped against her cheek, as his right drifted down to her neck. His palm laid flat against the wound now, and Lila realized the hand on her cheek was there to support her head up.

"Will this . . . will this hurt?" She bit her lip.

His eyes flashed to her mouth before returning to hers and then the wound.

"From what I've been told . . . yes. It might feel like something is trying to rip itself out of you from the inside."

Lila gulped. Hadn't she had enough pain for one lifetime? She didn't want to deal with more.

"I will try to make it as gentle as possible," he said, his expression softened. Lila wasn't sure if it was an act to comfort her—in fact, she didn't care. It was helping. "Would you prefer to be seated for this?"

"No, it's fine. Just . . . get Ciro's venom out of me. Please," she could hear her own voice quiver. She wanted to be done with the Reinicks. She knew she may be sent back to them very soon, but if she could be free of them, even for a day, that was enough.

Ambrose's jaw ticked at the expression on Lila's face, and he splayed his hand against the damage on her neck.

Fire. Hot, burning fire. Then ice. Then acid. It *tore* through Lila like a thorn ripping her from the inside out. The wound on her arm from where he had bitten her while she ran just nights before was exploding too, much like her head. Bright lights clouded her eyes, before nothing but black settled in, only to feel another burst of stars again. She wasn't sure when, but at some point she grabbed Ambrose's wrist, her nails gripping into his skin as an anchor. Lila screamed and begged him to stop, but just as the acid took over her—decimating the flesh on her neck—it was gone.

With haggard breath, Lila blinked the stars away. Her knees had given in at some point, dropping to the floor. Ambrose held her up, kneeling in front of her.

She looked at him then, as he watched her. His right hand pulled away from her wound, and in it swirled a string of green liquid.

"Th-that's Ciro's venom?" she asked weakly.

Ambrose looked between her and it. "Yes. Every vampire's venom is a bit different. Even when they are from the same manor," he explained. Looking back at Lila, he asked, "Are you okay?"

She nodded weakly, preserving her strength. She had to do this two more times.

"Let me know when you're ready for the next." Ambrose reached within his pocket, taking out a small vial. He placed the venom within and capped it closed before putting it away again. "I'll have to properly discard that later."

Without saying a word, Ambrose swooped his arms under Lila, and lifted her onto the bed. He gently placed her above the covers and as she sunk in, she felt his weight above her shift off and heard the sound of metal on wood. As she peeked her eyes to the side, she saw he had placed the dagger on the bedside table.

Lila relaxed her body, and gave a sigh of relief. This bed was exactly how she dreamed. It was *so* soft.

"Can I sleep now?" she hummed, her eyes drifting closed.

Ambrose chuckled, a low rumbling sound that did odd

things to her stomach and made her toes curl. "Unfortunately not, Little Mouse. We have to get two more cleared
out if your wounds are to heal in time."

"In time? For what?" she felt herself losing her grip on
consciousness.

"In time for our first favor, of course," she could hear
the smile in his voice.

This made Lila rise on her elbows.

"What is this favor?"

The vampire smirked as he sat close to her on the bed
and leaned over.

"You'll be my plus one to a masquerade party held at
the Arachnid Estate."

Lila's mouth opened and closed a number of times before she could think of what she wanted to say first.
"You're using a favor to ask me on a date?"

His smile widened. "Don't think so highly of yourself,
darling. I'm using a favor to take the most coveted murine
in the four manors to a party filled with vampires. If I'm
lucky, everyone there will be just dying to sink their teeth
into you, but I'll be the one at your side."

Lila's jaw dropped again. "So you want me to be your
prop."

"Essentially. And if someone makes a bargain for you—"

"No!" she shot up and gripped his arm. "Please. I'm
hardly coveted. What'll likely happen is that the Reinicks
will kill me the moment they lay their wicked eyes on me."
She heaved a breath. "I've . . . I've had enough of your
kind. I've had enough of being a murine. Look at me," she
ushered to the wounds coating her body. "Isn't this
enough? Haven't I given you monsters enough?!"

The fire in her core ignited again. Something inside her
wished she could just kill this vampire right now. Be done
with him and his stupid bargains.

But Ambrose cocked his head as his smile only grew. He inched closer.

"Darling, you're hot."

Furious, Lila let go of his arm and pulled back. "*What?*"

He leaned away from her, crossing his arms as he tilted his head down and watched her. "You don't know?"

"Know what?" she sighed.

"Why the Reinicks have kept you for as long as they have."

"You mean it's not for the pure joy of torturing me?" she said sarcastically.

He scoffed. "No, darling. As much as I'm sure they love your company, it's more your . . . sunny disposition that keeps them interested." He smiled, fangs glinting in the light of the fireplace.

"Yes, because I'm so cheery."

In a flash of movement, Lila was on her back, pressed against the bed. Ambrose was over her, holding her wrists by the sides of her head. His thumbs gently stroked her wrists as his eyes bore into hers and she realized his grip on her was feather-light, she could easily remove her hands if she chose to.

A fleeting thought, *Nothing like Hektor . . .*

Ambrose inched forward, their faces were only just apart. She could feel his white locks tickle her cheeks. He parted his lips just above hers but moved just before they touched. His lips rested by her ear, as he whispered, "You're the closest thing to sunlight I have felt in a long, *long* time."

Lila blushed furiously. Her heart beat like a hammer against her chest, trying to break out of its prison.

Ambrose rose, looking directly into her eyes again, only mere inches away. "Your body radiates heat, like sunlight.

You, my dear, are the only source of the same warmth sunlight gives off that *won't* kill a vampire. You are what we have longed for in the coldest of nights. And that is why the Reinicks would like nothing more than to touch you, lay with you, engulf themselves in you. They want your warmth; in any way they can get it." His arms drifted from her wrists, down her forearms and biceps. "Every vampire you encounter feels it, and the moment they do . . . you become like a magnet."

"So . . . my skin is warm?" It sounded so silly to her. All humans were warm blooded. Maybe she ran a little hot compared to others, but that was nothing for a vampire to obsess over.

He chuckled again with a grin that did more funny things to Lila's stomach. "It's not quite that simple. You *radiate* that warmth. Just being in your presence makes me feel like I'm basking in sunlight. It is the one thing we vampires are cursed to never feel again. We have eternal life, strength beyond measure, powers beyond thought, yet we cannot walk in the sun. We cannot enjoy its warmth. And like the greedy creatures we are, it only makes us yearn for it more," there was a look in his eyes, a look she had seen on him before but couldn't place. It looked like . . . need. But not like Hektor and Ciro, it was softer, warmer.

Lila was starting to like it.

"And because we yearn for it, we also yearn for *you*. If I take you to this ball, everyone will feel your warmth radiating. Everyone will want you. But you will be *mine*, and I will show you off like the accomplishment you are, unlike the Reinicks, who didn't realize what they possessed."

"And . . . what did they possess?" Lila asked, nervous.

"They possessed a descendent of the one who created the original vampire. Some say it was god or the devil, but

I believe differently. Regardless, you hold their blood in your veins."

Ice cold shock ran through her. *God? The devil?*

Lila opened her mouth to argue, to say how foolish all this was, but Ambrose swiftly lifted his hand to her cheek. The same cheek with the scar from Rebekkah's last bite.

Instant pain shocked through her as the venom swam through her body, electrifying every part of her. Her skin felt like it was melting off, and the flesh on her cheek was ripping apart. She screamed, arching her back and body directly into Ambrose. She felt his weight press down on her as he expunged the venom from her body.

"Hold on," he urged. In between the shocks of pain, she could see him gritting his teeth. "It's almost over, shh, shh," he comforted.

She screamed one last time and slumped back down against the bed.

Lila warily opened her eyes. Swirling in his hand was now a forest green, so rich in color, it almost looked like trees outside. Ambrose once again pulled a vial from his pocket and placed the substance within.

"All right, where is the latest bite from Hektor?"

Lila's eyes trailed down, looking at her thigh—now covered by a large man who was just too pretty to look at.

Not pretty.

A monster.

A monster willing to auction me off to the highest bidder.

That isn't very pretty at all.

"Thigh," she uttered as her head sagged to the side. It was the only thing she could get out. Her mind was barely working anymore, let alone her motor functions.

Ambrose gingerly lifted himself from her, before swiftly yanking her pants down to her knees.

Thank the lords I put on undergarments, she thought as her eyes squeezed close.

"Little Mouse? Stay with me. Just one more. One more and then we can put the ointment on, and then you'll be all better." His voice was soft, as though he were talking to a delicate child. Or a puppy.

"I'mnotadog," she slurred.

"What?" his voice was growing exasperated. "Look, we just need to get Hektor's venom, then you can sleep, okay? Just stay awake."

"Or what?"

"You have such a mouth on you, don't you. *Or* I'll feast on you till sunup."

The double meaning of his words caused her toes to curl again. "Jerk."

He smiled. "Am I doing this or not?"

She tilted her head back, not wanting to see how close he was to her body, how close his hands were to the apex of her thighs as they splayed against the wound.

But she also didn't want to see what Hektor had done to her. A part of her still felt his hands ravaging over her body. Her breasts felt uncomfortable at the memory of his hands on them.

"Get that bastard's venom out of me," she demanded.

"Your wish is my command." Ambrose pushed Lila's legs apart, resting her leg on its side to reveal her inner thigh. Ambrose delicately laid his palm against the wound and gently squeezed. Lila tried to focus on his long slender fingers gripping her, how his hand was nearly the size of her thigh.

But just as she was starting to focus on Ambrose and ogle at his hands on her—and not the bite from Hektor—the pain returned. And it was the nastiest pain yet. Most of Lila's body had been coated in scars and marks from the Reinicks, and most of those scars and marks had been from Hektor. He was rough with her, often forgetting—it seemed—that she was a mortal human. He pushed her against walls, forced her to her knees, pulled her against him, and he definitely had drunk from her the most. Whereas Ciro laid claim to her verbally, he only sought her out about once a week, feasting on others between. But every day Ciro didn't have Lila, Hektor did.

And his venom felt like tar in her body. Like acid. Like, well, venom. It clogged her systems and weighed her down and pulling herself free had become the most excruciating experience she had ever felt.

She screamed and reached for something to grab, finding Ambrose's free hand. She gripped as hard as she could until it was the only tangible thing she could focus on. He shifted his hand in hers and, suddenly, their fingers were interlocked. He gripped her hand hard—not roughly, just enough for her to focus her attention on. For her to see *through* the pain racing up and down her body and focus on that.

Lila screamed once more, and then the pain was gone. She turned from Ambrose, not wanting to see the color of Hektor's venom—she was sure it would be the ugliest thing she'd ever seen. She kept her eyes closed until she felt Ambrose shift to put the vial back in his pocket.

"You did great, Little Mouse. Truly," Ambrose's voice was soft, gentle, and a bit exasperated. "Now for your reward."

She peeked her eyes open to see him holding the tub of ointment again. Lila couldn't help but stare as Ambrose dipped his fingers into the tub and coated them in the white gel before he carefully rubbed it into the wound at her thigh.

A moan escaped Lila's lips. It *instantly* felt better. The sting, burn, *everything* was gone.

Ambrose's fingers worked her thigh, massaging it. He pressed his thumb deep into the muscles and rubbed until she didn't feel wound tight.

Lila bit her lip to stop another moan.

"Stop doing that," Ambrose's voice was low, husky, and his eyes didn't meet hers.

"Doing what?"

"You bite your lip too much. If you bleed, I won't be able to stop myself from taking them."

"Oh . . . right." Lila pressed her lips together, embarrassed.

"And even if you don't bleed, every time you do that *I* want to be the one biting them."

Lila blushed. This *flirt*. She wanted to argue, but all the fight had left her system the moment this vampire started massaging her.

Ambrose worked his way around Lila's body, lifting her pants over her hips the moment he was done with that wound. Everywhere he touched, he was respectful and kept her clothes covering her. Her arms, both the bite from Ciro and the slash from Rebekkah were coated. Her shoulder was coated, her cheek, the small cuts from Marcus's frenzy on her chest. Only one spot was left.

"Turn around," he rumbled.

And though she promised herself she'd never do anything a vampire told her to do again, she complied. With his help, she turned onto her stomach, and instantly felt Ambrose move the two flaps on the back of her top to reveal the wound there along the mark he left on her.

As soon as the ointment touched the angry slashes, she gasped. Immediately at his touch, the wound soothed. The pain on her back was like nothing she had ever known—until the venom extraction—and now it was finally being *cooled*.

"The mark on your back will look as it did when I put it there by tomorrow. In fact, all your wounds will be gone, save for the venom-extraction marks. Those will take a few days."

"Okay." Lila wanted to ask questions, but she couldn't quite think of anything. Not as her mind was drifting away. Not as Ambrose massaged the ointment on her back. Not as she lay on the most comfortable bed of her life.

Her eyes were already closed, and she felt the grip of sleep taking hold. She was fading, and Ambrose's warm hands massaging her were the open doorway she needed, especially as they traveled to her shoulders, her lower back, massaging more than just the wound.

"Sleep well, Little Mouse," his voice was once again like liquid gold.

And so, Lila did.

12

The waning light from sunset drifted into Lila's room. The fire still crackled in its place, warming her perfectly as the plush covers surrounded her. Lila didn't remember being under them when she had fallen asleep and realized Ambrose must have tucked her in.

Her cheeks warmed at the thought, drifting into the memories of last night, drifting to his touch against her back, her bare thigh. It was . . . so different than any kind of touch she had ever experienced. *He* was so different from the other vampires she'd been imprisoned by her entire life.

She slowly sat up, stiff from sleep, but found that she felt no pain in her body. She rolled her sleeves up, looking for the marks that had been there the night before—the scratches from Marcus, the bites and slashes from the Vipers. But she found nothing, just her arm, free from any marks. She got out of bed and ran to the mirror, turning swiftly to see Ambrose's mark unmarred. The tattoo Ambrose had put on her was just as it had been, she supposed—and it was even more beautiful now that it was complete. Black swirls around the birds made them look like they were emerging from the darkness. No ... They were breaking *free* from their darkness, flying across her back and up to her shoulder. Lila wished to be like these birds, wished to be free like them. She liked the tattoo when she had first seen it yesterday, but now she loved it.

Lila continued to inspect herself. As Ambrose had said just before she fell asleep, the only wounds left on her were those on her cheek, neck, and thigh. The extraction points. But even they seemed to be doing better.

The bite marks were finally closing, and they held no signs of infection. She wouldn't be surprised if they started scabbing over before the end of the night.

She gingerly placed her hand at the mark on her neck. It was wild to think that all this time, the Vipers' venom had been running through her body. They plagued her, staying with her even when she thought she was free of them. Every silent moment away from them, every pleasant moment with Marcus in their room—they were *always* there. Harming her endlessly.

Freedom had never been possible, no matter how hard she'd tried.

And now, thanks to the Lord of Crows, they weren't. She knew he'd only saved her so she would appear to be *his* during the party. She knew he was using her. But regardless, the vampire had *freed* her. Much like the birds on her back.

Lila looked at herself in the mirror again. Gone were the bags under her eyes, and her hair didn't look like string. She was *clean.* Hungry, yes, but she was sure she could mend that.

In the mirror, she caught sight of the room behind her.

On the small bedside table next to her stolen dagger was the tub of ointment Ambrose had used last night. She padded over to it and picked it up. The bottle was plain, just a clear jar, with the white medicine inside. She remembered how Ambrose's hand looked dipping into the ointment, but before she could focus on *that* thought, she wondered if she was meant to put it on daily or —

BANG!

Lila nearly jumped out of her skin and yelped when she heard a loud crash directly through the double glass doors leading out to a balcony from her bedroom. The doors had thick curtains, to keep out the sun, but they also blocked Lila from seeing what banged against her door. The doors were on the same wall as the bathroom door, but Lila was positive the sound came from the *outside*.

She carefully creeped over to the door.

BANG!

Again, Lila startled, dropping the tub of ointment onto the bed. The sun had just gone down, and she wondered briefly if it was Ambrose knocking.

Is he injured? she thought. *Maybe he needs help.*

Lila stood before the double doors, taking a deep breath and trying to gather her courage. She slowly pulled the curtain to the side to see the fading light of the sun and purple skies of twilight.

BANG!

Lila screamed loudly this time.

Crows. Crows were smashing into her window. Lila covered her mouth and looked at the floor of the balcony. There were now three dead on her porch. And she realized they weren't doing this to themselves ... someone was throwing them.

BANG!

Another one! Lila clumsily unlocked the room door and stepped onto the balcony.

And her heart dropped from her chest.

Above her, circling her door, were three large figures. Monsters. The Reinicks.

She could hear Rebekkah's cackling, Hektor's cursing, and felt Ciro's icy silence. She inhaled sharply, her breath lodging in her lungs.

"What's this? Is the fucking crow treating you like his new pet?" Hektor cooed, eyeing her pajamas.

At the sound of his voice, she felt her thigh pulse and her knees nearly buckled.

No, no, no, she pleaded. *I was free. I was* finally *free.*

Hektor swooped dangerously low, slashing at her as she fell backward to evade. She landed hard on her rear, and just knew there would be another nasty bruise on the tail of her spine in the morning. Yet another mark of pain from these . . . these *devils.*

Laughing, Hektor swooped again, throwing a crow. But before it could smash into the door, Lila leaped and managed to catch the bird. The impact took the breath from Lila as it crashed into her chest, but she quickly threw her arms around it. She felt the bird squirm in her grip and was just thankful it was alive. Lila looked down, a wing was bent out of shape, but the bird tilted its head to the side, looking back up at her with those inky black eyes. Black eyes like Ambrose's.

Would he come if she called him? Would he protect her? It was *his* house, and Lila knew the Reinicks couldn't step on the landing she was on. They hadn't been invited. A pesky rule for vampires but a godsend for Lila. They could still swoop low enough to grab her, but if she stayed flush to the ground, she may have a better chance to escape back into her room and find somebody to help her.

BANG!

Another crow, this time it flew right next to her head. It was Ciro who threw it, his expression was blank, but his eyes—oh, those eyes. He was *furious*. He would rip Lila apart if he got to her.

"Stop!" she called, mustering every ounce of herself into it.

But the siblings just laughed and laughed.

Until a force like thunder dropped in front of her.

He came.

Ambrose dropped, from heaven knows where, into a crouch before Lila. He was shirtless, wearing only low-hanging, black satin pants. He must've just woken up as well. His hair was still mussed from sleep, and it made him look like a wild beast. He slowly stood and faced the flying monsters.

"You *dare* defile my territory? You know what this means, don't you?" his voice dripped its own kind of venom. Lila had never heard him so angry before, not even that day in the market.

He waved his hand, indicating the fallen bird. The one in her arms gave a hushed squawk and nestled closer to Lila. She hugged it in return, her only comfort as she realized she'd been shaking since the moment she stepped outside.

Ciro dipped low but continued to keep his distance.

"I know the consequences of my actions, Draven. I'm declaring war."

"On whose authority? Daddy's?" Ambrose snarled mockingly.

"Daddy dearest was unfortunately too weak. Too old. And too ugly. Our brother here is the newest head of the

Viper Morada," Rebekkah sang, flapping her wings to be level with Ciro. But her brother only snarled at her till she backed away. Lila knew Rebekkah and Hektor were afraid of Ciro, but the fear that struck through Rebekkah's features in that moment was different. It was pungent.

Huffing a laugh, Ambrose cooly said, "So, you killed your father to take the title of Viper Lord?" Ambrose crossed his arms.

Ciro mimicked him. "It was time for a change. As my dear sister put it, the old man was weak. He didn't care when our property was *stolen* from us. He didn't want to wage war." Ciro flew lower, becoming nearly eye-level with Ambrose, hovering just beyond the railing of the balcony. "He actually wanted us to send her back to you. The moment he knew your mark was on her, he said she belonged to you. But I wouldn't have it. That murine is ours—*MINE*." His tone was the harshest Lila had ever heard it. She flinched at his words, remembering the hold he'd had on her mind just before he slashed her back to ribbons. "So, I killed him. And mother too, useless as she was."

The tension was palpable, and as Ciro spoke, Lila watched Rebekkah and Hektor. The latter only smiled, and Lila was sure he had no brain cells to think of anyone but himself. Rebekkah however . . .

"Well, your rule is already off to a great start, isn't it? Disobeying the oldest of vampire laws by ignoring a vampire bargain, starting a war over a human—"

"You know damned well she's more than that."

"And now, killing my birds. Trying to steal back what is properly mine," he motioned to Lila. "And killing your own father to do it all. The other manors are likely to love this, Reinick."

"The other manors are of no concern to me. I have other

means to get what I want. Give me back what's mine, and we will leave you be."

Ambrose placed his hands in his pockets as if this were an everyday conversation.

"You've seen the mark on her back. It cannot be undone. Once our bargain is complete, *maybe* I'll give her back."

Fear coursed through Lila's body. Lila decided, in that moment, she'd rather die than go back to being a murine for the Reinicks.

"Until then, fuck off. Get off my land. And don't you dare think about harming her or my birds again." Lila couldn't see Ambrose's expression, as his muscled back was still turned to her, but she could hear the sneer in his voice, see the tautness of his muscles. He was basically growling. "Or I'll fucking string you up, one by one, and watch till the sun comes up and crisps each of you. Now, *get out*." As soon as he said the words, a massive murder of crows shot from the manor, the trees below it, and Ambrose *himself*, it seemed. The crows cawed so loud, it radiated throughout the sky, and as they flew at the Viper siblings, they looked as though they were darkness itself. The crows dove toward the Reinicks, pushing them back. They pecked and clawed until the Reinicks were overwhelmed.

"Just remember, Draven. War," called Ciro, being pushed back.

"Don't get comfortable, Mouse. We'll be seeing you shortly," Hektor cackled, and Rebekkah followed suit.

And then they were gone.

Lila flopped back onto the floor, breathing for what felt like the first time since she heard the first bang on her door.

They're gone now, they can't hurt you. They're gone now, they can't hurt you. She kept repeating the words to herself until she believed them. She felt the phantom sting of her bite marks, their fangs plunging into her.

"Little Mouse," Ambrose called, turning to her and effectively pulling her from the phantom fangs.

He was . . . gorgeous. His body was like a painting or a sculpture. Muscles, everywhere, corded arms, protruding abs. And he was so lean. His dark skin now seemed to glow in the light of the waking stars. And his chest tattoo, she saw it in its full glory, and it was absolutely magnificent. A massive crow spread its wings from collarbone to collarbone, its tail ending right at the bottom of his sternum, and black tendrils and swirls—like those on her tattoo—encompassed the crow, as though it too was emerging from the darkness.

He kneeled before her, his gaze falling to the crow in her arms. "You saved one?"

But her mind couldn't come up with an answer as Lila's mind darted from place to place. The Reinicks said they'd see her soon. What did that mean? They also claimed she was more than human. Ambrose saved her, *again*. Where did he come from? Why were they attacking his birds? What vampire laws was he talking about?

All these questions, but there was only one Lila spoke aloud. "You said you'd give me back to them once the bargain's done. Did you mean that?"

His eyebrow shot up as he studied her. He stayed silent for a moment and the silence immediately flared Lila's anger.

"You *are*, aren't you?! To stop this 'war' Ciro was threatening?"

"No," he rolled his eyes and stood, surveying the dead crows around them.

"No *what*?" Lila was seething. She abruptly stood and walked up to him. "*You* brought me here. *You* made my situation worse!"

As he turned back to her, anger flared in his eyes now as well, but Lila didn't back down.

"*I* saved you. If it weren't for me, you'd be that fucker's little toy right now. The dumbass brother would've had his way with you in that hallway, is that what you want? Who knows how he would've hurt you while he—"

The bird in Lila's arms flapped its one good wing and hopped from her arms carefully onto the floor just as Lila took another step closer to Ambrose. She wasn't afraid of him, she was afraid of *them*.

"Obviously not, you *idiot*. But if you let them have me again, it'll be so much worse. They'll string me up with a noose and rip me apart, they'll drink me dry, and use me how they please. I *won't* be going back there. I'd *die* before I go back." She was directly in front of him, her gaze burning into him. They were so close she could feel the heat of his skin brush against her cheeks, her body. And the heat of his glare was hotter than any fire.

His jaw was working, and she could almost hear his teeth clench and unclench, before he took a deep breath. "I *won't* send you back there. And they will not bother you again. Not here. Here, you're safe." He swallowed hard. His fists still clenched. "Now, if you don't mind, I'm starving, and I'd rather not be near you right now. Your blood is pumping so loud, I can nearly taste it."

Ambrose took a hastened step back, but Lila wasn't done with him yet. She followed as if they were in a dance.

"What did they mean by I was more than human?" She closed the gap between them again. Ambrose inhaled deeply and closed his eyes. She rather liked doing this to him, pushing him.

"It's what I told you last night, sun child. You're a descendent of the one who created vampires."

"And what does that mean?"

"Different things to different people," he said coyly, shrugging a large, muscled shoulder.

"What does it mean to *you* then, vampire?" Lila seethed.

"To me? It means power. It means . . . hope." He took a deafening step, pressing his body flush against hers in a game of chicken she refused to lose. "Any more questions, Little Mouse?" He flashed a grin of fangs.

She huffed a breath. "One. Where did you come from?"

Ambrose's eyes widened in shock for the briefest moment. Clearly, it wasn't the direction he was expecting her to take this. "Oh, that." He placed his hand on her shoulder and gently forced her to take a step away from him. Then, his gaze turned up. "My room is directly above yours. I simply jumped from my window, onto your balcony."

Lila looked up, and there, above her, was an open window.

As Lila was turned, Ambrose leaned down, whispering in her ear, "Makes it easier to sneak into your bed."

Lila gasped and took a rushed step back, nearly tripping on her crow friend. He squawked and she quickly and carefully picked him up.

Tilting his head to the side, Ambrose hummed, "Huh."

"What?" Lila barked.

"He wants you to know his name is Pollock. And he also says thank you, for saving his life," Ambrose watched the bird.

Right. They can speak to their familiars, Lila reminded herself.

"Ah, hello, Pollock, I'm Lila."

"He said he's indebted to you and will remain by your side as long as I allow it."

Lila paused, feeling antsy by Ambrose's watching stare. She stuttered, "A-and do you? I mean—do you allow it?"

His gaze shifted up to her, as a slow smirk spread on his lips. "From vengeful goddess to quivering mouse. My, how you surprise me at every turn, darling." Lila blushed, though she wasn't quite sure if he was complimenting her or insulting her. "Yes, I'll allow it, if only to keep an eye on you as well. Now, if you'll excuse me, I'm going to have breakfast. You're more than welcome to join me in the dining hall. I'm sure Kaz has already whipped up a delightfully human feast for you." Ambrose sauntered past her, through the double doors, and into her room. Lila's gaze followed him, watching the muscles of his back work as he tucked his hands into his pockets.

Pollock squawked.

"Shh!" she hissed. This bird was going to give her leering away. "Come on, let's get some food and then I'll patch up that wing for you."

She couldn't tell if the bird understood her, but he gave a cheery chirp and hopped from her arms onto her shoulder.

Lila followed Ambrose into her room and shut the doors behind her, saying a silent prayer for the birds who lost their lives because of her.

As they walked down the halls and stairs of the manor, Ambrose spread his arms out in a lavish flourish, and a satin black robe fell around his shoulders, covering his bare back and chest.

Lila startled for a moment, wondering where it had come from. The Reinicks were never able to summon items like he had, and she wondered if it was unique to him.

Ambrose glanced over his shoulder and said, "Tell me, Little Mouse. Do you know how to kill a vampire?"

Startled once again, Lila hesitated, "I thought the only

way a vampire could die was if they were caught in sunlight?"

"That's *one* way. We are hard to kill, but it is possible."

They walked in silence for a moment more, Lila con-
templating his words. *Why is he telling me this?*

"It seems like you may benefit from knowing how to
defend yourself. While you are under our bargain, I will
protect you as much as possible, but—"

"Yes!" She didn't let him finish, and she didn't care.
"Please, I'm tired of being so . . . so weak. Teach me how
to defend myself. Teach me how to kill a vampire."

He turned to her abruptly, causing her to crash into his
chest.

"It seems like whenever the Reinicks are around, you
grow incredibly meek . . ."

There he goes insulting me again, she thought.

"But there is a fire in you, and I think I'd like to set it
ablaze and watch it burn the world down."

Lila felt her cheeks warm as his eyes held hers. She felt
warmth in her chest once again, spreading through her
body, down to her toes.

"I still haven't had my breakfast, so keep this"—he
cupped her cheek, running his calloused thumb over her
skin—"under control." Every time he acknowledged her
pink cheeks, they only grew a deeper shade of red. She
knew she'd soon look like a tomato at this rate.

Ambrose swiftly turned away from her and continued
to saunter to the dining room, and Lila jogged to keep up.

Damn those long limbs of his.

"Starting tonight. I'll teach you how to kill one of my
kind. I'm not saying you'll be able to, but it's better to
know than be as defenseless as you are. We'll test those
skinny arms and legs of yours first."

She gulped. She knew she was weak, her only defense for all these years had been her nails and her willingness to get out of dangerous situations while hurting herself in the process. She was a runner, not a fighter. But she was so desperate to be the latter. She didn't want to be meek Lila, the one the Reinicks walked all over. And if this damned vampire really was going to try to throw her back to those snakes, she'd go prepared.

"After breakfast?" she asked, hurriedly.

Ambrose chuckled, a sinful sound that ignited a different kind of fire in Lila's core. "So hasty, pet. I have some things to attend to during the night. Let's say midnight, I will come to get you, and we can begin. I'll send something more appropriate to wear to your bedroom beforehand . . . however, clothing can be optional if you so wish, darling."

"Scoundrel," Lila retorted without missing a beat.

There was that chuckle again.

The candles in the corridor they walked through came to life as the light of twilight disappeared. The halls were completely empty, and she realized . . . she hadn't seen anyone other than Ambrose, Constance, and Kaz since she got here—even though there were supposedly an entire vampire and human staff.

As the pair walked, Lila saw crows roosting in chandeliers, rafters and cross beams, and spotted tufts of feathers in every corner she looked. She didn't know how she hadn't noticed them last night.

"I have a question—"

"I'm sure you have many," Ambrose mused.

She smirked, because he was right. "Just one for now. What will happen to the crows on my balcony?" she saw Ambrose's pace falter, for just a moment, his features flashing with a bolt of sorrow.

"They should be gone by the time you return."

"That's not what I'm asking."

He sighed as his shoulders fell, "They'll be buried with the rest of the flock. We have a large grave site in the garden. The crows like to hold funerals. I know it might sound silly to a human, but those crows were like family. To a vampire, their familiar is part of their being, an extension of themselves while also being companions through the ages. They are every bit as part of the Crow Court as I am. So, I thank you again, Lila. Thank you for saving Pollock."

She grew flustered as she saw the sincerity in his eyes, the dip of his head, and immediately she felt herself warm.

"Of course. I only wish I could've saved more . . ." Lila paused. "Where did he get his name? I-I mean, did you name him or . . . ?"

Ambrose cringed. "That is quite an unfortunate question. The birds name themselves. But Pollock, here, thought *I* named him."

"Okay, I'm intrigued. Go on," she snickered.

"The damned bird misheard me cursing at him after he shat in my room—I said 'bollocks' and he thought I made a name for him."

Laughter rolled through Lila like a wave, bursting from her lips as she pictured the bird defecating on Ambrose. After a moment of feigned annoyance, he smiled genuinely, and Lila thought she heard a small snicker come from him.

Lila hated to admit it, but part of her was starting to like this vampire. She definitely didn't trust him. But he wasn't completely awful to be around.

As they entered the dining room, Lila gasped. Her question about the vampire employees was finally answered. Each of the seats at the table were occupied, and as Ambrose walked in, every person stood and gave a small bow to the lord of the manor. Lila didn't know what to do, so she awkwardly stood by him, wondering if she should bow also.

At the head of the table, the same seat Ambrose placed her in front of the night before, sat empty. As was the chair directly next to it, to the right. And those were the *only* empty seats. Pollock flew from her shoulder to the floor, hopping away. Lila hurried to follow Ambrose to their seats, and as she sat, she noticed Constance was seated next to her, already smiling widely.

"Good evening! How did you sleep?" the girl was practically bouncing in her seat.

"Better than ever, that bed was just to die for. Still going on a tour later, are we?"

Constance's eyes sparkled. "Of course! After breakfast! If that's okay with you?"

Lila smiled, "It's perfect."

She straightened and thought she felt the heat of Ambrose's gaze watching her. But when she turned to face him, he was already speaking to the vampire across from her. He was a burly man, with hands that looked even more calloused from work than Ambrose's. He caught Lila watching and smiled at her.

Fangs flashed, but instead of something malicious, the man smiled pleasantly. "Pleasure, ma'am. Name's Robin." As Lila assumed, he was one of the vampire employees.

"Hello, I'm Lila. It's nice to meet you."

"And you. Have you been to the gardens yet?" He leaned forward, conspiratorial. "They're quite the sight, if I do say so myself."

"Robin here," Ambrose cut in, "is our head gardener. And it *is* quite a sight, all thanks to him."

"I haven't yet, but I'll be sure to make that my top priority for the evening."

Robin beamed at her for a moment, and the simple expression skewed everything Lila had come to believe about vampires. She didn't know the man at all, but it didn't seem like there was a malicious bone in his body. He tended to *flowers*, after all.

Ambrose leaned back in his chair as he whistled for the table's attention. Lila turned to him, as did everyone else. He seemed so relaxed and somehow still managed to keep everyone at the edge of their seats, waiting for him to speak.

"Thank you, everyone, for joining us tonight, and every night. Let breakfast be served." Two vampires swiftly got up from their spots at the table, walked out of the room, and returned with trays full of large, silver goblets—more like chalices. They walked to the opposite side of the table and began to place a cup in front of each person sitting, working their way toward the head of the table. Behind them, Kaz walked in with two loaded plates of food. He carefully dodged the vampires passing out the cups and placed one of the plates in front of Lila with a wink before taking the seat opposite Constance and placing the other plate in front of himself.

So, everyone's a vampire. Except me and Kaz. Feeling a bit outnumbered, Lila felt her heart race at the thought. What if they all went into a frenzy the moment they began drinking and attacked her and Kaz?

Seeming to sense her dismay, Ambrose tapped the back of her hand, pulling her attention back to him. "You're fine. No one here likes to drink from humans, hence the already supplied goblets. Most of the vampires on staff live in the village you were in the other day, in fact, if not here in the manor. They live and work with humans daily. You're safe here."

He had said the words so many times in the hours she'd been here. So when was she going to start believing it?

"We all eat breakfast together every night. The humans do it too in the morning with Kaz. Ambrose joins them sometimes if he's still awake. And once a month, we all feast together—everyone in the Crow Court. Sometimes people from the nearby villages even come, just to partake. But this way, Ambrose can discuss anything urgent in the manor, and we all are more like a family," Constance explained, smiling at the men and women—vampires—around them.

Lila nodded. *It's smart*, she thought, *something the Reinicks would never even consider. But an act like this makes Ambrose's people loyal to him*. It explained why the village nearby had been so warm. As he said, many of the people who worked here lived there.

And then Lila realized, it seemed that here, in the land of crows, humans and vampires coexisted.

Once Ambrose was served the final chalice, he lifted his cup. Everyone followed suit, and Lila swiftly turned to Kaz to copy his actions as the only other human at the table. He lifted his glass of water, so she did the same. Then, Ambrose drank, and everyone followed suit.

Some of the vampires sipped, while others chugged at their glasses. Lila nervously ate her breakfast, but the last time she truly ate was when she first awoke yesterday, when Rebekkah fed her bits in her room. At the first taste, her stomach reminded her just how hungry she was, and Lila proceeded to gorge herself on the delicious food.

Thankfully, no one seemed to mind or really notice. Everyone was feasting at their own pace, as some stayed to chat once they finished, and others headed out to their nightly stations. Robin winked at Lila as he got up, and Constance disappeared out of the room.

Soon, even Kaz finished his human meal, bowed once more to Ambrose, and left the table.

"Take all the time you need. If you want more, just ask. There's plenty of food for you here." He watched her eat and then smirked. "We want to put *some* meat on those bones," Ambrose said as he stood from the table. "Remember— midnight."

"And you'll tell me more about this bargain?" she asked, remembering the masquerade he said he'd take her to.

Ambrose feigned thought as he rubbed his chin. "Perhaps. Don't get lost in my manor," he called, turning around and exiting the room, leaving her to finish her meal alone.

13

After a rather productive evening wandering the manor halls with Constance, and meeting all those working on the grounds, Lila was already exhausted, and she hadn't even begun any kind of training. This was the most she'd done in a night in years. Most of the time, in the Viper Morada, she was just holed up in her room until she was needed.

Her legs felt sore from her walk around the massive garden, one complete with a stunning rose garden and, as Ambrose had said, a grave for all fallen crows that had a large statue of the bird above it. It was all lovely to see, but she wished now that her lessons with Ambrose would begin the next night. She just wanted to crawl back into that fluffy bed and sleep. Maybe she had time for a nap . . .

As soon as Lila got back to her room, an hour before she was set to meet him, Ambrose was already sprawled on one of the velvet couches, waiting for her. He wore loose black pants tucked into black boots that looked recently buffed, and a flowing black top. He sat, with his legs crossed over at the ankles, reading a novel.

Lila couldn't make out the words, and truthfully had given up learning to read eons ago, when the Reinicks didn't give her any books. She could pick out some things, but she still took long to sound out each syllable, so most of the time she just ignored it all together.

"You're early," Lila said, walking past him as Pollock jumped from his perch on her shoulder, onto one of the small tables near the fire. He nestled in, warming himself.

"My duties ended sooner than I thought. I've been waiting for you for the last half hour. How did you like my garden?" He shifted to drape himself across the couch.

Lila didn't want to give him the satisfaction, but they *were* breathtaking. "I must admit, it was the most gorgeous sight I've ever seen."

"Other than me, of course." She could hear the smirk in his voice from the other room.

"You're deplorable."

Lila began to undo the simple dress she wore to roam around the manor. She had changed just after breakfast, before meeting with Constance.

She saw a bundle of leather-clad clothing resting on the bed. She picked a piece up and inspected them. The pants were leather, yet still stretchy. "Are these the—AH!"

Her dress was half undone, and she clutched it to herself as Ambrose strutted into the room, his hands in his pockets.

"Learn to *knock*, vampire. Aren't your kind not welcome unless invited?"

"If you try to uninvite me from this room, I'll uninvite you from my manor."

She grunted in exasperation. "*Child*," she hissed. "At least grant me the decency to change without worrying about you walking in."

"Soon you'll be begging me to walk in."

She rolled her eyes and grabbed the bundle of clothing, taking it into the bathroom. She closed, and locked, the door behind her. "So, tell me about this . . . party you're using me for," she called behind the closed door.

"It's in celebration of Sanktus Pernox."

"It's already here?" Lila, again, realized how much she lost track of time in her murine room at the Reinick's home.

"Yes. It's, of course, a masquerade ball, like every year. And I already have our outfits planned." He sounded like a child excited for his birthday.

"So, for the first favor to be complete, I just have to attend with you?"

"And dance with me, of course. But yes. Attend with me and let me show you off like the arm candy you are."

Lila grew flustered behind the closed door. The amount of flirting Ambrose did was disgusting. So why did it make her cheeks warm and her toes curl every time? Why did it sound like it wasn't a common occurrence and was meant for *her* ears alone?

"Tell me more about our bargain," she said in a way of distracting herself.

"What about it?"

"I mean, you practically forced me to agree. I don't quite remember the terms." The leather pants fit her like a glove, showcasing the curve of her hips. She studied her calves and thighs. *They'll need a bit more focus. They really are twigs.*

"Five favors, remember," he hummed.

"Yes, yes. But what *kind* of favors?"

"If you're asking whether or not these favors will be sexual in nature, I am sorry to disappoint you, darling, but I won't be asking you anything like that."

She released a sigh. Truthfully, it was something that had crossed her mind. Where vampires and sucking blood went, for some reason, so did sexual pleasures. She had seen her fair share of passionate encounters throughout the halls of the Reinicks manor, and after her encounters with Hektor and Ciro recently, she wasn't sure what to think.

"If you'll recall, I did say it would be within your power to do. So don't overthink it. I haven't even begun to think of what else to ask of you."

Lila, fully dressed, opened the bathroom door. The fighting leathers were skintight, and though it covered everything, she felt so . . . exposed. Ambrose turned to her, and his eyes immediately widened as he drank her in. His eyes scanned her body just for a moment before he put on his indifferent visage once again.

"Well?" Lila asked, placing her hand on her hip.

"Well, what? Is it comfortable, can you move easily?" He sat at the edge of her bed, one long leg crossed over the other, bouncing.

Lila tested her movements. "Yep, everything feels fine."

"Good. Let's go." He abruptly stood and walked out of the room and Lila hurried to follow.

The pair winded even farther down in the manor, past the third and second floor, through a set of stairs and halls, and down into the basement. The lowest level of the Crow Court manor was dimly lit, with sconces lighting the path and stone floor that echoed every step of their boots. It looked . . . rarely used. They passed a number of doors, until they reached the end of the hall. The door here looked drastically different from the rest—one that almost seemed more like the door to a cell than a room. Ambrose opened the iron door for her, leading her inside.

As soon as she entered, Lila bit her lips, holding in a gasp. All along the walls were weapons — weapons of every kind, weapons she'd never seen before, weapons that looked like make believe. The middle of the room had a large cut out divot, as the stone flooring shifted into a padded ring. In each of the four corners of the room were large cast iron fire pits. They kept the room warm, but not hot — as the basement seemed to have a chilly bite seeping through the stone — and they illuminated everything in the room as much as daylight.

"This," Ambrose said, startling her. "Is where we will begin your training." He walked past her toward the weapons along the walls, but she remained where she stood. "Tell me, Little Mouse. What do you know about vampires?"

"Uhm, you have fangs. You drink blood."

"Both correct, albeit obvious. Go on."

"There are four major vampire manors, each lord with a different familiar."

"Can you name them?"

"Reinick, Maronai, Nostro, and Draven."

"Good, and what are their familiars?" He pulled some kind of brass knuckles off the wall. Lila tilted her head, studying them.

"Um, snakes, spiders, maggots, and crows, respectfully."

"Correct again. Now, do you know what each of their bites does to a person?" He placed the knuckles back and picked up a gleaming knife.

Lila didn't know why but her heart was racing. She wasn't sure if his questions or the weapons all around them were making her nervous, or if she was just excited to get started.

She thought for a moment about his question. "I only

know the spider's bite paralyzes. Even though I had the snake's venom in me, I'm not sure what it caused."

"You're not going to like it," he said, flicking the knife in the air.

Lila felt herself gulp. *Will my torment by their hand ever end?* "Tell me," Lila demanded.

A glint of mischief flashed in Ambrose's eyes as he walked to the center of the room. To the space with the padded floors and stood directly in the center of it. "Make me, Little Mouse." He tossed the knife at her and, surprising herself, she caught it.

She timidly stepped down into the ring, feeling the soft ground below her. If she fell, it wouldn't hurt. At least, not as much as it would on solid ground.

Lila held the blade out, afraid to hurt him again. What if she actually cut him and he got mad at her? What if she stabbed his heart again and he sent her back to the Viper Morada?

"Don't worry, Little Mouse. You're not going to hurt me," he chuckled.

Lila felt both comforted and insulted by this. She slashed her arm in the air, aiming for . . . anywhere in his vicinity.

But before she could get a step in, Ambrose knocked the knife from her hand, and swept her feet from under her in a flawless move. In fact, it was so fast and soundless, she wouldn't have thought he moved at all if it weren't for her ass planted on the pads.

She now realized, every time he made noise walking, breathing, just existing, it was for her benefit. He could be as silent as a phantom if he wanted.

Lila looked up at him, reaching for the knife between them.

"You'll want to have an actual target this time, darling.

And you don't really want to cut with a knife, you want to *stab* with a knife. You know, the pointy end?" Though he mocked her, he still held out his hand. She reluctantly took it and let him help her to her feet.

"Again."

Lila lunged this time, aiming for the left side of his abdomen. This time, he simply side stepped, and she stumbled past him into the stone step.

"Better. Again."

As Lila tried for a third time, and swiftly failed, Ambrose explained, "The venom from the Vipers has lasting effects. They affect the internal, rather than external. The reason you bruise so easily. The reason you're so weak. It is because their venom is constantly leeching your strength from you — or they *were*."

Lila paused, mid strike. "They *what*?" She froze. But Ambrose didn't let her dwell on it, he again swept her feet from under her.

With a loud *umph*, she dropped the knife in her hand and again landed on her back.

Ambrose inhaled deeply, not that she thought he needed to. She didn't even think vampires *needed* to breathe, but they seemed to do it anyway to express and emote. *Feigning humanity.*

Ambrose stood above her. "You have a choice, Little Mouse. A choice you need to make right now. Will you continue to dwell on the past? Will you allow those who have wronged you to continue controlling your actions? Or will you let go? Will you let go and be *better*? Will you *show* them they were wrong about you, that you are more than just their murine?" He held out his hand again and Lila knew what it meant. If she took it, she had to let it *all* go.

His eyes, fathomless pits as they were, searched hers. "I

am not saying you have to let go of your rage. I am not saying you have to let go of your brother. Do not misunderstand me, pet. I am asking, will you let those who no longer control you still have power over you?"

She looked into his eyes for a long moment and something in head clicked. She finally understood the smallest piece of Ambrose Draven.

He had been hurt before.

He had been hurt and he had conquered instead of letting it weigh him down. He didn't get even, he got better.

Lila took his outstretched hand. "Again," she breathed.

They went on and on, for what felt like hours, until Lila sweated from places she didn't even know she could sweat from. Her muscles screamed for her to stop, but her mind told her to keep going.

With damp hair stuck to her forehead, she lunged again. "What—about—the—other," she took a deep breath, "manors?"

"Mine and the Maggots, you mean?"

Lila weakly nodded as she attempted to go for the throat this time.

"Well, the Maggots are a bit difficult to define. Gustov Nostro is one of the only true Maggots left alive, among a few others in his manor. The others in his house are half breeds."

"Half breeds with humans? Doesn't that—doesn't that just make them vampires?" She tried to kick him in the shin, but he just stepped away.

"Not humans—strigoi morte."

"Huh?" Lila had never heard that term. She knew Gustov Nostro's house was the farthest away from where she grew up, but she didn't know much else about his land, the Maggot Mansion, or the vampires that inhabited it.

"Strigoi morte. They're a . . . different kind of blood-sucker. Still in the vampire family, I suppose. But they're ruthless. Animalistic beyond measure. If you think *we're* the monsters, just wait until you meet one of them. They can turn anyone—even other vampires—with a single bite into the blinded, ravenous monsters, like them."

Lila winced at the thought. Something even scarier than vampires was out there?

"They may have more brute strength on average than we do, but their power is like an explosion. Chaotic and fast, they'll destroy everything. They have far less grace, or patience, than us. We can drain our victims for hours, days," he swept Lila's feet yet again, and she shut her eyes on instinct.

But when she prepared to land on her back, the impact never came. She peeked an eye open and felt Ambrose's strong, muscled arm underneath her. He had caught her before she landed, fully supported in arms. If he wanted, Ambrose could drop her at any moment, and she'd fall right where she was originally projected to. His eyes searched hers, "before ever even tiring."

Lila blinked a few times, her heart beating loudly in her chest, but she found it so hard to look away from those eyes. *Damn him.* If her cheeks turned pink again, he would surely notice *and* comment.

She pulled herself up and took a few steps back before looking down at her feet. "And your venom?"

There was pregnant silence. "I think I'd like to keep that a secret for now."

Of course he didn't want to tell her. He was being *nice* to her. Trying to gain her trust. But Lila saw through it, even if she was falling for it—just a little.

"In the meantime, I have another secret I think you'd like much more."

Lila looked up to see Ambrose had come face-to-face with her. She cleared her throat at the sudden renewed attention. "A secret?"

"It shouldn't surprise you that I have many. But I'll spare one of them for you now."

Lila raised an eyebrow. Something about his tone, the gleam in his eyes, the raise of his eyebrow, all of it was so . . . suspicious. And then she realized the catch.

"We're making a bargain, aren't we?" she said mutely.

"Darling, you're coming to know me so well."

She sighed, placing her hands on her hips, her biceps already whining at the action.

"What do you want this time? My soul? My firstborn child?"

The corners of his lips lifted. "One hundred squats. And fifty pushups. Once you are done, I will tell you."

"*What?!* I can barely stand as it is, yet you want me to do all that?" she yelled, exasperated. She would rather give him her soul.

"I was going to make you do them anyway, Little Mouse. At least now you'll get a reward out of it as well." He smiled a sick, sinister grin. Lila would've punched him if she could.

New goal. Get strong enough to punch Ambrose.

She took a deep breath and got to work. One hundred squats. Her legs screamed by the time she got to fifteen. But she continued to push herself and her limits. She knew Ambrose wouldn't settle for less. All the while, he sat comfortably on the top step to the ring, legs crossed, watching, commenting on her form, and very obviously staring at her ass. She cursed at him more than she'd like to admit, "asshole," "scoundrel," "cocksucker," "birdfucker," and some much more colorful things, but he seemed to love every second of it.

"Such a mouth on you," he muttered under his breath when she finished the squats.

During the pushups, she almost gave up after five. Then again after seventeen. By twenty-five, she felt like she blacked out and went to another universe.

"And that's fifty," Ambrose cooed.

Lila didn't bother lifting herself back up, she just let her arms and feet give up and she flopped onto the padded floor instead. She decided she'd sleep there. Screw the stairs she'd need to take back to her room; this floor was much more comfortable than the one in the Viper Morada. She could use her arm as a pillow and—

"Do you want your secret now, or when you awaken in this heap of your own sweat and drool?"

She weakly lifted her arm, and waved her hand, indicating for him to spill.

"It's about our bargain."

Lila opened her eyes. She inched up onto her elbows, curious, but still unable to breathe much, let alone speak.

"There are five favors between us, as you know. But those five favors don't necessarily have to come from me."

Lila's eyebrows scrunched together a moment, before her eyes opened wide as it all clicked. He never said he wanted five favors *from her*. He just said five favors.

Constance's words drifted through her mind *"They feed us, we feed them. It is a give and take."*

Just like their bargain. It was a give and take. Ambrose could ask Lila for favors, and she'd have to agree. But Lila could ask him, and whatever she'd ask, he'd have to do.

"Why would you—"

"We're done for the day, I believe." Ambrose's eyes shone a ruby red, just for a moment. "Go, take a warm bath, massage your muscles, put on the ointment, and rest, Little Mouse." His voice was like a sharp knife cutting through velvet. It eased all her muscles in the first note. She could die listening to his voice.

Lila felt a familiar haze drift through her mind. It was like when Ciro had enthralled her, only this time, it didn't feel . . . scary. She supposed it was because she had already wanted to do those things, maybe not at that moment, but still. She pushed herself off the floor, and as she walked to the door with him behind her. A light purple haze—a similar shade to her hair—drifted through her ears.

"You want to go to your room. You don't want to ask Ambrose more questions tonight. You want to take a bath and go to bed. You don't want to hastily use your favors."

Almost as if she were sleepwalking, Lila waddled to her room, all the while Ambrose followed behind her, hands in his pockets. Part of her wanted to argue, but she wasn't sure if what stopped her was the thrall or that she was just too tired.

As she walked into her room, he gently grabbed her shoulder, stopping her in the doorway. *"Sleep well,* Little Mouse," he commanded and with that, he disappeared from Lila's hazy view.

She walked into her room, kicked off her boots, peeled off the leathers, dropping them on the floor as she walked, took a warm bath, massaged her arms and legs, placed the ointment on the three remaining marks, and rolled into bed.

She dreamed of shiny knives and sharp teeth, of black eyes and wings. She dreamed of Ambrose Draven, and she did sleep well indeed.

14

L ast night—" she winced. "Last night, you said the vampires from the Maggot Mansion had been mostly half breeds with strigoi." Lila panted as she lifted heavy sacks of grain and placed them in a nearby pile, only to then return them, back and forth. She was already sweating, and they had just begun their second training session.

"That's correct," Ambrose mused, flicking invisible dirt off his gilded-lined jacket. It was a dark navy blue and the gold lines on the back swished into the form of a crow. It was probably the most expensive thing Lila had ever seen with her own eyes, and he wore it in the weapons room like it was nothing. It also showed that he wouldn't be sparring with her again tonight.

He wasn't going to make these training sessions easy for her, which she respected. She knew he kept up the conversation, kept prodding questions and answers from her, so she'd be forced to work on her breathing. "So, th-then what's the—shit, this is heavy—what's the Maggots' venom?"

He sat with a long leg crossed over the other, ankles

propped on the tabletop, which had been clad with more weights Lila assumed she'd be using later. The table stood parallel to the fighting ring on the far side of the room. It was circular and made of what looked like an old, incredibly durable wood. Something about its rustic appearance made the room feel like a fairy tale. She half expected to see knights in shining armor sitting around it.

"Good. I'm glad you remembered," he smirked. "The Maggot's bite is . . . grotesque. It has the *potential* to cause myiasis."

As she hoisted another bag of grain, she breathed, "What's that?"

"A parasitic infection. If the Maggot's bite isn't cleaned immediately, the venom becomes larva within the body. The larva hatches—"

"*Inside* someone's body?" Lila's jaw dropped and her eyes scrunched in disgust. She cringed, "Ew!"

"It is gross," Ambrose chuckled. "But the larva festers for a rather long time before the parasite just takes over completely."

Lila shivered at the idea. *He said there weren't too many Maggots left. Thank the heavens.* "Does a strigoi's bite"—she went to continue with her weighted sacks—"have special venom too?"

Ambrose thought for a moment, watching Lila work. She felt flashes of heat on her ass again and knew the vampire was peeking glances. "Not exactly, except for the fact that they can turn anyone drastically quick. I haven't seen a full-bred strigoi in hundreds of years, and I'm not quite sure there are any left." Ambrose thought for a moment, before he turned and studied Lila. His expression indicated there was more to be said, but he shook his head and continued. "Half-breeds with vampires from the four manors—rather than human half-breeds—get their venom from their manor, not the strigoi. For example, a strigoi from the Viper Morada will weaken their enemy, and one from the Arachnid Estate will paralyze them.

"Strigoi have a three-way jaw. It splits open at the chin, nearly full of fangs." He drew a line from his bottom lip to his chin right in the center, and then mimicked pinchers at his cheeks. "Their pincers carry the strigoi strain. If they don't completely drain the body, or maul the person to death, they infect their victims. One lick is all it takes, and the change happens incredibly quick. That's why there are so many of them."

Lila shivered as she heaved another bag over her shoulder. "They sound terrifying."

He grunted, "I told you."

"Do they also die from sunlight?"

Ambrose folded his arms over his chest and drummed his fingers against his arms. And then, in the blink of an eye, he suddenly appeared before her, easily lifting the bag she was carrying and throwing it to the ground.

"That's enough of that. Come," he turned and ushered her up the steps out of the ring, and to one the large back wall. It was filled with blades of all shapes and sizes— mostly knives, swords, and . . . "Are those pieces of wood?"

"Yes. Wooden stakes."

Lila eyed them—they looked out of place compared to the rest of the wall, all iron and steel. Everything shone, shimmering in the fire light. But those—they looked as rustic as the table in the room.

"Yesterday we covered what you knew about vampires. Was there anything else you could think of?"

"Um," she hesitated, racking her brain. "I know you have abilities, but I'm not sure what they all are or their limits. Strength and speed beyond human capabilities. Some kind of thrall," Lila tapped her chin.

Ambrose nodded, the only indication for her to continue.

"I know you can speak into minds, though the Reinicks have never done that—"

"Well, that's due to our bargain. You and I have an established link to do. Normally, a vampire would just enthrall you."

"Right . . ." She remembered the lavender haze from last morning. "Which I did *not* appreciate yesterday, by the way," she pointed a finger at him, scowling.

Ambrose chuckled. "What I did last morning was more like . . . light encouragement. I've already told you, Little Mouse, I won't be forcing you to do anything you don't want to do. You could've rejected it at any time."

"What?" Lila was growing more and more confused— and flustered—with his words. "How?"

He's not so awful, she thought fleetingly.

"The thrall—oh, how do I explain this?" He stepped toward her again and began circling around her, reminding Lila of a black jungle cat, the way his body stalked around her, muscles shifting, utterly silent, but powerful, deadly. "Imagine a dial when a vampire uses their thrall. I had mine very low, leaving it open for you to break out of. The other day, when Reinick was trying to have you kiss him, he had it very high—which was why you felt so confused during the whole ordeal. The higher the dial, the less it becomes simple hypnosis and the more it becomes a change in your *will*. He was *forcing* you into wanting him. And he almost succeeded," he said, stopping directly behind her. "But it was very evident you didn't want him . . . did you?"

Lila didn't hesitate. She shook her head violently. "No.

No I did not." She felt Ambrose close in on her, the heat of his gaze once again consuming her. "Is there—" she gulped. "Is there a way to fight against that?"

He looked at her from head to toe, and back up again— taking his sweet time on her ass. She began to turn around, to scold him, but he grabbed her upper arms, holding her in place.

"There is. Though it takes a lot. You're not ready." Lila huffed, ready to argue, but Ambrose pulled her flush against his chest. "What else do you know about us, Little Mouse?" he whispered into her ear.

"I know at least the heads of the manors can shift into their familiars—"

He slowly walked her forward to the wall of weapons. Her gaze drifted over the different ones—trying to avoid the feeling of his hands on her arms, of the broad warmth his chest was emanating, the idea of their similar tattoos touching—until it settled over one of the wooden stakes she had seen.

"Correct," he whispered. "Only myself, the three Reinick siblings, Nostro, and Maronai have that."

"And you can transform into . . . a giant gargoyle-bat-man-thing?"

Ambrose leaned back from her, and as she tilted her head back, she saw his eyebrows scrunch together from the corner of her vision. And then he burst into a rumbling laugh that sent butterflies to Lila's stomach.

"That is quite the unpleasant description of myself, but I suppose it is as accurate as any. Our features in our full vampire forms typically align with our familiars a bit as well. Hence, the viper eyes in the Reinicks, or the feather-like quality to my hair."

"I wouldn't want to see what Gustov Nostro looks like

as a bat-maggot. Do you think it'd be like a mermaid, his bottom half a little wormy?" Lila giggled, and as Ambrose continued to snicker behind her, his hot breath rushed across her cheek, her neck. She found herself leaning into her arms a bit, her toes curled, and her cheeks flushed.

Oh, no.

"It definitely is a sight to behold, I tell you. But, is there anything else?"

"I-I," she stammered, her tongue getting caught on her ragged breathing. *He's too close.*

Holding the back of her hand, he guided her to lift the stake she had been eyeing from the wall, feeling the weight of it in her hand.

"Anything else, darling?" he asked again.

She gulped, and then pushed herself away from him, trying to get some distance and breathing room.

"I know you can talk to the crows, so I suppose they can each speak to their familiars as well?"

He nodded, stalking back toward her.

"And I suppose they can control said animals. I've been surrounded by my fair share of snakes to know."

"Go on," he commanded, his tone like a blade. A blade slicing right through her.

"I've seen you walk on the ceiling. I've seen the Reinicks climb walls like nothing."

"Hmm," he mused. She turned to follow his sound, but he continued toward her, causing her to step back, pressing herself into the wall.

"Th-that's all I know." She held the stake close to her body. She gripped it so tight; she could almost feel the wood splinter in her hands.

"That's enough for now." He leaned down, and placed his hands on either side of her against the wall, caging her in. He kept his voice low, like that of a bedroom whisper, and said, "What I am about to tell you is a highly prized vampire secret most humans don't know."

Lila listened intently, eagerly waiting for—

"But first," *there it is*. "Yesterday we did one hundred squats and pushups, correct?"

"*I* did one hundred squats and *fifty* pushups, as you requested," Lila was still so sore, she didn't know if her poor arms could take another fifty, let alone one hundred.

"How about one hundred squats. That should suffice for today. And keep that in your hand," he pointed at the stake.

She raised her eyebrow again at him, waiting for some kind of trick. When none came, she shoved his arm out of her way, tied her hair in a high ponytail, and began her side of the bargain.

Lila felt his gaze roam over her the entire time. He leaned against the large table, crossed his arms, and just watched as her legs nearly gave out a number of times, as the muscles ached and twitched.

She couldn't decide what was worse, facing him or facing away. If she looked away, she felt the heat of his gaze on her ass. But if she looked directly at him—lords, she did *not* want to look directly at him.

By the time she was done, she was seething.

"There. Tell me,"

"So feisty when you're tired," he said, tossing her a towel. "There are three ways to kill a vampire."

Lila did a double take. "Three?!"

"You already know about sunlight, the most obvious. Not many know of the other two."

"How? Why?" Lila didn't know which was the more appropriate question here.

"We tend to keep our secrets to ourselves," he shrugged.

"So, you kill anyone who knows?"

He smirked, "Precisely."

Lila placed her hands on her hips. "Why are *you* going to tell *me* how I could kill you?"

Ambrose's smile widened, holding back a chuckle. "Darling, I've seen you 'fight'—you can't even touch me. And you know I *let* you stab me that first night here."

Ouch. It was rude, but not incorrect.

"I'm telling you so that if you ever find yourself in a tight situation, you can *maybe* survive until I get there."

"I don't need you to save me," she scowled.

"Really? 'Cause from my perspective, it looks like you do. Shall I count how many times I've rescued you now?"

"That was—"

"What? Different?" Ambrose took a step toward her. His eyes flared for a moment. He almost looked . . . angry.

Which immediately triggered Lila's *flight* response. She made herself small, hunching her shoulders, backing away. But Ambrose shot his hand out and grabbed her hand holding the wooden steak. "Stop running, Lila. *Fight.*" He angled the stake to his neck. "Running will only continue making you the prey. I'm teaching you how to *be the predator.*" His hand tightened around hers. "If you need me to be your punching bag till you learn to fight instead of run then so be it. Stab me, kick me, punch me, bite me—but do *not* recoil from me. Do not run away from me. As I've already said, Little Mouse, those Reinick bastards would've fucked you to death. They would have no qualms with hurting you as long as they got their way," his voice rose, and she realized—he wasn't mad at *her.* He was mad at *them.* And he was utterly terrifying when he was angry.

"Y-You're right," she stuttered, and his grip on her hand loosened.

"If you're going to learn how to kill one of us, you have to understand. We're *deadly*. You haven't even begun to see how cruel we could be. How malicious. How *evil*. The Reinicks? They're like puppy play. They whine 'cause daddy says no. They act out 'cause big brother gets all the attention. The other houses, Lila? Those are the real vampires. *I'm* a real vampire. The strigoi *are very real*. And if you want to survive this world, you need to be prepared for that."

Lila gulped. The only thing keeping their bodies from touching was the stake she held at his throat.

"This," he whispered. "This is your only hope to stop a vampire from killing you—other than me, of course."

"Wh-what? I don't understand. A piece of wood—"

"Steel can't. Nor iron. Nor silver. And most woods can't harm us either. This specific one can. White oak wood. Through the heart. Nowhere else."

He guided Lila's hand and stake right over where his heart would be. Right where she stabbed him the other night.

"All the way through. That's the second, and most convenient way to kill a vampire."

"*That's* convenient?" she startled. "I have to be this close?"

He gingerly placed his free hand at her hip and raised a perfectly elegant eyebrow. "Wanna hear the third way?"

Lila really, really didn't. But she nodded anyway.

With a deep sigh, Ambrose said, "The third way is to decapitate their head from their body, then burn the head in the north, and bury their body in the south. The farther apart, the better."

Lila was wide eyed by the time he was finished. "I was scared of your kind before but now—"

"Not scared enough," he exhaled.

Warmth from his hands seeped into her skin, the hand at her waist grounding her more than it should. "I-I'm not scared of you," she realized.

"Why's that?" He was still too close, still whispering. Lila didn't meet his eyes, knowing they would be on fire — she'd be afraid of *that* look more than anything else.

"Because of what you said. You've saved me so many times. Sure, you pushed me out a window. And you flirt with me every chance you get. But I've also seen how good you are to your people. I will not pretend to know you, Ambrose Draven, but that sentiment goes both ways. Until you show me you are unkind, I will not believe you to be. Until you show me something to be afraid of, I will not fear you."

The stake was still pressed to Ambrose's chest, pushing against his skin, as Lila finally looked into those familiar black eyes.

Only, they weren't black. They were shining in the fire-light. Shining a ruby red.

"Remember those words, darling. For I am the scariest monster of them all."

15

Freshly bathed and dressed, Lila paced in her bedroom. Her mind was reeling from the only three ways to kill a vampire and how difficult and oddly specific they each were.

But that wasn't what was keeping her up past sunrise as the rest of the manor had fallen asleep, and the day crew made their way into the house.

What bothered her was Ambrose. Why would he tell her how to kill vampires, and then kindly remind her he was one of them—the *worst* of them? Which, she truly wasn't believing.

She shook her head. Clearly, he was exaggerating. Boosting his own ego. She didn't necessarily think he was *nice* but at least he didn't treat his people horribly. And he didn't own any murine. *And* he made a bargain with her, one in which they *both* benefited from having—not just him.

Lila started chewing at her nails.

The Monster of Malvania was proving more and more to be a big softie.

Ambrose hadn't mentioned Marcus again. She knew it

had only been a couple of days, but he said he would help her. Didn't he? She squeezed her temples, trying to remember his exact words while he spoke to her in her dream.

The truth was, she didn't know much about the Crow Lord. Sure, she could ask around. But with how he treated his people, she doubted anyone would give her an unbiased answer. And maybe those unbiased answers would also be accurate answers—but maybe they wouldn't.

Pollock, now with a tiny wrapping around his damaged wing, hopped behind Lila as she paced.

"Do you know anything?" she looked at him, hopeful.

"*Squawk.*"

Lila took a deep breath, paced a moment more, and then looked back down at her animal friend.

"Wait—you can understand me, right?" She kneeled down, resting her arms on her knees.

"*Squawk, squawk.*"

"Hmm, can you bob your head for yes? Like this?" Lila mimicked bobbing her head. The bird copied. Lila gasped and jumped forward, now resting on her knees. "And can you tap your foot? Mmm, let's say twice means no?" Pollock *tap-tapped* his foot, causing Lila to squeal. "Oh, this is just excellent, Pollock!"

She lifted the bird into her arms and rose from the floor. As the sun peeked under the curtains of the bedroom, Lila walked to the sitting room area and placed Pollock on the arm of one of the velvet sofas.

Sitting next to him, she began, "Okay, Pollock. Yes or no questions. Do you know anything about Ambrose's past?"

Bob, bob.

Lila smiled. "Do you know how old he is?"

Tap-tap.

"Hmm, what might you know?" she wondered more to herself than to the bird. "Has he ever killed anyone?" She hesitated, "Wait! That's a stupid question, of course he's killed—he's a vampire." She sighed. This wasn't going as smoothly as she thought.

"We're leaving for the Arachnid Estate in just a few days, Pol. And I know *nothing* about him." *Except that he is very, very attractive, and may or may not be a monster . . . well he is a monster but perhaps he doesn't have a completely monstrous personality as well?*

Lila groaned, swung her body out of the chair, and began to pace again. "Okay, well. Is he a good person?"

Pollock started to bob his head when Lila stopped him. "Wait, wait. You're going to be too biased. He's like your father or whatever, after all."

Lila grunted loudly and flopped back onto the couch with him. She tried to think of more yes or no questions, but all the answers she wanted were more in-depth than a simple yes or no.

She flicked two fingers on her stomach back and forth and thought. The first night she stole away into his manor, she had confronted him in an office. *His* office. Maybe she could find something in there? She'd have to read, but if she played her cards right, she could take the whole day there, undisturbed.

She just wanted to know *something* before she went into even more enemy territory with him. Lila desperately wished he was someone she could trust. He'd never done anything to prove otherwise but . . . he was a vampire.

And for so long, Lila believed *that* was enough evidence she'd need. But this cursed Crow Lord had done things Lila found . . . unexpected.

"Up for a little espionage, Pollock?" The bird vigorously bobbed his head, and she smiled in return. "Come on, then."

Lila threw a robe over her shoulders, tied it at the waist and snuck from her room. The hallways were dim, not dark, as tiny bits of sunlight poured through underneath the curtains. She passed Constance's room, vowing to play with the girl that night, and then hiked down the stairs to the second floor.

Where she saw *people*. Actual humans—some dusting, others vacuuming.

One, a plump middle-aged woman, turned to her. She startled at first and then smiled. "Ah, you must be Miss Bran. Welcome to the Crow Court. Is there anything I could help you with?"

Lila blushed at the formality. "Oh, no, I'm fine. Thank you though. Just wanted to see the manor in daylight."

The woman giggled. "I never could fathom living on our lord's schedule, sleeping the day away. You and Mr. Kazimir are truly dedicated. My name is Sandra, dear."

"It's so nice to meet you," Lila smiled. "Do you live in the nearby town?"

"Asterim? Yes! Have you been?"

"Just briefly. It was beautiful." Lila felt her cheeks warm, and Sandra smiled at her.

"If you should ever like to go, I will be happy to accompany you and give you a proper tour. I've been working in the manor for nearly a decade now, so if you shall need anything here as well, don't hesitate to ask! In the meantime, go enjoy some sunlight, you look like you could use it." Sandra smiled widely, and gently patted her on the arm. Lila smiled back and desperately wanted to take the woman's advice, to go outside and sunbathe till dusk.

But she had a job to do.

Sneaking through the rest of the floor and winding down the next set of stairs, Lila carefully avoided running into anyone else.

The manor had been just as gorgeous during the day as at night, except now, an array of colors kaleidoscope on the walls and floors. Sun shone through the prism-like windows, warming and lighting every hall and room she walked through. It was more color than Lila had ever seen.

On the first floor, she made a hard left and turned for the door she had slammed through that first night.

The room was dark as the closed curtains swayed in a silent whisper. Lila looked all around her, making sure to check the ceiling this time. *No sign of Ambrose.*

She exhaled, closing the door softly behind her.

"Pol, stand by the door. Squawk if anyone comes." Lila scooched the bird onto a golden perch next to the door. She assumed crows sat in here plenty, as there were a number of posts and perches set up all around the room.

She inched to the narrow window—the same one she had been pushed from—and opened the curtains just a smidge, enough to illuminate the room.

The light immediately stung her eyes, and she squinted for more than a few moments as they readjusted. Trying not to strain her vision, she kept the curtain half closed as she searched for clues on her bargainer demon.

Lila turned to the desk in front of her and began to rummage through it. On top lay a map of Malvania. She saw the four vampire territories—the Crow Court was the only territory that shared its borders with each of the other territories. To their southwest was the Viper Morada, southeast the Arachnid Estate, and northeast the Maggot Mansion.

Lila's fingers ran along the Crow Court. She saw a small

dot with *Asterim* written close to the tiny picture of the Crow Lord's manor. But there were so many other towns and villages—cities even—marked as well all over the map. Ambrose ruled over *all* of this. A king without a crown . . . that's what each of the vampire lords were in Malvania.

And she was coming to learn *this* king was so different from those ruthless vampires she had come to know.

Shaking her head, Lila continued her search. Papers. Lots of papers. Quills, ink, unused notebooks. She grabbed a random paper and attempted to read the heading.

"T-To A-Am-bro-Ambrose Dr-Draven—urgh, this is going to be rather tedious," Lila sighed. She continued trying, muttering the sounds under her breath and Pollock made a small chirp. "Don't you go telling anyone about this, Pol," she scolded the bird. A week ago, she would've thought she'd lost her mind doing such a thing.

After several more attempts, she discovered what the paper's title had said.

TO AMBROSE DRAVEN: POPULATION COUNT IN ST. MARIGOLD CITY AND YEARLY GRAIN INTAKE

Not very telling of the intricate mind of the Lord of Crows at all.

"*Squawk! Squawk!*"

Lila's head shot up, dropping the paper from her hands. Pollock was vigorously flapping his wings. She expected the office door to open, but what she saw instead surprised her.

Sitting on the perch next to Pollock was a snow-white crow. An albino perhaps? But his eyes were just as black as Pollock's.

"Oh, hello," Lila said. She still felt silly speaking to birds, but then again she had been doing so all morning. And clearly, they knew how to respond.

The white crow flew from his perch onto a shady spot of the desk, landing right in front of Lila. He tilted his head, watching her.

"I wouldn't suppose you know any telling details about the Crow Lord's past, would you?"

The bird simply tilted his head to the opposite side.

"Right . . ." She sighed again, continuing to search through the desk drawers, as the white crow squawked.

"Oh, shut it. Don't judge me." She wandered to a wall of books, maybe he had some kind of . . . family memoir? Assuming he even had a family. The books were mostly dusty, save for a book on fairy tales. She plucked it from the shelf and flipped through the illustrated pages. Stories of princes and princesses, knights and maidens. The book had been worn down from use. Lila would have assumed it was just old, but the lack of dust indicated it was probably used a lot frequently.

"Do you think this belongs to Constance?" she asked the birds, her back still turned.

"Actually," that *damned* liquid gold, "that belongs to me."

Lila spun around on her toes, so quick she nearly lost her balance. Where the white crow had been, Ambrose sat on his desk, one leg crossed over the other. He wore the same black sleep pants, and yet again lacked a shirt.

"The Reinicks never taught you to read?"

She ignored his question. "You were the white crow?"

"I thought you would've figured that out the moment you saw me. But then you continued going through my things."

"What are you doing awake?"

"What are you doing in my office?" He crossed his arms, raising an eyebrow, and Lila couldn't help but stare for a moment at the bulge of his biceps.

Touché, Lila thought. "I'll be honest," she said with a deep inhale.

"Please," he mused.

"I don't trust you. I don't *not* trust you. But that masquerade is fast approaching, and you expect me to travel with you into enemy territory. And you're supposed to be *the Monster of Malvania* and it's—"

"Little Mouse, you don't need to trust me. The bargain doesn't need it."

"What happens if I don't follow through on my side of the bargain?"

"You die," he said simply, shrugging his shoulder. As if death was but a trip on the road.

Lila gulped. *Well, there's no backing out.* "Lovely."

"I'd rather you be at my arm willingly during the ball, and not by collar and chain—though, if you ask nicely, that can be arranged." A devilish twinkle sparked in his eyes with a smirk as wicked as sin.

Lila flushed, but quickly pouted as her response.

His eyes glanced down at the book in her hands again. "What can I do to help you be comfortable with me?" His voice was growing exasperated, but not like he was annoyed but rather . . . pleading.

Ambrose lifted himself from the desk and walked up to her, carefully avoiding the beam of light. With each step he took, Lila stepped back—right until she backed into the wall of books and a small gasp escaped her. His eyes shone with that same heated need that was so different from the Reinicks.

Lila couldn't help but yet again notice how truly massive

he was as he stood only a breath apart from her. Not only tall—well over six feet, maybe even six-foot-five, but his shoulders were so large and wide. Lila wouldn't be surprised if he could lift a horse, and that's without considering his vampiric strength or his monstrous form that was even larger.

Lila found her cheeks heating as she gazed up at him through her long lashes. "U-Um, I'm not sure," she stuttered, holding the fairytale book close to her chest.

"Ah, the meek mouse returns," he smirked. She saw, and felt, his gaze wander over her before he spoke again. "Let me show you something."

He took one of her hands, threading their fingers together. Yet again, it was warmer than she expected a vampire's hand to be. They were the undead, and oftentimes when she interacted with the Reinicks, she found them to be as cold as ice. And other times they were hot to the touch as though with fever.

But Ambrose's hand was warm and calloused as he held her gently. She could tell he worked with his hands often in his life, and she willed her own hand to not feel sweaty or clammy in his.

Lila's heart raced. They hadn't moved yet, and she felt like they were standing there for eternity, staring at their interlocked hands. Eventually, Ambrose cleared his throat.

"Come now. You can keep the book, use it to practice your reading." He turned and led her from the room before she had a chance to respond.

Pollock followed, but only for a moment, before hopping up the stairs to the second floor, and presumably back to Lila's bed chamber, as Ambrose guided Lila through the house, and down into the basement once more. She stiffened. *Is he going to make me train now? Again? In my pajamas?* she wondered.

The floor to the basement was damp and cold on her bare feet, but she didn't hesitate to keep walking. If they were going to the weapons room, it would at least be heated from the fire pits.

As Ambrose led her, Lila saw his back muscles move with each step, and was once again reminded of a jungle cat. Lila had seen illustrations once, of a massive black cat, she thought it was called a jaguar. That's what Ambrose reminded her of. All muscle, silent, deadly, a terrifying predator to no end.

But as his hand was in hers, she felt . . . safe. For the first time in a long time, Lila didn't feel like she needed to run and hide. The realization did something strange to her stomach and her chest.

Sure, this vampire could be leading her down right now to drink all her blood, killing her. Or he could be biding his time to throw her back in the Viper pit if they strike a better bargain.

But he could also be trying to *help* her.

And that was what scared Lila the most. More than vampire fangs, more than Ciro and Hektor. More than never helping Marcus.

What scared her, more than anything, was the hope she was holding out for this man . . . this monster. Should she trust him if that trust will only get stomped on in return? Should she not trust him only to find out he had been true and honest all along? And why was he trying so hard to simply make her comfortable with his presence?

Right now, as she held onto this man—*no, he's a monster as well*, Lila reminded herself—this *monster's* hand, she found herself *desperately* wanting to trust him.

How silly she was, someone showed her an ounce of sympathy, maybe even kindness, and it's like she lost all sense of direction. She felt her fingers tighten around his of their own will and she gulped.

Oh no.

"I had something ... adjusted for you," he said, his voice once again like liquid gold as it filled the damp hallway they walked through. Every time she heard that voice, she knew she was in danger of melting.

"Wh-what is it?" She wasn't sure how she found her own voice through her tumultuous thoughts but was thankful it came out in more than a croak.

"Something to make you feel safe. From vampires—from me, if need be. Something ... more helpful than that dagger you brought from the Viper Morada." He pushed the caged door of the weapons room open and led her inside to the round table. "Stay here a moment," he commanded, his voice turning from gold to the sharp silver of a blade.

So, Lila waited. She really hated her own resolve. She promised she would stop taking orders from vampires, yet here she was.

Putting the book down on the round table, she watched as he walked to the wall of knives and stakes. He pushed a panel on the wooden wall, a panel that looked just like every other brick in the wall, and out popped a hidden alcove. Ambrose reached his arm in and pulled back something long and thin.

And from what Lila could see, it was something sharp.

"I made this weapon for myself very, very long ago," he explained, gazing at the weapon and walking toward her.

Lila studied him once more. His body looked like he was in his late twenties, thirty at most.

"You snuck through my office to find out more about me right? Well, why not try asking the source?" His eyes reached hers and he smirked.

"How old are you actually?"

"Far older than I look, that's for sure." Lila pouted at his response, causing Ambrose to huff a laugh before continuing. "I lost count exactly, but I believe I am nearing my—what year is it exactly?"

Lila tapped her chin, thinking. She wasn't even sure herself. "If I am now twenty-two, it must be 264 AM. Unless my birthday passed as well . . ."

"What a dreadful pair we make. Can't even keep the year straight." He sighed sarcastically.

Lila giggled, "Truly dreadful. I didn't even know Sanktus Pernox was near, I thought we were already in the winter months. Which I guess means my birthday hasn't passed yet."

He chuckled, a sound that rumbled Lila's very core. "Well, I'll make note of that then. If it's *around* 264, then I assume I must be nearing my 465th birthday."

Lila's jaw dropped. He's been around since before the vampire rose to power? Since before the Mass Death? She quivered at the thought. She'd only been alive twenty-two years, and sometimes she thought *that* was even too long. But 465? "Wow," was all she could say. "How did you—" she hesitated, not quite sure what the proper question she was looking for was.

"How did I become a vampire, you mean?"

Lila nodded.

Ambrose pulled a chair out from the wooden circle table and glanced at it, indicating Lila to sit. Once he pushed her chair back in, he sat in the one next to her. He continued to obscure the weapon in his hand, so she still hadn't gotten a great look at it, only that it appeared to be made of a pale wood.

Placing it in the seat next to him, he propped his arms

on the table and rested his chin against his laced fingers. "Vampires are made in three ways."

"Hmm, vampires do lots in threes, it seems. Three ways to kill, three ways to turn," Lila observed.

"Very astute, darling. I don't know why that is, but you're right. It seems to be a balance of life and death.

"We can be changed by another vampire, sharing the blood back and forth; we can be born a vampire, like with the Reinick siblings; or—and this way is no longer in practice— we were once changed by your ancestor. At least, the original vampire was. Then he had three wives he turned, and those wives bore children, thus began the Mass Death.

"When I was twenty-eight years old, I was changed by the original vampire. Once the Mass Death occurred, he was killed, and I began one of the original manors."

Lila was enthralled by his story. What happened to his family, his life? What was he before he was bitten and changed?

Before she could ask more, he said, "But, enough about me. I want to give this to you. When I first turned, I learned how to defend myself from others, and, clearly, how to make a name for myself. I'm sure you've heard rumors about me?"

Lila nodded. "The Monster of Malvania. I thought you'd be a lot . . . scarier."

"Darling, you've only seen my good side," he smirked, sending chills down Lila's spine. "Before Malvania was made, all of us were united against humans under the original vampire and the House of the Bat. It was then I earned my title, the Monster of Malvania." Lila saw Ambrose swallow, his throat bobbing uncomfortably.

Lila opened her mouth to ask more about it, but Ambrose's gaze cut to her.

"I lived up to the title. That's all I'll say about that. When the House of the Bat was overthrown, we divided into eight manors. The Crows, Maggots, Spiders, and Snakes, as you know. But there were also Wolves, Bears, Lions, and Hawks. Over the years, the manors learned us critters have a way of . . . getting under the skin. We won and became four, establishing our laws and treaties under the new order of Malvania.

"But before the treaties, vampires were—well, blood-thirsty feels a bit apropos. We fought and killed one another to take our land and protect our people. That's when I used *this* most of all, to defend the Crow Court." He turned to Lila in his seat and held up a gorgeously carved wooden stake.

Her eyes went wide. The wood was so pale, and the details carved and whittled within could leave her studying it for days. It had the same swirls and feathers she had on her back tattoo and so much more. It reminded her of the stained-glass windows she had seen in the dining room.

But what really caught her breath was the hilt of the piece. It was the head and body of a crow, carefully made to still remain useful and comfortable to hold. Its gleaming black eyes made with a gem so black reminded her of Ambrose's, and the black feathers accented the wood beautifully.

"It's made of white oak and is as sharp as any blade on my wall. Eventually, I'll teach you to sharpen them and maybe even make your own. But I believe holding on to this may bring you the most comfort I can offer. As long as you don't use it on me," he smirked.

Lila reached her hand over the stake, scared to touch it. In her hesitation, Ambrose grabbed her hand once more, those calloused knuckles brushing her skin, before he placed it in her palm and her breath caught once more. The weapon was so light, so comfortable in her grip, despite its size.

"I didn't mention this before, but white oak is incredibly rare. After the Mass Death, many trees were burned by vampires to prevent anything from harming us—anything other than the sun. I have a small forest of them in the central region of the Crow Court, but other than those and the few remaining in the wild, the tree is all but extinct. Do you like it, Lila?"

The moment her name left his lips, she tore her gaze from the stake to his eyes. They bore into her, and Lila felt her heart racing in her chest at his hopeful expression. His eyebrows were turned up, his lips slightly parted, and his eyes—those *eyes*—were like the darkest part of the night sky. So *full . . .* of *everything*.

She immediately wanted to hear him say it again.

"Y-Yes. Very much. Thank you, I don't know how—"

"Don't concern yourself. Just keep it, and yourself, safe. I will add something to your outfit for the party where you can hold it on your person," he paused, tearing his gaze from her and scratching at his head. It was almost human. Almost. "I don't know if it'll make you see me any differently, Little Mouse, but for what it's worth, the Crow Court has never had human murine. *I* have never had murine."

Lila gasped, not realizing how badly she wanted to hear that.

Before she could fully process, Ambrose grabbed the book of fairy tales, stood, and offered his free hand to her. "Come. We should sleep before the night starts. We leave for the Arachnid Estate in a week, and we have to be well rested to train with your new weapon."

Lila knew what he wasn't saying. *I hope with this, you'll be comfortable with our trip into enemy territory. I hope with this, you'll come trust me.*

And as Lila's heart pounded when she took his hand; as her grip tightened on her new weapon; as she followed this dangerously gorgeous man up through the manor, she was starting to feel how doomed she had truly become.

She found that she trusted Ambrose with more than just her life—she was starting to trust him with her heart.

16

The carriage bounced, and Lila felt like at any moment she would burst through the small door and run far, far away. Or walk. She would rather walk barefoot the rest of the way than be in this horrendous thing for another minute.

"Are you still unwell?" Ambrose asked and she hurriedly lifted a finger, closing her eyes.

"Maybe we should lower the window?" Constance asked. Lila was happy the girl was traveling with them to the party. At least she'd be able to have someone there on her side.

Lila felt Ambrose watching her, the heat of his gaze lingering on her face.

"Maybe we should," he said, scooching over to one of the doors on his side of the carriage. Lila heard a window propped open and felt the instant cool breeze from outside brush past her face, immediately feeling the slightest relief.

"Better?" he asked.

"Better."

It had been five days since Ambrose gave Lila the etched

stake, five days of vigorous training and, though her muscles felt incredibly sore, Lila *felt* her body change over the last weeks. She had more energy, the slightest definition in her arms and legs. And her backside looked rather fantastic, if she could admit it. But they were finally on their way to the Arachnid Estate for the masquerade ball that would be tomorrow night, on Sanktus Pernox. She had yet to see what she'd be wearing for the event, Ambrose kept it incredibly confidential, which made her even more curious. She just hoped he wasn't expecting her to wear lacy underthings or a see-through gown to the party. Though, with this rake, she wouldn't be surprised.

Ambrose told her to keep the stake hidden. No one should see it unless she were about to end their life. She hadn't even shown it to Constance yet. But it was a great comfort as it sat in a leather holster—another gift from Ambrose—wrapped against her thigh under the layers of her skirts. She found herself placing her hand atop it frequently and, each time, it comforted her to no end to have it there.

"Once we arrive, Maronai will hold a feast in honor of all his guests just before sunrise. Then we will sleep, rest, and the ball will be held from moonrise to sunrise the next night. If either of you should need me, do not hesitate to ask. Remember, the other vampires fear me. Use that to your advantage," he explained. Then, with his gaze bearing into Lila, he said, "And remember, everyone in this manor will be a vampire. Everyone will be able to hear and feel your presence. *Everyone* will want a taste of you. There is no hiding here, Little Mouse. If you need me"—he paused, his eyes filling with a heat Lila only saw when he stared at her body—"come to me."

"Or me!" Constance giggled.

But Ambrose captivated Lila's gaze. So long, in fact, she didn't even notice they had already arrived.

"We're here!" Constance cheered as Lila finally turned her gaze from Ambrose and out through the window.

What she saw took her breath away.

Through the trees and early snow, Lila saw a structure she couldn't quite call a manor. A large building sat in the middle, elevated off the ground by imposing black pillars. These pillars reached from the ground high into the sky and bent in odd directions. Lila realized then that the structure strangely resembled a spider.

Gloved fingers delicately tilted her chin. "Save your jaw drops for me, darling," Ambrose grinned. But Lila felt like he wasn't teasing. He was serious. And the thumb he ran over her bottom lip proved it.

Is he jealous?

"So, will you two be sharing a room?" Constance mocked.

Lila jolted away from his hand, swiftly looking between the other young girl—who was currently wiggling her eyebrows at her with a wide smile—and the window. The window was safer. The cold air from the outside brushed against her warming cheeks as she chewed her bottom lip.

What in hell am I getting myself into?

The carriage finally rounded a large fountain with depictions of angels and demons fighting or making love, she couldn't quite tell, and stopped just in front of a large, obsidian stairway leading to the front doors. The entry stairs alone were so high up, they had to cover at least three stories.

Lila jumped in her seat, as the door to the carriage was opened by a terrifying man, incredibly tall and rail thin. He was even taller than Ambrose, but his appearance made him seem stretched, like he was pulled by his hair and feet at the same time in opposite directions.

"Welcome, Lord Draven. We are so pleased to have you and yours here." The old man's voice quaked as he gave a small bow, and Lila realized he must've been changed into a vampire many years into his life — or something to cause his decrepit look.

"Hello, Balzar, pleased as always." Ambrose ushered Constance out first. The young girl took Balzar's hand and climbed out of the carriage, greeting him as she went. Balzar guided her to the front door as Ambrose climbed out, following behind.

Lila inched her way to the door, ready to do the same, when Ambrose turned and offered his hand. She felt her breath catch in her throat as she looked up at him and saw he was so much closer to her than expected, their faces only so far apart. Lila slowly placed her hand in his and as his fingers closed around hers, he reached his other arm around her waist. Lila squeaked as he pulled her from the carriage and delicately placed her on the snowy floor in front of him. Even as her feet met the ground, Ambrose still held her close. Instead of continuing to hold her hand, he kept the arm around her waist, his hand gripped at her side, as he began to follow Balzar and Constance to the stairs.

Lila, once again, forgot how to breathe. She tried to blame the icy breeze, but her traitorous mind kept reminding her of his large hand at her waist.

"Relax, darling. If not, others will sense how taken you are with me," he whispered, leaning closer to her ear. "They'll be able to smell it off you too."

Clearly this monster did not know how to calm Lila's racing heart. He only boiled her blood and set her thoughts and body on fire. She blushed furiously and took a deep breath as Ambrose chuckled, apparently fully aware of what that rumble did to her.

He led her to the stairway and the two began the climb behind Balzar and Constance. Well, it was more like *he* began to climb for the both of them. With his hand around her waist, he slightly lifted her from the ground, just high enough for her feet to dangle above the steps. She gasped, but he just smiled, his gaze facing forward.

"I know you're sore. Save your strength, Little Mouse. You'll need it."

She once again blushed. This Ambrose was so different from the Ambrose that had pushed her out a window a couple of weeks ago.

His hand felt firm around her waist as she was pulled flush with his side. She wanted to argue, wanted to say *I can walk up these stairs myself.* But something about the way he held her made her keep her mouth shut. It was comforting, feeling him there for her just before the storm of chaos that was sure to erupt upon going into the manor.

So instead of fighting, she leaned into him.

Ambrose carried her to the top of the stairs, where Constance and Balzar waited, and set her feet down on the ground once more. She quickly brushed out her skirts and smiled at her friend, avoiding the stare Balzar was giving her.

"This way," he turned and led them to a ginormous black lacquered door. Lila had to bend her head all the way back just to see the top.

She felt Ambrose lean down as he spoke into her ear, "Don't expose your neck, darling. Remember your surroundings."

Lila's hand shot to her throat. He was right, that was stupid of her, like an open invitation to have *her* for dinner.

Balzar pushed the large door open and stepped aside to let them in. "Welcome, Lord Draven, Lady Constance, and Lady Lila, to the Arachnid Estate."

Like the door, the room beyond was massive, with stairwells as high up as the eye could see, all breaking off into different directions Lila assumed led to the leg-like pillars she saw outside. The room was dark, shiny black lacquer adorns the walls and floors, casting hazy reflections the lighting all around like a cacophony of fireflies. The accenting all around the room was a silver so bright it looked white, and a green so dark it could be mistaken for black.

And while the room was gorgeous in its gothic decor, to Lila's dismay, the room was just as cold inside as it was outside.

With each breath, she saw the cloud of vitality puff in front of her. And as she looked around, she realized she was the only one who could feel the cold bite on her nose and fingertips. She buried herself in her coat and stood closer to Ambrose.

Instantly, she felt heat radiate from his body, and found herself inching into him, till they were just barely touching.

"Ambrose Draven! Constance Lahmann! Welcome, friends." A tall man with broad shoulders and curly dark hair sauntered up to them with open arms. He was incredibly pale, and his black irises looked larger in his eyes than most. He was a classic tall-dark-and-handsome type and Lila had to admit, he was rather dashing in his light gray suit and cane. His dark eyes fell on Lila and his lips curled on one side, lifting a dark brown, well-maintained mustache along with it. "And who might this lovely being be?" He reached for her hand and placed a scratchy kiss on her knuckles. A flash of green shone in his eyes and he watched her through dark lashes, his lips remained pressed to her knuckles.

"This is *my* companion, Lila Bran," Ambrose stepped

closer to her, finally closing the remainder of the gap between them, and pulling her hand from the other man's. "Darling, meet Darius Maronai, Lord of the Arachnid Estate."

"And one of Ambrose's closest friends," Darius smirked and threw an arm over Ambrose's shoulder. "How have you been, you ol' buzzard? And Constance, dear, you look amazing!" Lila watched as the vampires all got reacquainted with one another.

Her eyes glossed across the room. She saw a number of enchanting faces all chatting amongst each other. Some glanced her way, and she saw flashes of gleaming fangs in the dim light of the room.

Ambrose stayed close to her, even as his attention seemed elsewhere for the moment, and she was beyond thankful as she tried to sooth her beating heart.

More than anything, seeing all these vampires in one room just reaffirmed that Ambrose was . . . otherworldly. He wore a thick coat made of black wool, and the neckline seemed to be adorned with feathers, like the cowl of Pollock and the crows. He also reminded her of a vulture, as his long white hair had been tousled by the wind outside, his dark skin perfectly complementing it. And those eyes—those *eyes*—Lila could stare into them all day.

They say when someone stares into the void long enough, it looks back, but looking into Ambrose's eyes was like being *engulfed* in the void; engulfed, consumed, devoured completely. Lila knew they must be incredibly powerful when he really wanted to enthrall others into doing his will. But when he looked at *her*, it was like she was the only existence in the world—it felt like *they* were the only two in a world entirely of their own.

Underneath the coat, Ambrose wore a tailored black-on-black suit. Even the detailing on his suit was a black velvet on his lapel and a matching tie that made up the wings of crows.

Both Lila and Constance wore similar coats, but where Constance had a plain black dress with similar velvet detailing as Ambrose underneath, Lila was dressed in a pastel lilac gown that matched her hair. The gown was mostly made of layers of chiffon with small studs of gleaming crystals throughout that sparkled in low lighting. Lila almost thought she looked like the sky at twilight, where the stars were just beginning to shine in the purple-haze. When she first put it on in the Crow Court, she had twirled and twirled—it was the fanciest gown she'd ever worn. Constance had done her hair for her, placing small gems hidden throughout the half-up hairdo.

Now, completely surrounded by vampires, she had rethought her dress and its sweetheart neckline and lack of sleeves. Her neck would be on full display once she removed the coat, and she even wore the thinnest chain that would only bring more focus to the long column—like an idiot.

She curled into her coat and looked to her feet. She wished she could just disappear.

A hand pressed against her back. Ambrose, still talking to Darius, kept his hand there, it was warm—even through her coat—and immediately eased her nerves.

"Come, let me show you to your rooms so you can freshen up from your travels. Then, we feast!" Darius said, turning to one of the stairways. "And, Miss Bran, I was informed you were attending so I had a more . . . human-fitting meal prepared for you. I hope it is to your liking." The man did a little bow, with his hand placed upon his chest. His voice had been serene, the expression he wore as he kissed her hand completely dispelled.

"Ah! Thank you. That is very kind of—"

"Please. It is no problem at all," he smiled. "I want you to feel at home here. If you should need anything, or are uncomfortable in any way, please inform me or one of my attendants, and we will assist in any way we can. Balzar can see to you at any time, night or day." The man turned to look at Balzar behind them, who nodded to his master.

Anytime in the day? Maybe he was part strigoi—but Lila suddenly had the suspicion that Balzar wasn't a vampire or human, but something else entirely.

Darius guided them through the dimly lit foyer, and Lila noticed the marble flooring was black and a jade green. It was mesmerizing, and the black lacquered railings and decorations reflected against the floor just beautifully. But as she continued to gaze down, she was the only person reflected back, the rest of the room looked abandoned, empty. An eerie sensation crawled down Lila's spine, and she suddenly felt the weight of every pair of eyes in the room staring at the back of her neck.

Ambrose kept his palm on her back, guiding her next to him. Constance stood on the other side of Lila, a comfortable and protective presence. She released a shaky exhale. At least Lila wasn't alone in this.

Ignore them, Ambrose's voice wove into her mind.

She jumped at the reminder of the Concord. *A bit easier said than done—especially when everyone in here wants to eat me.*

I'd say only half want to eat you. The other half want to fuck you senseless.

HA! Present company included? she pushed back sarcastically, already rolling her eyes. But she regretted it the moment it left her mind, as she realized she was only fueling the fire in Ambrose's needing eyes. Her cheeks warmed instantaneously as she felt the very overwhelming heat from his gaze on her caress the top of her head, the curve of her cheek, the tip of her ear. He was staring at her, devouring her with his eyes alone.

Present company is first in both lines, darling. You'd be forgetting your own name by the time I even touched you, and I would forget my every purpose—as though I was solely made for pleasuring you in this immortal existence.

She didn't meet his eyes. She didn't really believe him. There was no way he meant his words, when she was so very human, and he was so very . . . *him.* A vampire as gorgeous as him would never settle for a murine like her.

Still, she found herself chewing on her lips.

Please, he begged, his voice dipping into a tone she'd never heard before. It sounded desperate. She cautiously turned to him, afraid something had happened, something she didn't notice. Was a vampire approaching? Was she about to be attacked? She reached for the stake over her skirts.

But when her eyes finally fell on Ambrose, as they ascended the stairs behind a chatting Constance and Darius, his gaze was locked on her lips, where she had just bitten—begging *for her.*

Please, if I get another chance at life, let me be your lips. Let me be born again as those hypnotizing lips so I may taste you everlastingly.

As the words caressed her mind as the Concord tugged at her soul, Lila saw his eyes flare that ruby red she had only seen a few times before. She knew—when a vampire's eyes glowed, it meant their bloodlust was rising.

Lila's breath caught in her longs, as his crimson eyes drank her in. She tried to take a step back, but his grip at her waist didn't let her. Her heart raced, and she felt . . . afraid of him.

"Let go," she whispered.

But she was surrounded by vampire ears.

Constance and Darius turned back, looking at the pair—her blushing like an idiot, and him unable to take his eyes off of her.

"Tell me, Lord Darius, what are our room situations? Will I have to share a wall with these two?" Constance asked dryly, an eyebrow raised at the two.

Darius smirked; a dark eyebrow already raised in the pair's direction as well. "No, darling. You will have your own suite across the hall if that suits you. I promise, our rooms are soundproof."

"That won't be necessary," Lila quivered, stepping forward to stand next to Constance instead of Ambrose. "I'll be staying with you, of course."

Constance, scanning Lila's face, took her arm and walked ahead of the men. "Are you okay?" she whispered once they had taken a few steps forward.

Lila knew the men could hear every word they were saying, but she appreciated the sentiment regardless. "Yes—just still a bit queasy from our travels. I-I think I should rest for a bit before dinner if we have the chance."

"Ah, of course, dinner will be held in an hour, so please get all the rest you need in the meantime," Darius pipped in.

Finally, after ascending the seemingly infinite staircase, the Spider Lord led them off into a hallway, decorated the same as the foyer, except the walls were filled with paintings of beautiful vampires, their fangs gleaming.

"My manor," Darius explained. "All of the portraits in the halls are vampires that have once been or currently are in the Arachnid Estate."

"Constance, are you here?" Lila asked.

The two smiled. "No, though I'm technically a spider, he couldn't quite handle my bite."

Darius chuckled, "I would've tried harder if it weren't for that uncle of yours, he's scarier than us all. And you know you are always welcome here, love. Though it was an accident that brought this upon you, I shall always count you as one of my own."

"Though, she rightfully belongs in the Crow Court now," Ambrose grumbled.

Darius seemed to ignore him. "Your rooms are this way."

The four walked through the hall when Darius abruptly stopped between two more black-lacquered doors.

Darius really keeps true to his aesthetic, Lila thought.

He reached for the knob on one side of the hall, and opened the door, saying, "Ladies, these will be your quarters for your stay. Again, if you shall need anything let us know. Ambrose, you are on the other side. If you shall need extra cleaning services," he winked, "please let us know. See you all in an hour." With that, Darius Maronai, Lord of Spiders, bowed his head, and disappeared back down the hall.

Lila quickly turned, without looking at Ambrose, and walked into the room she was determined to share with Constance that evening. The first thing she noticed was how cold it was, just like downstairs. She shivered in her coat and thought about how she may have to wear it to bed.

But, to Lila's surprise, there was no bed in the room. As they entered, she found the room absolutely divine. It was dark, with large black, green, and silver drapes hanging from chandeliers and the sitting area had plush velvet chairs. But as they entered the bedroom, Lila was thrown aback.

"Oh, right. I forgot. I don't—um—I don't quite use a bed anymore, Lilac. I sleep in a coffin, as most vampires do," Constance said, embarrassment clouding her voice.

She quickly turned to her and reached for her hands. "I'm so sorry, it completely slipped my mind that I had requested this! It's just most comfortable, with avoiding the sun and all, and I didn't think—"

Lila's heart stuttered. "No, it's okay! Don't feel bad. It looks . . . comfortable? Do you like it?"

Lila was more curious about it than anything else. Though, in the back of her mind, she did realize it meant she'd have to share a room with Ambrose, assuming he didn't have only a coffin as well—or she could sleep on the floor. The latter may be the smarter option.

"It is rather comfortable. I like how dark it is honestly, it helps. Would you like to try it? I can wake you in an hour." Constance beamed, seeming excited Lila wasn't disgusted or repulsed. For a moment, Lila wondered how it must feel for the girl to have been human and forced out of it. Forced to live an immortal life of being a monster.

Like Marcus.

Taking a deep breath, Lila turned to Constance. The two smiled at each other and Lila decided, *why not?*

Constance led her to the coffin—it was a gorgeous thing. It was black lacquered, like everything else in this house, and the inside was a plush green velvet. It had a small pillow at the head and narrowed by the feet. Constance helped Lila get inside, smoothing her skirts flat.

"No blanket?" she asked, before realizing. "Oh, right! You don't get cold."

"Our bodies have their uses," she smiled bashfully. "If you feel cold I'm sure we could ask to start a fire or get extra blankets?"

Lila looked around the room. *No fireplace in sight.* Maybe they could ask for blankets later, but right now Lila just wanted to rest.

"I think I'll be fine for now."

"All right. Lie back and I'll close it for you. If you should need anything just knock, and I'll open it."

Lila nodded and rested in the coffin.

"It's best if you cross your arms, like this," Constance explained, crossing her arms over her chest so each palm rested on the opposite collarbones.

Lila mimicked her and Constance closed the door. Immediately, her breathing grew ragged as she was engulfed in the enclosed darkness. For a moment, she panicked—it was so dark and quiet in the coffin, and she couldn't properly twist and turn as she'd like. Her limbs felt stuck, and she didn't have enough room to breathe. She felt trapped.

Three deep breaths. She placed her hand on her stomach, remembering her first night at the Crow Court, remembering Ambrose guiding her through her panic attack.

In.

Out.

In.

Out.

In.

The initial fear faded, and Lila found the dark space almost . . . relaxing. It was so dark, she didn't know where her body ended and the coffin began, and her limbs felt like they were floating. Plus, Constance was just on the other side waiting for her.

And she knew—if she truly needed him—Ambrose would come for her if she called. She found her eyes blinked closed at the thought alone.

17

The darkness consumed her, and it was . . . oddly wonderful. It felt like a sweet embrace as warmth flooded from her body, starting from her chest. This warmth—the same warmth she felt on so many cold nights in the Reinicks' dungeon, the same warmth that allowed her and Marcus to survive all those years—was probably the warmth Ambrose had described to her. Her "sun warmth."

Lila didn't know how it worked, after all she still could get cold. She still got shivers. She still got goose bumps. But she knew she would never die from the cold. It was never unbearable . . . just uncomfortable. Just like the morning would be when she slept on the floor in Constance's room.

She wondered where her power came from—Ambrose had said she was the ancestor of the one who created vampires, but no one else in her family seemed to have any powers. Her parents were normal, as far as she knew. Maybe the odd color of her hair was connected to her power.

As Lila drifted into the dark, she eventually heard a faint knock on the outside of the coffin.

"Lila? It's about time to wake up," Constance said softly as she began to pull it open.

Lila slowly opened her eyes, the dim light harsh at first. "Thanks for that, it was oddly so relaxing."

Constance smiled and blushed. "I'm glad you aren't afraid of it. I know it's quite . . . monstrous."

"No! Not at all, it was so peaceful in there. I wouldn't have expected it. I thought it would be a bit," she hesitated, "claustrophobic?"

Constance snickered again, "Yeah, it does seem quite daunting initially." She reached her hand down to Lila, who graciously took it and got up and out of the coffin.

"Time really melts away in there. Has it really been an hour already?" she asked, stifling a yawn.

Constance nodded. "Yep, it's just about time to go to dinner."

As if on cue, there was a light knock on their door. Constance hurried to open it as Lila brushed out her skirts and hair, the curls still fell perfectly over her shoulders.

"Ladies," Ambrose called from the doorway. He was still impeccably dressed in that black suit. His long hair looked incredibly soft, and Lila briefly imagined running her fingers through it. Pieces of hair fell over his forehead and into his eyes as he looked up at her through his long white lashes, their eyes locking for a brief moment. "Are you ready?"

She gulped and then gave the slightest nod.

"Yep," Constance called, walking past him and into the hall.

Ambrose waited for Lila to reach him and then offered his arm. As she took it, he whispered, "Remember, you are powerful. And you are safe with me. Stay close."

Lila found herself gulping again and instinctively step-ping closer to him as heat radiated through his coat, warming her.

Or maybe she was the one radiating heat the closer she stood to him.

The three of them walked back the way Darius had es-corted them earlier and entered the foyer, where a number of other vampires were already waiting. A man and woman arm-in-arm smiled at Ambrose, Constance, and then finally settled on Lila in a way that felt genuine and friendly.

A loud *clap* echoed throughout the room, causing Lila to jump out of her skin.

"Ladies and gentlemen, undead brethren. Welcome to my home for the Great Masquerade of Sanktus Pernox." Darius stood on the staircase, a few steps up as though he were on a stage with his arms spread wide on either side of him, before bowing deeply. A round of cheers and ap-plause thundered through the room.

"While we anticipate a rowdy celebration tomorrow, I invite you all to dine with my manor tonight. We have pre-pared a lovely feast for you all, and I hope you will all enjoy it. Let the festivities begin!" He ushered the guests to a doorway that burst open at the exact moment he finished speaking. Within, the room was well lit, and Lila could hear the crackle of a fire warming the area. She breathed a sigh of relief.

The parties of people made their way in, and Lila found herself gripping Ambrose's arm tighter. There was a large table—bigger than the one in the Crow Court—that could easily fit over fifty people. On the table, she saw small name cards. *Maronai, Nostro, Lahmann, Draven, Bran, Bogdan.* They kept going.

Lila was so thankful to see her own last name directly

next to Ambrose's. He silently helped Lila remove her coat and then pulled her chair out for her.

The moment her skin was revealed, she felt the heat of vampire stares on her neck, her chest. She felt herself redden at the attention and took a deep breath, forcing it away as she sat down, and Ambrose pushed in her chair.

Once seated, Ambrose pulled her chair closer to his — so close the arms of both were touching. The scrape of wood on the marble floor caught the attention of some and Lila blushed at his forwardness. Ambrose leaned back and threw his arm over the back of her seat, his fingers and knuckles just barely grazing her shoulder as he curled a lock of her hair between his fingers. The touch was enough to send a shiver down her spine and heat through her core.

Lila looked everywhere to avoid the feelings tumbling through her. At the end of both sides of the table, giant fireplaces were burning with highly decorated mantels. The design and craftwork looked immaculate, all hand-carved and painted with intricate details of spiders and webs. On the table were ancient-looking candelabras, each with red candles dripping wax that reminded Lila of blood.

People began to find their seats, and a bald man, who looked much older than Ambrose, slid into the seat next to her. He looked like the personification of the undead. He had dark, bushy eyebrows that contrasted his stark-white skin, his ears were long and pointed, and his pale eyes were deeply sunken in. As he slowly turned to Lila, his pale blue eyes flared like icicles in the sun. His fangs were long and as he opened his mouth to speak, Lila saw that all his teeth were pointed sharp.

"Good evening, madam. I am Arnold Bogdan, it is a pleasure to meet you," his voice was husky as he gave a curt bow of his head.

"Good evening, sir. I am Lila Bran."

The vampire reached a hand out, with sharp, too-long nails. Lila carefully gave her hand to him, and he placed a chaste, rough kiss on her knuckles. Fear struck through her, but then she felt Ambrose's knuckles graze her against the curve of her shoulder.

Ground yourself, Little Mouse, he said through the Concord. She focused on where their skin met.

After introducing himself to her, Bogdan looked over her head and nodded at Ambrose. "Lord Draven. It is a pleasure to see you tonight."

"As it is with you, Bogdan. How's the family? And where is the Maggot Lord? I thought he'd be here already."

Ambrose didn't seem . . . intimidated. Or even on edge, as he had with the Reinicks. He almost seemed . . . friendly.

"Oh, they're doing well. Elizabeth should be here tomorrow, as will Alyssa. They wanted an extra day to get their costumes in order. You know how girls can be," he smiled. It was an eerie thing, but the twinkle in his eyes made Lila wonder if the man was more wholesome than his appearance suggested. "And Lord Nostro is sitting this year out. The old buzzard is reveling with the entire Maggot Mansion for Sanktus Pernox. I am here in his place."

Lila tried to imagine someone who would look even older than Bogdan, but all she could picture was a corpse.

With a small smirk, Ambrose nodded. "Typical Gustov. Elizabeth and Alyssa are Bogdan's daughters, Little Mouse. They're a part of the Maggot Mansion. Alyssa actually should be around your age. Elizabeth is just a bit older than Constance," Ambrose explained.

Before Lila could respond, she heard the dinging of silverware. Darius was calling everyone's attention.

As Lila turned to face him at the head of the table, she

noticed all but six seats had been filled — five across from Constance and one a couple seats down from Bogdan.

"Friends, I am sure we are all starved. Please, join me in a toast," Darius said, lifting a silver chalice.

Lila wondered if he was saying his cue early as no one had been served yet, but then she noticed. At every chair — save for hers — a matching silver chalice appeared. Ambrose slowly picked up the cup, eyeing Lila as he did. She jumped as a glass of red wine appeared in front of her. Lila picked it up and carefully sniffed it, making sure it was, in fact, wine and not blood. Ambrose smirked at her, a glint in his eye of amusement.

She joined the rest of the table, lifting her glass toward Darius.

"To Sanktus Pernox," he said.

"To Sanktus Pernox!" everyone called back, and then began to drink.

Lila sipped at her wine, watching those around the room. Eyes flared golds, blues, greens, and reds. She saw Darius's eyes shimmer the vibrant green she had seen earlier as he drank from the cup. She tried not to look at Ambrose, afraid of that intoxicating ruby glow. But his eyes were closed as he sipped from the chalice.

Someone cleared their throat behind her. She turned to find Balzar holding a steaming plate of food.

"Dinner, Miss Bran."

"Ah! Thank you," she said as he carefully placed the food before her, along with a set of silverware.

"Please let me know if you would like anything else, I can make whatever you wish," he said in a whisper, placing the napkin on her lap. She saw the ghost of a smile on his old face and returned one warmly. She had misjudged him.

"Thank you, Balzar, I really appreciate it."

The man nodded and disappeared back out of the room. As Lila looked back down at her plate, her mouth instantly watered. It was full of meats and cheeses, potatoes, and buttered vegetables. She carefully began to eat, trying not to call any attention to herself as the rest of the table drank from their cups and conversed with each other.

"How is it?" Ambrose asked, right after Lila took her first bite.

She wanted to moan. "Oh, my. It's delicious. These are the best potatoes I've ever had!"

Ambrose smiled at her, a warmth in his eyes that wasn't the need she felt from him before.

"Excellent."

She continued to eat as he spoke to Bogdan and others seated around them. The couple from the foyer—the Cambrias, Lila discovered—spoke about their latest vacation on a remote island just off the southern coast of the Arachnid Estate.

Lila, unexpectedly, found herself completely at peace—considering she was at a table filled with monsters who could kill her with as little as a slap. These people weren't terrifying, malicious beasts. They were friendly, and warm for being so naturally cold.

Mrs. Cambria—Dianne as she urged Lila to call her—was already inviting Lila to spend the summer months with her in the Arachnid Estate when a gust of wind burst through the dining hall, blowing out the majority of the candles on the table and one of the two fireplaces.

"So sorry we're late."

That voice. That horrible, uninvited voice yanked the rug from under Lila's feet and her entire body immediately tensed. Ciro Reinick was here, and where he went—

Lila looked up through her lashes, and immediately, her entire body felt like ice.

Ciro, Rebekkah, and Hektor all stood, as the latter had his arm around Marcus. He looked . . . wild.

Lila jumped back into her chair so hard, she nearly toppled out of her seat, when Ambrose placed his hand on hers. Immediately, his touch calmed her. And as she looked at their joined hands, she saw she was clutching her dinner knife hard enough to leave an imprint in her skin.

She sat, straight as a board, as she watched them round the table and fill in the empty seats across Constance. She stared down at her own plate as she felt eyes on her again, afraid to look up at them.

Phantom pains shot through her body, at her neck, her thigh.

They can't hurt me. The scars they've caused are gone. Their poison has been removed. Lila repeated this over and over, trying to calm herself.

At the same time, Ambrose flooded the Concord, over and over, *I'm with you. I'm with you. I'm with you, Lila.*

Hearing her whispered name through the Concord stilled her, and she focused on Ambrose's calloused hand over hers.

"Welcome!" said Darius warmly. "Where are Lord and Lady Reinick?"

Lila glanced up in time to see Ciro smirk, his eyes on her. "Oh, you hadn't heard? I'm the new Lord of the Viper Morada."

Gasps flooded the table for a moment as people glanced amongst themselves.

"I-I'm so sorry for your loss," Darius choked. "How . . . ?"

They don't know. They don't know!

Ciro's eyes shot to Lila, and a wicked smirk spread over

his lips. "I thought it was time for a change of pace. I killed them," he said matter of factly. She heard Hektor snicker, but she didn't dare turn to him. Instead, Lila's eyes drifted to Rebekkah. The girl seemed . . . meek. Especially compared to her usual self. She didn't cackle with her brothers, nor did she smile. She stood behind them, her eyes glued to her feet.

Darius, and everyone else at the table, hesitated. Clearly, they didn't know how to take the news.

Darius straightened. "That is . . . against our laws, Ciro." Lila remembered Ambrose mentioned something about vampire laws, and how they had been broken, but she didn't know them well enough to know what it might mean.

"Well, perhaps there should be some new ones. For example, why is there a murine sitting and feasting with us on Sanktus Pernox?" he asked, eyes falling to Lila once more. "Are you attempting to fatten her up, Maronai? So she may be our main course tomorrow?"

Lila shuddered at the thought, yet her blood boiled at the same time. Ambrose's hand tightened around hers as she heard him growl.

"Touch her and I'll—"

"Lila Bran is a guest of the Crow Court," Darius interrupted, "and therefore a guest to me. You *will* respect that, Reinick. I see you too have brought a guest not on my list." Darius's eyes fell on Marcus and Lila's heart fell through her chest.

"Ah, him? Yes, he's one of our newest additions. Everyone, meet Marcus Bran," Hektor sang, and pointed at Lila. "Her brother."

A cacophony of sounds echoed through the room, gasps, hisses, growls, and even snickers from few.

Hektor pushed the catatonic Marcus into the chair across from Constance and sat next to him.

"So are we still welcomed, Maronai, or will you be kicking us out?" Ciro asked, sitting next to Hektor. Rebekkah quickly sat on the other side of Marcus, eyes still locked down.

Darius hesitated once more, his gaze casting down the long table. "We will discuss your new lordship later. For now, yes. You may join us."

Lila felt bursts of heat caress her neck, her chest, her lips, her breasts. She knew the brothers' leering eyes were on her, drinking her in.

But her gaze was stuck on Marcus. The boy's eyes were still glazed over, in that unseeing golden hue, and when she focused hard enough, Lila could feel the thrall they held on him from here. He wasn't himself. She needed to break it and—

And as a chalice appeared in front of him, Marcus dove for it. He swung it back so ravenously, the blood in the cup poured down the sides of his lips, down his chin, and dribbled onto his white tunic. She found herself entwining her fingers with Ambrose's and squeezing tightly.

She had left her brother. Left him. And all the time she'd been gone, he's been like this. They had told her the frenzy would only last a short while, and now it has been weeks and he was still—

Lords, what was *wrong* with her! While her brother was being constricted by snakes, she was busy thinking about Ambrose's lips on her. Her breath became short, and her chest ached and twisted. Her vision clouded with black.

Lila, breathe, Ambrose's voice caressed her mind.

But it didn't help, the black only intensified as she looked at Marcus, his eyes so devoid of life.

Help me, she pleaded. *Help me help him.*

Ambrose stared at her for a long moment, she felt his eyes on her. Not the heat of his stare, no—it was softer than that.

"Darius," he announced, startling Lila. "I apologize, dear friend, but Miss Bran needs to retire to her room. I will accompany her." He stood, and guided Lila up by the hand.

"Of course," Darius didn't even feign ignorance, he was practically ushering them out as they walked past the table.

For once, Lila didn't feel eyes on her. All eyes were on the Reinicks. She saw Bogdan glaring at Ciro, as the Cambrias did the same to Hektor. Constance's gaze was fixed on Marcus, sorrow and worry etching her features, and Lila thought she saw concern flash in Darius's eyes as he glanced at Rebekkah.

Lila hadn't even realized she left her coat behind until it was too late.

Ambrose held her hand, his grip her only comfort as they left the room.

Ciro and Hektor's gazes burned into her back. It was different from when she felt Ambrose's eyes on her, that sent a jolt of electricity through her whole body. This scalded her skin as if she had poured boiling water on herself.

She quickened her steps, eager to get out of there.

As soon as they were out of the room, Ambrose turned to her. "Are you okay?"

She tried to speak, tried to say yes. But all she could manage was a nod before her eyes welled up and tears broke through. Ambrose's eyes bore into her, and she saw his jaw tick.

"I'll kill them. Say the word, and I'll go back in there and kill them."

Lila couldn't speak, so she shook her head. That would just cause more problems, and the Reinicks may be the only ones who could pull Marcus out of his haze, she wasn't sure.

Plus, she really wanted him to stay with her.

"No," she managed to say, just as the sobs broke loose. She felt her legs give out and realized how badly she just wanted to do nothing but cry. Ambrose grabbed her shoulders, holding her up.

"Ambrose," she sobbed. "It's my fault." She covered her face with her hands. He took a step closer and circled his arms around her back, pulling her to him. He was still so warm, and she was so very cold. He took his blazer off and placed it on her shoulders, just as she leaned into his chest.

His fingers dug into her hair as his other hand rubbed her upper back. He hugged her fiercely, protectively, and she swore she could feel him shake. Or maybe that was just her. They stood like that for a long moment, as she just cried and cried, soaking his dark shirt with her tears.

Poor Marcus. It *was* her fault. If she hadn't tried to run away, he would be fine. They wouldn't have changed him.

"Wh-Why is—" but she was still struggling to breathe as her chest knitted tighter with every sob.

Without a single sound, Ambrose swooped his arm under her knees, the other remaining on her back. He cradled her to him, his fingers digging into her skin. She felt like it should've hurt, but his touch only grounded her.

"You're freezing," he said in way of explanation, as he turned in the foyer, back to the looming stairwell leading to their room.

He walked with her in silence, her heartbeat and sobs the only sound between them. She felt her shoes slipping off as they dangled in the air, the hem of her dress falling over her feet, as her face buried into the crook of his neck and her fist balled the fabric of his shirt.

When they got to the black lacquered door, Ambrose

shifted her in his arms, holding her pressed against his chest with one arm scooped under her. He unlocked and kneed the door open.

The room was amazing, even more so than Constance's. It was one giant bed chamber, no sitting area, and the bed was huge, the largest she'd ever seen, with dark satin sheets. The ceiling was so high, and there were lit candles everywhere she looked.

Ambrose carried her through the doorway and her grip on him tightened. She didn't want him to put her down, she wanted his touch, but she figured he would anyway now that they reached their destination.

Instead, he sat on the edge of the bed and kept cradling her in his lap. His voice was as soft as rose petals as he said, "Little Mouse, tell me everything."

Lila knew he was asking about her brother. Knew he wanted to know what her life with the Reinicks was like. And so, she did.

"Ciro and Hektor . . . they're monsters," she gulped, scared to even say their names. Ambrose's hug tightened, pressing her closer to him as she shivered.

She continued, "My family lived just outside the border of a village in the Viper Morada. When my mother died having Marcus, Father seemed to have died with her. He couldn't work anymore. He still cared for Marcus and me. Still held us. But that was the extent of it. And with no money, there was no food. I began to steal away into the nearest village, scavenging for what I could find. It was then, I believe, that I was first caught in their sights. They stole me, once, to be their murine. I was gone for a week. A whole week that my brother and father went without eating. Marcus was still just a baby—he could've died." The sobs started to return, but she couldn't stop. "It was

so awful. I was still so young, but they had drank from me
till I was nothing but skin and bones.

"After they let me go, I realized *no one* would want to
be their murine. To the point where they might just pay to
get out of it. So I started to seek out the next murines. I
found people willing to pay if I went in their place. Eventually, I spent the better part of a month as their murine,
while the villagers supported my family.

"But that all stopped when Marcus turned five. I was just
Constance's age when my father died. They didn't even let
us have a funeral. Instead, the Reinicks plucked us from our
home, forcing us to leave all of our belongings—though it
wasn't much—and took us to the Viper Morada to live as
their murine full-time.

"I don't have anything from my mother. I was only
eight when she passed. I can't even remember the exact
shade of her eyes," Lila's voice quivered.

"You don't have to—" Ambrose began, but Lila just
shook her head.

"I want you to know." She met his gaze and warmth
filled her down to her very bones. His dark eyes were re-
served for only her at the moment, and he was listening to
every word she said.

"We knew they kept some murine at their manor but
being forced into it just felt . . . like they were dooming us.
We were slaves and there was nothing I could do to save
us from it. All I could do was try to get their focus on me
instead of Marcus and . . . it worked.

"As you saw that morning in your office, reading wasn't
a necessity. I learned young but it went unpracticed for
many years and eventually I lost it. Marcus doesn't even
know what his own name looks like.

"They were cruel. They didn't care. You've seen the

marks the Reinicks have given me. You've seen what they're capable of. Lord and Lady Reinick were less egregious in their actions, but they still watched as it happened, still laughed as Hektor tried to have his way with me on a number of occasions. But they always stopped him before it got far, and in a sick and twisted way Lord and Lady Reinick were the only ones holding the siblings back. I never knew why until—"

"Until I told you of your power," Ambrose finished, and Lila nodded her agreement.

"Ciro—I thought I was in love with him for a time."

Ambrose stiffened under her, causing the corners of Lila's lips to quirk.

"Relax, I quickly realized it wasn't love. I learned the few times he protected me from Hektor were for selfish reasons. He was always cold. His pain was ... mental more so than physical." She scoffed, "Aren't they a proper pair? Physical and mental assailants."

She saw his jaw clench again. She knew if she let him, he'd go down to the dining room and rip their throats out right now for all to see. But she didn't want that. More importantly, she didn't want him to leave. She rested her head against his chest again, playing with a string from her dress.

"They've known you were ... different," he said, his voice a low rumble. "They must've kept you longer than their other murine for that very reason. I'm sorry for what they've done to you and your brother."

"Is there a way to help him?" she asked, trying not to let hope get the best of her.

He stayed silent for a long moment. "There might be. It would be difficult. I'll look into it."

Lila nodded. She just wanted to rest. She knew it was

still early, there were still many hours before sunrise. But it had all been too much for her.

"Ambrose," she whispered. "I have a favor to ask." The mark on her back flared and she was sure he sensed it as well. But before she could second guess her thoughts she squeaked, "Will you stay with me today?"

With no hesitation, he squeezed her close once more, and said, "Of course."

She wondered for a moment if he only said yes because the bargain demanded it. "I've wanted nothing more than to share a bed with you, Little Mouse. Bargain or no bargain, I'd have said yes," he whispered, clearly reading her thoughts. She'd wasted one of her favors, but she knew it was worth it.

Lila smiled, her cheeks turning pink, as she eased out of his lap. She felt his warm eyes on her the entire walk to the adjoining bathing room and smiled at him as she closed the door.

She freshened up, splashing water on her swollen eyes, and replaced her dress for the sleepwear she packed—a soft pink nightgown that reached mid-thigh. Lila looked down at it, wondering if it would be too revealing. It was a bit shorter than she'd like, and also wasn't very warm considering the lack of a fireplace in the room. But it was all she brought.

She snuck out of the bathing room, trying not to draw any attention to herself, but it didn't work. *All* of Ambrose's attention was on her. The warmth in his eyes turned into a fiery heat as they raked over her body. She even saw his throat bob. At the same time, Lila studied his shirtless form—his body corded with muscles, the way his shoulders strained and pulled as he moved, the veins protruding down his arms to the backs of his hands.

Maybe this is a bad idea.

She awkwardly dashed to the bed, lifted the covers, and jumped under. She heard a soft chuckle escape Ambrose's lips as he watched her, awe in his eyes.

The satin sheets were cool to the touch, and she became increasingly aware of her taut nipples rubbing at the fabric of her dress. She saw Ambrose swallow once again as he lifted the comforter and followed her under.

"Can we train?" she abruptly asked.

"Now?" He raised an eyebrow, turning to her as he rested his head against his arm.

She hiccupped, "No! Of course not now. Maybe before sundown? Before the ball."

He watched her for a moment, thinking. "Of course."

Their eyes locked on each other for a moment before Lila turned to face the ceiling. The silence between them grew, and Lila found herself flicking her fingers back and forth, awkward and unsure.

"It's a bit cold, isn't it?" Lila blundered. She truly didn't know what to say or do, especially as she still felt Ambrose watching her.

"I think I can help with that."

She turned to him and in the blink of an eye, all Lila saw was dark gray wings ready to encompass her, causing a small squeak to slip from her lips. Ambrose lay still, watching her reaction.

He was massive. She forgot the size of him in this form, as his body took up nearly the entire bed. His white hair fell across his forehead, into those beautiful crimson eyes. He scooched one wing under her as he pulled her closer.

"It won't hurt if I lie on it?" she asked, worried about putting her full weight on his wing.

"Not at all," he breathed.

As his large arms surrounded her, she instantly melted into his embrace. He was so soft for being so muscular, and so warm against her skin. "If you get too hot, just push me away."

Lila nodded, too comfortable to speak.

He rested the other wing over her, like an extra blanket, cocooning her inside of his touch. As she rested on his massive chest and his arms wrapped around her waist, she felt her eyes drifting close. She rubbed her face against strands of his hair, absent-mindedly, and his long, clawed fingers gently wiped the tear stains from her cheeks. Heat flooded her chest and she felt so warm, mentally and physically.

Without thinking, Lila turned her head up. Ambrose was already looking down at her, studying her. Lila could live off that stare alone. She pulled herself up against him and gently placed her lips on his, cupping his sharp cheekbones in her palm. The size difference was alarming and had never been more obvious. Ambrose seemed startled for a moment, but then he returned the kiss. His lips were so soft, so delicate. He didn't try to deepen the kiss but was tender and warm. Lila—for the first time ever—felt truly cared for as he pulled her flush against him, wrapping his thick thigh around her tiny calves. His hand was the size of her back, and it made her feel cradled and encompassed even more.

She broke away, brushing her lips against his a final time, as she burrowed into his neck. Her eyes closed once more, and she felt his lips on her forehead as he nestled into her hair.

Before Lila knew it, her worries were cast aside, and her mind drifted into dreams of wings and kisses.

18

As promised, Lila and Ambrose were up an hour before dusk, training. She lunged at him over and over again, aiming for his heart with the wooden stake. She knew she still had leagues to go, but she was growing more confident in her skills. Ambrose evaded slightly slower, though she knew she still wouldn't be able to get him—not that she would stab him anyway.

At least . . . not again.

She felt completely refreshed, prepared for the whirlwind of events that would surely ensue tonight. Lila had the best sleep of her life, and was so warm and comfortable in Ambrose's embrace, she truly didn't want to get out of bed this evening.

But she promised herself she'd practice before the ball. Maybe an opportunity would arise to stab Hektor and kill him before everyone. Wouldn't that be grand?

"Good, watch your footwork," Ambrose instructed after another lunge and thrust. Lila was sweating, and she realized how much she preferred sweating from fighting to shivering from the cold.

A number of times, Ambrose swept for her feet but she managed to dodge each of them. She bobbed and dipped and hopped out of the way. She threw punches and kicks, each with more force than before. She was able to keep her pushups and squats consistent, and overall felt much stronger than before.

As the moon began to rise, Ambrose lifted a hand, stopping her just before her knuckles could meet his cheek. "I think that's enough for today. Can't be too sore for the big event," he smirked.

Neither of them had brought up the chaste kiss they shared before bed, nor how their limbs were wrapped around each other all day as they slept, but Lila found her eyes frequently dipping below his gaze. His lips were so welcoming as they smiled at her.

She wanted to take them.

A knock at the door interrupted her thoughts.

"Come in," Ambrose called.

Constance opened the door, smiling at the two of them. "Evening," she said cheerily. Her eyes fell on Lila and then the smile fell to something Lila couldn't quite place. "Can I speak to you for a moment?"

Lila nodded, took a deep breath, and followed Constance back into her room.

"I wanted to . . . apologize. For last night. I know it was uncomfortable, and the Reinicks suck," she said, looking down at her shoes. "And I'm sorry about your brother . . ."

Lila couldn't help but smile as the girl spoke. It felt odd to have people care for her, and Lila found herself still adjusting to the sudden warmth in her chest whenever she was comforted by people—vampires, nonetheless.

"I appreciate it. Please, don't apologize. I'll hopefully be able to find a way to help him soon."

"Help him?" She looked at Lila, her eyes glistening.

"Ambrose mentioned there might be a way. But I'm not sure yet. I just don't understand why he seems so . . . catatonic. Is that normal?"

Constance tapped her chin. "Hmm. The change is different for everyone. It's possible he's still affected by that. How long has it been now?"

"Nearly two weeks, I think? He was changed just days before Ambrose brought me to the Crow Court."

"Hmm," Constance concluded. "The initial frenzy should be over. It seemed like he was under their thrall. Keeping him this way so that he stays . . . cooperative. And, most likely, to bother you."

Lila's heart fell once more. He was in there, fighting them. But they were simply stronger.

"I noticed something odd last night," Lila said, shifting the subject. "Rebekkah Reinick. Something seemed . . . off about her."

"I thought that too," Constance agreed. "Normally when I've seen her at these parties, she's snickering alongside them, but yesterday she was quiet. Almost docile. I think I'll try to talk to her tonight at the ball. Remember, Lilac, I will be there for you. If you need me to knock someone's fangs out, just ask." She smiled widely and Lila wanted to hug her. In fact, she did. She threw her sweaty arms around the smaller girl's shoulders and squeezed her tightly.

"Thank you, friend."

Constance awkwardly patted Lila's back until she let go. Her cheeks flushed and her eyes flashed from their regular blue to a similar shade of green to that of Darius Maronai's.

"Sorry, still not one hundred percent in control. I'll be fine, but the contact was a lot for me."

Lila blushed in embarrassment. "I'm sorry," she mumbled, stepping back for Constance's comfort.

"Don't be. It was . . . nice. I haven't been hugged in so long because of this. And you're so . . . warm." She smiled. "Thank you, Lilac."

After a moment, she turned to face her room. "You can wash in here, if you'd like. I can do your hair for the ball. Do you have your dress?"

"Ambrose has it. I'll go retrieve it and then I'll be back. I don't know what to do with this mess," she said, tossing her wild ponytail around her. "Please help me, oh Constance, my hero." Lila mock bowed, shaking her hair wild, causing the younger girl to laugh.

After Lila bathed the sweat off, she sat in front of a vanity. Though her reflection did not show, Constance stood behind her, braiding her hair and placing small, golden flowers within. It was already gorgeous, but the image of Lila's gleaming amethyst strands weaving itself continuously brought a smile to her lips."

"Why is there a mirror if you cannot see yourself?" she asked after a small fit of laughter.

"Lord Ambrose specially requested them actually."

Lila's cheeks reddened. "S-so, what's my costume? A giant daffodil?"

Constance snickered. "No, I believe you'll see the whole picture once you put the dress on. Lord Draven likes to be . . ."

"Eccentric? Maddening? Arrogant?"

"I was going to say extravagant," she giggled, moving to Lila's face to apply makeup. "But any of those descriptions work too."

Lila smiled. He was a bit extravagant, and for that, she simply couldn't wait to see the dress he picked for her. She blushed even thinking about it.

"All right, just about done!" Constance beamed. Lila looked at herself in the mirror, and almost didn't recognize herself. Her lips were accentuated by a clear gloss that shimmered in any lighting, her eyes had golden flecks on the lids that made her brown irises look like golden honey, and her cheeks were so much more alive as they had the slightest pink to them. She looked like a storybook character, she realized, and she couldn't stop herself from smiling.

"Now, the dress, and then I have your mask!"

Constance helped Lila shimmy into the dress. The soft, brilliant yellow and threads of gold shifted with each fold. It was already a gorgeous thing and Lila hadn't even seen it fully on. It puffed in layers of chiffon at her hips, as the yellow corset of the top snuggly hugged her waist. Her breasts weren't large by any account, but the corset pushed them up rather nicely. But Lila's favorite part of the gown were the off-the-shoulder sleeves. They were made of the same see-through chiffon as the skirts and had giant slits along the tops so the skin on her arm would occasionally peek through the billowing fabric that cuffed at her wrists with thin gold bracelets. She knew Ambrose did this on purpose, making her flesh a tease for every vampire in attendance tonight.

Maybe even for him.

Constance pulled out a set of earrings for Lila to put on, large suns that hung on golden chains. "He said no necklace. Something about it taking away from your neckline,"

Constance explained. As Lila looked in the mirror, she understood why. The sweetheart neck made her feel . . . beautiful. Her hair was half up, showcasing the long column of her neck, and as the dress pressed tightly against her breasts, she knew it would drag every vampire's gaze to her neck tonight. She shuddered at the thought, but her resolve was strengthened at the idea that maybe Ambrose's gaze would be caught on her as well.

She was given heels of gold that strapped around her ankles, but what caught her attention last had her blushing furiously.

At the bottom of the box containing her dress and accessories, Ambrose had left her an ornate thigh strap for her stake that matched her costume. It was utterly mesmerizing with golden leather and metal, and it sent a small thrill through her as she snapped the golden sun buckle closed around her. Not only did Ambrose care enough to include it, Lila also couldn't help blushing at the idea that he knew she'd be wearing it.

The gold threads in the chiffon skirts shone with each move she made. Constance beamed at her as she walked and said, "You look like personified sunlight, Lilac. You're so pretty!"

The young girl was wearing an equally gorgeous dress, in blacks and dark blues and purples. As she placed her mask on, Lila realized she was dressed like a crow.

"And you look utterly divine," Lila smiled.

Constance's cheeks warmed and she turned around, gingerly picking something out of her own box. "I have the final pieces for you," she smirked. "*You* are going to look divine."

Constance held the mask Lila was to wear. Only, it was more like a crown than anything else. Constance walked up to her and indicated for Lila to kneel down. The headband was a brilliant gold with different sized beams poking from the main piece. It looked like rays of light as the sun said good morning and good night to the day.

Then Constance placed a thin golden lace mask around her eyes. She turned to a mirror and felt . . . ethereal. She didn't seem like the same Lila that woke up that evening. She twirled a few times, causing the dress to glow and shimmer as she did. Constance walked up next to her; the girl's reflection gone like every other vampire.

"You truly do look and feel like sunlight," Constance beamed, inching nearer.

"Does it feel . . . nice?" Lila asked.

"It feels like more than I could describe. It makes me feel alive again," Constance's eyes were beginning to tear. "I haven't felt the sun in so long, Lilac. Even being near you fills me with such a warmth I didn't know I could feel again. And now everyone will get the chance to feel it." She smiled widely and Lila restrained from hugging her again.

Soon, Lila promised herself. *Soon, I will hug her till she's had enough of me, and then I'll keep hugging her.*

"Ambrose is probably waiting, we should go." Constance grasped Lila's hand and the two exited their room.

As soon as they were out in the hall, Lila's breath caught in her throat.

Ambrose stood outside his door, leaning against it as he waited for the ladies to finish getting ready. His shoes were a polished black, so shiny and dark, they looked like crow eyes. His pants were tailored to fit him perfectly and were a rich, black velvet, matching the outer blazer he wore. His undershirt was a blue so dark, it looked like midnight, the top few buttons were undone to show off the crow on his chest, and he wore golden and silver rings on all his fingers. From his left ear draped a crescent moon earring, similar to Lila's suns. Immediately Lila bit her lip, stopping herself from running over to him and jumping on him and rubbing her hands all up and down his chest.

But what really had Lila gulping for breath was the mask he wore.

A black, porcelain bird mask, with a beak that reached far out, hid his eyes away, accentuating his lips. His white hair fell around his shoulders and over his forehead onto the mask, illuminating it and making those hidden black eyes glossy and endless. Over his blazer, he wore a half cape, in the same velvet material with a cowl of feathers, the inner lining was made up of an embroidered pattern of even more crow feathers. Lila wondered if his blazer had the same.

But as she looked up, finally meeting those inky eyes, and gold liner curved around the upper lids, igniting his eyes as he devoured her with a look.

Somehow, miraculously, she finally was able to gulp.

"You look . . ." he hesitated, his eyes roaming over her, swallowing every swish of her dress, every curve of her body. "Absolutely captivating. Radiant." He held a ringed hand up and she quickly took it. As soon as they touched, the entire hallway disappeared, it was only them as they studied each other.

They were like night and day.

His fingers tightened on her hand. "Shall we, darling?"

Lila forgot how to speak. She simply nodded, and as soon she did, he pulled her in close to him, taking her arm and keeping her at his side. He smirked at her, fangs peeking through those kissable lips, and she blushed.

Ambrose leaned down, whispering in her ear, "I want

to devour you whole." She felt his smile on the tip of her ear and the blush only turned into a violent red as heat flooded her lower belly.

She felt Ambrose silently chuckle beside her as he reached his free arm out to Constance, who was rolling her eyes as she smirked.

"You two had a room all night and you're still flirting? Jeez," she sarcastically sighed.

Together, with the two women holding the Crow Lord's arms, the three left the hallway and descended the staircase.

Others were exiting their rooms at the same time, all slowly making their way through the foyer and into the grand ballroom Lila had yet to see.

Everyone looked enchanting to Lila. She saw masks of reds and gold. Masks like devils and masks like angels. Dresses swished, suits shone. She blushed at the deep cleavage some women wore, or the thighs on full display, and some of the men had blazers open with no shirt underneath.

"Keep your eyes on me, darling," Ambrose smirked.

"Jealous you don't have my full attention?" Lila quipped.

He paused for a moment before he dropped her arm. She was afraid she actually offended him for a moment when his hand dropped to her lower back. His fingers trailed along her spine, dipping past the curve of her hips, and then firmly grabbed her backside.

She yelped, and he quickly pulled his hand away, snickering. "I'm rather convinced I could make you give me all your focus, love. But the point is to show you off, not keep you all to myself." He inched closer, whispering in her ear again. "If I wanted to do that, I would've tied you to my bed, and kept you all night, giving you *my* full attention."

Lila shuddered, heat spreading through her body and pooling inside of her, and suddenly she felt so much warmer than she had before. She smiled bashfully and playfully pushed Ambrose—he didn't even budge, but he chuckled in response.

Constance groaned in exasperation, "I wish Kaz was here so I wasn't just with you two. Look!" she exclaimed pointing. "Anyone else!" And with that, she ran down the stairs and into the party, trying to get away from the two infatuated idiots.

"Well, maybe I *should* keep you to myself. Would you like to go back to my room?" he asked, smiling wickedly.

Lila giggled and shook her head. "You rake! You dragged me all the way out here, no way will I be spending it sitting in a room alone with you."

"Darling, we'd do a *lot* more than sitting." He chuckled at Lila's balked expression, covering his lips with those gorgeously ringed fingers.

As they finally reached the bottom steps, they were warmly greeted by Edward and Dianne Cambria, who were dressed like matching monarch butterflies, Lila realized. They wore yellows, blacks, and burnt oranges, and they looked absolutely amazing together.

"Good evening Lila, Ambrose," Dianne smiled.

"Good evening. You both look wonderful," Ambrose smiled at the couple, and together the four of them walked to the doors of the great ballroom.

"As do the both of you. The sun and moon?" Edward smiled. "Bold, Draven. Bold and pristine. I expected nothing less."

As soon as the doors opened, Lila gasped, hearing a similar sound coming from Dianne. The room was absolutely *beautiful*. It looked like a forest in fall, everywhere Lila turned she saw reds and oranges and golds. There were faux trees lining the room, reaching as high up as the eye could see, dropping delicate leaves of fall colors. The marble floor was a deep red with gold veining all along that made it appear as though she were walking in a forest—she could almost hear the crunch of leaves below her feet. On massive circle tables, she saw pumpkins the size of her head, some even bigger. There were men in costumes and stilts walking through the room, dancing and prancing, with billowing olive-green fabrics and pumpkins over their heads. Dripping from the tree branches were more gauzy fabrics, in oranges, greens and browns and reds, as vampires twirled in them, elevated way off the ground, performing for anyone curious enough to watch.

"Madam," Balzar crept up behind Lila, causing her to jump as soon as he spoke. He held a silver tray with a golden chalice atop. "This is for you, from the master of the house. It's an aged red wine, one of the master's favorites from his time as a human. He said, 'Enjoy it for us all.'" He handed her the glass and smiled warmly. As she took it, Lila realized she was actually starting to like Balzar. "I will continue to bring them periodically, and should you have a change of taste, please let me know."

"Thank you, Balzar, so much. I truly appreciate it," she beamed, and noticed Balzar inched closer. "Is there anything I can do for you in return? I-I don't have any money but—"

"Just being in your presence is a gift enough, madam. Thank you," he bowed and turned away.

Lila blushed at the thought that her simply being there was enough for some people. But she wondered if that was why the Cambrias stood close to her. Or if that was why Maronai or Bogdan were kind to her. What if this warmth she supernaturally exuded was the only reason Ambrose remained close to her, basking in her?

The idea made a knot form in her stomach.

It couldn't be just that. Maybe for everyone else, but not for Ambrose. Not for Constance. They cared; she could feel it. And that was all that mattered.

Lila sipped at her wine as Ambrose went to grab a glass of blood for himself. She felt the alcohol immediately rush to her head and found the taste utterly delicious. She made a note to herself to ask Darius for the name—not that she would be able to find it anywhere but so she could at least know what to look for should the opportunity arise.

Throughout the ballroom, she felt eyes on her. She continued to look for the Reinicks or Marcus but didn't spot them in the crowd. As expected, most focused on the column of her neck, the mounds of her breasts. She blushed each time she felt the heat brush past her, but knew they weren't looking to *feel* her, but to consume her.

It was hunger, not lust—not like Ambrose's hungry gaze each time those haunting eyes fell on her. Looking at him was just . . . too much. It sent thrills through her body. Needs. Pulses. She had never felt this way and wasn't sure what exactly it was. Her brief, innocent kiss with Ambrose last night was her first. She had been able to avoid Ciro and Hektor's advances for so long and, here, a new vampire came, and she was sure that if he asked her just once more, she would let him take her wholly. She would give him her entire being, body and soul, if he only asked.

Suddenly, she felt very warm, considering she still saw no fireplaces throughout the room. She *should* be cold, but the more she thought of Ambrose—and more importantly what Ambrose could do to her—the warmer she became.

Maybe it was the wine.

But he just looked *so incredible.*

"Little Mouse, you're radiating," he breathed.

She mumbled her thanks, still avoiding his gaze.

Definitely the wine.

"No, not—yes, you're beautiful, gorgeous, a goddess on earth—but at this particular moment I am not talking about your looks. You're *literally* radiating your warmth like sunlight." He pulled her closer a bit, and that was when Lila noticed nearly everyone in the room was watching her, stepping closer.

"Oh." She stepped back, right into Ambrose, and then quickly ran around him to hide behind his back. He pushed her behind him, backing into a wall, and kept her behind his back.

Don't run. It invokes our predator instinct and makes *us want to chase,* Ambrose said into her mind, the familiar tug of the Concord pulling taut as she pressed against him. *Everyone here is like a fox waiting for the perfect moment to strike the little bunny rabbit that wandered into our den.*

Oh, that's reassuring, she rolled her eyes.

Don't worry, little bunny, they're all foxes but you have the big bad wolf protecting you.

Lila blushed despite herself.

"Everyone," he said quietly. She realized then the power he held. He didn't need to yell to get everyone's attention, they simply turned to him, listening already. "Please, enjoy the party."

His words were that liquid gold again and it made Lila feel like she was melting.

"Darling, you're only getting warmer. Can you, I don't know, turn it off?"

Lila saw even Constance inching toward her, her eyes beginning to glow that vibrant green once again.

Shit, Lila thought. *Think calming thoughts, calming thoughts—puppies and flowers.*

It wasn't working, not with Ambrose's muscled back pressing against her. Not as she felt her breasts pushing against him, each breath and movement he took rubbing against her hardening nipples.

"Lila," he warned, and she felt him begin to falter as well. She saw the rubies of his eyes begin to flicker under his mask.

Puppies and flowers, puppies and flowers, puppies and flowers.

"Mouse, what a pleasant surprise!"

Lila startled at the voice just to her left and, instantly, the warmth drained from her body.

It was Rebekkah.

Her eyes were glowing gold, but she kept herself restrained as she sauntered between the crowd and toward her and Ambrose. Something about her presence immediately dispelled the tension in the room.

Lila quickly looked around. If Rebekkah was there, it meant her brothers weren't far behind.

As Lila focused again on Rebekkah, she noticed she wore a red devil mask, with horns nearly masking into her fiery hair, along with a revealing dress of red and black lace. She looked gorgeous.

"For a murine, you clean up nicely," Rebekkah teased, causing Ambrose to immediately growl at her.

But, for the first time ever, Lila was actually *happy* to see the girl. Eyes from the crowd were shifting away from her, and the vampires seemed to be breaking their haze, going back to dancing and drinking.

Lila felt herself releasing a sharp breath.

"Lovely to see you as well, Rebekkah," she breathed.

"May I borrow her for a moment?" she looked at Ambrose, raising an eyebrow under her mask.

Ambrose turned to Lila, silently asking her if she'd be okay with it. Lila nodded and took the other girl's outstretched arm. They began to circle the dance floor before Rebekkah leaned closer to her ear.

"I want to . . . apologize."

This caught Lila by surprise. "For what?"

"Everything," Rebekkah said urgently. "I-I was awful. I know that now. My brothers, they . . . I'm just sorry."

Lila stopped, turning to Rebekkah. "Are they hurting you?"

She slowly nodded.

"Can you leave?"

Rebekkah bit her red lip, immediately puncturing her skin with her sharp fang. "I'm scared, Mousey. They killed our parents."

Lila slowly nodded and sighed. "I walked in just after it happened." Rebekkah gasped, clutching her hand to her mouth. "That morning, outside my balcony. You seemed totally okay with it."

"At first, I thought Ciro was so justified in doing so. But the more I thought of it, the more I realized that he didn't only kill the Lord and Lady of the Viper Morada—he killed *our parents*. And to make matters worse, I fear that he could kill me just as easily. Then I also realized it meant Ciro was in charge, and no one could tell him no anymore. And he— I tried to reason with him, on something silly too, not to kill a murine, but he didn't listen. And he only got angry."

"They've been hitting you," Lila realized. "Both of them?"

Rebekkah gave the slightest nod, her eyes looked like they were ready to well in tears at any moment. But then she smirked. "I guess you really were their plaything. And now that they don't have you, they've turned their aggression on me. They've killed all the murine in the castle. Even more villagers from the nearby towns are escaping in the middle of the day to evade the Morada. Ciro has an unquenchable thirst, and Hektor's like his rabid dog—killing and fucking anything in their way. Marcus and I seem to be the only ones in the castle relatively safe from those offenses." She sighed a long, exacerbated breath. "It's all different now, without Mother and Father to control them."

She hesitated for a moment. "I'm still a wicked thing, and perhaps I'm finally getting what I deserve, but Lila— please make sure you stay away. They've lost their heads, and if you returned, I don't know what Ciro would do. Kill you, that's for certain. But after? He might actually try to start a war. And I'm not foolish enough to believe we'd win. The Viper Morada would be no more."

Lila thought for a moment. "And Marcus?"

"What about him?"

"Why does he seem to still be in such a ravenous haze?" The two women started their third lap around, completely engrossed in their own conversation, though Lila felt Ambrose's eyes on her each moment she wasn't next to him.

"My brother has him enthralled to stay in that initial frenzy at all times. But I haven't actually seen him feed yet. I believe once the thrall is released, he will return to his proper se—" Rebekkah stopped dead in her tracks, pulling Lila along with her. "They're here," she said, without turning to the door.

But Lila felt it too. Felt the fiery, devouring glares lick up her back.

"Lila, darling, dance with me." She didn't know when Ambrose came up behind her, but suddenly his reassuring hand was at her back.

"Remember what I said," Rebekkah whispered in way of goodbye, as she dipped back into the spinning crowd and disappeared.

"They're here, Ambrose." She felt her body stiffen under his touch as he turned her and pulled her to him. One hand fell to her waist while the other delicately held her hand. She followed him, placing her free hand on his large shoulder, allowing herself to be led by him into the crowd of people.

"I know. Marcus is with them."

"Does he look . . . okay?"

He began to turn, spinning her with him. "The same as yesterday."

Lila felt the sobs from last night returning, tears welling in her eyes, and Ambrose immediately pulled her closer.

"I want to help him, Ambrose. I can't stand seeing him this way. He doesn't even know me."

"I know, love. I know. Remember, they can feel your frustration, your sorrow. Don't give it to them."

"How can I not—not *feel*?" She looked up at him then, those black eyes perfectly blending with the gorgeous mask on his face.

"Focus on me. Be *here*, dancing with me. My hand on the small of your back," as he said it, Lila felt it there, focused on it. It was warm through her dress, his fingers gripped her like she was a lifeline he needed to hold onto.

"Our fingers interlocked." She glanced over, their hands were woven together, and she could feel his callouses against her palm. They were the hands of someone who had lived a long life, fought his way through hell. She imagined these hands carving and whittling away at the stake on her thigh. She imagined these hands caressing her body, roaming wherever they wished to go.

"Focus on the sound of my voice." And, my lords, was she. She listened like there was no other sound in the room. She hung onto every word he said as it dripped through her, that molten metal.

"Focus on us," he finally said, his voice the only thing she could think about. She felt him pressed against her, their bodies flush with each other. She liked it and wished they could be even closer.

Lila was excited. Excited for the ball to be over. Excited to follow Ambrose back to his room, to lie in his bed, wrapped in his arms once more. She thought, maybe tonight she would kiss him a tiny bit more. Maybe she'd ask him to kiss her in return.

She felt, once more, like she was flying, as they danced together through the room. She wasn't sure if eyes were on them, she wasn't even sure if they really were spinning as much as she thought they were. But as Ambrose's eyes bore into hers, she knew *this* was where she wanted to be. With him.

She would save her brother—somehow, some way—and she'd do it with Ambrose if she could. She'd bring Marcus back to the Crow Court, where he could become friends with Constance, Kaz, and Pollock. She would train with Ambrose, hone her skills. Then she would help Constance and Marcus adjust to their lives. She would hug them as much as possible so they could feel the sunlight again. And during the days, she'd spend it wrapped in Ambrose's wings, as they slept in perfect bliss.

"Might I cut in?"

And the illusion shattered.

A shiver shot through her spine and her bones immediately turned to ice. She stilled, and the warmth in Ambrose's eyes turned into a cold so deep, they looked like frozen tundra.

"No," he said simply.

But Hektor didn't move.

"For ol' time's sake, Lila?" He placed a hand on her

shoulder, and she immediately shrank away, and stepped closer to Ambrose, who protectively encased her in his arms.

Hektor smirked, a wicked thing that haunted Lila's dreams. Though the wound was gone, she felt her inner thigh throb once more, her knees threatening to buckle in.

"*Do not touch her,*" Ambrose seethed, his eyes flaring a red so fierce it looked like bloodshed itself.

"What about a dance with her brother? He's been waiting all night for you." He flicked his hand to his side, guiding her gaze to somewhere behind him.

Lila gasped.

Marcus was at a table covered in goblets of blood. He ravenously drank from them, pouring them down his throat, coating his shirt in a gory mess, before tossing the cups to the ground and picking up the next.

Hektor whistled and Marcus's gaze immediately shot up, focusing on Lila.

In the blink of an eye, he dashed across the room and was directly in front of her, snapping his jaws desperately trying to bite her. His hands were outstretched, trying to grab and claw her.

But Darius Maronai was holding him back, his arm roughly wrapped around her brother's throat. "Is there a problem here?"

"Please, don't hurt him!" Lila yelped.

Darius raised an eyebrow, his silver mask hanging from his neck as Lila realized it was meant to resemble a spider's web. His suit was made of a silver chiffon with an overlay of black lace making a webbed pattern. "I wouldn't think of it, Miss Bran. But I also will not allow anyone to get hurt on Sanktus Pernox." He shot a glare at Hektor and seethed, "Do not make me ask you to leave, Reinick."

Hektor put his hands up in mock surrender before roughly grabbing Marcus by the collar and pulling him away. "My apologies, Lord Maronai. Won't happen again." But the smirk spread across his face told Lila otherwise.

Lila still felt Ambrose stiff in front of her, his arms caging her in. She looked up at him and saw his face was morphing, desperately trying to stop him from shifting into the monstrous-like form she knew would rip the heads off of everyone in this room. She carefully placed her hand on his chest, trying to get his attention. His eyes burst open, and he stared at her splayed fingers, his face calming to normal.

"I'm sorry, friends. Please, enjoy the party," Darius sounded unsure of himself, as he bowed and disappeared back into the chaos of spinning masks. Lila caught the quickest glance of Darius walking in the direction of Rebekkah, who was making herself small in the crowd.

As Lila's gaze turned, following Marcus and Hektor, she saw them walk toward Ciro. He was leaning against the wall near the entrance to the ballroom, and his eyes were already on her, watching. He smirked at her as Hektor shoved Marcus, and pulling him along, they all stepped deeper into the crowd.

They were pulling her brother like a damn dog on a leash.

Lila stepped forward, attempting to go after them with little thought. But she just met Ambrose's arms.

"You can't stop them, Little Mouse. Not right now."

Lila was seething. She knew she wasn't strong enough— not yet.

But she would be.

19

"Calm down," Ambrose stressed as Lila paced back and forth in his room.

After another hour at the party, Lila couldn't take it any longer. She asked Ambrose to leave, and he obliged. The majority of the Sanktus Pernox festivities were still going on below them, but Lila couldn't bear to wear a brave face anymore. "Constance is keeping an eye on him at the ball."

"He's down there, unaware of what's going on. Unaware of who he even is. Meanwhile, I've been doing lords knows what! Dancing! I've been *dancing*!" Lila vented. She wasn't able to stop, as she paced back and forth, feeling all of a sudden too hot in her skin. "I left him, Ambrose. *Left him*. This is all my fault."

"You did not leave him, love." He leaned against the bedpost, arms crossed, his blazer and mask now thrown onto the bed alongside hers. "If it weren't for our bargain, you would be—"

"Dead! I know! You've said that already," Lila seethed.

"And I know, a dead murine can't save her brother. But, you know what? Neither could a living one!"

"You are not a murine, not anymore," He began to roll up the sleeve of his dark blue shirt.

"Yes! I am! And you know that. No matter what kind of fantasy we have created for each other here, do *not* forget what we are." Lila's voice hitched, her chest was pounding, and her mind was so scattered, she wasn't even thinking before she spoke any more.

"And what are we, darling? Hmm?"

"A *filthy fucking murine*! And . . . and the Monster of Malvania." She was at a breaking point. Maybe death would be easier. Maybe she could run right back downstairs, offer herself to Ciro. Switch places with Marcus. He could owe Ambrose her bargain, and she could slit her wrists in front of all the vampires in the room and simply be devoured.

Lila didn't see Ambrose move, but before her brain could catch up, she was pinned against the stone wall. Her arms were pressed above her head as he held her wrists in one hand, his other hand firmly pressed against the wall by her head. She refused to meet his gaze, so she watched his chest rise and fall. With the top few buttons undone, it looked as though with each breath, the crow's wings moved.

"Look at me," he ordered.

She refused, biting her bottom lip.

"What did I tell you about doing that?" his voice was closer, and soon she felt his breath against her cheek, her ear.

And then she gasped.

"Do that, and it'll drive me to do things like this." His lips kissed a sensitive spot directly under her ear. His lips were so incredibly soft and warm against her.

"Wh-What are you—"

Ambrose hummed against her neck, shushing her as he flicked his tongue against the sensitive spot. Lila bit down on her lips harder as Ambrose began to travel along her jaw.

"I can help you," he said, his voice a rumble against her skin.

"H-How?" her mind was muddy for all new reasons. She tried to focus on Marcus, but the sensations coursing through her body were making it incredibly difficult.

"I can distract you."

"I don't want to be distracted." But lords, was she lying through her teeth. She *very* much would like to be distracted. By him. As soon as possible.

"Then what if I told you we could save him."

"Marcus?"

Ambrose nodded, his hair tickling Lila's cheek as it cascaded over her chest. He continued to kiss and lick her jaw and neck, carefully avoiding nicking her with his teeth. The hand gripping her wrists eased down her arms, bringing them down with it, as his free hand pushed the sun crown from her head before twisting into her hair as it clanged to the floor. She saw her strands of lilac curled around his dark fingers, and her entire body shook at the sight.

Then his hot mouth was on her throat again, licking up the column of her neck. She pushed her hands on his chest, only to find there was no budge. Her hands were on fire as they touched him, and it was the warmest she'd felt since training.

He groaned against her neck, which did funny things to her stomach.

"You're so warm," he breathed.

"Y-you're distracting me," Lila stuttered.

"Is it working?"

She felt him smirk against her neck, and she bit back a moan. "This is—this—I—we can't do this," she finally managed to say.

"Why not?"

Lords, she wanted to do this—whatever *this* was. But her brother needed help.

"Marcus. I need to help Marcus."

His tongue curled around her ear lobe before he pulled it into his mouth and sucked. "I told you, we'll help him."

"How-How do we do it?"

Another tortuous lick.

He hummed against her ear. "What will you give me for it?" His lips dipped to her collarbone as he sucked at her skin there. His voice sounded far, distracted, completely focused on her skin against his tongue.

And because of that, finally, she let out the barest hint of a moan, "Anything."

Ambrose rose to his full height. His hand twisted in her hair moved deeper, pulling at her scalp, forcing her head back to look up at him. His other hand dominated her waist, pulling her roughly against him.

She felt *all* of him at that moment. His hard, marble-like abs against her stomach, her breasts aggressively pressing against his chest, and the intoxicating hard length of him push against her thigh.

Lila moaned again as his lips met hers, swallowing the sound whole.

Their lips entwined like they were meant to be connected, meant for kissing each other. He carefully bit her bottom lip and sucked it into his mouth before dipping his tongue between her lips. As their tongues danced hot, and their breaths grew only heavier as he pushed her harder against the wall.

Lila ran her hands over his chest, needing to touch that fiery skin. He was so warm, and she wondered how it would feel if all of her could touch all of him. She wrapped her arms around his neck as his hand on her waist dipped to her hips with hungry fingers, roughly grabbing at her.

Lila noticed, despite how ravenously he kissed her, he was so careful. Each time she got near his fangs, he moved so she wouldn't scrape against them.

Lila needed him. Needed more of him. She pulled on his neck, and Ambrose immediately understood her silent request. His hands untangled from her hair and dipped past her hips. He cupped her ass in his strong hands and lifted her. Instantly, Lila wrapped her thighs around him, kissing him harder. "I've wanted to grab this ass every moment of every night," he breathed hungrily against her.

She gasped for breath before diving in to kiss him more.

"Breathe, Little Mouse," Ambrose chuckled against her lips, which only sent her head spinning more, desire thrumming through her. She kissed him deeper, sucking on his tongue to give her more, and before she knew it, he carried her and threw her onto the bed.

Lila stared up at him, breathing deeply. She felt her face flush in the heat of him, her body aware of the limited distance between them. Distance she wanted to close.

"You're so goddamn gorgeous. *Fuck*," he cursed. His eyes were glowing like rubies again, but Lila didn't care.

She felt her body go taut, tension coursing through her. She pressed her thighs together, seeking some kind of relief. It only helped for a moment.

She needed *him*.

Ambrose stood over her, watching her, his eyes glowing as they fell on her pressed thighs. He carefully slipped the golden dress up her legs, sending electric tingles all across Lila's skin. Once the skirts met her thigh, he carefully removed the wooden stake—*his* wooden stake—from where it was held and tossed it to the ground. Without breaking eye contact, he ran his thumb under the leather strap, massaging where it rubbed against her flesh, and unsnapped the sun buckle, tossing it carefully as well.

She knew he could smell her lust pooling between her thighs, knew that he reveled in the fact that *he* had done this to her.

And she wanted more.

So, she bit her lip.

Ambrose's lips were on her in a flash, as he lay on top of her on the bed, pushing himself against her. She moaned against his lips as his dragged against her jaw, down her throat. Lila felt the briefest amount of pain as two sharp fangs bit into her neck, and though it hurt, it was so different from the bite of the Vipers. This bite was . . . pleasant.

She moaned at the mix of pain and pleasure, and arched into him, grinding against his body. But as he sucked on her throat, her mind completely hazed over into something like euphoria.

She moaned, without constraints, as she ran her hands along him, pushing his shirt open to feel along his muscled core, his strong chest. She had never felt emotions to this level before and it was driving her absolutely mad. She pulled his shirt over his head, the need to touch him stronger than anything else.

Lords, he smelled divine. He *felt* divine. She wrapped her legs around his waist as he continued to kiss her neck. She felt something hot and wet trickle down to her shoulder.

In a twist of motion, Ambrose was beneath her, and she was sitting on his lap, facing away from him.

"You're *perfect*, love." Ambrose taunted her with another lick as his hand palmed her breast. Lila moaned, leaning back into him. She felt his length press against her ass and had the sudden desperation to ride him till sunup.

She continued to jive against him until he nipped at her neck again. "Soon, Little Mouse. One step at a time. I want to do *everything* to you."

The hand padding her breast taunted her, teasing the hard nipple under her corset. She gasped and tossed her head back onto his shoulder.

"Do you like that?" His voice rumbled in her ear, dripping molten liquid gold all over her.

She vigorously nodded.

"I want to hear you say it," he breathed into her ear.

"Yes, I like it," she moaned. "Please, touch me."

"Touch you?" he chuckled, sending waves of heat through her, down to the apex of her thighs. "Where, Little Mouse? Where do you want me to touch you?"

It was like nothing she'd ever felt before. All of him engulfed all of her, and she *wanted him.*

The hand at her breast dipped into the neckline of the dress and she felt his calloused hand palm her breast whole, playing with the pink bud between his fingers that had Lila whining with need.

She reached for his hand on her waist and guided it to the hem of her dress.

Slowly, cautiously, they lifted it together, revealing her pale thighs once more, and her lacy pink undergarments were soaked already from her desire for him.

"Here," she said, placing his hand over her center.

As soon as his hand touched her, he cursed again, "Fuck, you're so wet for me." His fingers grazed her damp folds through the thin fabric, teasing the sensitive bud at the top. He drew lazy circles around it, sending shivers all along her body. She arched into his touch, begging him. Her head felt like it was about to explode, everything was spinning, and it was too hot.

He licked the wet liquid on her neck as he twisted her nipple between his fingers so roughly, she shrieked.

His finger dipped under the seam of her underwear, toying with her, rubbing the soft skin of her pelvis. "Are you sure?" he breathed against her neck.

"Touch me," she demanded.

His hand moved past the seam, and he slipped a thick finger between her dripping lips. Lila immediately moaned. *Finally*, she thought.

His finger continued to slide across her, teasing the bud that felt like it'd burst at any moment. Each graze against it sent Lila bucking into that rock hard length under her. She felt like she was on fire.

"You're delicious," he said, licking and sucking at the wound on her neck. Lila felt lightheaded just as Ambrose pushed a finger inside of her and immediately growled against her. "Fuck. *Fuck*, you're so warm and tight." He slipped a second in, and began to work her.

She moaned with every press, every touch of his thumb against her clit as her body felt completely cared for, spoiled, as she leaned into every ounce of his touch. With each pump, Lila found herself riding his hand, holding onto his wrist and bicep.

"*These*" —he slipped his fingers out of her, eliciting another needy moan, and grabbed the crotch of her underwear—"are in my way." With a violent movement, Ambrose tore the lace from her body, pulling hard enough against her before she heard the *rip* of fabric.

"Ambrose," she moaned as pieces of the fabric fell to

his lap. A cool breeze swept past her hot center a moment before Ambrose drove his fingers back inside her. She gasped, her entire body going taut.

Something was rising in her, she wasn't quite sure what it was, but she was sure at any moment her entire body would combust. He pumped his long fingers into her, carefully stroking her so as not to nick her with his rings or nails, as she began to moan loud enough for the entire manor to hear. He turned her head to him, hand at her jaw. She gazed into those ruby red eyes, white hair dangling in front of them, hungrily taking her in.

"You're beautiful," she said between moans to him.

She was reaching the combustion. His fingers pumped and pumped, she felt her tight slickness all around them, the pressure pulled her apart.

"You're so warm," he said against her lips. He took her mouth once more as she moaned into him.

"Don't stop," she begged. And he listened.

Taking her mouth, Ambrose continued to fuck her with his hand until she was crumbling at the edge of a climax. She moaned his name over and over again, screaming it, as he ran his tongue against hers. She shook her ass on his cock, hoping to give him even an ounce of as much satisfaction as she was receiving before screaming and buckling into him, feeling herself come undone around his curling fingers.

Breathing heavily, she pulled herself from his kiss, watching him. His gaze bore into her with heat and need and desire and everything she needed to fill the hole in her heart.

He slipped his fingers out of her, causing the oversensitive bud to send more shockwaves through her body as his thumb grazed over it once more.

Ambrose's fingers were covered in her slick, hot orgasm. He smiled, gazing at them as he brought them to his lips and tasted her on his tongue, sucking his own fingers clean, not breaking eye contact with Lila. He watched her reaction as he licked her up—and suddenly she needed more. She needed his tongue on her, needed him to taste her right from the source.

She pleaded, "Ambrose—"

As he drank her from his fingers, the red in his eyes quickly faded, and his expression shifted to her blushing expression.

She was overwhelmed, she wanted more of him. So why was he moving her off of him? Why was he standing up?

"Lila." He didn't face her. Lila's finger trailed down her dress, grazing over her nipples, searching for that feeling again, searching for euphoria.

"Ambrose, touch me, please," she begged.

"No." He still wasn't looking at her. Why wasn't he looking at her?

"Wh-Why?" Her fingers found the bud, adding pressure to it before she moaned, already close to a second wave of a climax from its hypersensitivity.

Ambrose turned and pushed her back flush on the bed, gripping both hands by her sides. *That's more like it.* She smiled, leaning up to kiss him again.

"Sleep, Little Mouse."

She felt an instant compulsion, and as haze glossed her vision, she thought of the invisible dial he described so many nights ago.

He was trying to enthrall her.

"I don't want to."

"*Sleep.*"

Lila's mind suddenly went very blank. She found her

eyes closing without warning, her mind drifting away. Everything was fading.

"I don—"

"I'm so sorry, Little Mouse." Ambrose sounded pained.

She could make him feel better. She didn't want to sleep. She wanted to be with him. To make him feel as she did.

"*Sleep*," he whispered, and she felt a wave of demand rush over her. She *needed* to sleep.

She *needed* him.

But her body didn't listen to her lust nor her heart. Her eyes drifted close as she felt Ambrose's weight ease off of her, suddenly cold from his absence.

"Come back," she managed to beg before completely fading to black.

20

L ila didn't dream, there was nothing in her mind
except the creeping darkness of sleep. Pain struck
through her body, her neck, as lust and euphoria
left her body, making an empty cavern in her chest. She
felt the need for more—aching for more.

There was no warmth as she slept, though she could
feel herself sweating as she tossed and turned. And between the hot flashes, cold bouts that left her shivering
plagued her through the day.

Lila tried to call out, but no sounds would escape. She
heard pacing, footsteps falling back and forth. She felt heat
on her neck from watching eyes. *Bang,* the sound of wood
breaking.

She heard silence.

She heard her name.

"Lila. Wake up."

Someone was shaking her.

"Hmm?"

"Wake up," Ambrose mumbled, easing her into consciousness.

Her head was pounding as she saw colorful explosions behind her eyes. Her entire body felt sore, her neck hurt, her lips were swollen, and her thighs were shaky. She slowly sat up, Ambrose's hand on her back supporting her. As she sat upright, she realized how sore her center felt and then everything came flooding back.

The kiss, Ambrose, his hand between her thighs, her insatiable need for him.

"Wha-What happ—"

"It's my fault," he interrupted, unable to meet her eyes. "I . . . I don't even know what to say." He sat at the edge of the bed with his back to her and leaned over, his elbows propped on his knees as his hands rubbed at his face and dug through his hair. "I bit you last night. And on top of that, we made another bargain."

"I . . ." Lila didn't know what to focus on first. Why did either of those things come before what else they did?

"I got carried away. I bit you. And my venom—well, you experienced the venom of a crow last night."

She hesitated, carefully running her fingers along the wound on her neck. It didn't hurt. In fact, it seemed to already be scabbing over.

"My bite is . . . some have described it like a drug. It makes you want to give into your needs. Its—"

She squeaked, "Euphoric."

"Yes. An aphrodisiac. Meant to charm my victims into a false sense. And I used that on you."

"But, I—"

"You only reacted the way you did because of that," he said, not waiting to listen to her.

"No, I wanted—"

"Little Mouse," he said, turning to her. "It was a mistake."

Lila's heart stuttered. She heard what he was saying

but . . . it wasn't true. They were kissing well before he bit her. And Lila *liked* it. She wanted more *before* his venom.

"We can pretend it didn't happen," Ambrose said, turning away again. "If that'll make you feel more comfortable with me."

Finally, he let her speak. "What are you talking about?"

Ambrose took a deep breath. "Well, it should be no surprise that you . . . intrigue me."

Is that what you call it? she thought. "Obviously, I do—"

"I got carried away. At some point, the blood lust took over. I bit you, you reacted, and then so did I. I should've noticed sooner it was due to the bite. I—" he hesitated. "I'm sorry, Lila. I don't mean to make things uncomfortable."

He continued to shoot it down, like it was all an accident. Like he didn't want her—though she so wanted him.

"I removed the venom as you slept. The bite is already healing . . . but about our bargain . . ."

"Is this about my brother?" Lila vaguely remembered that as Ambrose had begun kissing her neck, she told him she would give him anything if it meant saving him.

"Yes. I will help you save him. In exchange, you said you'd give me anything. I—That's too much power to give anyone." His eyes found hers again. There was no warmth in those endless pits. "So, instead, I've already decided what to ask of you."

"Oh . . . wh-what is it?"

"In exchange, I want you to travel with me to the vampire manors."

Lila was surprised by the request. Why would he want to go to them? She started to ask but he cut her off.

"I just need you to be there. You don't have to do anything. We're already here at the Arachnid Estate."

Lila wanted to ask a million questions—most importantly: *Did last night mean nothing to you?*

He was acting colder than he ever had to her. No longer was the mirth in his eyes as he looked at her. Nor the heat as he watched her. He wasn't even flirting with her or teasing her. It made Lila just feel . . . cold.

Her heart was pounding in her chest, and it ached more and more with each passing second. What was she hoping for? To live happily ever after with her vampire prince while her brother's corpse rotted away as an enthralled monster?

"Okay. Do I need to formally agree or anything?"

Ambrose's eyes swept to her neck, just behind her ear, and then down to her collarbone. "You already did. I . . . I marked you as we kissed." Lila remembered his tongue flicking against her skin, the heat it sent through her body.

And he regretted all of it.

She touched the mark, but she couldn't feel it, and she wasn't about to go study it in a mirror—not with the awkward tension filling her lungs.

A sad smile spread on her lips as she realized how similar this mark was to their kiss. She knew it was there, knew it happened, but the feeling of it was no longer tangible.

"The mark is a black feather . . ." Ambrose mumbled, his eyes falling down to the bed.

Lila dropped her hand. She looked down at her lap, realizing the dress she wore last night was swapped for her pajamas. She was cleaned, the residue from everything they did last night gone.

Light slipped through the covered windows, and Lila realized it must still be daytime. A chair lay in pieces in the far corner of the room and a washcloth rested on the night table.

"What do we do now?" she asked.

Eyes still downcast, Lila heard Ambrose lift something from the floor, the wood scraping underneath, before he tossed her stake next to her.

"It's an hour till sunset. Let's train."

The training that evening was rigorous. More so than it had been in their first few sessions. Lila wouldn't be surprised if she found bruises all along her body and had difficulty walking over the next few days as her aching muscles recovered.

She was hunched over herself, leaning on her thighs and trying to regain her breath.

"I recommend you stay in here for the night. I'm going to have a conversation with Darius you won't be needed for," Ambrose said coldly.

He had been distant the entire evening—cruel even. She didn't think it was a coincidence he pushed her harder while training right after their . . . tryst.

Lila blushed at the thought of their night, before utter embarrassment and a little bit of rage seeped in. She was still fuming from how he reacted, how he disregarded it and made it seem like it was all a mistake *he* made, and not a mutual joining. She had wanted to bring it up, but each time she even thought of it, the cold look in his eyes shot her down.

Even now, he didn't look at her. And it drove her mad.

"What are you going to talk about?" she asked.

He paused, clearly thinking. He was withholding something from her, she just knew it.

"Why do you need me to travel to the vampire manors with you?" she prodded.

"The same reason I used our bargain to bring you here. To show off what I have, and they don't," he shrugged. Lila knew it was a nonanswer, but it still stung.

She gulped before asking the next question. "And what do you have, Ambrose?"

The room was silent, save for Lila's heartbeat, which she heard pounding in her chest. She wished for it to silence itself—she knew Ambrose could hear it. But like the rest of Lila's body, it acted of its own accord, beating even faster as those dark eyes *finally* met hers. It felt like a burst of cold air smacked into her, the icy look in his eyes sending gooseflesh all over her skin.

Ambrose smirked at her then—a wicked grin that didn't reach his eyes, of sharp teeth and amusement. She knew she would not like what she was about to hear.

"The ultimate desire," he said, waving his arm toward her, as though presenting Lila to an awaiting audience. "The one thing no one can have is now attainable just by standing in a room with you." His hand fell to his side.

Heat flooded Lila's cheeks—embarrassment for their tryst last night, rage for how he was treating her. "So I'm still just an item to be sold to the highest bidder?" She folded her arms over herself, really wishing she could use the stake against him at the moment.

Ambrose shrugged again. "Perhaps. Now that I know you become even more radiant when you're turned on, it might make you more valuable."

Rage filled Lila's entire being. This *absolute asshole.* "Hopefully they won't need to use their supernatural power to make me want to fuck them."

"Ah, but you do make for a good fuck as well. Another

addition to the price." He placed his hands in his pockets as he turned to her.

Lila's blood turned cold, while her entire body felt like it was on fire. She wanted to scream, she wanted to attack him, she wanted to run away.

But she held her tongue. She knew he would sense the anger in her, but she wanted to *hurt* him.

"Well, at least I'll be able to get a decent fuck if you give me away."

Her words only brought a wider smile to Ambrose's face, infuriating her further.

Impossibly fast, he moved to stand directly in front of Lila. He pressed her against the desk in the bedroom, both arms at either side of her. He inched down, his cold gaze warming into a fiery, red heat, as he whispered into her ear, "Ah, do tell. Was I lacking in anything as you screamed my name? I'm pretty sure you were dripping for me, darling, before you came all over my fingers. Or was I imagining the delicious taste of you as I sucked them clean? Was I imagining you begging for more as you fucked my hand?" Lila's first reaction was to push him away from her, but when her hands met his chest, he didn't budge, he only smirked. "I like it when you fight back, Little Mouse."

Lila's whole body shook. She couldn't quite tell if she was afraid, angry, or incredibly aroused, and she hated herself for it as she knew it was a violent mix of all three.

"Hektor said the same thing," she seethed, hoping her words would be like a knife. She met his eyes as he stiffened and prepared to twist the blade. "It seems you two are more alike than I thought. You only know how to make me scream when you're inflicting pain."

Ambrose straightened, removing his arms from around her. Lila stood a little prouder, taking a step from the table, toward him. "You're quite like Ciro too, it turns out. The only way to have me is by forcing me into it with your powers. Isn't that right?"

She watched as Ambrose gulped.

Good.

"Isn't that what you said? The only reason I wanted you was because of your *euphoric* bite? Well, the more I think about it, the more I realize you must be right. How could I ever want to be with someone who treats me like I'm something to be sold? How could I ever be foolish enough to think I—"

Lila stopped herself, exhaling a sharp breath. When she met his eyes again, she glowered, "I would rather be caught in between Ciro and Hektor than *ever* let the Monster of Malvania touch me again."

And it was a boldfaced lie, a lie she knew he wouldn't believe, but she wanted her words to hurt more than a stake to the heart. She wanted him to hurt just as much as he hurt her.

By the destroyed look in his eyes, it worked.

Ambrose stiffened once more, his gaze becoming like a tundra. Lila saw his fists clench and unclench, his nails prolonged to a dangerous length. With each flex, they cut into the meat of his palm, drawing out droplets of black blood.

"Very well," his voice was far away, any sense of the molten gold was gone, only leaving behind ice in its wake. "Sending you back to the Reinicks can be arranged if you prefer to be their murine. Consider our bargains nullified, Miss Bran."

He turned and grabbed for his coat, shoving it, his hair still tucked into it, and stalked toward the door.

Lila held her breath the entire time.

As he reached for the knob, he glanced over his shoulder. "If you do not wish to be touched by others as well, you will stay in here until I return," he snarled and whipped the door open, slamming it behind him, causing the entire room to shake.

Lila felt her blood fluctuate from pure ice to raging heat, back and forth, until she felt dizzy.

What had she just done? Why would she say those things? She clearly wanted him so desperately, why wasn't he seeing that? And, like an idiot, she spoke before she could even think, telling him she preferred the touch of the Reinicks—and he *believed* her?!

She pulled the chair from the desk and flopped into it, throwing her face into her hands.

They were both wrong, she knew it, but he just got under her skin, and she reacted *so* poorly. What a fool.

Tears welled in her eyes as so many emotions ran through her. Anger, frustration, disappointment, sorrow. She wanted to explain herself, wanted to fix the mess she created before it was too late.

The door to the bed chamber opened, causing Lila to jump out of her seat.

He came back! she thought.

"Ambrose, I'm sorry—I didn't mean any . . ." she hesitated, surveying the room, ". . . of . . . it . . ." Her eyebrows knit together.

The room was empty, save for the swinging front door. *Perhaps it opened again because he slammed too hard,* she thought, feeling more disappointment wash through her as she watched it slightly swing on its hinges.

Lila sighed, wishing Ambrose *had* returned, and closed the door. She pressed her back against it, surveying the room just in case.

But no one was there.

Still, something didn't feel quite right. The room's air felt . . . stagnant.

Lila spotted her stake on the nightstand. It may be better to hold on to it, even if it was only a comfort.

But the moment she took one step, a large, horrifying figure dropped from the ceiling in front of her. Immediately, her eyes were snagged on skin paler than the moon, ears that were so long and pointed, and limbs that appeared abnormally long. As the figure's eyes met Lila, she couldn't help but gasp. His eyes were all black, looking as though ink flooded his vision—there were no whites, nothing distinguishable from pupil and iris. Lila couldn't even tell where exactly he was looking, as his head jutted from left to right in sporadic movements.

The man, if Lila could even call him that, looked old. But she knew it was just a facade. The line down his chin told her everything she needed to know.

It told her this creature, at least in part, was a strigoi.

And he was blocking the path to her only defense.

The creature took a step toward Lila. She knew he was being deliberately slow, as he took deep inhales of the air. He was smelling *her*.

"My, my. I've been waiting for him to leave," he took another step toward her, and she took one back, pressing herself against the door. "I followed you from the masquerade last night. I waited outside as he had his way with you. It sounded like you enjoyed it." The creature sniffed the air again. "In fact, I could *smell* just how much you enjoyed it," he smiled, and it was the most horrifying thing Lila had ever seen. "Just over there, correct?" He pointed a long, sharp finger to the bed. All jagged teeth, red tongue and—and something otherworldly.

As he smiled, the split in his chin began to peel open, revealing his three-way jaw. The two lower jaws had fangs, almost like pinchers of a spider, sticking out. The bottom jaws swooped out like wings, revealing rows upon rows of jagged sharp teeth reaching to the back of his throat.

Lila gulped, trying to steady herself as the creature closed his mouth again and began to laugh. He closed his eyes as he stood in front of her. "Ah, to feel that warmth again. Ambrose really should've known better than to bring you to a den of vampires."

"Constance!" Lila called against the door, hoping the other girl would be able to hear her.

The strigoi only smiled. "Ah, the young lady followed her master. In fact, no one remains in this wing. There is only you and myself here now."

"Who are you?" Lila asked, even though her voice quivered.

Ambrose! she screamed through the Concord. But there was no response.

"That is not important," he smiled.

Lila couldn't tell if he was full strigoi. She didn't believe so. He was terrifying, yes. But not as menacing and animalistic as Ambrose conveyed full-blooded strigoi to be. He had a sentience she wasn't expecting from the death creatures.

Which meant she had a chance as long as she avoided his venom.

If he managed to bite her, there would be hell to pay. It was a gamble on which kind of half-breed he was, one from the Arachnid Estate or from the Maggot Mansion. If he were from the former, then she would get paralyzed, and he would be able to feast on her alive.

She thought of Constance, her horrifying story of how she almost died, how it was too late by the time Darius and

Ambrose found her. She wondered if this was the same vampire who turned her. And there was always the possibility of her becoming a strigoi if he bit her. Lila couldn't remember what Ambrose had said about half-breeds turning others. Heavens, why couldn't she pay more attention?

Any moment now, the strigoi would leap, and Lila wouldn't be quick enough to dodge. But, if she acted first, maybe—just maybe—she'd be able to surprise him just long enough to reach her stake.

Adrenaline pumping, she didn't think twice.

As the strigoi closed the distance between them, Lila threw a hard punch aimed directly at his throat. The vampire gagged, and as his hand instinctively went to his Adam's apple, it was just enough time for Lila to dash past him, toward her only weapon. She knew his recovery time would be quick, but she tried anyway.

The strigoi swung a clawed hand at her, managing to grab a fistful of her ponytail. He yanked her back, but Lila managed to use the momentum to sweep her feet below him. Her foot hit his ankle, hard, and the strigoi lost his footing, releasing her hair.

Lila plunged forward, jumping and rolling over the bed, as the vampire ran around it. Just as her hand grasped the familiar wood of the stake, the strigoi was on her, tackling her down to the floor beside the bed.

Ambrose, there's a strigoi—

"The more you fight, the more it'll hurt," the strigoi smiled, his sickly almost silver saliva dripping from those jagged teeth onto Lila's cheek. "Not that I'm telling you to stop. I like to play with my food. Isn't that what your pretty vampire said?" The strigoi snapped his teeth before flaying his three-sided jaw.

Lila used all her strength to hold him back as he got

closer, her arm like a bar over her body at his neck, pushing him back. His saliva kept dripping, as his teeth neared her face. They were in a standstill and Lila knew her strength would eventually give out, leaving her completely open.

Leaving her stuck.

She had an idea, but it was a risky one. More than risky. If she missed her only chance, it could lead to death.

Lila took as deep a breath as she could, with the strigoi on top of her. With her free hand, she pressed the stake against her body, the sharp end pointing up, directly at the strigoi's chest.

Ambrose's voice solidified in her mind, the Concord a comforting tug. *I'm coming, Lila.*

Without so much as a thought, she took a leap of faith.

She let her arm barring him go slack, and the vampire plunged down, sticking his pincher-like fangs and then the rest of his numerous rows of teeth, deep into Lila's shoulder.

But the moment he bit down was also the moment Lila's stake stabbed right through the strigoi's heart.

Agonized screaming escaped the strigoi's mouth as blood as black as tar dripped down Lila's fingers and wrist. The vampire spit blood, coughing out the black ooze all over Lila—her face, her neck, the bite mark, her eyes.

She tried to block her face or smudge the blood from her eyes, but that was when Lila realized she couldn't move.

The vampire was seizing atop her, and she couldn't scoot away, she couldn't even turn her head, she could only shift her eyes back and forth as the panic settled in.

Lila was paralyzed.

The strigoi straddled Lila as he sat up, clawing at the

wound on his chest. Already his skin was charring, as if he had been out in the sun. His black eyes went wide, milking over with a white haze, as the tar continued to drip down his mouth, his nose, his ears, and out the gaping wound.

He shrieked and began to steam as his skin turned as black as night, cracking and crumbling away. His body was looking more and more like the corpses of Lord and Lady Reinick, and Lila realized this must've been what happened when Ciro murdered them.

She was a murderer now too.

And it felt good.

After another moment of the beast's wailing, it flopped back onto her, knocking the wind from her chest.

She couldn't move as the creature had its last twitches and spasms of life over her, as the stench of death settled in, as the gore spread all over her, as her own shoulder wound singed and burned in pain, making her want to cry out.

All she could do was sit, watch, wait, and hope—hope that Ambrose would be there soon.

21

As the body still twitched in rigor mortis atop her, the sound of the bedroom door crashing down made Lila jolt. Or it would've, if she could move at all.

"Lila!" Ambrose yelled as she heard his footsteps hurry into the room. She strained her eyes, trying to see him through the strands of lavender bangs blocking her view.

He came.

Immediately, Lila was filled with a guilt heavier than the strigoi's weight against her. It felt like an anchor on her chest, constricting her ribs and her lungs.

She shouldn't have said those things to him. If she hadn't managed to luck out as she had, she'd be dead right now, and Ambrose would think she hated him. Would think she wasn't absolutely smitten with him, that she didn't want to be touched by him.

Lila would apologize. She would explain herself. She had too.

Ambrose dashed across the room, around the bed, and cursed as he saw the shriveled, decomposing body on top of her.

Ambrose! I'm—

And then those red eyes met hers.

Worry. Fear. Anger. Sorrow. Guilt. Relief. Pride.

Every emotion played across his features as he watched her, as his eyes went from hers to the wound on her shoulder to the staked strigoi above her. She watched as the glow of his crimson eyes dimmed, turning back to their deep, velvety black.

"Draven, how is she?" Lila hadn't noticed Darius enter the room. He stalked up beside Ambrose, looked down at Lila and the corpse, and gasped. Somehow, he became even paler. "Dear lords. Again?"

Ambrose hurried to Lila, shoving the body carelessly from her and gingerly lifted her into his arms before placing her onto the much-more-comfortable bed.

She knew she would be stiff for days after this, only adding the soreness from last night and the evening training session.

With delicate fingers—the same he ravenously thrust inside of her last night—he carefully moved the fabric from her shoulder, ripping and stretching the pieces needed to get away from the wound.

She winced as the fabric pulled at the wound, and his jaw clenched, studying her.

Are you all right? he asked through the Concord.

Y-Yes. It hurts but it's not too bad. He came right after you left. I thought it was you.

Ambrose's eyes fell to the body on the floor. *Judging by the stake through his chest, it looks like you've actually learned something.*

I was still bitten.

It was your first real experience protecting yourself, Little Mouse. You did very, very well. Not dying is winning. His eyes met hers again, boring into them. He wanted her to think on his words. To embrace and be encouraged by them.

Wa-was he a strigoi?

Again, Ambrose's gaze shifted. From the corner of her eye, Lila saw Darius observing the body as well.

Half. He was a half-blood who must've joined the Arachnid Estate.

Does that mean I'll turn?

Ambrose paused for a moment, studying the wound. *If my theory about you is correct, I don't think you* can *be changed into a strigoi. I believe, unlike the rest of us, you are immune to the venom that so easily changes us.*

Why?

"I'm going to remove the venom," Ambrose said aloud. "Remember, it'll hurt but it'll be over in a moment."

I'll explain later. I promise.

Lila readied herself as he placed his palm against her shoulder.

White-hot pain seared her shoulder as milky green ooze crawled from her wound. It felt like millions of tiny spiders scuttering against her torn flesh, under her skin, shifting and bumping into each other as if they were running away.

Lila wanted to scream, but her mouth wouldn't budge open. She felt tears rain uncontrollably down the sides of her face, but she kept her eyes glued on Ambrose.

Remember to breathe, he reminded.

His eyes were so dark, and she couldn't help but miss the warm mirth that filled her soul every time he looked at her.

Slowly, she was able to move her fingers and toes. And then her arms. She buckled her legs impulsively at the pain before Ambrose leaned against her thighs.

I'm so sorry, Ambrose. About earlier—

"Almost done, darling."

His voice calmed her. It always did. That golden voice pulled her from the peaks of pain, fear, loathing, and anxiety, down to a calming, warm place. His voice was like a warm blanket on the coldest of days.

Lila felt his grip tighten against her skin, his fingers digging, nearly bruising. But it didn't hurt. It felt . . . comforting. Possessive. Grounding.

She was *his*.

This strigoi's bite couldn't claim her.

She fought through the pain, feeling the millions of imaginary spiders leaving the wound as the sickly sting of green ooze left her body.

She jolted up, finally in control of herself again, and threw her arms around Ambrose's neck.

"I'm sorry. I didn't mean any of it. I was mad and I just—I just said things! I don't believe any of it!" she pleaded, pulling him closer to her. She buried her face into the crook of his neck, watching his Adam's apple as it dipped from a swallow. She didn't want to meet his eyes, afraid that maybe . . . just maybe, he *did* mean all he said. Or that he might not be willing to forgive her.

Ambrose opened and closed his mouth once, twice— but before he could actually say anything, Constance dashed into the room.

"Lilac! Lilac, are you all right?" the young girl's face was twisted with worry. Her haunted expression survived the room and studied Lila, the wound on her neck, and the body on the floor. Lila could see the memories of the girl's own history replaying in Constance's features, and she released her hold on Ambrose and gazed at her friend.

"I'm fine, just a bit sore now that the adrenaline's worn off."

Constance leaped onto the bed and threw her arms around the girl. "Ambrose said your name and disappeared so suddenly—I thought you were . . ." she hesitated. "I should've stayed with you, I should've—"

"Constance, it's all right. Truly, I'm fine. Better than fine."

It was true. What Ambrose said was true. She *won*. Sure, she was bitten and put herself in a compromised position, but she'd successfully killed a strigoi! It proved all her training had been for *something*.

"Lila, I cannot even begin to apologize . . ." Darius said as he walked up to them. "To have one of my own guests attacked by someone under my house . . . I don't know what to say."

Ambrose eyed him. "Who was he?"

Darius shook his head. "I have no clue. He's not someone I've turned . . . I have a theory, however."

"Drusilla?"

Darius nodded. "That woman has been a thorn in my side for centuries."

Constance gave a small squeak, but Lila had no idea who they were talking about.

"Who's Drusilla?"

Ambrose's eyes fell on her again as Darius began to explain, "To put it lightly, she's my cousin—and she believes *she* is the rightful Lady of the Arachnid Estate, as if bloodlines had anything to do with it. She tries to kill me every few decades. Her latest endeavor is trying to build her own manor. But without her own people, she's decided she'll take whoever she gets her teeth into—including the strigoi." His eyes hesitated on Constance for a moment.

The one to change her must've been one of Drusilla's as well . . . or maybe Drusilla herself, Lila realized.

"She's built a small strigoi army off the northern coast of the Crow Court. My intel hasn't given me much, but this seems exactly like something she'd do. Did the vampire say anything to you?"

Lila shook her head, glancing at the body. "He said it wasn't worth me knowing anything and just that he'd been waiting till I was alone." Lila lifted her chin in defiance. *Alone, but not useless.*

As she turned back to the vampires, she saw Ambrose smile, pride welling on his features, before he quickly hid his emotions once more.

"It could've been an attack, or it could be Drusilla's faulty leadership," Ambrose observed. "Either way, you'll have to put her in her place soon enough. I can help . . . as part of our bargain."

Something shifted in Ambrose at that moment. As he spoke, he released her and stood from the bed, lifting to his full height.

Lila wasn't sure what it was, but he almost seemed regal.

Darius took a moment, but he slowly nodded. "All right, all right. You know I was already going to take the deal," he smirked.

"Well then, it seems like we have an agreement." Ambrose grinned, sticking his hand out. Darius took it, shaking it firmly before they clapped each other on the back and smiled.

As Lila looked between the two men, she saw a small black feather form along the curve of the fleshy part just under Darius's thumb knuckle and index finger. She knew whatever bargain was struck between them had to do with why Ambrose wanted her to travel with him to the other manors.

Turning back to Lila and Constance, Ambrose placed

his hands in his pockets. "Well, I believe our time away from home has been quite . . . eventful. If we leave now, we should arrive back at the Crow Court before sunup. Ladies, are you ready to depart?"

It took them only a few moments for Lila to freshen up, change into her travel clothes, and pack up her belongings. They left with little fanfare, only saying a quick goodbye to the Cambrias and Balzar. The three were soon back in the carriage, traveling along the bumpy roads to . . . to *home*.

Though it had only been three nights and two days away from the Crow Court, Lila missed her own bed, her own room. She missed Pollock and Kaz, she missed the gardens and the weapons room.

But what Lila missed most was the feeling of constant safety that surrounded her while in the walls of the Crow Court. The knowledge that the Reinicks couldn't touch her there.

She exhaled, easing into the cushion of the seat under her. Lila didn't know how to relax, exactly. There had been very few exceptions when her body wasn't tight from clenching, wound up from being ready to run at any moment, nor sore from being on edge.

And this was not one of those rare moments. The sick feeling she got whenever traveling in the coach didn't help and she also felt a pair of eyes lingering on her.

Ambrose studied her as he leaned against the covered window. He seemed . . . tired.

They had taken a risk leaving when they did, racing

against the sun. But Ambrose had felt comfortable in his decision, so Lila had also. Worse come to worse, they would all just have a cramped day in the carriage as they waited it out.

It seemed like they were in the darkest part of night, just before dawn. Of course, Ambrose and Constance had no problem seeing a thing, but for Lila's human eyes, she found she could only just-barely make out the vampires near her. And as she looked back into Ambrose's black eyes, she found that she wasn't actually sure where the darkness began, and he ended.

They hadn't spoken about anything. Not the bite, not the strigoi, not their argument, not the night before, and surely not about what will happen between them once they arrive back at the manor. Not since the brief exchange in front of everyone.

Lila fidgeted with her hands, worried that Ambrose *had* meant what he said. Worried he would send her back to the Reinicks, as she had so stupidly requested.

But even as Lila turned away from Ambrose, she felt his eyes still on her, staring. It wasn't a hot glare like usual, surveying her body lustfully. It wasn't cold either, with disdain that could kill like that afternoon.

It was . . . warm, and it encompassed her, as though he were simultaneously looking at her entire being.

It felt like her back was being rubbed in slow comforting circles, like she could sleep and be safe and nothing would ever harm her.

I'm not mad, he whispered through the Concord. *You do not have to worry.*

He smiled sheepishly at her.

I—

"Ambrose," Constance hissed in a panic.

Ambrose jolted. The warmth and comfort were gone. "I know. I sense them too," he said, calmly. "Lila. Pull out your stake," he ordered, still calm.

She fumbled with her skirts to pull the sharp wood out. It still had the black stain from the strigoi at its tip.

The horses pulling them reeled and bucked, causing the carriage to bounce lightly.

But then everything went silent.

She followed Ambrose's line of sight, not seeing anything, and then did the same to Constance.

"What's—"

The carriage shook violently.

Ambrose's eyes flashed red, as did Constance's green.

He lifted a finger, indicating silence—stillness. "Don't move," he commanded. Lila and Constance froze in their place, ready for anything.

Another bang against the side of the carriage followed by silence.

Lila, no matter what you see, what you feel, remain completely still.

Lila wanted to question him, wanted to know what the threat was. But before she could ask, the door opposite her was torn from its hinges.

She fought the urge to yelp or flinch, stilling herself as Ambrose commanded.

The dark outside was quiet. Too quiet. The crickets weren't chirping, the cicadas weren't singing. It felt . . . eerie. Like something was looming just out of sight.

And then there was an explosion of energy.

Constance burst from her seat beside Lila into the night, her dress shifting into a pair of fleshy wings behind her as she bore her claws and teeth to whatever was stalking them.

"Stay here," Ambrose ordered once again, only his tone was growing more gravelly as his face began to shift into his monster form. Lila had almost forgotten what it looked like, tall and hulking. His muscles were nearly impossible, and his new mass took up most of the car, his thighs pinned hers between his and his huge arms could go nowhere but forward, perfectly caging her in. He was massive, terrifying, and utterly gorgeous.

She saw the animal in his eyes, the animal that would rip anything apart that even looked at her the wrong way. "Listen to me, for once. Please," he breathed; his fangs so close to her. "You don't want me to punish you, do you?"

Lila flushed as Ambrose shifted his body, darting out through the broken carriage door. She swore she saw a glint of a smirk on his lips as he left. As curious as she was to find out what Ambrose's "punishment" would be, she heeded his warning, and remained perfectly still.

She couldn't see much outside from her side of the carriage, but what she could hear sent shivers down her spine. Ripping flesh, teeth, yelps. She could only hope the noises were coming from their enemies.

As her ears focused on the sounds outside the busted door, she almost didn't notice the clicking sound of something just beyond the still-intact door to her left.

Click, click, clack. She couldn't tell what it was. It sounded like . . . rocks maybe? Pebbles hitting one another?

Then the sound of dragging nails against the wood struck her ears, just before the door tore open like the other.

In the background, she still heard the sounds of the fight going on above her, but what was *before* her made an instant sweat break along the back of her neck, her hairline.

Before her stood a monster *nothing* like the one she faced earlier.

It moved its three-pronged jaw into the space the door took before, searching for something. Searching for her.

Click, click, clack.

22

The monster rattled his teeth together as it studied Lila. *Click, click, clack, snap.* Lila remained completely still, trying not to even breathe as the creature crawled onto the floor of the carriage. It was bald, and as it looked at her, she saw the same defining line along his chin the strigoi had. Only, this creature was much, much uglier. And his eyes . . .

Unlike the half-strigoi she fought with inky black eyes that reminded her of a spider, this creature's eyes were all white, clouded over—as though it were blind.

Click, clack, snap. It snapped at the air around her, its teeth looking more like razor blades than anything else. And that's when she realized why Ambrose had begged her to listen to him—it couldn't see her, not if she remained still.

With the stake in her hand, Lila felt confident. She knew she took down the half-strigoi by chance, but maybe luck would strike again. If she remained patient and bid her time, she could attack the beast before it even realized she'd moved. But for her to be able to do that, she'd have to time her attack perfectly, and wait until it got very, very close.

Outside, she could hear the sounds of the fight continuing. She wasn't sure how many strigoi had surrounded them, and based on everything Ambrose had said, she was sure it would be an ugly battle.

But Lila had solace. It was soon to be dawn, which meant the vampires would have to take cover, to hide from the sun. If she could fend them off, just till sunrise, she'd survive.

So, she waited. She let the creature snap its teeth at her as she held her breath, didn't blink, and remained perfectly statuesque.

Until the creature was eye-to-eye with her.

She could smell its rancid breath fill her lungs, and she held back a gag. The stake was still in her grip, aimed up, directly at the creature's chest—at his heart. All she had to do was thrust it upward.

Just a little closer.

The strigoi opened its three-way jaw, its pincer-like teeth surrounding Lila's face. It hissed and then inched closer, splaying its tongue out down its nonexistent chin.

Just a little closer.

Her knuckles were white, and her hand was growing numb from how tightly she was squeezing the stake.

It shifted its head, the three-way jaw nearing her ears now, as it ran its tongue along its top teeth, coating them in a sickening saliva. It sniffed the air, brushing the bangs on Lila's forehead back with each exhale.

And then it licked her.

It ran its wet, scaly tongue up Lila's cheek, from her jawline to the outer corner of her eye. And just as his tongue flicked off her skin, Lila finally moved.

She threw her fist up, plunging the stake directly up, into the chest of the creature. It reared back but Lila thrust her weight into the wood, pushing the stake in till the creature's flesh met her hand.

The creature jerked away, but Lila followed, pushing it to the other side of the carriage and straddling it as it fell on the opposite seat. The momentum helped her dig the stake even deeper into its chest when she heard a loud *crack* and felt bone break under the weapon. The strigoi spasmed below her, thrashing at her thighs and trying to shove her off him. She took the hits against her arms, her chest, but pushed deeper, pressing against the wood in her grip until the creature's skin heated and burned below her, turning charred and black, as it spurt up the rancid vampiric blood from his lips. The strigoi collapsed in on itself, and Lila felt the creature crush underneath her.

Though it was much harder to kill than the one she faced earlier, it was dead. She successfully killed the strigoi. Now she only had to fend for herself against who knew how many more.

As she pulled the stake from the corpse, she could still hear the fight outside. Sitting still in the carriage was like a waiting death trap, so she hiked her skirts up, tearing the bottom so it wouldn't get in her way if she needed to run, and jumped down onto the road.

The moment she left the carriage, regret settled in. Regret and fear. The scene was like that of nightmares, a number of strigoi were crawling on all fours around the horses, biting and eating the poor creatures alive. Up above, Ambrose and Constance ripped, slashed, and tore three or four strigoi each, some clinging to their body parts.

Lila had never seen Constance fight, but the girl seemed ravenous as she dug her teeth into the strigoi latched onto her and gripped another's neck with her claws. She was smaller than the other vampires she had seen in this bat form, but still just as ruthless.

Next to Ambrose, however, Constance looked like a small bunny rabbit—a small rabbit covered in black blood.

The hulking beast tore at the strigoi hanging on him. Lila heard the crunch of bones breaking as he violently kicked the one gripping onto his foot, his heel digging into the vampire's face.

She knew this was his true body, his true face. Ambrose was massive, terrifying, his muscles bulged under the taut, thick charcoal-gray skin. His normally well-kept hair was wild, falling into his face and over his shoulders.

It looked like moonlight.

This was the Monster of Malvania.

Click, clack, snap. Lila heard the familiar sound of teeth to her right. Her head snapped back down to see a strigoi's attention fall onto her. His mouth was covered in gore from the horse, but clearly it wanted more. It slowly crawled on all fours toward her, snapping its jaws. Lila's fist tightened on the stake, and she lowered herself into a fighting stance, ready to lunge.

But just as she shifted her weight to her feet, she heard a loud growl. Her eyes impulsively snapped up at the sound Ambrose made, seeing blood gush from his chest as a strigoi tore into it with long fingernails. He caught the beast by the base of his neck and gripped his skull between his claws. And then he *pulled.* Lila watched as Ambrose ripped the head of the strigoi clean from its neck, black blood splashing down onto her and the strigoi before her.

The strigoi.

Lila turned suddenly, remembering the monster stalking toward her. She jerked her weapon in the air, ready to strike, but it was too late. The strigoi was close now, right in front of her, and it smacked the stake from her hand. Lila didn't wait a single heartbeat. She threw her leg at the beast, kicking it hard in the ribs and managing to push it away from her. But the strigoi only seemed more excited.

And worse, more began to notice her.

She slowly backed up, gauging where the stake would've landed, when the strigoi leaped onto her, tightening its arms around her neck. She flipped it over her, throwing it to the ground and then took off down the road.

More strigoi were catching up to her now, and she knew running on the dirt road would do nothing. There was nowhere to lose them, nowhere to hide.

She could run into the forest, the trees would make for decent cover, and she could lose them around the —

Lila felt something tug in her loose hair, but she didn't slow until it yanked her back.

Another strigoi gripped Lila's hair in his clawed hands, pulling her head far back to reveal the long column of her neck. She punched and kicked out at it, but another strigoi was there in seconds, grabbing her arms and pinning her body to its own. She thrashed, but it only made the two strigoi hold her tighter. She felt the claws of the first digging into her scalp as the second clacked his teeth in her ear. She heard the whinnying of the horses that were still alive, the fight going on above her between Constance, Ambrose, and the strigoi.

And then more were on her. There had to be at least six of them surrounding her, reaching for her. She felt scratches burn along her skin, but none of them had bitten her, so she continued to thrash, continued to fight.

She kicked out and one of the monsters caught her foot, before it rubbed its face along the length of her calf. Lila felt shudders race across her body, but then another grabbed her arm away from the second strigoi and did the same.

In a moment, they were all rubbing themselves against her.

Lila shrieked, trying to pull away from them, trying to wiggle out of their grasps, but her attempts were useless. They had been overrun by these monsters—she wasn't sure any of them would make it out of this alive, let alone her, the weakest of the weak.

She screamed again. But it came out gruff and angry. It wasn't a scream of pain or of fear. It was of anger. Why was she born so weak in a world so strong? Why, no matter how hard she tried and trained, was she so useless?

Lila's scream wasn't a scream at all.

It was a battle cry.

She tore her leg away from the strigoi still rubbing its face against her leg and used all the strength she had left to kick it against one of the creature's side jaws. The teeth from its jaw met the sole of her boot and dug into the meaty flesh of her foot, but she pressed on until she heard the loud crack as its jaw came loose from its hinges.

As soon as the beast was down, she threw her arm back, crashing her elbow into the second strigoi's throat. It finally loosened its grip on her, and she jumped up, crashing against the strigoi holding her hair. She smacked and clawed and punched until she felt its nail scrape against her scalp and let go. She jumped off of it and scrambled to the stake, lying so close she could reach it if she moved quickly. She felt hands try to grab her ankles, but she didn't stop crawling until she rolled onto her weapon and brandished it before her.

The strigoi were mostly recovered, clicking and clacking at her once again.

Her hand was shaking, from exertion or fear she didn't know. But Lila was done playing the role of the scared little murine. She would go down, but she'd go down fighting.

She held up the stake just before a large shadow crossed over her.

Another strigoi?

Wings. That's all Lila saw at first. Leathery wings of a bat. Ambrose crashed to the ground before her, crouched, his wings splayed behind him, blocking Lila from the several strigoi that had just been stalking toward her. Blood was sprayed across his body, up his arms, even in his moon-white hair. She couldn't see his face, but she could only imagine the look of pure rage on it as a low growl came from his throat.

23

ila lowered the stake slowly, and Ambrose immediately shuffled back toward her, his wings nearly
surrounding her now as the warmth of his back
radiated on her face. Now that the adrenaline was wearing
off, Lila's entire body ached and burned. She felt cuts and
scratches she didn't realize she had received, and her foot
stung from where she kicked the strigoi in the teeth. Without thinking, her head flopped onto Ambrose's back, just
between where the wings met on his shoulder blades. He
tensed, and his skin immediately changed from a burning
furnace to a piece of marble left out in the cold. It felt good
against her warm forehead.

The growl coming from Ambrose grew deeper as he
spread his arms and wings wide to the sides before her. Lila
heard the strigoi shuffle farther away rather than closer.

The growl turned into a roar as the murder of crows
flew from the flesh on Ambrose's chest, from the tattoos
inked across his torso.

The crows flew at the strigoi, pecking and tearing away
at the monsters with no remorse. It was like the time on

her balcony, when the Reinicks had come to torment her the evening after Ambrose took her. She had rarely seen that power, but it dazzled her nonetheless.

Within moments, the number of crows grew exponentially, and only heartbeats after that, the strigoi were gone. Just, gone.

Nothing but bones and teeth and black ooze were left on the dirt floor.

The crows had eaten their way through them, going for the hearts first. And then they moved, swarming like a bloodthirsty cloud toward where Constance had been protecting the last remaining horse of the four. The crows flew over them, attacking only the strigoi.

"They're amazing," Lila breathed, still slumped against Ambrose's back. He shifted then, turning toward her, and holding her shoulders steady.

"A fourth way to kill vampires I forgot to mention. Complete and utter eradication. A little harder to come by," he smirked.

His eyes shone the brilliant red she had seen so infrequently. The color that symbolized hunger and bloodshed.

And she found herself growing to like the monstrous shade.

"Are you hurt?" he asked, his voice hoarse. Facing her, Ambrose pulled her to lean against his chest. He was still wounded from the gashes earlier, so she carefully rested against his arm as his wounds were already healing.

"Nothing too bad. I think one of their fangs bit through my shoe though. My foot feels like it's burning." Lila noticed their size difference, his hand was the size of her entire stomach. If they were standing, she'd probably only reach to his abdomen. And his thighs—they could crush her like a bug.

And at the thought, Lila found herself crawling into his lap.

"You did good. You fought like hell." He wrapped his arm protectively around her waist. "Even if you did disobey me," he smirked.

"There was one in the carriage!" she tried to argue, but Ambrose only pulled her flush against him.

"Guess I'll just have to come up with a suitable punishment for you." He stood, scooping his arm under her rear, and carried her—*with one arm*—back to the carriage.

Immediately, Lila flushed at how easily he handled her—how easily but also how gently.

The murder of crows flew toward them, and as Lila tucked her head into the crook of his shoulder, they were swarmed with the birds as they flew back into their lord's tattoo. Lila thought some would hit her along the way, but the only thing she felt was the rush of soft feathers. It felt like being cuddled by a dozen fluffy puppies.

"Why didn't you use the crows when they first attacked?" Lila asked, looking up into those crimson eyes that seemed to be slowly dimming.

Ambrose sighed, "It takes a lot of my energy to do it, leaving me vulnerable. Plus, once they're out, they're out. The initial impact is gone. So I try to reserve it as a last-ditch effort."

The idea of this giant beast being vulnerable nearly made Lila laugh. She just couldn't picture it. Not with his massive, warm arm wrapped around her, effortlessly carrying her like she was a doll.

His hand tightened on the back of her thighs, and she blushed at the realization that her thighs, together, fit perfectly in his monstrous hand.

She gulped and he only gripped tighter, as though he

was reading her thoughts—teasing her. She realized she *still* had no idea what the scope of his abilities were. Maybe he *could* read her mind.

"Do you—"

"Your thoughts?" he smirked. "No. Just emotions. It doesn't work on other vampires. Only humans and animals."

She frowned. "Then how did you know that was what I was going to ask?"

"Well, one moment you were ogling at me, then I did this"—his hand slid from the back of her knees closer to her rear before he squeezed again, causing her to squeak—"and while your dirty thoughts peaked for a moment, you then became confused, upset, but mostly embarrassed. I only put two and two together. And I could tell it is a question you've asked yourself a few times."

Lila opened her mouth several times, trying to come up with something to argue, but words failed her. So, instead, she crossed her arms, pouted, and turned her head from Ambrose. Which didn't do much considering she was pressed against him, in the crook of his arm. "Well, stop it."

"It's a bit hard to do that, my dear, when you project every emotion you have to the entire surrounding area. Your face speaks volumes before you even open those pretty lips of yours," he used his free hand to turn her face back toward him, pinching her chin between his fingers. His thumb rested on the hollow dip of her chin, his sharp nail just barely pushing into her bottom lip. "And when your face doesn't say much, your body does the rest of the talking."

Lila dipped her eyes to his mouth. Sharp fangs peeked through lips she suddenly, desperately wanted to kiss.

She tore her gaze back to his eyes—the red glow coming back to life—but he was staring at his thumb. Or rather, her lips under his thumb. She felt him gently pry her lips apart with the sharp tip of his nail, rubbing the bouncy flesh against the calluses of his skin. Lila wanted him to claim her lips, claim all of her, right there on that dirt road.

"*Those* emotions will be the death of me," Ambrose breathed, eyes locked on her lips.

"Umm—" Constance said in front of them, pulling them from their daze. It shocked Lila so much, she actually jumped, feeling herself press deeper into the crook of Ambrose's elbow, hiding herself between his arm and his torso. "Sorry to interrupt whatever . . . that was. But the sun is going to come up soon, and our carriage is broken." The young girl was already back into her regular state, brushing invisible dust off her torn skirts. She pointed to the sky, and she was right.

Within the hour, the sun would be up.

"Shit," Lila grunted. "How far are we from home?"

Ambrose studied the sky and then their last remaining horse. "If only one of us takes the horse, then I would say just under an hour. Ideally, the lighter, the faster." His gaze fell on Constance.

"I can do it. I'll have Uncle Kaz send a new carriage the moment I return." She walked over to the horse, patting it.

Lila tapped Ambrose's shoulder, indicating that she wanted to be put down, which he gently did.

As soon as her feet touched the hard ground, pain shot up through her foot where the strigoi tore through the sole of her boot. It didn't feel deep as far as she could tell, but it stung all the same.

"Will you be okay going on your own?" she asked.

Constance nodded. "Yeah, we're not *that* far. But what will you do? Ambrose shouldn't be in the sun either."

Lila thought for a moment and then hobbled over to the

carriage and assessed it; both doors were gone, but other than that the carriage itself was fine. She didn't think the single horse could carry all of them, so they'd have to travel by foot once the sun went down or wait for the carriage Constance would send upon traveling along to the manor.

"Ambrose," she called over her shoulder, "can you take the carriage over there?" Lila pointed to the side of the dirt road, where it met the trees. The shade provided by the trees should be enough to make them comfortable for the morning—as long as it didn't pass noon, they should be fine.

Ambrose nodded and lifted the carriage from the ground. Lila leered as she watched his back muscles flex with the weight.

As he moved it, Lila forced her attention to Constance. "I think if we could find something to act as a placeholder for the door, it could work. Got any ideas?"

Constance tapped her chin. "Maybe . . ." She walked up to one of the trees and gingerly touched the wood. Then she dug her nails into it, tearing off the bark in a clean break. Constance had torn a plank of wood about the size of the door. "Will this do?"

Lila nodded. "Yes! It's perfect," she beamed at the younger girl who smiled back.

"I hate to leave you behind," she said solemnly. "If more strigoi come—"

"It's fine, I know we won't have to wait long for the return carriage. But you should get going if you're going to make it before sunrise." Lila ushered Constance back to the carriage and helped her ease the plank over the broken door space that faced the road.

"Well, I'll see you both tonight," Constance said, leaping effortlessly onto the horse's back. "Try not to tear each other's clothes off as soon as I'm gone." She smirked and started forward.

Ambrose uttered, "Safe travels," before hiding in the carriage. The sky was a light indigo, and the stars were as bright as glitter, but Lila knew the sun was close behind. She waved goodbye as Constance rode away and then followed the vampire inside.

Ambrose had remained in his monstrous body as he sat within the dark, tight space. Lila hesitated a moment and then crawled over his thick thighs on the bench across from him. She kept her knees close to her chest on the bench, giving his massive form space to stretch out.

"Why haven't you changed back yet?"

She heard a few cracks and pops as Ambrose rolled his neck. "I'm sure you've gathered this already, but this is a vampire's true body. Once the change happens, we keep our human appearance, but it is not our true face—not anymore. The humanoid body is meant to lure, make humans comfortable. They know we are ... *other* no matter how much we look alike. But it is that otherness that makes you intrigued, attracted, and obsessed with us."

"What makes *me*?" Lila balked.

"Not *you* you. Figurative you. Humans. Humans have been fascinated with vampires since we came to be," he smirked, catching her eye. "But, because *this* is what we truly are, it is sometimes ... comforting to rest like this. To stretch our wings."

Lila studied him as he spoke. It must've been uncomfortable to constantly focus on remaining human-looking. It didn't make sense in this world they lived in, dominated by vampires. She would've expected them to be free of their human glamor but, she guessed, maybe it was just part of their customs now. Or maybe they were still trying to keep hold of whatever humanity they had left.

"Remember what I told you, Little Mouse. Vampires are creatures of desire. And we will always desire that which we cannot have." He stared at her again, his eyes dipping to where his thumb had been only moments ago.

But then he cleared his throat and looked down. "Humanity. Every vampire unwillingly strives for it. We don't know why. We detest it yet crave it. That is why you are so coveted. Being near you . . . it feels like life itself. Like warmth and sunlight. All which we are constantly denied."

Lila thought back to the strigoi surrounding her. They didn't hurt her, not mortally anyway. They were rough with her, yes, but in reality all they did was rub against her.

"Is that warmth . . . physical?" she asked sheepishly.

Ambrose looked back up. "What do you mean?"

"The strigoi. They rubbed their faces against my skin." Ambrose bristled, so she quickly added, "Not anything inappropriate necessarily. More like a . . . cat or a dog rubbing its owner. Or like a child with their blanket. They just rubbed their faces on my legs and arms."

The vampire squinted his eyes, looking at her skin, before he gingerly took her ankle. Lila shuddered at his touch, and blushed as she remembered his comment about sensing emotions. She tried to pull her leg back to her before the warmth in her lower belly grew any hotter.

"I have to make sure your wound is all right," he explained dryly.

He was the one just looking at me like a predator ready to eat his prey alive, she thought, pouting.

Ambrose smiled as he unlaced her boot and carefully removed it. "Those strigoi . . . they were blind."

"I noticed."

"Just being around you feels like sunlight, Lila," he admitted, looking deep into her eyes. "It's warmth and comfort and life and—" he hesitated. His eyes were now the deep, endless black void and they were sucking her in. "And I'm sure the strigoi just wanted to get closer to that. They wanted to *feel* it. And since they couldn't see, they relied on touch."

He pulled off her boot quickly, causing her to flinch and yelp all in one moment, grabbing the nearest thing to her—which happened to be his thigh.

With a coy smile, he tossed the boot onto the floor below him. "Touching you enhances that warmth."

"Do you . . ." she began, afraid to continue. "*Did* you feel it too? Last night?" Her voice was almost a whisper, but she knew he could hear her. If it weren't for the shift of his long hair on his shoulders, she might have missed him nodding.

"More than ever."

They both sat in silence, Ambrose kept his eyes locked on her foot. "The wound seems fine." He picked up a piece of her torn dress on the floor and wrapped it around the wound. "When we arrive home, have Kaz look at it."

She nodded quietly.

The sun rose, and they could see the light through the cracks of the wood on the floor. Ambrose inched away from the light, and closer to Lila.

"I'm sorry for how I behaved, both this morning and last night," Ambrose whispered.

Lila had wanted an apology, but not for last night.

She pulled her foot from his warm hand and brought her knees up to her chest once again.

"It's not that I didn't want to kiss you . . . but I let myself get carried away by the moment," he explained gruffly. His voice was gravelly, and he didn't make eye contact. But Lila noticed that he was *actually* twiddling his thumbs. "I felt your warmth, and like those damn strigoi, I wanted to surround myself in it." He finally looked up at her. She blushed at the implication. "But I shouldn't have bitten you. The moment I did, it ruined—"

"Nothing. Your bite, or venom, or whatever you call it, didn't ruin a thing, Ambrose. I . . . I wanted you too. I wanted you to kiss me and touch me. It's not like you drugged or enthralled me. So stop apologizing for something we both wanted."

In the blink of an eye, Ambrose's arms were caging her in, pressing her against the back of the seat. They were eye to eye then, and his form suddenly took up way more space than she thought possible. His eyes bore into hers, and she could almost describe them as pleading as they heated quickly from a black so deep to a red so vibrant. "Lila, I wanted to *bury* myself in you and be completely engulfed in you. Do you know how hard it was to step away from that?"

She blushed, feeling her blood race to her cheeks, as his jaw ticked. "If you hadn't, I might've let you."

His eyes flicked between hers, dipping to her neck, then her lips, and finally back up to her eyes. He visibly gulped, his Adam's apple bobbing in his throat.

"I got carried away," he mumbled. "I could've hurt you." He slowly leaned in.

"I thought it'd be evident by now . . . I can handle a little pain." She angled her head toward him, ready to kiss those lips, fangs and all. She wanted to feel his muscles against her breasts, wanted his massive hands to run over her body, grabbing and groping. She wanted him to bury himself inside of her and feel all the warmth she had to offer.

If he considered his bite euphoric, she had to assume her warmth was equally so. They were on even playing grounds and she knew, in that moment, they both wanted each other, despite their abilities.

Lila pushed him back into his seat, and he let her. She slowly, carefully, climbed on top of him, straddling his hips. Their faces still weren't even while he remained in his natural body, and she came just under his chin.

His skin was hot to the touch, as she was sure hers was too, like their bodies were radiating in harmony.

And then she felt . . . something pressing against her thigh. She squeaked. *That couldn't be . . . could it?* It felt huge, and as hard as a rock. She had felt his cock against her the night before and it was large by human standards, and thick enough to send her over the edge just thinking about it.

But this? This was . . .

Monstrous. It was the only way to describe it. She wasn't even sure if she'd be able to take it all. She rocked her hips against him, testing. Ambrose groaned into the small space between them, his hands tightening around her waist.

"Lila," he breathed. His eyes were pleading, just like a greedy beggar, as he slowly thrust his hips up, his massive heat cleaving between her center.

She released a soft moan, and decided she needed more of *that*. More of *him*. And she was ready to beg for more, on her knees if she had to.

With another slow rock of her hips, she grabbed the two long pieces of hair framing his face and pulled, her fingers locking around the silken strands. As Ambrose followed her movement, leaning down, he wrapped one large hand around her bottom and squeezed.

Lila let out a soft whimper and she could feel the breath of Ambrose's snicker on her eyelashes.

He shoved her skirts up her thighs, their lips just hovering over each other—so close, she could feel the warmth of them ghost against hers.

The patter of her heart was so loud in the tiny carriage, she thought it may explode from her chest.

It was getting louder and louder and . . .

Closer?

The patter of hooves beat against the dirt road.

"Lord Draven!" one of the human employees of the manor called out. "Miss Bran! Are you in there?"

With a sigh and a giggle, Ambrose and Lila both slumped down, the moment of heat broken by their inevitable interruption.

Ambrose leaned back against his seat, a smirk across his face as he gazed into Lila's eyes.

"Your eyes really are gorgeous," he hummed.

"My eyes?" she balked, still straddling his lap. "*You're* the vampire. Your eyes are like-like—"

"Bottomless pits? Droplets of blood?"

She giggled. "I was going to say like the night sky and rubies. Mine are just brown . . ."

He shook his head. "Oh, Little Mouse. If only you could see what a vampire sees. Your eyes are billions of shades of yellows and oranges. Like the leaves in fall, or like the setting sun. They are warmth incarnate. Much like you."

She blushed and he pressed a chaste kiss to her cheek. As he did, his massive body shifted underneath her into his human body.

Lila still straddled him, and he was still tall, lean, and muscular, but now her knees could rest on the pressed velvet seats, and they were much closer to eye level.

Ambrose leaned back and eyed their makeshift door. "We're in here," he called.

Lila heard the hooves of the carriage stop next to them, and moved to get off Ambrose, but he grabbed her hips, stopping her. She quickly turned her head back to him, but he was still turned toward the door. Waiting.

The footman, with a large black umbrella in hand, pushed the wooden plank from the door and held the umbrella up to perfectly block out the sun.

"Master, I—" as the footman's eyes looked up to them, noticing Lila's precarious seating position, her hiked-up skirts, and the even more precocious placement of Ambrose's hands, he gave a small squeak and quickly averted his gaze. "I'm so sorry to interrupt!"

The Lord of Crows gave a hearty laugh. Seated so close, Lila could feel the vibration of each exhale of air.

"It's no trouble, Ivan. Is the replacement carriage ready?"

"Ye-Yessir," he stuttered.

"Excellent. Darling, you'll have to get off of me now," Ambrose smirked.

Lila's cheeks turned hot as she scurried off his lap and through the doorway. "Little Mouse, you have one bare foot," Ambrose called after her, holding her boot up.

She huffed and snatched it from him before stomping to the other carriage, pouting once again.

After being escorted with the umbrella by Ivan, Ambrose joined her in the coach, that smirk still spread across his lips.

24

The moment Lila walked through the manor doors, she was greeted with a flurry of feathers to the face.

"Pollock!" she squealed. She hugged the bird as it flapped in front of her, nuzzling the top of his head against her chin and nipping at her shoulder. "It's good to see you too."

"That crow has gotten awfully close to you," Ambrose crossed his arms.

"He's a conversationalist, what can I say?" She looked at him. "The great Lord of Crows isn't jealous, is he?"

Ambrose grinned. "She-devil."

"Master Draven, Lady Lila. Welcome home," Kaz stood at the end of the foyer, bowing deeply to the vampire. It had only been a few days since they had been in the manor, but it felt like weeks. She missed the warmth of the halls, and the humans and vampires who worked them. *Maybe I'll find Robin at nightfall and see if he needs help in the garden*, she thought.

"It is good to be home. Kazamir, the lady has a simple

injury on her foot. Please assist her in cleaning it and then meet me in my study."

"Certainly, sir." Kaz nodded. And with a tilt of his mustache—which Lila assumed meant her smiling— he turned to her and said, "How many times do I have to tell you to not come home injured?"

Her cheeks reddened, both from embarrassment and the admission. This *was* her home.

Ambrose turned to Lila. "You must be tired, my dear."

"Aren't you? Shouldn't you sleep before—"

He cut her off. "I have boring matters to discuss with Kaz about the Crow Court while we were away. Please, rest, refresh. And whatever you need, do not be afraid to ask. I will retrieve you at dusk for training." Ambrose turned away and began walking toward his study by the kitchen.

"Wait—training?" Lila called.

"Well," he stopped, glancing over his shoulder. Those wicked eyes lighting up as they roamed all over her. "Of course. There is much more I have to show you. Go, rest— and get ready for me."

Heat shot through Lila, and she wasn't sure if it was from his stare or the toe-curling reaction she was having to his words.

"Can you do that for me, darling?" Ambrose cocked one of his gorgeous eyebrows.

Lila forgot how to speak. "Ye-Yes," she nodded.

"Good girl," he smirked and continued walking to his study.

The steam from the hot water smelled simply divine. There was just no other way to put it. Lilac flowers floated on the water's surface as purple petals clung to her skin and hair. She desperately wanted to take a bath upon arriving at the Crow Court, and after Kaz had properly attended to the wound on her foot, he sent for the human employees— Sandra, the kind maid from the other morning, was one of them—to attend to the bath. They were the ones who sprinkled the lilacs into her water. *"Per the master's request, dear,"* Sandra had said with a smirk.

Now alone, Lila blushed, playing with a flower as it floated in front of her. He had done this *for her*. He knew how much she simply needed to soak her aching body. Her muscles had ached so much, from the fighting, their journey, and—

And . . .

The apex of her thighs clenched. She had been sore there, rubbed to ecstasy, pumped to her body's content by Ambrose's fingers. If she thought about it hard enough, she could almost feel his calloused finger still rubbing her—

Lila shook her head and dunked herself completely under the water to clear her mind until her lungs needed air again. She pushed the wet hair from her face, massaging her scalp. She would *not* think about Ambrose. Not here, not like this . . . not while she was nude and—

Her hand slipped below the water's surface, tracing down her body. She bit her lip as her fingers clearly had a mind of their own, completely and utterly uncooperating with her brain.

Her fingers grazed over her hardening nipples, striking the memory of Ambrose's fingers toying with them, his sharp nails pinching them. She wondered how it'd feel if he took them into his mouth, lashed his wicked silver tongue over them.

Before she knew it, Lila moaned.

She glanced around the room, remaining perfectly silent, waiting to see if anyone would walk in to check on her. Did anyone hear her? Would anyone come searching?

After a moment, and complete silence, Lila knew no one would come. She eased back into the water, and her hand followed suit, drifting deeper between her legs. Her forefinger grazed the small bud between her thighs, and she immediately shuddered, biting her lip hard.

Lila, in all of her twenty-two years, had never touched herself. It's not that she *hadn't* had these kinds of thoughts, she just never had the time—or space—to do so. The closest she had come was imagining herself kissing Ciro Reinick when she was just fifteen.

Now, things were different. Ambrose Draven awoke something inside of her. Something that was starved, untamed, and completely unnurtured. It was toe curling, and mind maddening, and it made her entire body actually feel like a fiery sun, lit up from the inside. She felt like an animal in heat trying to burst out for that wicked vampire with a voice like melted gold who did things to her thoughts only a devil could do.

Lila slipped her fingers inside of her, thinking of Ambrose and his careful hand. She remembered how terrified she was that he would cut her inside with his sharp nails, but there wasn't anything uncomfortable about it.

She pumped herself, trying to mimic the rhythm Ambrose had set, rubbing the pink bud with her thumb as he had done.

"Ambrose," she moaned.

She wondered what else he could do to her, what his tongue would feel like against her skin, against that warming bud. She wondered what his cock would look like buried inside of her.

I wanted to bury *myself in you.*

Her fingers pumped quicker.

She wondered how many of those giant fingers he'd be able to fit inside of her when he was in his natural form. How he would take her like the animal he was and how much she would love it as he thrust into her, splitting her completely in half. She thought about riding his cock till *he* was yelling *her* name and how she would make him beg for release, and equally imagined being toyed with enough that she was begging him to ruin her.

The feel of his cock sawing through her folds had her eyes rolling back, as she thought of the hungry thrust he took before they were interrupted.

All along, her fingers teased her, slick with her pleasure.

She remembered how he tasted her and called her divine as he licked his fingers clean of her. She remembered how his lips felt against her and wanted to already experience it again. She remembered his teeth sinking into her.

"Ambrose," she cried out again.

Faster, faster, her fingers curled inside, finding the perfect spot, and then pulling out of her to rub at her clit before diving back in again.

Lila thought about her supposed punishment, the punishment he said he would inflict upon her if she didn't remain still in the carriage when the strigoi attacked. She wondered what it could be. A spanking? She imagined his hand spanking her ass until it was red, and she was begging him to stop. She imagined he would keep going, spanking her pussy until she screamed in ecstasy.

Or maybe it'd be a different kind of punishment. Maybe he would tie her to the bed and lick and bite and kiss every part of her, torturing her until she was falling apart at the seams, begging for him to just *fuck her already*.

Something was rising in Lila, the same something that rose when Ambrose plunged his fingers into her the other night. *Ambrose, Ambrose, Ambrose,* was all she thought of as sense left her mind and all that remained were her fantasies. She pictured him, his eyes, his hair—how gorgeous he was. Those taut muscles all over his lean, dark body. Those large shoulders she'd love to wrap her thighs around, that wide chest that could hold her, the abs that she could lick for days, and those hips that drove her absolutely mad.

And then her imagination continued.

She saw him then, in his monstrous form. Even bigger, scarier, and stronger than that of his human disguise. But just as breath-taking, just as beautiful. Lords, she liked him like that just as much. She would let him, in either form, do anything to her if he asked. She remembered the feeling of his massive cock against her in the carriage.

The idea of trying to fit *that* inside of her sent her over the ravage edge of euphoria. Her fingers curled roughly inside of her as her body released all the tension that had been building. She moaned his name loudly, as her toes curled against the bath's walls and her back arched out of the water, the cool air piercing her hard nipples. She jumped from the peak, feeling just how much he affected her slip down her fingers.

It was bliss.

With a smile on her panting lips, she slowly slid her fingers from between her legs, shuddering from the after waves. Her center throbbed and pulsed so pleasantly, Lila took a deep sigh and relaxed deeper into the water.

But the smile on her lips faded as she felt her heart thumping.

She was fucked.

Her feelings for the vampire were growing, and based on his actions, she still wasn't sure if he even remotely reciprocated. Sure, he was clearly attracted to her, and it was evident he was seducing her. But did he just want her warmth? Did he *like* her? Did he want her as she wanted him?

The thought of the answer being no, hurt. She pulled her hand from the water and properly washed her body, washing away the evidence of her desire.

She washed her hair clean, drained as much water out of it as she could, tied the lilac strands into a soft towel, dried the rest of her body, and threw on a plush robe the maids had left for her.

As Lila left the bathroom, she noted the sun, still high in the sky. She figured it was most likely after noon, and her body was suddenly hit with a wave of exhaustion. She slumped to the massive window and closed the shades, leaving the room in a cozy and warm shaded light. She pulled the towel from her damp hair and curled under the soft blankets of her bed. Lila remembered feeling her body easing into the plush mattress, feeling her bones settle, her aches rest, before she slipped from consciousness.

A few days of training turned to weeks. Every evening, before breakfast, Ambrose would come to Lila's room to wake her. They would then train in the weapons room, using stakes and daggers, bows and arrows, swords and weapons of all kinds. Lila's body had gone from thin and breakable, to so much more. When she punched, she felt her fists cut the air in half, and as the days passed, each impact grew stronger and stronger.

She felt muscle on her arms and legs, and her ass was well rounded. But beyond that, she *felt* strong. She wrestled with Ambrose and other willing vampires in the manor every night. She even went toe to toe with Constance—the latter still winning every time. She went from being able to barely push one hundred squats out, to doing one hundred squats, pushups, and sit-ups every day.

After breakfast, Lila would spend time with either Constance, Kaz, or Ambrose, or a handful of others in the manor. She spent time in the gardens with Robin at night, and his human employees during the day, walking through the halls and learning their secrets with Sandra, and tending to the horses with Ivan.

She kept her feelings for Ambrose in check, using her fingers whenever she got any ideas.

But Lila was determined. She was on a mission.

She would save Marcus. She would be strong enough to fight off strigoi on her own. And she *would* take down Hektor and Ciro.

25

Lila was dreaming. She knew it. But that didn't make the fear pumping through her blood any less real. She ran, her bare feet pounding against the wet dirt below her. She felt small pebbles jab into the soles of her feet, but she knew she couldn't stop.

Why can't I stop?

Dreams were fickle little devils. The best of them could make an entire reality seem worthless, leaving dreamers to always want more. And the worst? Well, they were called nightmares for a reason.

And Lila knew this was a nightmare.

Her heart was pounding in her chest, and she knew her body felt the same anxiety in the comfort of her bed. Her feet hurt from each rock, and her muscles already felt tired—yet all of these were phantom feelings, pains that would disappear as soon as she opened her eyes.

And yet, here she was. Running for her life in a forest she'd never been in before, from something she hadn't yet seen.

But she could hear it.

Loud gusts of wind continuously tried to trip her off

balance. The thing was above her, and she feared that at any moment it would land directly in front of her—or worse, on her, sinking her into the mud.

She knew, in her real body, her newly muscled legs would be able to run this terrain with no problem. But in this dream, her body was once again weak. Her legs were tired, and she felt a stitch in her side threatening to squeeze tight enough to stop her in her tracks. Her heart was hammering in her chest, and she wasn't sure where the fear began and where the adrenaline ended. She just knew, *I have to keep going.*

But the little trickster that was her nightmare continued to act against her.

The wet dirt beneath her grew increasingly more like mud, and with each new step she took, Lila found it harder and harder to pull her feet out. Soon, her feet were sinking into the mud up to her ankles, as her run became more of a slow trudge.

By the time Lila was calf-deep in the mud, she felt the strongest gust of wind yet directly above her. She tried and tried to pull her legs out, but even so, there was now nowhere to run.

She was stuck.

The beast—for it certainly was a beast—screeched loudly and landed with a thud on the ground before her. Its clawed feet managed to stay above the mud that was slowly pulling Lila to her knees, bringing her eye level with the creature's hulking thighs.

Thighs that looked oddly familiar.

Her gaze shot up, realizing the beast was Ambrose in his monstrous form.

She smiled as her eyes met his, feeling genuine relief wash over her body.

"I'm so happy to—"

But the Ambrose in front of her growled, flashing a horrifying set of teeth in her direction. He threw his wings wide behind him, looking larger than normal—larger than life. And his eyes seemed almost unseeing.

Lila fell back into the mud, her knees awkwardly and painfully bending as her rear began to sink into the mud.

Ambrose dropped to all fours and crawled on his hands and feet over her.

She froze, the only movement was the hitching of her breath. She had never seen the absolute predator in his eyes—at least not directed at her. She had seen him hungry, she had seen him thirsty, she had seen the look of lust for her in his eyes.

But this was different.

This wasn't sexual.

This was murderous.

How closely the two lines danced together, attraction and fear. She was allured by this creature above her, maddeningly so. But, right now, she was also afraid. So afraid, she felt her body shaking.

Lila hadn't felt fear like this since Ciro controlled her mind.

Ambrose continued to crawl, ascending ever closer. She was so afraid to be face to face with him, to see that look in his eyes head-on.

But her nightmare didn't care about her feelings.

He crawled above her, clawed hands at either side of her head, his knees pinning her legs together, completely caging her in.

And those eyes.

They were as red as blood as they bore into her. Ambrose was snarling like a rabid dog, saliva dripping down his chin. Lila couldn't slow her panicked breathing, no matter how hard she tried to calm herself.

The monster's eyes darted from hers to a spot on her neck and his eyes grew wide.

Thump, thump, thump.

In a flash of movement, Ambrose had his arm digging through the mud, wrapping around Lila's waist. He pulled her out of the mud and pressed her flush against his body, falling back onto his heels.

They were once again face to face, and for a moment Lila thought he was the Ambrose she knew again. *Her* Ambrose. He watched her, his eyes darting back and forth between hers. Slowly, he lifted his free hand and pressed it against her cheek, trailing his nails against her scalp through her hair.

For a moment, she leaned into it, relaxing. Forgetting this was a nightmare. Forgetting she should be afraid.

The monster fisted her lilac hair, a stark contrast against his dark gray skin, and yanked it to the side, leaving the column of her neck on full display.

And then, he bore his fangs and tore into her.

He broke the skin above her veins, and she screamed out. She hit and kicked and squirmed, but his bite only dug deeper the more she fought. At any moment, she was sure her shoulder would be ripped clean off from the rest of her body.

"Ambrose! Ambrose, please!" she panted. "You're hurting me!"

But he didn't let up, he drank and drank and drank— he drank until she felt her limbs go limp. Her arms stopped punching, her legs stopped kicking.

She became a doll. A doll to be thrown around.

Ambrose finally pulled back from her, his lips and chin dripping with her blood down to his chest.

It wasn't till then that his eyes went wide again. It wasn't till then that *he* really saw her.

"L-Lila?" he whispered. "Lila!" his voice cracked, hoarse. He freed his grip on her hair, and wrapped it around the wound on her throat, gently applying enough pressure to slow the bleeding. "Lila, talk to me please."

His body shifted then, the dark gray skin became an ashen brown, his wild hair became slightly less wild, and her knees finally were able to reach the ground.

She was too weak to respond to him. Too weak to do anything but watch. She saw his pained expression, the tears streaming down his face. Her vision was growing hazy, but Lila could see Ambrose returning to himself, to his senses.

"Lila, please," he begged, holding her closer. Her blood still dripped from his chin onto her bodice. His eyes were solely focused on her, darting back and forth between her eyes, her lips, and the blood gushing from her neck.

Ambrose was so focused on her, he didn't notice the sky changing color.

"A—" she tried to warn.

"Lila?!"

The sun would rise, any moment now. He had to get out of there, he had to—

"Lila, I'm not leaving you. I'm right here," he said gently, trying to soothe her.

"Ambr—" she tried again, still too weak.

"I can make you a vampire. Right now. If you'll let me, I can save you," his voice broke on a sob, still too focused on her, those crimson eyes glowing from tears. "It'll only hurt for a moment. And then—then you won't feel pain anymore!" He rubbed her cheek with his thumb, and all the while the dark sky was turning a warm shade of orange. "You can be with me—forever—but only if you say yes, only if this is something you want."

The sky was bleeding, maybe even more than she was.

"Ambrose . . . pl—" she begged before her voice cracked. She looked to the sky, trying desperately to get him to turn around, as tears pricked her eyes.

But it was already too late.

The ray of sun illuminated the ground they rested on. Ambrose's dark, ashen skin became so warm, so rich, but only for a moment. His hair in the light radiated—so much so it almost hurt to look at.

He was gorgeous.

And then the burning began.

"Lila, I won't leave you," he repeated. There was conviction in his voice, even as the flesh on his hands began to burn away, bubbling and boiling until it turned to char and ash.

"Run—please," she begged, trying to push him away even though her limbs wouldn't work. He only held her tighter.

"No, my love, I'm staying with you."

There was no convincing him.

The sun rose, the light illuminated over them, and as the blood drained from her neck, the man holding her burned away. He gripped her tight, holding her till the line between them blurred.

And as Lila breathed her last breaths, Ambrose became a husk of ash.

"Lila!"

Ambrose was there, kneeling over her on her bed, shaking her shoulder gently. "It was just a dream," he soothed, all too aware of the nightmare she just had. For a moment, she batted her eyes, unsure when the dream ended, and reality began.

He shook her once more and, in a sudden burst, she woke. She shot up and took deep breaths. Her lungs were on fire, as though she had been underwater for too long and was fighting for air. Ambrose sat on the bed and rubbed her back as she regained her breath.

"Breathe, breathe," he mused. "You were having a nightmare. I came as soon as I—"

"You're alive," she breathed, cutting him off. She turned to him then, cupping his face in her palms. His eyes were as black as a crow's feather, his skin still ashen brown, his hair a long white mane, and most importantly, no burns.

He leaned into her palm, his eyes fluttering closed for just a moment. "So warm," he breathed.

Then, looking at her again, he scoffed, "Well, as alive as you could count me."

Lila scowled.

He laughed, grinning wide. It was so . . . warm. "Not one for vampire humor. Got it. Nice to know you were dreaming of me," he winked. Ambrose studied her for a moment, then settled on her bed. "Do you wish to talk about it?"

She dropped her hands into her lap. "Not particularly."

Ambrose nodded. "I believe it has been a stressful few weeks. The rigorous training schedule, Sanktus Pernox, your brother, the strigoi attack . . . the other strigoi attack—"

"Our tryst."

He raised an eyebrow and smirked. "I'd like to believe that was stress *relieving,* dear. Not stress inducing."

"I'd like to believe that as well. However, you did behave like a complete ass afterward, and that *was* rather stressful." Lila flopped back onto her pillows with a sigh. After a moment of silence, Ambrose followed her and flopped next to her, and they both stared at the red velvet curtains connecting at the top of her four-poster bed.

"I suppose I did," he muttered. "I think . . . I believe we both need a break—a night of solace. I know I promised you training tonight, but one night off won't hurt."

Lila nodded. She knew she *should* continue training.

"But," Ambrose continued, "I have a different proposition in mind."

Interest peaked, Lila turned to him. "Oh?"

"I would like for us to share a meal together. Tonight. Alone."

Lila blushed and was too stunned to even say yes.

"I realized there is much of me you still do not know." He turned to look at her then, their faces only so far apart. "And I would greatly like for you to know me. All of me." His eyes drifted to her lips and remained there. "If, of course, you'll say yes." He inched closer to her, ever so slowly.

"Does this mean," she said, shifting her eyes from his lips—those teeth—to his eyes, an endless abyss she would happily fall into, "that I'll need to drink a goblet of blood if I say yes? Or can I have real food?"

His eyes darted back up to hers as he processed what she said. In another moment, those fangs were on full display as he burst into a raucous laughter, shaking uncontrollably as he tried to hold it in to no avail.

Lila began giggling too, and then more so from the contagion of Ambrose's laugh. She watched as he quickly covered his mouth behind his hand, but she pushed it away, enjoying his face too much to let him cover it.

"Little Mouse, I will be sure the chefs prepare every delicacy your heart desires," he cooed.

"Then I'll request the finest of finery, Lord Draven," she sang.

Still chuckling, Ambrose rolled up and off the bed and walked to the longer sitting couch Lila had in her room. From it, he lifted a long dress bag that had been hidden by the back of the sofa.

"Another request, love." He lifted the bag, revealing a breath-taking dress underneath. She caught sight of golds and yellows and burnt oranges, but it wasn't until he fully pulled it out that her breath caught in her lungs.

The dress was billowing with layers and layers that she just knew would make her look like a wildflower. The entire bodice was a warm, golden yellow, with small, embroidered flowers and sunbursts all around. The panels of the bust were two large pieces of the yellow fabric, dipping low into the cleavage before flaring into the skirts. Connecting the two strips between the cleavage was a lace design of black flowers. The design continued through the bodice, following the seam of the backless gown, as the lace trailed the hem that would fall on her lower back.

The gold continued down the waist and then began to break into deep slits at the hips, like that of a flower blooming, with layers of tulle spread between. Below that layer, the thick fabric of burnt orange cascaded down to the floor, all embroidered with white, black, and yellow flowers.

Once again, Ambrose managed to find a gown that encapsulated warmth, and she couldn't wait to put it on.

Lila hopped out of the bed and ran to him—well, to the dress. She tightened her robe around her silk sleep set, and reached a hand out to touch the fabric. It was alarmingly soft, something she had never felt before. It wasn't quiet velvet, nor was it suede, and it certainly didn't look like either.

"It is custom made . . . for you." He watched her as she took in the dress, the black in his eyes gleaming.

"And this material? It is unlike anything I have ever seen . . . or felt."

"A vampire secret," he smirked. "Will you wear it?"

"Of course!" she uttered without a second guess. "Thank you, I—I don't even know what to say."

"There is no need to say anything. Just wear this and join me tonight."

For so long, she has been fighting her feelings, questioning how he felt for her in return. And this felt like the clearest indication that he returned her feelings.

That he wanted her as badly as she wanted him.

She nodded.

"Excellent," Ambrose smiled, a menacing thing full of fangs that made Lila's toes curl. She knew she was truly deranged, lusting after a monster such as this. But he was gorgeous and kind, and there was something electrifying between them. "Then, Little Mouse, I'll see you soon." He took her hand, lifted it to his lips, and pressed a kiss to her knuckles. His lips lingered on her skin, sending a shiver down her spine, before he turned and exited her room, leaving Lila's cheeks flushed and legs shaking.

Maybe she needed another bath time fantasy session sooner than she thought.

Or a fantasy come true. His mere presence had the power to make all of her nerves feel electric. Her hair stood on end, as though each pore of her skin was begging him to touch her. Every time he entered the room, a heady, confused feeling washed over her—not like the heady, confused feeling of a vampire's thrall, but of arousal, fear, distrust, and utter desperation.

Lila wanted to be loved. It was something she had wanted her entire life, to just be treated warmly. After her parents passed, she yearned to be tucked in at night. To be held. After the Reinicks, she wasn't sure if she could tell what love was even if it had a glowing sign.

But she felt like that was changing. The thought of Ambrose's lips, his teeth, against her skin, sent a warm feeling through Lila's blood, coiling in her lower belly. His skin against hers, those tattoos across his chest, she wanted to see every part of him—*feel* every part of him.

Her fingers twitched as she pressed her thighs together. *Knock, knock, knock.*

A sound at her door startled Lila from her thoughts. She quickly pushed the idea of touching herself away and tightened her robe against her as she went to the door.

Constance was on the other side, dressed already for the night. She wore a long violet dress, her golden hair assorted in pigtails.

"Evening, Lilac," she yawned, walking into the room. "Breakfast?"

26

Lila's evening had been filled with activity. Breakfast with Constance, gardening with Robin, playing in said gardens with Constance, chatting with Pollock, and tea with Kaz. And though she kept her eyes peeled for him, she hadn't even caught a glimpse of the white-haired crow throughout the evening.

By the time Lila returned to her room at midnight, just after lunch, she was exhausted. She took a quick bath, even though it was still hours till her dinner with Ambrose, and sat at her vanity brushing out her hair, when she heard a light knock on her door.

Surprisingly, Sandra stood on the other side, a playful smirk across her face, and a paper in her hand. As she handed the paper over, she stated, "If you wish to read this, Lord Draven says you are to go to his study, immediately."

"Sandra? You're working a night shift?" Lila took it, seeing the neat scrawl of Ambrose's handwriting. She squinted at it, but before she could even attempt to read it, Sandra spoke up again.

"I have been specially asked to work tonight," she winked and threw a coy smile in Lila's direction. "Do you want my assistance in dressing, miss?" She pushed past Lila, walking into the room with a giggle. "I never knew the master to be such a romantic!" she said with a blush.

Lila, still too startled to say anything, just turned to her, holding the note. Sandra, taking things into her own hands, began opening dressers and pulling out varying fabrics. She threw lacy white undergarments at Lila, giggling even more. As Lila lifted the panties, she realized they weren't really panties at all, but just a bunch of strings.

"It's called a *thong*, dear. And trust me. Men go crazy for these."

"Huh?" Lila blushed, as Sandra pushed her to change from her evening wear.

"The color will suit you well, I think."

"I hate to ask this, but . . . what's all this for?" she cringed. "Can't you just tell me what the note says? O-or give me a moment, I may be able to try myself."

But Sandra shook her head. "Dear, the entire manor has seen the looks you and Lord Draven share. Everyone is waiting to clear out tonight to give you two the privacy you need —"

"What are you talking about, exactly?" Lila interrupted.

Sandra gave her a sympathetic smile and took her hand, patting it lightly. "Don't panic, dear. These things" — she motioned to the undergarments — "are . . . a just-in-case scenario. It's better to be prepared now, even if nothing happens, rather than have something happen and not be prepared." She winked.

Lila blushed, flashing back to the only other time Ambrose had seen her undergarments. She hadn't necessarily been *ashamed* then, they were still lacy and cute by all means, but had she known *that* would happen, she probably would have picked something a little more . . . devious.

"Plus, if anything, I find that wearing pretty under-things makes me feel better—braver. So I hope it will do the same for you."

Sandra's warm smile was so infectious, Lila couldn't help but return it, nod, and slide the thing up her thighs. The straps rose high on her hips and hugged them snuggly. She removed her robe and, with Sandra's help, fastened the corset top into place. It was a strapless piece that stretched from the mounds of her breasts to her upper waist. She went to look in the mirror and immediately understood what Sandra had been saying. She looked . . . good—no, great. Lila would even say beautiful if she also didn't feel so . . . naughty. The string of her thong disappeared into her ass, leaving it on full display, before revealing itself again at the curve of her lower back and splitting into the two straps on her hips. As she looked at herself, she *did* feel bolder. She *wanted* Ambrose to see her like this, and she almost felt daring enough to show him herself. Especially with her newly added muscles on such display.

"I found it suspicious when Ambrose deigned to pick all of your clothing out himself. But, my dear, I fully understand why now. You look bewitching."

Lila turned to her in a frantic blush. She had never even thought about where all these clothes came from. She knew he selected the dress he showed her early that night, and the dress for Sanktus Pernox. But *all* of her clothes were from him? He, personally, selected them? Each dress, each stocking, each coat . . . each panty?

Will he recognize these? Her face warmed at the thought.

Smirking, Sandra turned away. "Let's find you a dress." The woman began shuffling once more. "We don't want something too busy, after all you're just supposed to be studying. And we do not want to take anything away from the beauty of the gown you will be wearing to dinner. Aha!" She pulled something from the wardrobe and spun it toward Lila. "This would be perfect!"

As Lila walked up to it, she saw how right Sandra had been. The dress was a simple cut. A strapless, sweetheart neckline, and a cinched waist with skirts that fell to mid-calf. But what really made the dress was the color. It was a pale, dusty lilac, a shade darker than her hair, and it sparkled silver anywhere light touched, as though pieces of starlight were stitched into the very fabric itself. She eagerly put it on and twirled. The skirts flowed back and forth, and Lila realized that the skirts had an ombre effect, becoming more and more translucent, revealing her thighs and legs through the material, but keeping her hips tastefully covered.

"I love it," she mumbled in awe.

"And Lord Draven will too. Now, you best be going! Take the note, dear. He should be in his office."

Lila plucked the note from the bed, and scuttered out of the room so quickly, she didn't even put her shoes on. She darted through the hall, cascaded down the stairs, and came to an abrupt stop just outside the door to Ambrose's office. Lila adjusted her hair, tossing it over her shoulder, and smoothed the dress out below her. She clutched the note in her hand and gently knocked.

"Come in," the sultry voice on the other side of the door called. Ambrose was seated in the ornate chair behind his desk. Crows sat all over the room, feathers ruffling as they cawed, and she caught sight of Pollock, pruning his feathers. A desk light was on, dimly illuminating the room.

He looked up at her then, his eyes roaming over her

dress as she felt the heat from his gaze glide over her skin. She saw him swallow hard as the lines of his neck bobbled, the Adam's apple dipping. As his eyes reached hers, he splayed a hand out to the empty chair across his desk. "Sit, please. I see you got my note."

"Ye-Yes," she said entering. Lila was finding it hard to tear her eyes from him. He was dressed simply, in an untied white shirt that revealed the crow on his chest, and slim black pants that tied at the waist. He was dressed like every day, and every other man, comfortable at home . . . and yet . . . he was unlike any other man.

Her eyes dipped to his chest. The black ink of the crow, its wings spread wide, seemed to be teasing her, calling her in.

His long white hair fell over his shoulders as he studied the pages before him. One thick piece by his ear looked more curled than usual, as though he had slept on it wrong or had been leaning on it for too long and it folded under him. Lila wanted to twirl it around her finger.

"I thought you said we were taking a break from training tonight," Lila folded her arms over her chest.

"Physical training, yes. But now we work on your mental training." He smirked and Lila immediately huffed a breath. "Can you read it?" he asked, not looking up at her.

"Read what?" She sat in the chair.

"My note, Little Mouse. Can you read it?" He put the paper he had been studying down, interlaced his hands, and watched her, those black vortexes pulling her in.

"O-Oh," she squeaked, quickly opening and rubbing the paper against the edge of the table, trying to flatten it from her tightened grip.

Ambrose chuckled. "My lords, what you do to me. You *sound* like a little mouse."

Lila blushed, trying to ignore his teasing. "For your

information, I *can* read . . . it just takes me a bit longer to get the words."

"I know you *can,* but you still have to sound everything out. What if I were to send you a note while in another's manor with private information? Would you just read it aloud, for all the other vampires to hear?" he raised an eyebrow, once again sending that coiling heat through Lila's body. She blushed, and hoped Ambrose would take it to mean she was embarrassed by her lack of skills. But then he smirked, and she knew he was looking right through her. He cooed, "I read emotions—remember?"

Lila bit her bottom lip, averting her gaze.

"Oh, don't do that, Little Mouse." He leaned forward across the desk, and whispered, "How many times do I have to tell you? It only makes me want to take your lips for myself and suck on them for eternity."

She gasped at his boldness, so different from the laughing Ambrose that was in her room earlier that evening. Well, not different but . . . direct.

Lila straightened. If he was bold, she could be too. She felt attractive in her undergarments and remembered the feeling that washed over her as she saw herself in the mirror.

"Then do it," she breathed, biting her lip again, looking up at him through her eyelashes.

She saw him falter for the briefest moment. His mask of ease slipped as his eyes fell to her lips again and a ravenous hunger overtook his eyes. Those black pits shone red for just a moment, before he cleared his throat and returned into the icy exterior.

"First, read. Then, reward." He pointed to the note.

Lila scoffed. "As if a kiss from you is a sufficient reward," she teased. She purposely was egging him on. A *look* from him would be enough of a reward.

Ambrose raised his eyebrows and sat back in his chair, smirking. "You're right, of course. In fact, I don't know why I even mentioned rewards when I have something much more pressing to give you first. If memory serves me correctly, I believe it is actually a punishment in which I've promised you."

Now Lila gulped. "P-punishment?"

He sat forward again. "Yes, for disobeying me in the carriage. Against the strigoi. Remember, darling?" He waited a moment. "I think now would be as good a time as ever to punish you."

Lila was shaking, with anticipation or arousal, she didn't know. She thought back to her daily fantasies, of him spanking her ass, spanking her—

"Ah, yes. You've had quite some fun in the bath lately, haven't you?"

Lila froze, her eyes widened as she stared at him. He reached over the table, grabbing for her hand that's been inside of her. He pulled her fingers into his mouth, swirling his tongue around her middle and ring finger, sucking on them.

"Mmm . . . your taste still lingers. Was it just after sunrise? You're so fucking delicious, love." He watched her expression and smirked. "You thought you got away with it too, didn't you? Touching your pretty pink clit to the thought of me? I have felt your arousal every time, the moment you even think of touching yourself. Then I smell you, and it takes everything in my power not to tear your door down and trade your fingers for my cock in that bathtub, that bed, or that garden—yes, I know about that too. But when I hear your sweet little moans, I lose it. I use my own hand, pumping myself till I feel you coming at the thought of me."

Lila was stunned, her toes curling at his words. "Wh-why haven't you said anything all this time? Why save it for now?"

Ambrose leaned back and shrugged. "I didn't want to give the wrong impression, Little Mouse. Not everything I do is to get you naked. You've had priorities these last few weeks. Priorities that I support and admire. I do not want to be a cause for distraction. It's as simple as that." He propped his elbow on the arm rest and leaned his cheek against his knuckles. "However, since we are taking the night off from training, it seems like you may have found yourself some free time," he smirked, his wicked grin displaying his sharp teeth, as he ran his tongue over them. "Now, for your punishment. I want you to take off that pretty little dress."

Lila's cheeks must have been stained red at this point, as her mouth fell open.

"Keep those lips closed, Little Mouse, unless you want to give me other ideas on how to use them."

Her jaw snapped shut, maybe a little too hard, as she tried to give him the visual of what she wanted to do to *him* right now. But he just chuckled.

"And if I don't?" she folded her arms, trying to act tough. Trying, and failing.

"It's your choice. Do it yourself or be forced to do it yourself." His eyes sparkled red, showing his exact meaning. If she didn't do it, he would thrall her to do so.

With a huff, Lila stood, shoving the chair back so hard, she cringed as it scraped the floor. She reached along her back, feeling the laces, and began tugging at them. Within the blink of an eye, her sexy—and ideally tortuous—strip tease turned more into what she could only assume looked like a fish flopping out of water.

"Do you need assistance, love?" Ambrose smiled. His liquid-gold voice made Lila squirm. As stubborn as she was, she had the rejection on the tip of her tongue, ready to throw it at him. But she bit it back.

Pride be damned.

"Yes. Untie me, please," she batted her eyes. *Two could play at his game,* she thought. She walked around the table, stopping at his side, and turned her back to him. She pulled her hair over her shoulder, fully displaying her upper back, the tattoo he left on her, and the column of her neck.

Ambrose rose, standing behind her. She jumped as he grazed her shoulder blades with his knuckles. "Say that again," he murmured into her ear.

She began to turn. "What are—"

Ambrose didn't let her be sassy. In a flash, the hand at her back wrapped against her neck, only holding tight enough to keep her head from moving, and his other hand grabbed both of her wrists, pinning them to her lower back.

She gasped as the hand at her neck slightly tightened. Or maybe it was a moan. She wasn't sure exactly, but this new position they were in was doing funny things to her core.

"I said. Say. It. Again."

Without hesitating, she repeated, "*Yes. Untie—*"

"'Not that part."

Lila paused for a moment, thinking. But Ambrose tightened his grip again at her throat, still not tight enough to actually restrict air, but she felt the pressure in his hand, his fingers at her neck, his thumb rubbing into the base of her head. She knew that, with a twitch of a muscle, he could probably snap her neck and kill her before she had time to blink. And some sick part of her liked the idea that he *could*, but *wouldn't* do that to her. It drove her crazy with desire.

"*Please,*" she moaned. "Please, Ambrose," her voice was breathy, as she took a step back into him. "Please."

"Do you like my hand around your throat, Little Mouse? Do you like being choked?" His grip tightened.

It was hard to speak, and she felt her body quivering with much more than the dull sense of fear. "Only. Yours."

In another blink, Lila was lifted by the waist and seated on his desk. Her wrists were freed and the hand at her throat was now tangled in her hair at the back of her head.

They were so close, she could feel the presence of his lips on hers. He nudged her knees open and stepped between them, standing flush against her.

She felt like she was going to faint, she couldn't handle his gaze any longer, and she feared that if her cheeks became warmer, they'd simply melt off.

Keeping his gaze, Ambrose pulled his chair to him with his foot, and sat back down. Because of their height difference, he still sat only a bit under her.

The hand not in her hair traced up her thigh, her hips, her waists. She felt each finger and cursed the fabric between his skin and hers.

As his hand reached to her back, and began undoing the laces of her gown, her breathing hitched. Her lip was quivering, and she instinctively sucked it between her teeth as she turned away her gaze.

"What did I just tell you about that, Little Mouse?"

He lightly pulled the hair at the nape of her head to look at him. His eyes dipped from hers to her lips, licking his own slowly. She felt him undo another lace as he leaned in, pulling her head down to meet him.

Lila fluttered her eyes closed, feeling the heat emanating off him nearly as much as it was her. She peeked through her lashes to see his eyes closed as well, fangs poking ever so slightly through his parted lips.

Her mouth parted too, ready—*desperate* to kiss him. She could feel his lips ever so lightly brush against hers.

"You've been a very bad girl," he said softly against her lips.

The moment the words fell from his tongue, he yanked the last of the laces at her back free and the dress fell from her chest. She hurriedly scrambled to clutch it to herself.

As Ambrose sat back in his chair, smirking, she realized he never meant to kiss her. He was teasing her the entire time. She scowled at him, ready to throw a bounty of curses his way.

"Little Mouse, it's time for punishment now. Not rewards. Remember? Maybe I'll reconsider *after* you read my note."

Still feeling the heat on her cheeks, Lila hopped to the floor and let the dress fall from her body in front of him. She stepped out of it and kicked it aside as she watched Ambrose drink her in.

For a moment, he startled at her undergarments, before his eyes roamed over her, and she felt every wavering glance with the heat of his stare. They lingered on the mounds of her breast before dipping to where her pink nipples were poking through the lacy white fabric. He looked as though he wanted to swallow them whole. Swallow *her* whole.

Then his eyes trailed farther down. Down her belly, down the curves of her waist, across the lines where her thong straps sat, over her hips, and back up to the apex of her thighs.

He licked his lips again, and she imagined he wanted to push her over that table and run his tongue between *her* lips. She wondered how his teeth would feel on the sensitive bud between her legs.

His breathing was growing ragged as his eyes consistently stayed a vibrant shade of red. She watched as he gripped the armrest, digging his nails deeply into the cushion, tearing the fabric apart.

He was holding back the monster within, and she thought maybe he wasn't winning the fight—not after he bit his lips. "I feel every emotion you have, plus mine, Little Mouse. This is as much a punishment for me as it is for you."

But Lila wasn't done getting revenge. She huffed once more and turned from him before bending over his desk, pushing her ass closer to his face.

She felt his eyes stare at her center, so much so, she could almost feel his gaze alone penetrating her. Would he take her like this, bent over his desk like an animal?

Lila knew her ass looked good in the thong. She knew it did little to properly cover her. And she knew he was salivating at the idea of burying himself—whether his tongue or his cock—inside of her. "Punishment? I thought seeing me like this would be a reward for you."

Lila plucked the note from her side of the table and looked over her shoulder to face him, smirking as she leaned against the desk.

"You mean, this note?"

Ambrose didn't take his eyes off the pretty white lace before him, and as he focused on her, she found her eyes falling to the impressive bulge in his pants.

It was alarming in size but *so* hot. She wanted to see it. She wanted to taste it. She wanted it buried inside of her to the hilt.

"You know, one of the major flaws with white undergarments is that you can just see about *everything*," he said, eyes still on her. "Those little pink nipples are so hard.

These plump lips are dripping from that pretty pussy of yours. And it's all for *me*."

Without warning, he reached a single finger out, and slid it between the folds, to the damp part of her panties, pressing hard till he flicked against her clit.

Lila immediately shuffled back, choking down a moan.

Ambrose put the finger to his lips and sucked it with a loud *pop*.

"Your desire for me is evident, darling. But it'll have to wait. I won't budge, no matter how much you beg. Now. Read me the note or you'll be getting a spanking."

Lila's lips quivered once again. "Wh-what if I want a spanking?"

Ambrose chuckled, making her legs nearly buckle under her. "You naughty little thing. I want to fuck that little mouse right out of you till you're the one telling me to beg." His hand glided up her thigh until his thumb slid under the strap of her thong. "You have that power over me, you know. I would wear a collar for the rest of eternity if it meant you'd send me down on my knees and tell me to feast on you forever."

Lila opened her mouth, ready to beg him to do so, but he quickly pulled and snapped the thong strap against her skin, causing a sharp sting of pain.

"But . . . I'd only do that for a *good girl*. Now, are you going to be good for me?"

Lila hesitated a moment but nodded.

He smirked. "Excellent."

27

Lila was cursing herself for her body's desires. They were overtaking her mind and soul, making every decision *for* her. She felt how wet she was between her thighs at the thought of a "punishment" or "reward" from Ambrose Draven. His words were like a spark igniting her mind with wicked thoughts and ideas that she could only hope would come to fruition.

So she would play his little game, but she wanted to do so on *her* terms. She held the paper up to her face, twisted around, and gingerly sat on Ambrose's lap. She felt his hard cock against her ass and inched herself higher, as if she was getting comfortable, when really she just wanted to feel it rub against her.

"Little Mouse, what are you doing?" But he knew exactly what she was doing, especially as he wrapped his large hand against the flat of her stomach and pulled her closer to him.

"Reading. Shh, please. I need to concentrate."

Lila felt Ambrose chuckle, his body shook underneath

her, as his cock twitched at the apex of her thighs, causing her to gasp.

Lila squeezed her legs together, trying to ignore the sensation, but all it did was cause a groan to release from Ambrose's throat, as her thighs had also tightened around him.

He dug his fingers into her hips, causing the slightest amount of pain, but she feigned ignorance.

"Wh-Whe-When. When." *One word down, ten more to go,* Lila thought.

She sounded out everything, struggling here and there. Ambrose assisted her when she struggled too much, reaching around her and pointing to syllables and showing her how to pronounce them.

"When you learn to read, I—elle,"

"No. Here, it is *I'll*—as in *I will.* The two *L*s here make the *ul* sound, not a hard *L*, like in your name."

Lila nodded. "When you learn to read, I'll g-gi-vu—I'll give you a . . ."

She paused again. There was only one word left and it started with a letter she hadn't practiced in his note yet. "Is—is that a *T*?"

Ambrose nodded, his lips dipping dangerously close to her shoulder. He was tracing his finger in tiny circles around her belly, and though time had passed, Lila still felt the warmth between her legs and the hard length pressing against her.

She continued to sound out the last word. It was the hardest to pronounce thus far, but she tried and tried. She grew frustrated and sighed, tossing her head back, against Ambrose's shoulder.

"This is stupid," she groaned. "Why do I have to read anyway?"

"So that you can help me read through all these," he said, ushering to the walls of books around them. "I'm sure one of these has a key on how to undo the vampire transformation, and if we are to save your brother, we need all the information we can get."

Lila jerked up, causing another deep groan—almost a growl—to erupt from Ambrose's throat.

"All this time, you've been working on helping my brother?" Lila asked, turning toward him.

He looked into her eyes. "Of course. I promised I would." His eyes dipped to the feather along her collar bone—a tattoo she had come to love just as much as her first—and then rose back up to her lips. He promised her he would, for a kiss. And a kiss she gave him . . . and some more.

Lila wanted to kiss him again at that moment. She wanted to do much more than kiss him. *He* was the one that deserved the reward.

"Don't get sappy with me, darling. Finish reading that note. Now." Ambrose grabbed her shoulders and angled them against his chest once more. He drifted his hands up and down her sides, kissing her shoulders.

Then, one hand delicately grazed her breasts before he pinched her nipple between his thumb and forefinger, rolling it between the calloused pads.

A whimper came from Lila's throat. "You're distracting me," she mumbled, feeling her lips quiver.

"I know. Read," he ordered.

She felt his tongue against her flesh and her spine straightened, digging her ass farther back against him.

"Fuck," he mumbled, and massaged her breast before roughly twisting her nipple.

"W-when you learn to-to read, I'll give you a . . . a tr-tree-tru-eat. I'll give you a treat," she finished.

The moment she did, Ambrose blew out a low whistle. The door to the office cracked open and immediately, the crows surrounding the room all flapped their wings at once and left the room. He flicked his wrist again and the door slammed shut.

Instantly, Ambrose's lips were against the shell of Lila's ear as he kissed and whispered, "Be as loud as you'd like, no one can hear you."

And as Lila startled at the idea, blushing furiously, Ambrose nipped at her ear, careful to only use his front teeth.

His hands dipped down her sides again and over her pale thighs. She watched his hands against her, saw him fighting himself to squeeze her flesh, and was so turned on by the sight, she thrust her hips against ever so slightly. He gripped her inner thighs, his strong hands making little divots in her skin, and slowly spread them wide, till each leg draped over the armrests of the chair they sat in.

"Wh-what are you going to do?" Lila breathed out, scared and excited for his answer.

"Well, you've been *such* a good girl for me, I think you deserve your reward now." His hand, feather light, grazed against the wet spot on her panties. With her thighs spread wide, both Ambrose and Lila could see exactly what reaction he had on her. She buckled under the light touch, wanting him to add more pressure. But instead, he lifted his hands from *there* and roamed over the rest of her body. One large hand cupped her breast and pulled at her nipple again.

"I want to see them."

Lila nodded, not even fully knowing what to say other than *Yes, please, yes.*

His hands dipped behind her back, unlacing the corset

she wore. He worked quickly as the lace fell away from her body, leaving her completely nude save for the damp thong.

"You are so fucking beautiful, love." He cupped her breasts again, with both hands, pinching the tight pink peak between his thumb and forefinger as he looked down on her, over her shoulder. "I want to suck on these till they become an array of bruised skin, till they match that lovely hair of yours. Would you let me do that, Little Mouse?"

Lila nodded again.

"Say it," he commanded.

"I would let you . . . ah!" she moaned. Ambrose pulled them both at the same time, causing a yelp to escape her lips, before he kneaded them back to comfort.

As one hand remained toying with her, the other trailed down her body. He ran his index finger along the seam of her panties against her hip, before crooking a finger around the thickest part, and lifting the lace away from her body. He traced his finger up and down the damp fabric, pulling it between her folds and then away from her as his finger was so close to her core, she could feel the warmth radiate against her. Each time he pulled the panties taut, a building pressure against the sensitive bud sent her head spinning.

"Don't torture me," she said grabbing onto his arm. "Touch me, please." She was okay with begging, if it was begging him. She felt justified in asking him for what she wanted.

It was her reward, after all.

Ambrose carefully nipped her shoulder and then licked the tender area, before working his mouth up, to that wonderful spot behind the ear. But his finger didn't move any closer, it just kept trailing along the wet seam of her thong as his other hand still toyed with her nipple.

"What is it you want, Little Mouse? Tell me, and I *might* give it to you." His voice vibrated against her, causing her to let a moan slip. Fuck, even his voice could pull that from her.

"You. I want *you*."

"What do you want from me? My fingers?" he finally, deliciously, grazed his knuckle against her folds, slipping in and grazing her swollen clit.

"Oh, *fuck*," she breathed.

"My tongue?" he licked the column of her neck, cupping his tongue at her earlobe, indicating *exactly* what he would do with it between her thighs.

"Or my cock?" he pressed his hard length against her then, pressing against where she wanted him most of all. She threw her head back against him, grinding her hips into him.

Fuck, she wanted him bad.

"Can't decide?" he cooed. "Shall I choose for you?"

Lila's thoughts wouldn't work even if she tried. She didn't trust herself to say "yes," let alone make a decision. So she nodded her agreement.

In a rush and swirl of movement, Ambrose stood, twisting Lila in his grasp so that they were face to face. One arm gripped under her ass, forcing her legs to wrap around his waist.

His eyes bore into her, and for a moment, Lila thought he would take her right there, right then.

But he seemed to have other plans.

Ambrose kicked the chair back from under him and walked to the window—the same window he had thrown her out of not so long ago. He unlatched it with his free hand and grabbed the outside of it.

He whispered against her cheek, "Hold on, darling."

Lila yelped and threw her arms around his neck, as Ambrose climbed out of the window and began to crawl alongside the stone exterior of the manor. At first, Lila could not believe what was happening. With all the things she had seen from this strange man—this *monster*—why had this felt the strangest? And why did it excite her down to her very core?

The cold air nipped at her bare breasts, causing her nipples to become even tighter peaks. It was almost painful, but each rub and press against Ambrose's chest sent her head spinning and she knew he could feel the very same sensations as she did. Knew that he felt every part of her against him, as his hand gripped her ass firmly.

His fingers and toes latched to the edges of stone, almost like that of a bat, as he climbed. The higher they went, the more her breathing hitched as she bounced against his hard cock. She wanted it so badly.

Sensing her arousal, Ambrose halted mid-climb and faced Lila. She felt the cold stone dig into her back as he pressed himself into her against the wall.

"So needy, Little Mouse," he smirked. Ambrose parted his lips and brushed them against hers. "And so shaky. A quivering little mouse." She felt him smile against her before kissing her. He sucked her bottom lip between his teeth and overtook her. She kissed him in return, nipping at his lips, attempting to fight for dominance. He smiled again, and then parted her lips with his tongue as he forcibly claimed her, body and soul. Their tongues clashed as they drank each other in. Lila sucked his bottom lip into her mouth, mimicking his movements before biting them.

He chuckled and squeezed her ass so hard, she knew she'd have a bruise the shape of his hand there tomorrow.

Ambrose continued climbing, their lips intertwined until they reached the roof of the manor. He pulled away from her, moving down to kiss her neck.

"Look up," he ordered against her throat.

Lila's lips were already swollen from their kiss, but as she looked up, her breath caught once again. Ambrose stood, with her in his arms, on the very top of the manor, and to Lila, it seemed like the top of the world.

The sky was cloudless, as stars shone through, twinkling and sparkling. It was dazzling, breathtaking, and Lila found that she couldn't look away.

Ambrose lifted her higher against him, her legs wrapped around his upper waist, as he angled down. He nipped and sucked at the mound of her breast, leaving hickeys and bruises all over her, so careful to not use his fangs—though, at this moment, she wouldn't have minded.

When he pulled her nipple into his mouth and sucked, her attention was finally pulled back to him.

"These little pink buds will be the death of me," he mused as he bit and pulled one before licking it. "They have been haunting my dreams since I first saw them peek through that rag of a night gown when I took you from the Vipers." Another bite and she gasped, digging her fingers into his shoulder.

"Ambrose," she breathed.

"Yes, Little Mouse?"

"Wh-Why are we up here? It's beautiful but . . . will anyone hear us?"

"I want you to watch the stars while I feast on you. I want you to have a view at least half as gorgeous as mine will be when I see that gorgeous pussy of yours." He laid her down on the stone. The cold ground warred with the raging heat of her body, and Lila was afraid she would melt right through it. "And I want you to be as loud as you want. I want to hear every cry, scream, whine, and moan come from those lips. Every sound of pleasure, every call of my name, I want to drink it in, I want to devour it as much as I want to devour you."

He slid his hand up her thigh and curved his thumbs into the straps of her underwear, slowly pulling them away from her core, and off her thighs. The cool night air wafted against Lila's hot center, causing a shiver to rake down her body.

"I'm keeping these," he said, pocketing her soaked panties. Ambrose sat over her, and Lila was struck with the embarrassment of being fully nude under his watchful eye—especially while he was still fully dressed. She wanted to cover herself and began to raise her hands to do so before he pinned them back to the sides of her head.

"No. I want to see you. All of you."

"B-But I'm the only one undressed . . . Y-you have to take your clothes off too," she stuttered.

Ambrose only smiled. He neared her face and dragged his tongue along the side of her cheek. "Being naked in front of me was *your* punishment. Remember, darling? I may be rewarding you now, but that still stands."

Slowly, Ambrose again worked his way down her body. He licked and kissed and carefully bit every part of her. Her swollen breasts, her flat belly, the curve of her hips, her pelvic bones.

And then he reached her center. He pushed her thighs apart, leaving a trail of hickeys along the insides, and lifted one over his shoulder, giving himself a better angle to the sight of her.

"Oh lords," Lila breathed, feeling his hot breath against her.

"I am the only lord you should be calling out for tonight, Lila."

Another wave of heat flooded her senses. She had been

anticipating this from the moment she removed her dress in his office. From the moment she put on those ridiculous undergarments. She wanted his wicked silver tongue all over her, *inside* of her. She watched his expression shift as he finally spread her folds with his index and middle finger.

"Fuck," he cursed. His eyes were hungry, that same ravenous hunger she saw a few weeks ago when he fucked her with his fingers. They shone red as his eyes completely and utterly devoured her. "I think pink is my new favorite color. You're so fucking beautiful, love." He let the folds of her pussy close again before rubbing his thumb up, along the seam and pressing into her sensitive clit.

Lila bit her lip, holding back another moan.

"I want to hear you screaming my name, Lila."

As soon as her name left his lips, he dragged his tongue along the seam of hers. Lila's back immediately arched with a breathy moan.

"You must be a witch," he breathed. "You've enchanted me with this magic between your thighs." His words warmed her clit as he mumbled against her. He dragged his tongue up her center once more and flicked at her awaiting clit. It was swollen from the pressure of her want and every touch sent a wave of pleasure right to her tightening core.

He sucked her clit into his mouth, gripping the thigh at his shoulder almost painfully tight. She felt like she was beginning to see stars—and not the ones above her in the sky.

"You are the most delicious thing I have ever tasted," he said after her clit popped from his mouth. Lila was shaking, feeling her arousal build inside her. He had only licked her a handful of times and she already felt the orgasm building. His tongue lapped against her dripping pussy, and she knew he was tasting exactly what he did to her.

"You're so fucking wet for me. You smell and taste so sweet." His tongue dipped inside of her core, teasing at her entrance.

Lila buckled against his face, begging for more. "So eager, Little Mouse." He dipped his tongue farther inside of her, cupping his tongue to lick even more of her.

Lila's head popped up and she watched him as he feasted on her.

"Ambrose," she moaned.

Again, he said through the Concord. He pulled his tongue from her, slowly dragged his tongue from her entrance to her clit.

Ambrose! she screamed through their link, over and over.

He bit down on the mound above her swollen bud, scraping his teeth against her before sliding his tongue against it. The mix of pleasure and pain sent shockwaves down Lila's body, and her eyes threatened to roll in the back of her head.

A feral groan released from Ambrose's throat as he lapped at her again. "I could do this forever. Would you like that? Do you want me to feast on you forever?" He nipped on her bruised clit.

"Ah—fuck—*yes.*"

Ambrose opened his eyes and watched her from under his white lashes.

"Do you like watching me devour you?" His deep voice vibrated through her, causing her to suck in another breath.

Lila forgot her words again and nodded vigorously. She felt her own juices drip down her inner thighs, down her ass. "*Fuck,*" she moaned. She felt her pussy throb under his full attention.

"Watch the stars, love." He reached over a long arm and gently pressed it between her breasts, pushing her back down against the cold stone.

Lila's breath was deep and labored, her entire body rocked with each inhale. She wasn't sure how much more she could take of this, the building pressure inside her lower belly was becoming intolerable as her toes curled.

She needed release.

Ambrose removed her thigh from his shoulder, and pushed both of her knees toward her chest, barring her legs under the knees with one arm. This position forced Lila to lay all the way back, as her ass hung a bit in the air. It also gave Ambrose a much better view of just how wet she was.

Immediately embarrassed by *how* much he could see, she yelled, "Ambrose! Not like—"

"*Fuck*, Lila. You're beautiful." Another long, torturous lick as his tongue squeezed into her entrance from her pressed-together thighs.

Ambrose licked the entirety of her core, curling his tongue inside of her entrance and dragging it up the bundle of nerves that had her back arching. Finally, she jerked her hand out and grabbed a fist full of his hair.

"Ah, *fuck—Ambrose*," she moaned.

"Show me where you want me."

She followed his orders and used her other hand to grab another fistful of hair. She guided his head up, his tongue to her clit.

"There, *please*."

Ambrose did as he was commanded. He sucked her clit hard into his mouth, his tongue pushing and flicking against her as Lila screamed into the night.

"A-Ah! I think—I think I'm going to—"

Ambrose stopped then, releasing his arm barring her legs up, and crawled over her, kissing her deeply. She could taste her creaminess on his lips.

"See how fucking delicious you are?"

She shook, feeling the orgasm at the tip of her being.

"Ambrose, *please*," she begged, clutching onto his shirt.

"Please what?" he teased. "Beg."

Lila hated him at that moment.

"Make me come. *Please, Ambrose*," she moaned, heady and desperate.

In a swirl of movement, Ambrose was on his back with Lila on her knees above him, straddling his face.

"I'm going to fucking drown in you, love." He licked between her folds. "I'm going to fuck you with my tongue till you scream to the stars." He nipped at her clit. "I'm going to worship this sweet little pussy of yours like it is the only god I will ever know." She shivered again, nearly unable to stay upright as she felt her arousal flood at her core. "I want you to sit and come on my face, darling, use me like your fucking sex slave, let me devour you," he growled, low and deep, as he took her into his mouth.

"Ah, Ambrose. I'm so close, *please*," she panted.

With one hand at her hip, holding her upright, he reached the other hand beneath his chin and between her thighs. Lila gasped as she felt his large, thick finger enter her, his tongue still sucking on her sweet bud. His finger curled, hitting her inner walls and the exact sweet spot she liked so much, and he quickly added another.

Her hips buckled against him, grinding against his tongue, as she slipped lower, unable to keep herself up.

Ambrose groaned in pleasure, taking longer, deeper licks and continuing to curl his fingers as she dripped down his hand, down his chin.

"I-It's too much, A-Ambrose!"

"Come for me, baby," Ambrose groaned, as he curled his fingers even deeper inside of her. He flattened his tongue against her, meeting his pumping fingers and dragged it dangerously slow up her cunt until it slowed on her pulsating bud.

Lila's eyes rolled to the back of her head as she bent forward, unable to hold herself up any longer. Her hands fell in front of her, elbows to the stone below her, as Ambrose held her up with one hand, the other still diving into her. She pressed her pussy against Ambrose's mouth, grinding against his face, and yelled out his name over and over.

The more he lapped his tongue against her, the more Lila arched her back, bliss coming in violent, earth-shattering waves. He licked and fingered her through her orgasm until she was a twitching, wet mess.

"Ambrose!" she screamed, as she came around his curled fingers, on his face. He licked and swallowed it all up, not leaving a single drop as he cleaned her up. The after waves rocked her body till she felt like nothing more than a puddle.

Lila yelped as he pulled his fingers from her. The sensation was too much, almost threatening to send her over again.

"Fucking delicious," he moaned, sucking each digit clean. He shimmied Lila down his body, so they were face to face, her body limp and twitching, then sat up, wrapping his arms around her. "You're such a good Little Mouse." Ambrose kissed her, soft and sweet, as he adjusted her in his lap. She still felt his straining erection under her, and after taking a few deep, recollecting breaths, she gently placed her palm on it.

"Do you want me to—"

"No, love. This reward was for you." He kissed her again. Her body wanted to thank him, but she wasn't sure if she could do much in her current state. Both of them sat there, watching the stars as they tried to catch their breath. Lila's legs still shook from the after waves of the most intense orgasm she had ever felt.

"I don't think I can walk," she admitted.

He chuckled, tightening his arms around her. "Good thing you don't need to." He rubbed his palm against her arm. "Are you cold?"

She shook her head. "The opposite. I feel like molten lava."

"I thought that might be the case. Your pussy was like fucking sunlight."

Lila's brain was too muddled to understand what he meant.

Still panting, Lila asked, "Are-aren't you supposed to take a lady out to dinner *before* you tongue fuck her?"

The vibrating chuckle from Ambrose rocked through Lila's quivering body. "Darling, you *were* my dinner."

28

After carefully climbing from the roof, back into his office, Ambrose assisted Lila in getting dressed once more. He laced her corset and dress back into place, but the cheeky bastard kept her panties in his trouser pocket.

"These are mine, darling. A memory of the best feast I've ever had," he smirked, arching one of those gorgeous eyebrows. Lila blushed but was too exhausted to argue.

Somehow, Ambrose managed to get Lila back to reading. He gave her a children's book that she successfully finished a couple of hours later.

"It is almost time for our dinner plans. Shall we resume this lesson tomorrow? We can practice from that story book I gave you."

Lila nodded before saying, "Actually, there is something else I want you to train me on."

Ambrose shot up an eyebrow. "Hmm? And what might that be?"

Lila thought about how to form the words for a moment. "Is there a way for a human to be strong enough to fight against a vampire's thrall? I know you mentioned it is like a dial."

Ambrose studied her and then tapped his chin. "Yes. It's difficult though. Have you ever heard of people growing immunities to poison? They ingest micro doses that increasingly get bigger over time. At first, the poison does the same thing to them as everyone else. But as their body gets used to it, the poison no longer affects them. The Reinicks did the same to you with their poison, as over time it became less effective," he explained. "Well, the same could be done for our thrall. You can train your mind to realize when it is being placed in a trance, and how to get out of it. It's more of a strength of will than physical strength. Is that something you want to do?"

Lila nodded. She wanted to become more than physically strong. That had already done so much for her. But becoming mentally strong as well? After all these years of being weak, protecting herself felt like something finally attainable.

And it was all thanks to the Crow Lord.

Lila's heart fluttered with what could only be described as wings.

"All right, we start tomorrow. We'll alternate your physical and mental training to keep your strength up. And you must read before bed, every morning."

Lila nodded. "And when do we go to the next manor?"

Ambrose thought for a moment, tapping his finger against the wooden desk. *Thunk, thunk, thunk.* "Ideally before it gets too cold with winter. Snow would make the trip to the Maggot Mansion rather difficult. Impossible, even. And waiting till after the cold months would be too long."

Too long for what? Lila wondered but kept the question

to herself. She knew the strigoi and Drusilla Reclus were threatening to rise, and there was the attack when they were traveling home from the Arachnid Estate. But was that a coincidence? Or was it planned?

Sensing her curiosity, Ambrose focused on her again and smiled warmly. "Come, let us speak at dinner." He stood from the seat they had been embraced in just a couple of hours ago and reached his hand out toward her.

She took it and felt like she was giving him not only her hand, but her whole heart.

Sandra was eagerly waiting for Lila in her room upon her return. As she entered, Sandra squealed and jumped toward her.

"So?! How was it? Did he like the dress?"

Lila immediately blushed and lifted her fingers to her lips. "Oh . . . yes."

Sandra made an unearthly screech once more, and as soon as the sound escaped her lips, Lila's bedroom door burst open, and Constance ran in.

"I knew he would! I could hear your racing heart from my room!"

"And that flush on your cheeks! Darling, you're glowing!" Sandra winked.

Constance put her hands on her small hips, "Have you two finally confessed your love yet, or are you still 'just flirting.'"

Lila laughed, "No, no—none of that. Goodness, what have you ladies been thinking of?" She walked deeper into her room, seeing her dinner dress hanging in front of her armoire.

"Much tamer thoughts than what you've actually been up to, that's for sure," Sandra snickered as she assisted Lila in removing her gown.

Sandra gasped as soon as the dress fell from her body. *"Dear,"* she whispered, *"where's the thong you wore?!"*

Sandra looked at Lila wide-eyed and her cheeks reddened, as she quickly turned back to the thirteen-year-old in the room. "Constance, dear, I think Lila would prefer a bit of privacy as she gets ready."

"Ah, that's right!" Lila quickly agreed. "I promise to tell you all about it later, okay?"

Constance sighed and crossed her arms over her chest. "Fine. But you should know none of us will be in the manor till tomorrow evening for breakfast. Ambrose asked to empty the castle for your date. Only the cooks are remaining, and even they're leaving right after they're done. Uncle Kaz and I are spending the day at a luxurious inn in town. I heard they have an indoor swimming pool for vampires!"

Lila glanced back at Sandra, "Is that true?"

Sandra nodded and smiled. *Completely alone? With him?* Were they going to—

"Lilac, you're kind of a perv, you know that?" Constance snickered, causing Lila to immediately blush from embarrassment again. She turned to the door and began to leave as she called, "Anyway, tell him you love him already!"

Sandra waited a moment after Constance left the room, and then whispered in a rushed voice, "Okay, tell me *everything*! Did he keep them?"

And, blushing, Lila told Sandra that the two of them had shared a kiss, and maybe her dress came off, and maybe he did see her undergarments—and kept them—but she dared not mention anything further than that. She wanted to keep their rooftop escapade to herself.

"And was this the first kiss between the two of you?" Sandra asked eagerly.

"Ah," Lila stuttered. "N-No. At the Arachnid Estate. That was our first kiss."

Sandra lightly smacked Lila's arm. "And you're only telling me this *now*?" she laughed. Lila blushed again before Sandra smiled widely at her and squealed. "Well, no bother. Now that I know, I understand why he had that beauty of a dress made for you. I wouldn't be surprised if he properly declares his feelings for you tonight."

The thought of Ambrose's tongue praising her body felt like declaration enough.

But the thought of hearing his words, his . . . professing . . . it made Lila's heart skip. Suddenly, her entire body felt warm, like a fever without the head cold.

While Lila was lost in thought, Sandra helped her choose a new—much simpler—pair of undergarments and prepared a slip skirt for her to wear under the gown. Once the gown was on, Sandra sat her down at the vanity and began to twirl Lila's hair into perfect ringlets, placing shimmering pins and clips throughout to look like sunlight peeking through her lilac tresses.

She adorned Lila with a simple, gold necklace that hung just above the girl's collar bones, just above the feather marked on her. As she gazed into the mirror, Lila realized it brought much attention to her long neck. She wanted to ask if that was the best idea in the company of a vampire—not that she feared Ambrose would hurt her—but then Sandra moved on to makeup.

"Close your eyes, dear," she murmured, fully focused

on her task. Lila did as she was told and then felt a soft brush against her eyelids, her cheeks, and then paint against her lips and charcoal around her eyes.

"All right, you can open now."

As Lila's eyes blinked open, she felt her breath catch in her lungs. She almost didn't recognize herself in the mirror at first.

"Do you like it?" Sandra chirped.

The charcoal around made the brown in her eyes pop, as did the reddish and orange powder on her eyelids. Her lips were painted a light pink, perfectly pulling attention to them.

"I-I love it!" she stuttered, her lips spreading into a wide smile. "Do . . . Do you think Ambrose will like it?"

"There isn't a shred of doubt in my mind that he won't go absolutely mad when he sees you," she grinned, tucking a curled strand behind Lila's ear. "Especially after the events this evening. He won't be able to keep his hands off you."

Lila hoped that would be the case. He had fully tended to her needs every time something had happened between them. She was hoping, tonight, she could be the one to tend to *him*.

After tying golden sandals to her ankles, Sandra said, "Well, dear, I believe it is just that time for dinner to begin. Shall we go?" Sandra held her arm out to the girl.

Lila's heart was pounding as she took Sandra's arm and was guided out of the room, through the hall, and down the stairs. As she neared the door to the dining room, her heart went from beating too fast, to not at all.

It was ridiculous, this effect Ambrose had on her. After all they'd been through with each other. He had seen her sweat, bleed, cry, snort, scream, beg, moan, and in turn, she had seen him for what he really was—a monster.

But instead of being afraid, she was even more enam-
ored by him.

And even though he had made sure he'd seen *every* bit
of her, she was still fearful of how he would react seeing
her in this dress.

She wanted to scoff at herself.

Marcus ran through her mind at that moment. His cute,
dopey smile when he made a bad pun, or his voice when
they whispered in the middle of the day, snickering to
themselves. Her brother was somewhere, still suffering at
the hands of Ciro and Hektor. And she was too busy thinking about whether a vampire would find her pretty.

She was ridiculous. A ridiculous fool who couldn't
keep her priorities straight whenever she saw this man.
Did that make her a bad person? Forgetting all about her
brother and his new teeth, while this vampire's teeth rav-
aged her? Now wasn't the time for romance, it was the
time for action, for fighting for his life. And here she was—
going on a date with her Monster of Malvania.

"Lila?" Sandra said. Her voice sounded like it hadn't
been the first time she was trying to snag the girl's attention.

"Sorry, what?"

"I was asking if you were ready, dear. Are you all right?"

Lila could see the concern on her face. "Ye-Yes, I'm fine.
A bit nervous, is all," she lied.

"Ah, well, don't be. There is nothing to be nervous
about," Sandra smiled, and Lila wished down to her very
being that Sandra was right, but really there was very
much to be worried about. "Just take a deep breath. I'll be
leaving the manor shortly, along with everyone else, as requested by Lord Draven. But remember, we are all rooting
for the two of you. And you must tell me *everything* first
thing tomorrow, okay?" She smiled warmly. Being alone

with Ambrose wasn't necessarily what she was worried about. But rather how much she *enjoyed* being alone with him, while she shouldn't be enjoying anything.

"O-Of course," Lila said hurriedly.

Sandra lightly patted her shoulder and then pushed the dining room door open. The room was empty save for the fire blazing in the hearth and before it, the man stood tall, watching the flames dance.

As Lila passed the threshold of the room, the door closed behind her, enclosing just the two of them inside. It reminded her of her first official night at the manor, when Ambrose carried her to this very room. Ambrose had been helping her, even then, healing her wounds through his salacious remarks.

She took a step deeper into the room, causing Ambrose to finally turn. His gaze danced over her, and she felt the heat in his eyes as they roamed over the dress. Yet, as scorching as his gaze was, she couldn't quite place his re-volving expressions. Awe? Lust? Maybe even . . . love?

"You look . . ." he began, his eyes warming her neck, her lips, her waist.

"Pretty?" Lila asked.

She watched as Ambrose visibly gulped. "Like the stars cannot compete." He took a step toward her. "Like the earth and heavens were made just for you." Another step. "Like the sun's warmth is cold in comparison to you." *Step.* "Like the heavens were made in *your* image, not the other way around." *Step.* He was standing just before her, eyes locked on hers. "You look like life itself. Devastating, beautiful, painful, ethereal. Darling, you could tell me you were about to destroy the entire universe, and I would ask to be the last in line, only so I may be able to watch you that much longer." He clawed at his chest as though it physically pained him. "Darling you *are* the entire universe."

His eyes were drinking her in, and his words were utterly intoxicating. He looked as though he could not contain his emotions for her. His face shifted, as his eyes widened and grew glossy. They were sparkling, like the night sky. And she could see *exactly* how he felt about her. And she felt it too. She had not felt this much nor this deeply for him, even when he bit her and infused his venom inside of her.

And now?

But she also did not know how to respond. It was . . . overwhelming, the feeling his words caused inside of her. What they did to her. Her lungs still couldn't catch up. She watched as Ambrose smirked at her expression, and for once she was thankful he could sense exactly how she felt. She wasn't as eloquent with her words as he, but she wanted him to know that she felt the same about him. He leaned down and placed a soft kiss against her cheek, finally snapping her out of her daze.

If she didn't know any better, she would almost think he had enthralled her.

He took her hand and began to lead her to the dining table, already laid out with an assortment of food.

She stopped, pulling on his hand to force him to look at her. "Y-You also look . . . universey," she tried, causing Ambrose to crack into that wondrous laugh of his. Her cheeks were on fire, any warmer and she was afraid her skin just might start melting off. "You do things to me . . . make me feel ways I've . . . never felt. I don't know how—" She wasn't sure if it would work, but she *pushed* the feelings she had for him through the Concord. She wanted him to know *exactly* what she thought of him, wanted him to know that words weren't and would never be enough to express how she felt.

He clutched his chest again with his free hand and she

thought she saw the smallest well of tears in his eye. He knew how she felt. He *felt* it. She didn't need to put it in words.

"Thank you." He smiled, guiding her into her seat and pushed in her chair. It was the chair closest to the head of the table where he normally sat, and she was thankful he didn't try to place her at the other end. As he sat, he continued, "I hope everything here is up to your liking? As promised, I had our cooks prepare the very best."

Lila had been so distracted by watching him, her eyes hadn't even made it to the table yet. But as soon as they did, her mouth dropped open.

"Oh ... my . . ." she let slip. The smells hit her all at once, rich meaty scents, freshly cooked bread, roasted garlic. The sight of ripe fruits, condensation dripping down plump grapes. If she could eat with her eyes alone, she would gobble the entire table down in a heartbeat.

"Am I expected to eat this all?" Lila said, her eyes as large as the stars. "'Cause I think I can ... if I have to of course."

She heard Ambrose chuckle beside her. "Only if you wish. Otherwise, we can save the rest for leftovers, or I can have runners deliver it to the village."

Lila felt her heart leap. She liked that idea. She liked it a lot.

As Ambrose poured her a glass of wine, she began to fill her plate, a piece of juicy-looking meat, plump grapes, a wallop of mashed potatoes, a small block of cheese, and other foods Lila had not seen but only heard of in all her years living in the dungeons of the Viper Morada.

"*Salute,*" Ambrose said, lifting his chalice. It was much larger than Lila's wine glass and was decorated with small rubies all around the metal cup. She knew it was filled with blood. "To that dress and our first private dining. Hopefully, the first of many."

"*Salute*," she repeated blushing, clinking her glass against his.

As they both drank, Ambrose's eyes remained on her. Once his chalice pulled away from his lips, she could see the remnant stains of red, fresh on them. She had no desire to drink blood, or really be near it, but that didn't stop her from wanting to lick his lips clean.

She plopped a grape in her mouth to distract the thought.

Ambrose leaned over, picking up her fork and knife, and began to cut the thick steak that sat on her plate for her. "Before you entered the dining room, you felt . . . off."

His eyes didn't meet hers, and she found herself thankful to avoid it. It made telling the truth a bit easier.

"I'm . . . worried."

"Worry wasn't *quite* the emotion I sensed."

Lila's gaze followed the sawing of the knife. "It's my brother. I'm worried for him, but I suppose it's more than that. I feel . . . I'm not sure what to call this exactly."

"Guilt," he clarified. "You feel guilt. Resentment toward yourself . . . and toward the joy you've experienced here."

That made sense. *Good thing he knows my feelings better than I do.* "I feel like I am distracted. By you," she admitted, finally looking up. Ambrose nodded his head but continued to watch as he cut through the piece of meat.

She expected one of his quick-witted jokes. Something along the lines of *I am quite distracting, I mean, look at me* or *Yes, yes, my tongue can be quite distracting when it's sending you to oblivion.*

But he didn't say any of that. Instead, he nodded, understanding what she meant.

"We should be focusing more on your training. Coming up with actual solutions to saving your brother."

"It's just . . . everything has been happening so quickly. It feels like I have left him with those monsters for an eternity. I know it's only been a few weeks, but every second he's alone with them—" She didn't even want to begin imagining what they were doing to him. "Rebekkah suspected Ciro and Hektor to be constantly enthralling Marcus. Forcing my brother to do anything those demented savages wanted." Lila felt herself shaking, her hand firmly closed in a fist.

Ambrose gingerly placed his hand atop hers. Warm, calloused, and large, it covered her fist completely and instantly soothed her straining muscles.

"There are . . . rules between the vampire lords. Rules with little to no loopholes," he began. "But, I swear, as I did on Sanktus Pernox, I *will* find a way to save your brother, Lila. I *will* turn him back into a human if that is what you wish. I *will* help the two of you be free of the Reinicks—forever."

She loved him.

That's what it was.

She loved him, she loved him, she loved him.

A shy smile Lila had never seen before spread across Ambrose's lips.

She trusted him, but she wasn't sure he even knew how to accomplish any of these goals. "How, Ambrose?" her voice had gone quiet.

"Eat, love. Don't let the food get cold." He handed her the fork and knife, encouraging her to take it. Lila began pecking at her food, and once she tasted a bit of everything, the pecking turned to devouring. Everything was beyond delicious and filled the hole in her heart—at least temporarily.

29

"id you have any siblings?" Lila asked through
bites of food.

Ambrose was silent for a moment, took another glug of his drink, and spoke. "Yes, once. I was one of four. Second oldest."

"Brothers and sisters?"

"To my poor mother's dismay, all brothers."

"What happened to them?"

He hesitated a moment. "Remember how I mentioned I was turned?"

"You were . . . twenty-eight? It was the original vampire."

He nodded. "Before becoming a vampire, I was a slave. A human slave. Not unlike murine now."

Lila's eyes widened. She had no idea. "Why?" was all she could get out.

Ambrose smirked, but the grin didn't reach his eyes. "Why indeed. To this day, it's unclear. In those days, society judged based on a person's skin color. And my skin was rather unfavorable it seems."

Once again, Lila startled, scrunching her eyebrows. She

felt a lump in her throat as she said, "B-But you're beautiful. Stunning. Why would—"

"Hate is venom, love. It spreads and spreads, hypnotizing the masses. Even before vampires, society always found a way to do stupid things in the name of others," he explained mournfully. She watched as his fingers tightened around his chalice. "Most of my scars are from that time."

Lila wanted to hug him. She wanted to embrace him and never let go.

He cleared his throat. "When I was a boy, my mother and father were very poor and too kind for their own good. When I was eight, white men we couldn't understand stormed our village. They raped my mother before killing my father, in front us all. Forcing us to watch." His fist clenched harder around the metal chalice, bending it under his grip.

"A-Ambrose, I-I'm so sorry . . ."

"They took us . . . all of us. We were separated shortly after that. Then came the buying, the trading. I was able to stay with my youngest brother for a time, but he was eventually sold elsewhere also."

Ambrose had lost his siblings. He knew the pain she struggled with and experienced even worse.

"I never heard of any of them again. About three hundred years ago I looked for them. Records. I knew it was unwise to hope they were still alive, made to be vampires like myself. But that's the pesky thing about hope. It manages to creep inside anyway."

"And did you? Find them, I mean."

He shook his head. "They had all died within five years of being sold."

Lila gulped.

"I was sold back and forth for years, auctioned and bartered off. When I was twenty, I was finally purchased by a very notable man—a count—of a small region of Malvania, back before the continent adopted the name, back when it was known as Europe and was divided into countries. Now ... to know the rest of my story—and perhaps the beginning of yours—I think I must tell you of this man."

Lila perked up. *My story?* she thought.

"This count was the original vampire. And when he purchased me, he was still very much a human."

Lila's eyes widened. "You were there when the first vampire was made?"

He nodded. "Oh, I was there, all right. In the eight years before I turned, I watched the count wage wars, defend his country, become a hero, and a villain. But the most defining moment of his life—of all our lives—was when he fell in love."

Lila took another bite of her food, listening to Ambrose with rapt attention.

"Before he became a vampire, the count had a wife no one knew about—no one save for the people who lived through it ... people like me.

"Most just know of *after*, just before the Mass Death, he stepped out from the shadows with three new vampiric wives at his side. All bore him multiple children, who eventually corrupted the human world. You know the rest of that story. But his first wife—she was a mystery to vampires and the old families. A fable more than a reality. But not to me.

"As I served the count, I saw him and this woman—she was ... a nobody. A healer in the town. No notable family to speak of. No status. No money. But this maiden was much like you,"

"H-How?"

He grinned again, "To start, she was beautiful. Sunlight personified. And warm. Like you."

"Do you mean in looks and personality? Or—"

"I mean she was *sunlight personified*. Like you. She had the same ability. And even before the count became a vampire, he loved it and was drawn to her through it. They met by chance, and he immediately was smitten, as was she. Many in his family and his region believed them to be an odd pair. He was a ruthless ruler who did the worst of things for the betterment of his people, he was a murderer, and prestigious in battle. On the other hand, she healed people, had dirt on her hands, and was a poor village girl.

"They were each other's opposite in every way, sun and moon, day and night, life and death. And it was that opposition that attracted them so fiercely to one another. The couple foolishly, naively, believed others would see them and understand."

"But they didn't?"

Ambrose shook his head. "They didn't." He looked up, noticing Lila's empty plate. "Are you done? Would you like anything more?"

Lila glanced down before her, "O-Oh, no thank you. I'm okay."

"Would you like dessert?" Lila imagined having something sweet and nodded at the idea. "Then I'll be back in just a moment." Ambrose stood and left the room.

Lila began to pile her used dishes to make it easier to clean and just by the time she had finished, Ambrose walked back in with a small plate, and something made of chocolate atop it.

He placed it before her and chuckled as her eyes went large.

"This looks . . . heavenly!"

"Well, I hope it tastes as good as it looks. I know you do," he teased.

"And I certainly hope you taste as heavenly as you look," she teased, cheeks going hot.

"There's my firecracker. Would you like to find out?" He raised an eyebrow.

She did. She really, truly wanted to find out how sweet he tasted. But she wanted to know more about the original vampire and his wife too.

And she *desperately* wanted to eat the syrupy cake before her.

So, instead of answering, she picked up her spoon and took her first bite of the cake. She wanted to moan the second the chocolate syrup touched her tongue but refrained, fearing she'd only be teasing Ambrose more.

But by the second bite, she let a small gasp slip.

He scoffed. "You're dealing with an animal, remember? I won't be able to control myself if you keep making that sweet face and those little noises, darling. I just might have to get those plump lips of yours around my cock." He leaned his elbow on the table and inched closer to her. "Or maybe I'll bend you over this table and feast on you once again. Now, that would make for a delectable dinner spread, don't you think? I still have your taste on my tongue and I'm already hungry for more."

Lila squeezed her thighs together, feeling a pool of wet heat flood in her core.

With cheeks on fire once again, she urged Ambrose to stay on track. "Tell me more about the count and his wife."

Ambrose swallowed, took a breath, and then swallowed again. She saw veins popping on the back of his hands, his wrist, up the column of his neck, and his jaw clenched. Lila knew, then, that he hadn't been exaggerating when he said he wouldn't be able to control himself.

"First, finish your cake. Then, I propose we walk through the gardens. I am in need of . . . fresh air. All I can smell is you and it's making me want to do very, *very* naughty things, Little Mouse."

Ambrose's hand clutched the stem of his chalice as Lila quickly finished her dessert, and with a still-full mouth, said, "Done!"

He snickered at her and stood before pointing to her wine glass. "Would you like another for our walk?"

Lila nodded and he poured the red wine from a beautiful and ornate decanter. "This *is* wine right? You're not secretly sneaking me blood?"

"No, darling, I wouldn't give you blood in such a civilized way. I'd make you lick it off my skin and take it from me yourself."

Tempting, she thought.

He put his hand out to her and helped her from her seat before taking her arm and handing her the wine glass.

"My favorite color is white, by the way," Lila stated.

"Sorry?" Ambrose raised an eyebrow.

"Earlier tonight. You said *my* shade of pink was becoming your favorite color. Well, mine is becoming white. This shade, exactly." She pulled on a strand of his hair.

A low chuckle escaped his lips. "Ah. I did say that. Well, being honest. It seems to be a three-way tie as of late. That pink, definitely. But also, the shade of lilac your hair shimmers at night, and the red of your cheeks when you think naughty thoughts."

"Hey!" she playfully yelled, pushing into him. But Ambrose only took it as an excuse to hold her closer.

He opened the door from the foyer to the backyard, and

once outside, Ambrose took another swig of his chalice before continuing with his story.

"During the times of the count and his wife, there was a mass epidemic of hysteria . . . religious-centered hysteria. Society was ruled by Catholicism at the time, and when those in leadership roles would claim something, the majority would listen—whether they were right or wrong.

"One of the count's power-hungry relatives worked for the church. In order to try and force the count's hand, he claimed to his congregation that the count's maiden was a witch, and that she had cast a spell on the count to make him fall in love with her. The region immediately took it for truth—after all, that was the *only* explanation why a man of such a position would fall in love with a peasant." His voice dripped with sarcasm, and he rolled his eyes.

They arrived at the gardens, Ambrose's arm clenched tightly to Lila's, not enough to cause pain, but she knew he was tense. This story must be bringing back awful memories for him.

The moon was bright outside, full, and the sky was clear of clouds. She could see the same stars twinkling she had been under only a few hours before, when she was screaming his name. And even though the sky was breathtaking, and the gardens were mesmerizing, Lila found it difficult to take her eyes off her companion.

"So, they did whatever greedy man would do when they are given an ounce of power—they snuffed out that wonderful light. A mob led by the count's relative dragged her from her house in the middle of night and tied her to a crucifix in the middle of the town square. Just as the count finally arrived, his loyal guards in tow, they set her aflame, condemning her back to hell 'from which she came.' The original vampire watched as she burned to death right in front of him, and there was nothing he could do to save her. So, instead, he decided to die with her."

Ambrose paused his stride next to a gorgeous wisteria tree, the flowers in full bloom under the moonlight. Beneath the petals, there was a small, stone bench.

"Ever since you came here . . . I look out at this tree, and it only reminds me of you. Will you sit with me?"

Lila nodded and followed him to the bench. They both fit comfortably, but Lila scooted closer anyway. She wanted to be as close to him as possible.

"The count leaped onto the flames with her, burning away with her. But once the fire cleared away, and all that was left was the smoke and scent of charred bodies, the count opened his eyes. He was . . . different. You could see it, his eyes were no longer black, but a vicious red. And his teeth were long and pointed. His charred skin crumbled to reveal a gray like that of a stone gargoyle. And soon, he began to look like one too."

"That's where your monstrous form comes from. House of the Bat was the original manor of vampires and you all stem from him."

Ambrose nodded. "Some more than others. As soon as he came to, he attacked anyone and everyone around. Even his own men. I was able to hide, but I witnessed it all before escaping back to his manor. For nights, we heard the agonizing sounds of a man mourning for the love of his wife. He lost his heart and his humanity based on the delirious decisions of a greedy man. Those sounds of a man in agony slowly became the wailing of a beast.

"When the count returned home, he was unrecognizable. He changed me then, eight years after first serving him. Originally he was just going to kill me, drink my blood. But I don't know what made him change his mind.

He gave me his blood to drink after taking mine, and changed me, teaching me to be like him. He was angry—blinded by rage at the death of his beloved. He made terrible choices in that rage. Became an entirely new being.

"There are reasons why people believe vampires to be created by the devil, Lila. I never understood how it drove him to such madness, but now," he looked at her, eyes boring into hers. "Now, I fully understand. I would burn the entire world back to the dirt in which it came if someone hurt the one I cared for."

Lila swallowed the lump in her throat. But . . . she felt the same. She wasn't a monster, not like Ambrose—not a literal beast. She wasn't a killer either. Yet, if he were hurt . . . if he were killed, she would destroy *everything*.

And once again, she felt a pang of guilt. Why hadn't she been able to destroy everything for her brother? She wasn't strong enough now, so what would make her strong enough to do so if Ambrose were hurt?

He placed his hand on hers, and she immediately entwined their fingers, leaning into him.

"There is a reason they call me the Monster of Malvania. I am not proud but . . . when he first changed me, I was much like Marcus is now. Ravage, hungry, and blinded by fury. I killed *everything* that had a pulse. Women, children, animals, the elderly. It didn't matter. The world was my dinner plate, and mine for the taking. I cared for nothing, no one. Not until the count told me of what happened to him *after* he jumped into the flames."

"What happened?" Lila asked, her entire mind engulfed in his story, his life before, and the life of the count and his wife.

"*She* saved him. Well, part of him. They died together, but once they entered the doors of the afterlife, her light . . . did something. The way he described it, it is as though his love and rage turned him into a monster — a monster of death."

"A monster of death . . . a strigoi morte?" Lila discerned as her mind worked.

"Exactly. That is why I said his wife was the one to create vampires. In that same moment he became a monster, he felt a warmth as hot as the sun wash over him. He claimed she changed him from a strigoi, blinded by bloodlust, to keep a semblance of his humanity. To keep his *light*. His heart was broken, but his soul was saved."

It was so . . . disturbingly romantic.

"Am I her descendent then? How do I have this . . . power as she had?"

"I am unsure. I didn't think she had any children, but perhaps they did in secret? Or maybe it has nothing to do with blood at all."

Lila tilted her head.

"Maybe you just . . . *are*. The world needed a new light, and you were it. Your hair . . . it's not common. It's unnatural to everyone else. So how is it that you, the Sun Child, is born with hair of lilac?"

The idea weighed on Lila. She didn't feel worthy enough to be the world's light. She had never given much thought to her hair thinking, if anything, it was a birth defect.

Ambrose gripped her hands. "And I have a theory. I believe, like the original vampire's wife, with your power you could change strigoi — "

Loud screeches broke through the overall silence of the gardens. Crows flew from the trees, gathering in the sky like a dark storm cloud. Ambrose abruptly stood and held out his hand as Pollock soared from the masses.

Caw, caw.

Lila stood, coming to Ambrose's side and watched as Pollock landed on his arm. The crow bobbed its head up toward Ambrose, making a number of chirps.

"It's a message from Darius," Ambrose explained. After hearing a bit more from the bird, he turned to her with sad eyes. "He needs help. The manors are officially at war."

30

A-At war?" Her mind immediately flashed to Ciro Reinick. He had threatened war between the manors that night on her balcony. He had threatened war—over her. He killed his own father over the fact he wouldn't go to war. "*Too scared,*" he said. And now, only weeks after seeing her at the Sanktus Pernox ball, war had been waged.

"Ciro?" she asked. It was the only thing she could say. Ambrose didn't meet her eyes. He simply nodded. And that slight bob of his head sent her heart spiraling.

"Pollock, call the others back home. Tell them it's urgent," Ambrose commanded, jerking his arm in the air. Pollock went soaring, cawing frantically at the dark cloud above them. Once he was gone, Ambrose walked ahead, back toward the manor. "We need to prepare."

He didn't turn to her, he didn't even look at her. His back was so straight, so stiff, as he walked away from her. She saw his hands clenched in fists.

Did he think Ciro was bluffing when he threatened war? Did he think he could just keep me and Ciro wouldn't—

And then it hit her. The solution to this problem.

It was rather simple.

Just . . . give me back to him.

She thought of voicing it. To do so would be brave, an act of ultimate courage. But . . . Lila was feeling very *unbrave* right now. She wanted to stay with Ambrose. She didn't want to go back, not at all. In fact, the idea of going back made her sick to her stomach. Her head spun and she felt her knees shake. To go back would be worse than death.

But was her sanity worth the lives of thousands? If war struck, surely many would die—humans, vampires, and strigoi.

She wasn't worth that . . .

"Ambrose—" she began, ready to speak her mind.

"Hurry. We need to prepare and leave tomorrow before nightfall."

He didn't stop or turn around. He didn't wait for her to join him. And a little part of Lila's heart was happy he didn't hear her idea. If only it meant she was able to spend a bit more time with him.

Lila's dress fell to the floor around her feet. When she first imagined doing so, she thought it'd be in front of a smoldering Ambrose, his hands sliding all over her skin as he helped unlace it from her body, tension high.

Instead, her room felt like ice.

Lila dashed around her room, grabbing the travel bag Ambrose had given her when she was packing for their trip to the Arachnid Estate. Only now, instead of gowns and jewelry, she was stuffing it with the training clothes he had given her. Leather leggings and tops, belts, pieces of thick armor, boots for climbing, boots for running. She packed extra holsters for her stake and a number of plain stakes and daggers Ambrose had given her.

Everything that made it into her bag was about practicality. Thick socks, instead of dainty stockings, hugging undergarments instead of anything with lace. The nicest thing she packed was a robe, just in case it was needed. Within minutes, she was packed for their trip, and just as she was snapping her bag closed, a rush of wind cooled her back.

"Lila." Ambrose hadn't knocked. In fact, she didn't even hear him come in. She turned around and he was just . . . there. Inside her room. The door behind him remained closed.

For a long moment, he held her gaze and she felt like he was seeing right through her. All her fears were on full display. She stood in the simple undergarments she had on under her dress, and a small part of her felt so bashful. Ambrose was still dressed in his dinner finery, the velvet coat and pants, his chest tattoo hidden under all the clothes covering him. Yet here she was, practically nude before him for not the first time that night. His eyes dipped to her body, but only for the briefest moment. She felt his gaze warm over her skin, but he quickly concealed any lingering desire as his eyes met hers once again.

Her breath caught from his stare alone—but not in the same way it had earlier that evening.

It felt more like the night before Sanktus Pernox, when she broke down after seeing Marcus and the Reinicks at Darius's dinner party.

"It's been . . . such a long night," she breathed.

"I'm afraid it is only going to get longer." Ambrose was still just watching her. His voice sounded regretful.

"D-Did something more happen?"

Ambrose shook his head. "No. But, if you are to come with me tomorrow, there is something we must go over."

Lila straightened. "A-And what is that?"

Instead of an answer, he tossed something in her direction she instinctively caught. Lila looked at the weighty item in her hand—a simple wooden stake.

"Another one? I already packed—" as she looked up at Ambrose, she noticed he was gone. The room was empty once more.

At least, that's what she believed until the fire in the mantel was snuffed out, leaving her in pitch darkness.

Fight like your life depends on it, said his liquid-gold voice through the Concord.

"B-But I can't see."

Chances are, in a real fight, you won't be able to see a vampire coming either.

She felt a sharp shove on her right shoulder and quickly spun around, arching her stake in a downward thrust. But it only met air.

A leg kicked behind her knee, sending her thudding to the wooden floor.

I like you on your knees.

A hand gripped her hair and tugged, pulling her back up.

Lila reacted without thinking, she reached for the wrist holding her.

That's not what I taught you.

He lifted her by her hair and wrapped a corded arm around her neck, bringing her flush against his body.

Don't make me bite you, he licked up the column of her neck and Lila knew she would *not* want this bite. He wasn't trying to seduce her right now. He was trying to show her what it would be like going against a monster.

She flipped her grip on the stake and plunged it into the back of Ambrose's hand, pushing her body roughly against his before using the extra space to squeeze out.

Good.

Lila relied on her other senses. *Don't panic,* she thought to herself. If she remained calm, surely there would be a way to feel his presence.

Heat glided up her free hand before blazing on her armed hand. The same heat she felt whenever a vampire looked at her.

She side-stepped Ambrose as he lunged for the stake, and then thrust it at him. He blocked, but she didn't relent. Over the weeks, he had taught her to use her strength, to use her stature, to use everything she had to her advantage. She was small, but fast, it turned out, and she used that now.

Lila ducked low, and swiped at his feet, then jumped up and jabbed into his rib cage while he was caught off guard from the first punch. She wasn't as fast a vampire, but it was still fast enough to surprise them.

And, luckily for her, she was learning to be unpredictable.

Lila, instead of dodging yet again, moved in closer to Ambrose. She shot the heel of her palm up, chucking him directly in the chin. He sprang back, and she got out of arms' reach.

"Good," he said aloud before he lunged at her again.

They kept on like this in the darkness, panting and sweating. They each landed blows, and more than once Lila had delivered what would be a killing blow.

Unfortunately, Ambrose had also.

In a swirl of limbs being thrown out, Ambrose had

knocked the stake from Lila's hand and leaped onto her. He held her arms down above her head with one large hand and slammed the other next to her head. Both of them were breathing heavily as the flames in the hearth came roaring back to life. Ambrose had abandoned his coat and frilly shirt at some point, and now the crow on his massive, sweaty chest was staring down at her. With each shallow breath he took, it looked as though the bird's wings were flapping.

Her corset was tight against her ribs, her skin underneath damp and sticky, and her underwear was soaked with sweat.

"You-You've done well," Ambrose said between breaths. "But not—"

Before he could continue, Lila tucked her knees close to her chest, and kicked her feet up against Ambrose's abdomen with all her might. He stumbled off of her, and in a rush of movement, she reached for her stake and straddled him with the wooden point over his heart.

"I should be stabbing you right now. The pointy end, remember?" she smirked as she panted.

Her thighs were barely long enough to reach the floor, and it felt a lot more like sitting on top of him than caging him below her. But, nonetheless, if this were a real fight, she would've just killed the bloodsucker.

Ambrose smirked. "Excellent, love. Excellent." He rubbed the back of her thigh, sending a different kind of heat coiling through her body, as he dropped his head back on the floor. "You did well. Really well. You've improved beyond measure."

His praise did funny things to her heart and her stomach. She felt her cheeks warm even more.

"Lords," he said under his breath. "Is this what it felt like to bask in sunlight?"

Lila cocked her head. "Do I feel . . . warmer?"

"Darling, you're radiating. You feel like a summer day. I regret taking it for granted for so long."

She wondered if her overall warmth had more to do with her body temperature or her feelings.

"You feel like summer when I touch you." His hand rubbed her upper thigh, nails grazing over where her thigh met her rear.

"W-When you touch me?"

"Every time you blush, you flare. You felt like lava when I feasted on you earlier."

"*Oh.*" Lila felt her cheeks warming.

"Like that," Ambrose chuckled. "Unfortunately, Little Mouse, we can't have playtime just yet." His hand gripped Lila's ass and squeezed—hard. She still felt the bruised spots from where he grabbed her earlier.

She nearly yelped, but before a sound could escape her, her entire body stiffened.

"At least, *you* can't have play time. Get up, doll."

Lila stood without hesitation. In fact, she stood without realizing she was doing so.

"Spin around."

She did.

Why did she?

Ambrose stood behind her, running a hand over his sweaty face, pushing his damp hair from his forehead. "Bend over."

Her mind felt hazy, but she did as he said, and a hard spank landed on her ass.

The flare of pain sent a shock wave through her. She wanted to flinch and yelp—maybe even moan as her fantasy was coming true. But she didn't fight back, didn't moan in approval. She didn't say anything. *Couldn't* say anything.

What are you doing? she asked through the Concord.

Ambrose smirked.

"Face me."

She stood upright and turned again, her mind fogging over. What was happening? Why was she—

His eyes were glowing red.

He was enthralling her—hypnotizing her to do whatever he wanted.

She took a step back but then felt the compulsion to get closer.

"Shall I make you kiss me like Ciro tried?" He studied her, smirking. If he compelled her to do so, it would be nothing like her time with Ciro. Lila *wanted* to kiss Ambrose. She didn't need supernatural power to make her do so.

And Ambrose knew it.

"Hmm. Perhaps that's too easy. I need to pick something you really, *really* don't want to do." He turned his back to her and moved to the sitting room area of the bedroom, where the couches were warmed by the fire, and then plopped onto one, draping his arm over the back of the chair and spreading his legs comfortably wide. "Ah, I've got it. How about you dance for me? Give me a show."

Lila felt her heart drop. The idea of enticing him, seducing him—she liked that. But dancing for him? Just the two of them? While he *made* her? It was utterly embarrassing.

She hesitated.

"Dance for me, darling."

His voice was at once liquid gold and cold metal.

The heat of the fire blazed against her skin uncomfortably as she stepped before him. Her cheeks warmed, and she wanted to squeeze her eyes shut, bite her lip, *something* to hide from this.

Her hips began to sway.

"I've imagined this...quite often, in fact." Ambrose rubbed his own thigh, his hand trailing over the bulge hardening in his pants. "I like the idea of you dancing for me."

Lila felt the urge to keel over and die as her hip-swaying turned into more. There was no music, yet she felt rhythm within her. Perhaps she was dancing to the beat of her own heart thumping within her chest.

"Take off your corset," he ordered. Lila did as she was told, and she felt the heat of his eyes rest on her breasts, her nipples. Her cheeks flared and her mind reeled as her hands moved without her command. "I can never get enough of those." His hand gripped the bulge, and he threw his head back. "Unlace my trousers."

Lila walked in front of him and stooped to undo the laces. Her breasts hung over the bulge, and she felt his eyes glued to her as his breathing grew ragged.

The embarrassment mixed with a pleasure so thick, she felt like she couldn't breathe. She was so incredibly humiliated yet so incredibly wet.

She badly wanted to grab his cock and pleasure him, to have him break apart inside of her.

But he stopped her the moment the lace was undone.

"You're only allowed to watch, Little Mouse. Break out of the trance and maybe I'll let you touch."

Him and his stupid bargains, she cursed.

"Now, back to dancing. And add more gyrating."

So, Lila continued. She felt weak each time she shook her ass before him. She liked it, liked what it was doing to him, but she wanted to do it *for* him, not *forced* by him.

And then he pulled his cock out.

Lila gasped, stuttering in her dance for only a moment. It was the first time she'd seen it and it was . . . glorious? Terrifying? Mouth-watering?

All of the above.

She knew he was well endowed, but it was massive and . . . perfect. *He* was perfect.

He started to pump himself slowly, his thumb brushing against the head.

"Keep dancing," his voice was gruff—nearly a growl. Lila fought against it for a minute, but he pushed harder. *"Take off your panties. Slowly."* His eyes were illuminating, glowing in the firelight. Lila shimmied the underwear past her hips and down her thighs till she was completely nude.

Ambrose licked his lips and squeezed himself tighter. "Fuck, baby. *Dance.*" As he spoke, his hand behind the couch gripped the back so tightly, veins popped from his arms and the fabric under his nails tore.

She could tell he wanted her to do much more than dance, he was hoping she would break free from his control, to run to him, and take over.

But she kept dancing.

"Remember," he said, still jerking his hand up and down his shaft. "Remember how it felt when I spoke in your mind when that bastard was about to force you to kiss him. Remember the turmoil you felt. Remember the feeling of the haze breaking in your mind." He was panting, even more so now than he had been when they fought. And through his words, his eyes stayed glued to her.

It was hard, because *some* part of Lila enjoyed dancing for him. Enjoyed watching him work himself. She didn't feel as strongly motivated to break it.

She once again pushed that feeling to Ambrose through the Concord as she shook her ass for him.

Ambrose smirked. "Such a little devil. Fuck it. *Pick up your stake."* She did. *"Come here."* She did.

She stood over him, the apex of her thighs so close to the tip of his head. She was so tempted to just sit on his lap and saw her wet folds over his cock. She could feel his pre-cum on her thigh and she desperately wished she could just lick it up.

But her body wouldn't let her.

He grabbed her hand with the stake and pointed it at his neck. *"Stab me."*

All the heat from Lila's body immediately evaporated and all that was left was an icy chill.

"Wh-what?" she asked.

"Stab me." Ambrose's voice was full of command. "You've done it once. You can do it again." His eyes glowed, piercing right into her. She felt her hand dip, the point digging into his neck, breaking skin.

No! she thought.

But her hand pushed a little farther. Ambrose clenched his teeth. He would sit there and take it. If she stabbed this through his neck, *he would take it.*

She felt tears prick at her eyes, her hand shaking.

Don't make me do this.

"Little Mouse," Ambrose ground out, orders ready to slip from his tongue.

NO!

Her free hand shot to her wrist. She was fighting herself, mentally and physically.

The stake drew blood.

But only a drop.

"Stab. Me."

She felt it then. The dial. She knew he had it at the highest level, testing her will.

And somehow, Lila found her will to be stronger.

With a burst of heat erupting the room, Lila threw her

body back, landing hard against the tile floor below her. The stake went skidding across the room, under the bed and out of sight.

She huffed, feeling as though she had been underwater, and she needed to refill her lungs.

"You . . ." Ambrose began. When her eyes met his, she saw the shock and awe on his face. "You did it. You did it!"

He jumped up from where he sat, fitting himself back into his trousers, and scooped her into his arms with ease, twirling her around.

Lila didn't hesitate, she wrapped her arms around his neck and squeezed herself tightly against him, not caring one bit that she was still nude.

"Don't *ever* make me do that again. Next time you make me want to do something I don't want to do, have me lick the floor, or chop my hair off." She punched his chest. "Don't ever make me hurt you again unless we're sparring, okay?" She glared at him.

"I promise, love." He snuggled her closer and kissed her forehead. "You did so, so well. I'm so proud of you."

She blushed at the praise. "Can we be done now? I'm exhausted." Lila let herself go slack in his arms. The night had been *so* long. She had a horrible nightmare, was asked out to dinner, was forced to read, had her entire world blown up by Ambrose's tongue, was forced to read again, had the best dinner of her life, *started a war*, fell into a pit of despair, fought for her life, and then fought for her mind.

Ambrose chuckled, patting her head as his hot breath tickled her forehead.

"Let's clean up. Then we can sleep."

31

L ila gasped when Ambrose kicked her balcony
doors open, walking out into the fresh night sky.
It was nearly morning already, past the darkest
part of night, and she could see the sun was just minutes
away from peeking out.

Ambrose jumped, causing Lila to grab onto him tighter,
and landed on the smaller balcony above hers—the one
that led to Ambrose's room. She held her breath, anticipation growing. She had never been in Ambrose's room, she
knew the majority of the top floor was his living space. But
as the glass doors opened, Lila saw the balcony leading to
Ambrose's bathing room.

He carried her inside and placed her on the marble
counter of the sink before running the hot water in the
massive, golden tub. The cold marble soothed the heat
from before along with her already aching limbs.

As he filled the tub, Lila looked around. The room
wasn't very different from her own bathing room, but
everything was so much . . . larger. The bath would easily
fit four to five people, the ceilings were incredibly high,

and the room overall felt so much wider. She wondered if the size of the bath was to accommodate Ambrose's true form. It certainly looked large enough to allow him to spread his wings a good bit.

Ambrose tested the water with his fingertips before shimmying out of his pants. It was the first time seeing him fully nude and it just looked so . . . right. His body was complete perfection. Every corded muscle, dip, and curve—he was so much more than she could've ever imagined in her mind. And she still wondered how a being as beautiful as this was attracted to her—her! So thin and frail, so . . . so human.

"The water's ready," he called, pulling her from her own thoughts, even though she had a difficult time pulling her eyes from his butt.

Lila nodded and felt her bones give out a little more. She truly was exhausted. Ambrose walked over to her—intimidating as ever, but now for a whole new reason. How could he ever love her?

He stood before her, her eyes at level with the bird on his wide chest. She reached her hand up and placed her fingers gently against its inked head. He shuddered under her touch, but only for a moment.

"Do all vampire lords have these markings?" she asked, thinking of her own marking her back and collar, thinking of the Concord between them.

Ambrose shook his head. "Only me, as far as I'm aware. The markings from bargains, like yours, are different. This," he said, placing his hand over hers, "originally served as a reminder."

He lifted her into his arms, where she nestled against him. Lila traced the bird's beak to his wings. It was so much more intricate up close, full of details she had never noticed. It appeared as though each feather had been drawn within the crow, each unique with their own details. Like a real bird.

Ambrose stepped into the tub and lowered them both inside. The moment the hot water touched Lila's rear, she felt herself melt in his arms further.

She was officially jelly.

"A reminder for what?" she managed.

He sat her on his lap, massaging her shoulders and working down her spine. "When all manors were united under House of the Bat, I still felt my . . . connection to the crows. Back before the Mass Death, many religions and superstitions believed crows and ravens to be a sign of ill things to come, a bad omen, a sign of death. But not mine. Back when I was human, my mother used to tell me crows were messengers from the heavens and from those in the afterlife. That stayed with me always. When I became an undead, *I* was to be the messenger."

Lila leaned her head back against him, the crow markings on their bodies touching. "A messenger for what?"

"For myself, for those weaker than me, for those I love. I have not always been a good man, Lila. In fact, I still do not believe I am. But I will always, *always* fight for what I believe and for those I care for. I will never allow something I cherish to be taken from me again." Lila knew he was talking about his family, the brothers that were taken from him. And she thought about Marcus. About Constance and Kaz. And about Ambrose. And she understood. She relished the tattoos he had given her, and felt she wanted them forever.

"I would like to be a messenger as well. For those I care for and those who cannot fight for themselves," she admitted.

He brushed her hair behind her ear. "You already are."

She remembered his hard length before she broke free of his thrall. She still wanted to please him, especially after all he had done for her. Lila turned in his lap and reached for his cock. "Would you like me to—"

He grabbed her hand, entwining their fingers. "Not tonight, love. I will not have you in this near-unconscious state. When you take me, I want you to feel the power you hold on me. I want you to watch as you make me wholly undone just by your touch." He squeezed her hand reassuringly and planted a kiss on her knuckles. "Tonight, let us just bathe together. This is more than enough for me. It's perfect."

Lila grinned and pushed herself against him, planting a gentle kiss against his lips.

It was soft. The softest they'd had yet. And though it left her hungry for more, it also felt . . . innocent.

"Well, then, if you won't let me . . . *please* you, then at least let me wash your hair."

Ambrose grinned widely and chuckled. "If you insist. Though, you will find my hair to be the softest thing you've ever felt. I think it might be more pleasing to you than me."

"Yeah, yeah, of course it is." She rolled her eyes playfully.

"Then you must let me wash yours after. And your body . . . if you'll allow me."

Lila bit her lip and nodded.

It turned out his hair really was the softest thing she had ever touched. She had felt it so many times before, but now, in the water with shampoos and conditioners, she discovered just how silken it truly was. And so well kept. It was softer than all the pajamas, robes, and blankets, and she just wanted to rub her face in it. It was feather-soft. She made a mental note to twirl her fingers within it more often—as often as she could, in fact.

"My turn," he whispered, turning her around once more. As he dug his fingers into her locks with the shampoo, she felt her entire body relax at once. It soothed every part of her and didn't take long for her eyes to feel incredibly heavy.

This. She liked this.

Ambrose's nails gently scratched against her scalp as his fingers rubbed and lathered. It was pure bliss and she felt herself slipping between the line of conscious and unconscious.

"Ambrose."

"Mmm?" His voice vibrated against her back.

"I'm falling asleep," she slurred. At least, she thought she said it.

"Sleep then, love. I'll finish up here. Rest. You've had a long night and we have another before us." She felt him kiss her soapy temple, and then the spot where her neck met her shoulder. "Rest well, darling."

Lila stopped fighting the weight of her eyes and limbs. She felt his hands scratch and rub her head for a few more moments, and then she succumbed to her dreams.

Lila was thankful her dreams were quiet unlike the last time she'd slept. No blood, no vampires, and no dying. Nothing that made her wake in a cold sweat. But one thing was the same, she was still waking up to Ambrose.

The first thing she noticed was how completely comfortable she was. Warm but not too warm. She was wrapped in Ambrose's thick arms under blankets of soft fur. Their bodies were pressed flush against each other, and it seemed she had used his massive chest as a pillow for the majority of the day.

The second thing she noticed was just how dark it was—almost otherworldly dark. They were in a coffin, much like Constance's in the Arachnid Estate. It was plush underneath her, even more comfortable than a bed, and though they were both in there, it did not feel confining, which led her to believe it was a rather large coffin. She wondered if it was sized to fit Ambrose in his natural form, and if he found it more comfortable to sleep in one form rather than the other.

The third thing Lila noticed was that they were both still very nude, and both still had damp hair from the morning. He must've finished washing them both and then immediately carried her to the coffin to sleep. She vaguely remembered him climbing inside, his arms cradling her like she was delicate glass.

She cuddled closer into him. He smelled amazing, clean from last night's bath, but still like himself. Like the forest and smoke.

As her eyes adjusted in the coffin, the final thing Lila noticed was his cock growing so hard, it looked painful. Veins bulged under his skin, and Lila began to imagine how they would feel inside of her. He didn't allow her to touch him during their reading session, nor did he let her finish him in their bath.

She wanted to do it for him, though. She wanted to touch him and the idea of not being able to was driving her absolutely mad. She knew pleasuring him would do just as much for her, and she wanted him to understand that.

She squeezed her thighs roughly, attempting to allow herself even a morsel of relief.

But that hope crumbled when she saw *it*.

Her breath hitched and her eyes went wide as she watched just a drop of precum drip from his head. She felt her mouth salivating as if she were looking at the juiciest piece of steak she had ever seen. Lila's tongue slipped from her mouth, and she mimed licking his tip, desperate as the drop trailed down his length.

"Little Mouse," Ambrose hummed. His voice was like gravel from sleep—gravel made from gold. He squeezed her against him, trying to turn her to cuddle her better. "Don't pay me any mind. It's just . . . from the morning," He sounded so . . . sleepy. So human.

She pressed her breasts against his chest, causing him to finally, slowly, open his eyes. Inky pits she would happily get sucked into.

"It's not from sharing a coffin with me wrapped around you?" Lila raised herself high enough to lightly drag her hard nipple against his chest. "In the nude?"

Ambrose chuckled under her, causing the entire coffin to vibrate. "Hmm? That could be part of it. Waking up next to a beautiful goddess—in the nude, no less—is definitely worthy of morning wood."

Lila snickered and trailed her hand along his body. He stiffened under her touch.

"You don't have to." The gravel in his voice nearly made her come on the spot.

"I want to. If you'll let me?"

She watched Ambrose open his mouth and close it a number of times before his Adam's apple bobbed in his throat, clenched his jaw, and gave her a stiff nod.

Lila smiled wickedly at him and removed her hand from his body. He quirked an eyebrow, confused.

Good.

She ran her fingers along her own seam, grazing feather-light over her clit. A shuddering moan released from her lips, and as Ambrose began to shift, ready to touch her, she pushed him back with her free hand.

"No. You watch. I'm going to please you."

"You already do. You have no idea, but I have come more for you in my eternal life than I can fathom. By you, I am completely undone."

Lila inched down, kissing his chest, then his abdomen, his pelvic bones. "It's unfair. You already know how much you affect me. How much I've come screaming your name at the thought of you. Let me see you come for me." And then she finally swiped her tongue over the bud of precum that had her mouth watering.

Ambrose stiffened, a grunt escaping his lips.

"You look so hard. Does it hurt?" She planted a soft, teasing kiss against the ridge of his cock.

"Fuck. Yes. Yes, it hurts."

"Then let me make it feel better." She wrapped her lips around his thick head and sucked.

Ambrose's hand slammed down against the side of the coffin as another grunt rumbled from his throat. "Fuck."

She played with him, hollowing her cheeks, and flattening her tongue against him with each stroke. Lila had never done this before but by the way he was reacting, she assumed she was doing well.

"Heavens, you're so big."

She sucked him deeper, till she felt him in her throat, and it still wasn't deep enough to consume all of him. With a *pop*, Lila let him fall from her mouth, and she immediately went to lick up the length, wrapping her free hand around his base, and stroking up to meet her lips.

Ambrose buckled underneath her, and it seemed like the animal was let loose at that exact moment.

His hand shot out, gripping into her hair at the back of her head roughly, guiding her head down.

"Fuck, love, you're doing so good."

Lila rubbed herself just a little bit harder from his praise. She was doing well, driving him mad as his stomach tightened.

She opened her eyes and looked up at him through thick lashes. Red heat was staring back at her. His eyes were glowing in the dark coffin and watched her with a hunger she had never seen. Ambrose cupped her cheek with his free hand and held her face to watch him.

"You're going to make me come, Little Mouse," Ambrose moaned. "Are you touching yourself?"

Lila nodded.

"Good. Touch your clit for me, love. Rub your fingers over it in those little circles you like so much."

Lila did as he commanded, and for a moment, it felt like he was touching her instead. She moaned on his cock, and it sent the vampire buckling again.

"Fuck, baby, you sound so good around my cock."

He guided her head along his length as he thrust into her mouth. She couldn't even take all of it, with each thrust she gagged to the point where tears were welling in her eyes, but she didn't care—she loved every second of it. His nails dug into the back of her head, and she loved being controlled like this. It was so different from being enthralled, so . . . animalistic. And she knew that she was controlling him just as much, if not more.

Her clit felt plump from her fingers' abuse. She was so close to coming, she wanted to wait for him, but she wasn't sure she could as she moaned around his cock more and more.

She curled her tongue around his head, pulling a moan from Ambrose. "Lila, love."

It sent her over.

She moaned around him, feeling her hot slick coat her fingers. She shuddered everywhere, riding the waves as she continued to lick and suck his cock. The orgasm felt weak in comparison to the one from their night before. It was nothing like what Ambrose could draw from her. But she was satisfied nonetheless. She just wanted to give him the same earth-shattering orgasm she had been given.

Lila pulled her hand from her pussy, her fingers dripping her fresh orgasm, and wrapped it around the base of Ambrose's cock.

He threw his head back. "Fuck. Cover me in your come, Lila." But before Lila could continue, he shifted his position, sliding his hand between her legs. Before she could protest that this was for *him*, not her, he said, "Just ride my hand. I just want to feel you. Please."

His voice was dripping with needy desperation.

"So needy," she cooed, mimicking his words from their scale up the side of the manor.

Lila positioned herself so his hand was between her wet folds and rubbed her swollen clit on his coarse fingers and knuckles. She jerked her hand up his length, met her lips, then jerked back down again. Each stroke had his stomach tightening even more, and each time his groans were coming closer and closer to unhinged. And with each lick and suck, she rubbed her pussy on him, already feeling another orgasm building in her belly.

He tightened his grip on her head, still guiding himself into her, but now his thrusts were uncoordinated, chaotic, and his fingers under her cunt were growing greedy.

Lila felt his undoing was near. "Ca-Can I finish in your

mouth?" he choked out. And she felt ready too. Ready to finish all over his hand yet again, the friction on her clit too much for her to bear any longer.

She nodded and then once again flicked her tongue against him and knew that was what did it.

His eyes squeezed shut as he gripped her hair impossibly tight and thrust all the way into her for the first time. His cock went impossibly deep, and she could feel him constricting her throat as her lips met the base of his cock. At the same moment, his fingers grabbed her cunt, and he feverishly rubbed her sensitive, sore pussy to a breaking point.

As he began to pull out, he erupted in her mouth as she erupted on his hand. His hot come filled her mouth and she hungrily drank him in, swallowing mouthfuls as more dripped down her chin.

He was absolutely delicious, something she hadn't expected at all. But she drank and drank, till there was nothing left, and he curled his fingers inside of her one last time, causing another wave of violent shivers through her body.

Ambrose's entire body went slack under her as she *popped* him from her lips once more.

"Fuck," he said between heaving breaths. "That was . . ." he took a deep breath. "Amazing. Lila, you're perfect. Too perfect. Are you sure you aren't a goddess?"

She smirked and shimmied herself up his body. "Who knows? Maybe I am."

"You must be. It's the only explanation." He was flustered, his cheeks a darker shade, blushing and exasperated, and Lila thought it was the cutest thing she had ever seen. "And this," he lifted his hand coated in her. "I will *never* get over this." He licked all but his index finger clean and then guided it past her lips, into her mouth. "Taste how good you are." She took his finger, swirling her tongue around it, and licked it clean. All while keeping her eyes on his.

The coffin had grown steamy from their encounter, and as he finally pushed the lid open, a burst of cool air hit them both. Lila sat up, crawling between Ambrose's thighs to give him more room.

"Did you sleep well? I know the coffin is a bit jarring at first."

She stretched her arms and back and felt like it was the best night of sleep she ever had. "No, I slept wonderfully. I think I want to sleep in a coffin for the rest of my days." She smiled. Lila glanced around the room for the first time, and it was just so perfectly . . . Ambrose. Black and gold were everywhere. The coffin sat in the center of the room, large and imposing, on a dais of black marble. All around there were ornate candelabras, statues, and tapestries. It was at once dark and sinister while also being comfortable and sensual. Which expressed Ambrose so well.

He ran his long fingers up her spine as she was turned from him, if he added any more pressure, his nails would slit her skin open. "But only if I'm there, right?" he smirked a devilish grin.

"Of course. I wouldn't be as comfortable without you." She poked the crow on his chest. "Plus, you're more comfortable than any pillow I've used." Ambrose smiled and watched her for a moment, the heat still in his glowing crimson eyes. He slowly leaned forward, wrapping one large hand around the back of her neck, and bringing her lips to his.

At first, he kissed her softly. Their lips rubbed against each other as if they were breathing the other in. Then he opened his mouth and licked along the seam, sucking her bottom lip into his mouth.

She moaned as their tongues clashed and found herself pushing him back down into the coffin, crawling on top of him. Their lips stayed interlocked as she laid down next to him, digging her fingers into his shoulders, as the arm around her waist pulled her closer.

His free hand trailed down her body, dipping at the curve of her waist, raising with the curve of her hip, and then stopping at her thigh. He gripped her thigh harshly and guided her back over his hips to straddle him. She felt his impressively hard-again cock underneath her, pressing against her entrance, as her breasts squished into his chest.

He groaned into her mouth as he pushed himself against her wet center. Their tongues danced around one another, drinking each other in and he thrust his hips, ever so slightly, just enough to push the head of his cock against her clit. She moaned in his mouth, deciding she wanted to have him, there and then. She wanted him inside of her. Wanted to be seated to the hilt. Wanted to feel him plunge and claim and *own* every part of her.

Ambrose thrust up again, sliding between the seam of her dripping pussy, enveloping him in her wet, slick warmth. Heavens, it's like nothing she had ever felt before.

"Ambrose, take me," she breathed between kisses.

He sucked her tongue into his mouth before answering. "Are you sure?"

She nodded. "Yes, I want you to fill me. Take me as yours so I may take you as mine."

"I'm already yours, darling," he whispered against her lips. He pushed his hips up once more, driving the head of his cock just into her.

She moaned at the immediate pressure. "Ambrose, you're so bi—"

Ambrose suddenly went very still under and inside her. He stopped kissing her, stopped pushing himself into her entrance, stopped everything.

Lila reeled back to look at him and noticed his eyes were wide, worry etched over his entire face.

A shrill scream pierced through the room, through the manor, through the air itself.

He gulped, and in a voice clearly trying to remain calm, he uttered, "It seems we have company."

32

Ambrose eased her off, jumped out of the coffin, and pulled Lila into him before steadying her on her feet.

"Get dressed, now! Grab every weapon you can hold. I'll meet you in your room in just a moment."

Lila didn't wait to ask what was going on, nor who was at the manor. She saw the desperation in his eyes and knew that now, more than ever, she just needed to listen. He tossed one of his shirts to her, and after quickly slipping it over her head, she ran out of the room, down the first flight of stairs she spotted, and found herself in the hallway to her own room.

In the back of her mind, she realized she hadn't seen anyone in the manor. Normally, there would at least be *someone* cleaning at this time. And if Constance was in her room, wouldn't she have come out? They were all supposed to be back at sundown—and the sun *was* down. So where were they?

Another loud shriek pierced the air. Lila couldn't tell if it was the crows or those attacking. It didn't sound human, but it sounded much louder than any noise Pollock could make.

She quickened her pace as soon as she shut her door behind her. Ambrose's shirt was lifted over her head and tossed onto the small couches as she ran past.

"Fuck, fuck, fuck," Lila cursed as she began to dig through the bag she had packed. Deciding it was taking too much time, she flipped the bag and emptied its contents onto her mattress. She slipped on underwear and the snug leather leggings she used for her training.

CRASH!

Something loud rumbled the house from below her and a moment later, a rapid knock came from her balcony door. Lila jumped out of her skin, grabbing the stake, and eyeing the door.

"Lila, open up," urged Ambrose from the other side.

She sighed and relief filled her muscles. She dashed to the door and opened it, and he didn't waste a moment. As he walked past her, she saw he was dressed in his usual garb, slimming black pants, a black shirt—the collar hanging in a long, open v-cut, leaving the crow tattoo on his chest fully exposed—black boots, and a long black coat with little frill.

"Are you ready?" He looked down at her then, noticing her bare breasts were still on full display. "Never mind. Hurry." He followed her back to her bed, tying belts and strapping holsters over her waist and thighs as she pulled a top on and covered her torso with a thick leather plating. This all-black outfit usually made her feel strong, powerful. But all she felt right now was fear.

Breathe, Ambrose commanded through the Concord. He delicately brushed her hair behind her ears and then pulled it up into a high ponytail, tying it for her. *I am with you. We will get through this.*

Lila took a deep breath, grounding herself. "Who is it? Who's here?"

Ambrose stayed silent for a moment. She felt him hesitate behind her, his fingers pausing in her hair. "The strigoi. I believe Drusilla Reclus is here as well. And . . ."

She turned to face him. "And?" He didn't meet her eyes and instead strapped a harness over her shoulders and chest to hold a number of extra stakes.

"Ambrose, who else is here?"

She saw his jaw work before he swallowed. "The Reinicks and Marcus."

Lila's eyes went wide. She wasn't surprised. Not a bit, of course they would be. But the confirmation did nothing to settle her nerves.

They were here for her.

Finally, he placed a thick, ornate gorget around her neck. It was rustic gold with a crow etched into it. It was also much heavier than Lila thought it would be, but at least it would protect her neck. "Lila, there's more—"

Just as he was about to tell her something, another loud *boom* shook the manor. Ambrose grabbed Lila's arm, steadying her.

"Sorry to interrupt, dears." This voice, a woman's voice, boomed through the manor, through the air surrounding, maybe even through the nearby village. It sent chills down Lila's spine, like that of nails on a chalkboard. "But your presence is required outside. Now."

Ambrose grabbed Lila's hand. "If I asked you to stay here, would you?"

Lila thought about it for a moment, but ultimately shook her head. She wanted to help—as much as she could.

Ambrose smiled, though it didn't reach his eyes. "Dammit,

Little Mouse. Now's not the time to be the crow I know you to be." He placed a kiss on her hand, then turned, guiding her out of the room.

"I-Is that Drusilla?"

"It is." He squeezed her hand. "Lila, I want you to stay next to me. No matter what happens."

She nodded even though his back was to her.

"We didn't—fuck, we didn't prepare enough. You broke my thrall but keep on guard. Remember, it was only once, and at the expense of my death."

They winded down the stairs, through the halls, and to the front of the manor. Still, she saw no one.

"Ambrose, where is—"

"Remember, keep your stake up. Aim for the heart. Protect your neck."

They were at the door, standing side by side. Ambrose clenched her hand once more, loosened his grip, and then clenched again. He reached for the door, but instead turned to face her.

His black eyes peered into hers, drinking them in. Lila felt her lip quivering under his stare, and she knew he was afraid too—though, for very different reasons. He cupped her face, rubbing his thumb along her cheek.

"You'll be okay. We'll be okay."

Lila nodded, lost for words. Would she? Would they?

Ambrose kissed her, hurriedly and intensely. It wasn't soft, but desperate. It wasn't hungry, but afraid. His lips brushed and pressed against hers, speaking for them-selves. It wasn't a kiss of lust like she had come to know from him, it was more.

And too quickly, he let go. Before Lila even had the chance to open her eyes, he was already turning from her.

"Ambrose, wait—"

But as the words fell from her lips, he turned the handle to the grand door—the same door she had slipped in through to escape her tormentors, in the same foyer she had first laid eyes on the Crow Lord.

It was too late, their final moment was gone. She couldn't hold him longer, kiss him, tell him she loved him. Not now with the monsters of her nightmares before her.

Ciro and Hektor stood, one scowling and one smiling, like that of the comedy and tragedy masks of theater. Their gilded eyes slid under Lila's skin, drinking her in. Ciro's eyes focused on her face, while Hektor's eyes drooped to her newly formed hips and curves that came about from training. Where Ciro's gaze turned to a heated anger, Hektor licked his lip, ready to take his murine back to his bed.

Lila shivered, forcing her eyes away from them. Behind them, Rebekkah stood. She looked worse than on Sanktus Pernox. Her eyes and cheeks were gaunt, her lips were paler than usual, and her neck was covered in bruises. She remembered what the girl had said at the ball, her brothers' focuses had shifted to her. Her and—

Marcus stood next to Hektor, attached to a thick silver collar and chain. And something was different. His teeth were snapping ferociously, as his once-brown eyes were pitch black, unseeing, like that of the half-strigoi from the Arachnid Estate. She saw a thin seam run from his lower lip down his chin.

Lila couldn't breathe, as her eyes focused on that line. That line meant so much. It meant her brother was truly an unsavable monster. It meant—

"What do you think," Ciro asked gruffly, "about having a strigoi for a brother?"

"No!" Lila yelped, leaping forward, but being caught in Ambrose's arms.

We can fix this, we can fix this, we can fix this, was all he
kept repeating in her mind, but Lila felt the tears slipping
free as she let her body become limp.

Another voice chuckled. In the middle, stood a tall, thin
woman. She had platinum blond hair, curled around the
ends, but otherwise straight. Her dark hazel eyes seemed
bored, watching Lila and Ambrose as they emerged from
the manor and their reactions to Marcus. Her thin arms
were left exposed in the dress she wore, and a tattoo of a
viper coiled around one of them, from her shoulder to her
wrist.

The viper of the Morada.

Lila immediately thought of the mark on her back, and
realized this tattoo must've been the mark of a bargain
struck as well. "Well, nice of you to finally join us. I hope
we didn't interrupt anything important." She planted her
talon-nailed hand on her slim waist, before a striking and
terrifying smile spread across her lips. "Oh, well, it seems
we *did* interrupt something. I can still smell it on her." She
ran her tongue over her fangs. "Ciro, dear, I believe the
two of them were about to have sex. Can you smell how
wet she still is?"

Lila felt so small, smaller than she ever had. She impulsively squeezed her thighs, taking a tiny step back into
Ambrose, as Ciro's gaze darkened still. His rage was palpable—in fact, if she focused, she could hear him growling, even from this distance.

"Well, then, good thing we arrived when we did,"
Hektor cooed, that same sickly smile on his face she remembered so well—the smile she used to see every time
she closed her eyes. "We wouldn't want a soiled whore,
would we, brother?"

Lila didn't even see it happen. One moment, Hektor

was patting Ciro on the shoulder, and the next the bastard was missing his lower jaw.

"You never know when to shut up," Ciro ground out, his hand now slicked in his brother's blood. Lila watched as teeth fell on the ground, his tongue pulled straight from his mouth.

But what was worse, was seeing the bottom jaw grow back. Lila felt the urge to vomit as muscle and sinewy stitched back together again. New teeth and fangs sprouted up, as his lips finally formed, able to speak again. "That wasn't very nice."

Ciro turned to him again, but Drusilla silenced them both with just a glance. "Enough, both of you." As she turned back to Lila and Ambrose, her face of scorn changed to something mimicking pleasantry. "So, Draven, let's cut to the chase. Surrender, join us, give back the girl, and we'll spare you, your manor, and all the villagers currently being held by my strigoi."

Drusilla snapped her fingers, and a number of strigoi morte crawled from the trees, dragging a number of figures in their wake.

Constance, in her full form, was fighting with everything she had, but the strigoi threw her to the ground and four grouped on top of her. Kazimir was dragged out as well, as were a number of vampires and humans Lila recognized from the manor.

"And if you don't, I'll turn all of these lovely blood bags into strigoi for my army, kill you, and *still* take the girl."

"I'll fuck her on your corpse," Hektor sneered.

Lila flinched. Ambrose speaking so vulgarly had always excited a certain part of her, even when she denied it. But hearing such things from a man who was so far away from being her Lord of Crows made her cringe into herself. It brought back unwanted feelings and memories, and she could feel the new Lila slipping back into the meek little mouse she had always been before him.

But Ambrose tightened his grip around her, before helping her straighten and entwining his hand with hers once more, pulling Lila's attention to him and fortifying her new strength.

However, as she looked up at him, the lump in her throat grew. Ambrose's eyes were a red so vibrant, they looked like they were glowing—not unlike how they were a few moments ago while she was pleasuring him. But now, instead of his gaze being filled with adoration and what she hoped was love, it was only filled with a hatred so violent, it threatened to rupture the heavens. His jaw clenched more than she had ever seen. Ambrose's gaze was pointed at Hektor, who took a tiny step back. He gulped, and Lila felt a profound admiration for Ambrose at that moment.

"Drusilla Reclus. The hag of the Arachnid Estate."

Drusilla scowled.

"What are you doing at my doorstep?" Ambrose's usual liquid-gold voice was cold, hard. He seemed so much . . . bigger. Scarier. The Monster of Malvania, the Crow Lord.

The scowl was quickly replaced by another sickly smile. "I already explained, silly. I'm here to have you surrender to me and the strigoi. We vampires work so much better when we're united under one manor. You remember those days, don't you? Vampires fighting humans," her gaze fell to Lila. "Not vampires fighting vampires. Once we unite as one House of the Bat, we'll be so much stronger, so much *more*. We'll finally be able to have all of the murine under our thumbs. No longer will you need to confine yourself to drinking donations or living by their rules."

"Ah. Now it makes sense," Ambrose said, catching Lila off guard. She spun her head to look at him at the same moment Drusilla responded.

"It does, doesn't it? We are hunters, and we should live like—"

"You misunderstand me, Reclus. I do not mean your ideals make sense—they are undoubtedly unhinged. What makes sense is why you have aligned yourselves with these fools," he ushered at the Reinicks. "Both so foolish. You fail to understand that we cannot live without the humans, yet the humans can very easily live without us. We may be more powerful, but without them, we are nothing." His hand squeezed Lila's once more.

Drusilla's smile slipped away, revealing a look of disgust and boredom once again. "So you choose to be a romantic instead of the monster you truly are?"

"Oh, do not misunderstand me. I am a monster—a monster driven by romantic ideals. Those driven by anything less are merely vermin scrounging for purpose."

Lila saw Rebekah smirk from where she stood, Constance and Kaz did as well.

And it made Drusilla feel like an absolute fool. The hag from the Arachnid Estate yelled in frustration, literally huffing and stomping her foot like a child. "Fine, if you do not want to join us by choice, then it will be by force."

33

The breeze was cold against Lila's skin, whipping strands of loose hair from her ponytail against her cheeks. There were moments when all she saw was lilac. She preferred it to what she *was* seeing. Her brother convulsed as Hektor dragged him by the chain and collar around his neck to stand before Drusilla.

"I am told this boy is your brother. Is that so?" Drusilla smirked, not waiting for a reply. "Marcus, isn't it? He's such a pretty boy." She ran her long talons down his cheek, and though her touch seemed delicate, dark welts marred his skin. Small onyx drops appeared, and Lila felt her heart plummet, her instinct to run to him, to protect him, kicking into full gear.

Ambrose unwove their hands to grip her wrist. He sensed her desire to run toward danger but was holding her back.

Drusilla's wicked grin widened as her eyes moved between Ambrose and Lila. "It's a shame his beauty won't last much longer." As soon as the words left her lips, all Lila could hear was the tearing sound of nails on skin, and then the crunch of bones, and the gush of blood, as Drusilla tore her way through Marcus's back and pulled his heart through his chest.

Lila's eyes widened in terror as she saw the still-beating thing in the bloody talons of the vampire. A scream she didn't realize was hers tore through her throat, her lungs. Drusilla bore her fangs and slowly lifted a wooden stake in her free hand.

At least, it looked slow.

In reality it was probably normal speed, but everything was going so fast around Lila, it all seemed to be slow motion.

At the same moment, Ambrose released Lila's wrist and a flurry of black feathers dove past her. The crows from his tattoo. They shrieked and cawed, talons and beaks aimed right at Drusilla and the surrounding strigoi holding Constance, Kaz, and the others.

In the blur of wings, Lila saw the stake fall to the ground. She leaped into action and ran toward it, as hard as she could, dropping down and skidding along the dirt to grab it. Drusilla was there, batting away the crows and still clutching Marcus's heart in her hand. She growled at Lila, but as soon as the wood touched Lila's palm, she twisted her grip and plunged the tip into the thin spot of the vampire's ankle. With a hiss, Drusilla let go of the heart. Lila caught it, midair, and scurried to her feet.

But as soon as she stepped back far enough, she felt strong arms constrict around her and was pressed against a strong, wide chest. The heart fumbled from her bloody hands, and she angled her leg so it would gently roll down her body instead of smashing to the ground.

She didn't need to look to see who was holding her, the chills running up her spine and utter disgust by his touch told her instantly. Hektor.

"Our little murine, acting all tough. I've never seen you run like that and, oh, you know how much I love it when you run from me. If I let you go, will you let me chase you?" He pressed his nose against her cheek and deeply inhaled, sniffing her. In the past, she would've nodded just to get him off of her. She would have agreed to anything.

But she wasn't the weak little murine anymore.

She threw her head back, hard, smashing into the tip of Hektor's nose. With a grunt, his grip loosened but didn't fully release, so she used the slight freedom to reach for the stake at her thigh that Ambrose had given her and drove it deep into Hektor's thigh. The moment his arms moved from around her, she pulled it out and dashed away. As soon as she was out of arm's reach, Constance — in her full monstrous form — flew in with her knee bashing against Hektor's cheek.

"Go!" she screeched at Lila, continuing her assault.

Lila turned and saw Ambrose fighting a number of strigoi, fending them off from Kaz. He pulled and tore throats out, two long stakes she had never seen in both hands. Then she saw Ciro, walking toward him with nothing but malice and hatred in his eyes. Ambrose was still weak from using the crows, she could tell by his movements, and Ciro was sneaking up on him. At this rate, she feared Ambrose wouldn't notice. She needed to tell him, to warn him. "AMB—"

Cold, long fingers closed around her throat, hard enough to stop the words on her tongue, hard enough to stop her breath from coming at all.

"Never turn your back on one of us, dear. Didn't your lover teach you anything?"

Drusilla lifted Lila into the air from behind, holding her

by the throat. She watched as Ciro turned into a huge ser-
pent, wrapping his body around Ambrose, who was too
busy pushing Kaz out of the way from the strigoi, still trying
to bite him. Ciro constricted, holding him firmly in his grasp,
and that's when Ambrose's ruby eyes finally met Lila's.

He bit his lip.

I . . . failed. I couldn't protect you, his voice seeped
through the Concord.

*No. I couldn't protect myself. I was dumb. This isn't your
fault!*

After a swift movement behind her, Lila felt her shirt
and skin tear. Blood welled and the hot liquid began to
ooze down her back.

Nearly everything around her went quiet. The fighting
strigoi stopped in their places, chattering their teeth.

Click, click, clack.

The sound haunted her, bringing back a flood of memories
from the night after Sanktus Pernox. The only movement she
noticed came from Kaz, running into the tree line behind
them.

Hot breath stung the wound on her back just before she
felt Drusilla's tongue lick at the dripping blood.

"Mmm, delicious. Now I know why he's so smitten by
you. You taste absolutely divine." Another lick. "He must
find it so difficult to control himself around you." She
pressed her lips against the wound, sucking out blood.
Lila gasped at the sudden sensation and started to squirm
in her grip. She scratched at the hand at her throat, and
kicked and buckled, but nothing worked.

Ambrose writhed in Ciro's coil, clawing and biting,
shifting into his monstrous form and then his crow—but
nothing worked. The snake had him trapped. And all he
could do was watch.

His eyes haunted Lila. They were sad, desperate, and defeated.

"Lila!" Ambrose yelled.

"I'd like for you to see something," Drusilla's voice was coated with a wicked, proud sneer, and though she couldn't see it, she could perfectly visualize the grin spreading on her lips. Her talons loosened on Lila's neck, just enough for the barest amount of breath to filter in and out. Drusilla turned, bringing Lila with her, forcing her to turn away from Ambrose.

As soon as her back was to him, Lila's stomach fell.

Before her, in an oozing black mess, Marcus sat on the floor with Constance between his legs, his bifurcated jaw biting into her shoulder. She saw the gaping wound on his chest was now closed, and Constance's bloodied palm told Lila she must've just placed his heart back in his chest when he attacked her. Marcus's split jaw opened and the two fangs at the ends detached from her skin as her head slunk back against his shoulder.

Lila wanted to run to both of them. To save *both* of them. She kicked her legs more, but the grip around her neck didn't loosen.

"NO! Constance, Marcus!"

Drusilla only cackled.

Marcus watched the girl in his arms, black blood dripping down his chin. His breathing was ragged but this was the first time since he'd turned that Lila saw him still. In fact, he was almost calm as he watched Constance.

"No!" Ambrose yelled behind her. A struggle ensued, and she heard clawing and tearing. But she couldn't look. She couldn't turn to see if Ambrose was getting torn apart just behind her, or if he was doing the tearing.

And then she saw the hair-thin seam form down

Constance's chin. The same as Marcus's. In just moments, Constance lifted her head and turned to face Marcus.

Click, click, clack. He chattered his teeth to her.

Her split jaw opened, revealing the fangs within. *Clack, clack.*

She was a strigoi. That was how they turned Marcus. It was that easy, that fast. And just like that, their humanity was gone. The venom that had no effect on her worked *this* quickly on *everyone* else.

Both of their all-black eyes fell on Lila and then, too fast, Constance began to crawl toward her, jaw opening and snapping shut.

Drusilla threw Lila against the ground, hard. Her shoulder took the brunt of the impact and felt dislocated, but she couldn't be sure. All she could focus on was filling her strained lungs with air. She breathed deeply, coughing as though she were a fish out of water.

When she finally got it even enough, she looked up and Constance was just before her, her split jaw opening wide, ready to clamp down onto Lila's face. Her venom would paralyze Lila, leaving her to be an open target to all the vampires and strigoi around her.

And she wouldn't be able to do a thing about it.

She squeezed her eyes shut, hoping that at least she wouldn't have to watch her own demise. And as she heard the *crunch* of teeth on skin, she waited for the inevitable excruciating pain.

But it never came.

Lila blinked her eyes open slowly. She saw Constance in front of her, just as close as she had been before. But her fangs were biting another. A massive, charcoal gray arm barred the girl from Lila. Black ooze dripped from where her fangs pierced skin. Another strong hand grabbed Constance's shoulder, holding her back.

As her eyes followed the figure's arm to his shoulder, then his neck, and finally his face, she saw ruby eyes staring into hers, pleading.

"Lila, love. I need you to run." His voice was barely higher than a whisper for such a huge monster.

She didn't know what to do, but she knew she couldn't do what he was asking. She wouldn't leave them. She wouldn't leave *him*.

"I'm going to turn, any minute now. I will lose myself, like her. I *need* you to run for me."

She didn't move.

"Lila." His voice grew harsh. Constance still dug into his arm. "I'm using the bargain. My next favor is for you to run from me, darling. *Run.*"

Lila felt a tingle all along her upper back. A tingle that turned into a burning sensation. It was where her tattoo had been. The one he gave her for their deal. It was making her do her half of the bargain.

Constance unclasped her bite, sitting back against Ambrose, then quickly scurrying under his arm and behind him, back toward Marcus. The moment she was gone, Ambrose leaped to attack Drusilla, his claws boring into her face. She screeched, trying to dodge as she ripped into her own grotesque monstrous form, but the Monster of Malvania was loose and angry. He pulled her hair and smashed her face into the dirt, as she scratched and clawed at his quickly recovering skin. And then he threw her, with what seemed like all his force, away from the sight. Lila realized it was just to buy her time to run away, to get a head start before Drusilla *and* Ambrose attacked her.

Lila stood then, compelled by the burning of her tattoo.

Ambrose turned back to her, taking a slow step back before convulsing and landing on a knee. His red eyes turned an inky black—but not like the normal universes he usually contained. These covered his entire eye, the whites and all.

These eyes weren't never-ending possibilities. They were haunting. As his gaze trailed over Lila, she didn't feel the usual heat that came from his gaze. It was just . . . cold. An icy chill.

She stumbled back. "Ambrose?"

The thin seam cracked his chin, forming the bifurcated lower jaw.

His eyes met hers once more. In a hoarse voice, he said, "Run, my love."

With heat licking up her back once more, Lila Bran turned around and ran away from Ambrose Draven.

34

S he didn't know where she was running to, only that
she had to keep going. Her body wouldn't let her
stop, no matter how much she willed her legs to. He
was behind her, wings flapping painfully in the air, each
creating a boom that nearly threw her off her feet as she
ran left, pivoted right, and ducked behind large trunks of
trees. Low-hanging branches slapped and scraped against
her cheeks and arms, leaving behind small cuts. Ambrose
growled behind her, thirsting for her blood that teased
him with each new slice of skin.

Lila slid underneath a fallen-over tree and took a deep
breath. This entire moment, the running, the woods, even
her exhausted body, it was all reminiscent of her nightmare just yesterday. Had it been a prophetic dream? The
heavens warning her of the upcoming turmoil?

In the nightmare, she and Ambrose died.

She would *not* let that happen. She didn't know how
she would stop it, but it was nowhere near morning yet,
he was still safe from the sun.

She, however, was very unsafe.

Just then, a loud slam clawed through the bark she was under, and Ambrose's ruby eyes shined through the opening. He snarled as he reached for her, and she could see he had completely lost himself.

"Ambrose!" she yelled desperately.

But the sensation on her back only burned more. She yelped and scurried to her feet, running away again.

But even though she was much faster than before, she didn't get far. Ambrose grabbed the ponytail he had tied and yanked her back. He did it so roughly, she fell to the floor instead of into him. But, like the night before, she fought back with all her might. She swept her feet against his thick ankles, and though it didn't trip him, he stumbled over her, loosening his grip on her hair.

She used the moment of reprieve to scurry back and get on her feet. She stayed low, making herself even smaller in front of him.

He had to be two, maybe even three, times her size in this form, and it wasn't like he was the big-but-slow type. He was big *and* fast, so her best option was to make herself as small of a target as she could be.

Lila kept her stake at her thigh, not daring to cross that line, and instead pulled a small dagger from her hip. The silver glittered in the moonlight as she brandished it toward Ambrose. He growled at her, snapping his wild jaws. His white hair looked savage, messy from his crazed daze as it fell into his eyes. His muscles were taut, and for a moment, Lila wondered if he was fighting himself. It was the only way to explain it. Was he still in there?

"I don't want to hurt you, Ambrose."

Normally, he would make a snarky response, something about how she couldn't even if she wanted to.

But now he said nothing, his eyes were devoid of any and all reason.

He was a mindless, bloodthirsty monster.

And he had turned her into a monster killer.

Ambrose lunged at her, claws ready to slice her to ribbons, but she dodged and rolled under him, slashing her dagger through the skin behind his knee. Instantly, Ambrose crumbled, his wounded knee crashing to the dirt, but his wings splayed, smacking Lila in the face as he shielded himself. In just moments, his leg was healed, and he was crawling toward her once more. She slashed at his cheek, and he didn't balk but kept moving toward her, snapping his teeth.

"Ambrose, please!"

He grabbed her thigh and pulled her down under him, caging her under his arms.

Her nightmare flashed before her, when he climbed on top of her and bit into her neck. Now, she squirmed under him as he leaned down, deeply inhaling her. His huge body pressed against her, showing her just how small she was compared to him. She threw her elbows up, creating some space between his snapping jaws and her face. She punched him, with all her might, and was surprised to find that it was enough. His head snapped to the side, away from her. It was the perfect opening to get up and run.

She dashed between trees, leaping over branches, and found a small, tight alcove, big enough only for her. Lila ran to it, wedging herself within and waited. She knew Ambrose could still hear her breathing, smell her sweat and blood, but she hoped he wouldn't be able to get in, not until she figured out what she was going to do.

His huge body slammed into the opening of the crevice and his hand immediately shot forward trying to reach, grab, or scratch any part of her he could. She was just far back enough for him to barely graze his nails against her abdomen, but it was enough to tear at the fabric protecting her and carve a thin slice into the skin below.

Lila grunted as a fresh wave of pain hit her in the abs and back, as the bargain was trying to force her to keep running while the new wound bled. But there was nowhere to run. She was trapped between rock and Ambrose.

"Ambrose, please. Please, this isn't you."

Another long tear and she screamed, as nails trailed from her abdomen, all the way down to below her belly button. All she could hear was the snarling, snapping, and scratching sounds beyond her own screams and each time she closed her eyes, she saw a rabid animal, not the Lord of Crows she had come to love.

As her blood dripped down her stomach, Ambrose slammed the palm of his hand against her, coating his hand in the warm, red liquid. Each touch of his calloused hand against the wound sent fresh, striking pain against Lila's skin, as her legs forced her to move back, to run away. But she was already pressed as close to the wall behind her as possible.

She truly felt like a mouse caught in a cage with a large cat waiting outside, ready to play with his food before devouring her.

Ambrose pulled his hand back and savagely licked at the blood, not letting a single drop go to waste. His black eyes, already so large, seemed to increase in size even more.

Though she had never seen one, he reminded her of all the terrifying things she heard about sharks in the ocean. A blood crazy, lethal predator. She heard Rebekkah talk about them once, gray and massive, black beady eyes, slipping into a frenzy when they tasted blood. This was *exactly* what Ambrose reminded her of as he lapped his tongue between his fingers, sucking on each digit to get as much as he could.

Then, he paused. He watched his hand for just a moment, before those black beady eyes shifted up to her. Lila startled at the resolve on his face. It was the first semblance of emotion he had since becoming strigoi. He watched her, then turned his attention to the crevice itself . . . almost as though he were sizing it up . . .

Lila yelped, sensing what was going on through his crazed mind. In a blink, the hulking mass of Ambrose became the white crow she had first seen in his office. The white feathers flapped in the wind as he ferociously cawed, diving between the hole of rocks. Lila shot her arms up, defending herself, as the white crow clawed into her forearm.

"Ambrose! Stop it!" she begged. And much to her surprise, the flapping did stop. There was a new kind of pressure against her forearm. A calloused hand, wrapped around her. Ambrose pulled her arm from her face, and she saw him, just before her, bodies pressed tightly against each other. He was staring down at her, those large black eyes drinking her in. She had seen him hungry and had seen the look of lust in his eyes.

But this was different.

This wasn't sexual.

This was murderous.

He was drinking in her fear, her blood, her scent, he was ready to devour her—just like he was in her nightmare.

His human body caged her in, her thighs pressed together between his, her wrists grabbed by his hands, and their chests were pressed snugly against each other. Lila wondered if he could feel her heartbeat against him. If he recognized, somewhere inside of him, that it was hers.

"Ambrose . . ." she squeaked, hoping, begging to get through to him. "Please. Don't do this."

He pinned one of her hands between them, and reached up, touching her cheek. His white hair was a mess, nowhere near as tactfully disheveled as it normally was. His dark skin was made even darker by their small alcove. And his lips were parted, showcasing a ton of jagged, pointed fangs, the seam from the bisecting jaw closed. The nail on his thumb lightly scraped her cheek in an *almost* gentle caress.

But his eyes gave him away. He wasn't back to himself.

Lila pushed herself against his chest, trying to create space between them, but it didn't work. He was as solid as stone and there was nothing behind her but more stone. The hand on her cheek lifted, grazing over her brow, her temple, and then grabbing a fistful of the loose lilac hair coming undone from her ponytail. Ambrose then pinned her other arm between them as well, and as she wiggled, he leaned into her, pushing her even farther against the wall.

With his now-free hand, he slashed through the leather binds holding the gorget together on her shoulders, and the metal clanged down between their chests. Ambrose grabbed it and tossed both pieces over his shoulder out of the crevice, making sure nothing was in his way.

He jerked her head to the side, revealing the long column of her neck, and tearing the high neck from her collar away. He ripped the fabric down to the rounded top of her breast.

Ambrose held her head firmly, an unbreaking grip, and Lila struggled. The nightmare was becoming real, and she didn't know what to do to stop it. She felt so helpless. She had tried so hard to change the outcome, yet somehow, they ended up in the same position.

The three-way jaw split open as he moved in on her

neck, the two fangs at the ends already poking against her. Ambrose slid his tongue from his mouth and licked slowly over her tender flesh, marking his target. Lila buckled, trying till her last breath to get away.

And then he couldn't control himself any longer.

His fangs pierced her skin, and it was akin to being set on fire. Her entire body felt like it would combust under his bite as he tore into her. Slowly, he sucked from the wounds, the feeling of blood being pulled from her body sent gooseflesh all over her skin, even though she felt hot with fever. And just as quickly as he bit her, a new sensation of emotion coursed through her.

His venom.

35

The familiar waves of euphoria raked through her body, sending shivers down to her core. With each pull from his mouth, she felt the apex of her thighs grow needy with desire. She wanted—no, *needed* to be touched. By him. Right now.

"Ambrose," she tried. She knew it was the venom. Knew now was *definitely not the time.* "You're hurting me." Her words came out as a moan.

Right now, she loved the pain. The pain turned her on.

Instead of pushing against him, she pressed herself to him. His rock-hard chest against her nipples made her so, so wet. She wanted his cock, and she whimpered as she sought it out with her body. She drove her hips forward, trying to press against him, when she felt her knees buckle.

"Fuck," she groaned, and she wasn't sure if it was from pain or from how desperate she was. She was losing blood, quickly, and she didn't seem to care.

Grinding her teeth, Lila squeezed her own thighs together, giving her the barest breath of release, as she reached for another blade at her hips. Thank lords

Ambrose had strapped so many weapons to her before they left the manor.

Lila was able to grip the blade and lift it behind him. She almost dropped it as another wave of euphoria hit her, her eyes rolling to the back of her head as a loud moan escaped her lips.

She was about to come, just from his tongue and hot breath lapping at her throat. It felt . . . divine.

But wrong.

With another press of her thighs, a moment of solace rushed over her, and she used that to drive the dagger into his back.

Ambrose screeched, releasing the grip his teeth had on her. She pushed him forward, and out of the crevice, diving to the side as he feverishly reached for the blade to pull it out, just as a loud squawk sounded above her.

Pollock dove down, talons forward as the crow attacked Ambrose's face.

"Pollock!" she cheered. The bird attacked Ambrose, buying her enough time to escape. Lila didn't stay to watch if he pulled the blade free, she just ran. She hated hurting Ambrose and watching him in any kind of pain, but she knew the blade nor Pollock would do much damage. Nothing like what a wooden stake of white oak could do to a vampire's heart.

She dashed back through the trees, her heart and body begging her to run right into Ambrose's arms and waiting jaw, but her legs and mind forced her away.

He compelled her to run from him, and the birds on her back were making her do just that.

Her legs were on fire as her feet pounded the ground below her. Each step sent sharp, fresh pains to the large wound on her neck, and she felt herself losing a lot of blood. Too much blood.

It felt the same as it had in her nightmare, and Lila was afraid that maybe . . . maybe she wasn't going to make it.

Pollock screeched above her head, warning her that if he had returned, it only meant Ambrose wasn't far behind. In less than a heartbeat, she heard the loud, terrifying sound of heavy footsteps bounding directly toward her. Surely, the monster was right behind her.

It was the most frightening sound she had ever heard — it sounded like doom. There was no way she could outrun him.

And then, because the heavens decided to have their own kind of fun, her legs gave out under her. She'd lost too much blood and no amount of training could prepare her for numb limbs and the toxin coursing through her.

Lila fell to the ground, hard, landing on her face. She cursed as she felt more blood drip from her surely broken nose. But she didn't have time to worry about it, as a huge beast's shadow appeared behind her.

Ambrose.

She turned to see the massive form once more, wings splayed out, three-way jaw open and salivating.

Her insides turned to jelly as the venom reminded her just how euphoric his touch was, just how enthralling his bite could be as he drank from her. She was nearly ready to give herself over to him.

Pollock flapped toward her, grabbing onto her hair and pulling with all his little might. It snapped her out of the love-stricken thrall his venom continued to put on her and she scurried back, trying and failing to stand up.

"Ambrose—"

He didn't let her get far. He walked forward, grabbed her by the belt at her waist, and with a strong burst of his wings, skyrocketed into the stars.

Lila felt her stomach leave her behind, as he tossed her in the air and caught her, carrying her in his arms as he had when he first brought her to the Crow Court. But it was so *unlike* then. His claws dug into her, his grip too rough, and she felt like he was holding her like a cumbersome doll.

Pollock tried to keep up, tried to soar right behind them, but Ambrose quickened his pace, dipped to the trees, and soon he was but a speck in the sky. Ambrose banked left and right, zooming so quickly, the trees surrounding them looked like only a blur.

And then the trees turned into bodies.

Ambrose came to a sudden halt in the large space before the manor. Drusilla, the Reinicks, Marcus, Constance, and all the numerous strigoi stood, watching.

Waiting.

As Ambrose threw Lila to the ground, Drusilla cooed, "Good to have you back, darlings. How was your little adventure in the woods?"

Lila spat at her feet and sneered.

"Urgh!" Drusilla grunted in disgust and kicked the soiled foot into Lila's bleeding shoulder. "*Disgusting murine.*"

Pained, bruised, bleeding, and sore, Lila pushed her battered body up. She faced Drusilla, her true enemy, and kept the scowl on her face.

"Disgusting but brazen. She doesn't know how small she is." One corner of her smirk rose, and then she snapped her fingers.

Strigoi all around Lila began chattering their fangs, crawling and scurrying toward her. Lila backed up, only to back into stone. Ambrose stood over her, the black in his eyes just as hungry as before as they trained on the blood dripping from her neck. He looked up at the other strigoi, dropped to all fours, caging her between his arms, and bellowed out a growl so loud, it shook the earth. She knew he was claiming her as his own prey. After all, he had done all the work to bring her here.

He looked back at her and pulled her closer to him like a ragdoll, not really caring where her limbs went. His eyes watched her, for just a moment, and an overlay of her nightmare drifted into her thoughts as Ambrose tore into her.

His ginormous fangs broke the skin once more, above her veins, as she screamed out. She hit and kicked and squirmed, but his bite only tightened.

"Ambrose!" she panted. "Wake up!"

But he didn't let up, he drank and drank and drank—he drank until she felt her limbs go completely limp. Her arms stopped punching, her legs stopped kicking.

His lips and chin dripped with her blood down to his chest, and back onto her. She felt hot all around her, inside and out. So hot, she thought she would burn up. Was it the venom? The bite? Her impending death?

Lila felt like she was melting as sweat pooled on her forehead, with each drag of blood he took from her, and her clothes became too sticky, making her feel as though she were roasting within.

Her eyes were batting closed, trying to stay open, but the heat was just overwhelming.

Next to her ear, she heard the faint sound of sizzling flesh, and then Ambrose let go of her, hissing in discontent and pain.

She was carelessly tossed back onto the ground, too weak to stay upright, but even the dirt was too hot.

Lila was sweltering, and within a moment, she couldn't handle it anymore.

A scream erupted from her throat, and as it did, something else erupted from inside of her. A burst of the sizzling heat tore through her. Not quite like fire . . . but rather energy burning through her, combusting like tiny explosions.

The heat completely engulfed her, and then flared all around. She watched as waves rushed past the vampires surrounding her. The strigoi all shrieked, withering in their spots. Withering, but not burning. Changing. The Reinicks and Drusilla shielded their faces, but that was all they could do.

Another scream tore through Lila as a fresh wave of heat bombarded her like sunlight bursting through every pore of her skin.

36

S uddenly, arms wrapped around her, and though the
heat was still unbearable, this touch was not. The
arms scooped her up and held her tightly.

"Lila," the holder called. "Lila, I'm right here." It was
Ambrose. He was speaking so gently, trying to soothe her.
But . . . wasn't he just a strigoi trying to kill her? How was
this possible?

The line bisecting his chin was gone, and his eyes were
the shiny ruby red she had come to love so much.

Lila broke into a sob, shaking in his arms. It was all too
much. Too much physical pain, too much emotional heart-
ache, and too much confusion.

She felt his grip on her tighten, grounding her.

I'm here, I'm with you. The Concord ignited her heart,
her mind, he was *him* again.

"H-How?" she uttered.

"You. *You* saved me. And look—" he pointed beyond
where she was looking, and then angled her to see all of
the strigoi, *all of them*, were . . . normal. Or as normal as
they could be. Marcus, Constance, Ambrose—they all

seemed to be regular vampires again. And other strigoi had shifted back into humans and vampires as well. Most of her wounds, save for the place Ambrose bit her, had also been healed.

She did this?

She groaned in pain as she had shifted in his grip.

"I need to take the venom out of you," he said solemnly. She knew what that meant. More pain. Lila grievously nodded, and Ambrose lifted her onto his lap. "Bite down if you need to," he whispered, and without waiting, she bit his shoulder.

Ambrose pressed his hand to her neck and began to pull the venom from her. Waves of euphoria were leaving her body, pulling sensations and lustful thoughts she had been battling since he trapped her in the crevice. But unlike last time, emptiness wasn't left behind.

She bit down harder, squeezing her eyes shut as tears wet her lashes.

"I'm almost done, love. I-I'm so terribly, awfully, stupidly sorry for what I did. I don't think I can—I don't know what I would've done if I—"

Lila bit harder, then kissed the same spot, shutting Ambrose up on his self-loathing tirade. He continued to pull the venom, and Lila went back to biting his shoulder. His skin tasted oddly sweet.

As he pulled the final strains, Lila unclasped her teeth, leaving a number of bruises and bite marks on his skin. The venom swirling around his hand was a color eerily similar to her hair. A light lavender or lilac, and it too glistened under the moonlight. Her eyes widened at the color, and she looked up to him.

"Interesting, isn't it?" His eyes glowed that same ruby shade that did funny things to her belly and toes.

"Lila?" a small voice called. A voice she hadn't heard in what felt like a millennium. She spun her head around to see Marcus, stumbling toward her. His big brown eyes quickly filled with tears, as he rushed to her side. While she was still on Ambrose's lap, Marcus threw his arms around her and squeezed. "Lila! I'm so sorry! I-I-I didn't know what I was doing. It was like-like I was in a nightmare. I was so scared—"

Lila lifted a hand and brushed the back of his head lightly. "Shh, shh. It's okay now. You're finally safe."

His squeeze tightened and Lila felt herself relax into him. Her brother, though still a vampire, was finally free of the mental prison the Reinicks had locked him in. He was Marcus once again.

"Well, I wouldn't say *safe*, loves." Drusilla scowled, an angry shrill slipping through her words. "What the hell did you do to my babies?"

Ambrose spoke up, his voice defiant. "She is a descendant of the first vampire's human wife—the creator of vampires."

Drusilla gasped and took a step back.

Lila wasn't quite sure what this meant for her, only that someone in her past had also fallen in love with a vampire. With *the* vampire.

"What about the villagers? The strigoi—" she began.

"I believe you cured everyone in the territory of the Crow Court, darling," Ambrose answered. He pulled Lila closer to him protectively. "Your warmth touched everyone."

Lila saw Drusilla's eyebrow twitch. "Well, I can't have a murine ruining all my plans. I've cultivated an army and I will *not* let you ruin that."

"Drusilla, step down," Ambrose ordered.

"And why should I do that? You're still weak, are you not? I could do whatever I want."

She was right. Ambrose had just shifted from a strigoi, *and* he still hadn't had time to fully recover since letting the crows attack. And who knew what her "warmth" did to everyone affected by it.

Ambrose's jaw clenched, and Drusilla cackled. "I was willing to let you live, murine, for the sake of the Reinicks, but now you seem to be a bigger problem than your worth." She stood for a moment and then in a blink, Drusilla threw her fist out, her claws and hand brushing past Lila and wrapping around Ambrose's throat in a tight grip. Ambrose immediately reacted, striking against her but . . . Drusilla wasn't exaggerating, Ambrose was significantly weaker than usual.

Yet that didn't stop him from fighting. He grabbed the stake at Lila's thigh and jabbed it into Drusilla's wrist. She hissed and pulled away, smacking Marcus in the process. Marcus flew back, crashing against Constance.

"Kaz, get the kids in the manor," Ambrose demanded. Out of the trees, hidden in the dark, Kazimir ran out, dashing between the dazed vampires and humans alike, and helped Marcus and Constance up, grabbing their wrists, and pulling them up the manor steps toward the doors.

"B-But, Ambrose, I can help!" Constance called, but Ambrose just shook his head.

"You're still weak too."

Kaz pulled the girl to him, mumbling comforts like, "It's going to be okay. They'll be fine."

Marcus pulled his wrist free and turned to Lila. "I won't leave you again!"

Ambrose stood, lifting Lila to her feet with him. Her legs were still wobbly from the excess energy release, but Ambrose kept his hand around her waist, steading her. She turned to her brother and nodded reassuringly. "It's okay, go with them. I need you to protect Constance and Kaz now."

The once-strigoi humans and vampires around were beginning to snap out of their dazes.

"What's going on?"

"Where are we?"

"It's her . . ."

The other strigoi are riling, Ambrose said through the Concord. *If we can hold off for just a few more moments, we may have a lot more allies than we planned.*

Lila looked around. Many of the cured strigoi seemed incredibly weak, they must've been strigoi for much longer than Ambrose and Marcus. To be in that state for months, or even years, it must take a serious toll on the body and mind. But some of them were already eyeing Drusilla. Eyeing her with disgust and hatred.

Unfortunately, Drusilla seemed to also notice how far outnumbered she was now.

"This was just a taste of my strigoi, Draven. My world *will* come to fruition." She pulled the stake from her wrist and leaped forward. "And I won't let *you* ruin this for me!" She plunged the blade at Lila's heart but was blocked as Ambrose threw his hand up to shield her. The end gushed into his palm, dripping black blood, but Drusilla used the stabbing as a distraction. In the same breath, she pulled Lila from Ambrose's protective hold.

Lila struggled in Drusilla's grip but was spun around, her back to Reclus's chest. She was held down, as though truly in a spider's web, as Drusilla used one hand to bind Lila's wrists, and the other was at her throat, ready to drag her incredibly long, sharp claws through her neck.

Her nails pierced Lila's skin, as droplets of hot liquid dripped down Lila's throat.

"Drusilla," Ciro stepped forward, "we had a deal." The tattooed viper coiled tightly around the arm squeezing Lila's neck. "Kill her and you die too. You know the rules."

Drusilla's grip tightened, for just a moment, before she screamed in frustration and then pushed Lila toward the Reinicks.

Just as she did, Ambrose dashed forward, ready to grab her, but Drusilla stepped in his way, nails at his throat. Ciro caught her before she fell, and the sensation of being in his arms again sent shivers down her entire body.

"We won't let her leave the Morada again. We'll keep her in a thrall. You won't need to worry about her." Ciro didn't take his eyes off of Lila.

"Fine. But if she does, I'll kill her."

Ambrose growled, "You will do no such thing. And she will *not* be returning to the Morada." The usual-liquid gold turned to an icy metal. His fury was palpable. But Ciro didn't care, he just smirked at the Lord of Crows.

"*She* won't have a choice. And if you do anything against that, we'll tear her pretty little head off." Ciro pulled Lila to meet his gaze, his golden eyes piercing into her. "Lila, you want to come with us, don't you? Back to the Viper Morada?"

"Fuck, no!" Ambrose yelled, trying to run to her but was blocked by Drusilla as Ciro held Lila's chin firm. She couldn't look away.

"You want to come with me to the Viper Morada."

"I want to—" she felt the familiar lure of his words, the caress on her mind. She wanted to go, of course. She wanted to be with the Reinicks, she always had.

Hadn't she?

"Lila!"

Ambrose's voice shook her. She didn't want to be with the Reinicks. She hated them! Why would she even—

She was being enthralled. And she knew it. She could *taste* it on her tongue, feel it weave into her mind.

But her will was stronger yet.

The moment she realized the thrall was engulfing her, anger flushed her mind, something sparked in Lila. Something wicked, and bold. Something a little mouse would never do. But Lila wasn't a mouse—she never was.

She was *better.*

Lila was a crow. And crows had a knack for surviving. A greed for revenge.

Play along, she said through the Concord.

Wha—

"Yes. I want to go with you, Ciro."

Lila, what are you doing?

Ciro smiled and caressed her cheek with his thumb. "Excellent." He took her hand.

Don't do this. Don't go with them.

I have to do this. For me. And remember our bargain, part of it was that you would have access to the Viper Morada through me. You can come get me—at any time. But I need to go with them. Let them think I'm under their thrall, and then I will strike.

Ambrose's eyes were grief-stricken. *Why choose now to stop being a little mouse? You don't have to prove anything to me.*

I don't want to be a mouse, Ambrose. I need to get them out of my head. I need to fight back. I need to prove it to myself. As you said . . . I need to be better. *I know you'll take me as I am . . . but I'm not sure I can take myself as I am.*

She heard him sigh in her mind. She knew she had already won him over. He *had* to let her do this.

Okay, then. If you are positive you want to do this, love. Only crows can hold grudges as much as you.

That almost made Lila slip from her act to smile.

But you must *keep our line of communication open. Do not shut me out. And if either of them so much as touch you—*

I'll call for you. I promise.

Ambrose stopped fighting Drusilla. Took a step back and fell to his knees.

Okay. I don't like it. But okay. I'll play along.

"Please, Lila. Don't go. I-I can't . . . not without you. I-I . . ." His performance was admirable. If Lila hadn't just heard his agreement, she would've thought it was genuine. In fact, some part of her felt like it still might be.

The previous strigoi were beginning to rile, demanding answers.

"Draven?"

"What are we doing here?!"

"What did you do to us, Reclus!"

The Reinicks and Drusilla put their backs to each other, shifting into their beastly forms, reading to fly away.

"Murine," Hektor cooed. His voice was thick from his thrall, but it felt like heavy, gross smoke as it waved over Lila. Smoke she was all too aware of as his thrall wasn't working even a little bit. "How about a parting gift to your Crow Lord? Stab him through the heart." Lila hesitated but fought herself and plucked the metal dagger from her hip. "Not with that. With this." The damn bastard thrust a wooden stake into her hand.

You know where my heart is. Stab next to it.

But—

You have to.

"No, Little Mouse. Break through their thrall. It's me!"

Lila stepped toward him, still hesitating.

"Well, this *is* interesting," Drusilla cooed.

I don't want to hurt you, Lila thought to him.

I know, love. I know. You won't hurt me though. You never could as long as you—

Ambrose stopped himself, just as Lila stood right before him.

"Lila. Please . . ."

She lifted the stake, aiming it just next to his heart, sure to be completely clear of it.

"I told you I'd let you do anything to me, and I meant it." His eyes sparkled as he watched her. With him on his knees, she could look down at him with all the privacy, as her hair curtained her off from the other vampires.

And I mean anything . . .

Ambrose, I don't want to stab you again.

He held her wrist. "If this is the way it must be. I don't want to live in this world without you."

Lila felt tears prickle her eyes. She wanted to sob and throw her arms around him. But they couldn't fight Drusilla, Hektor, and Ciro right now. They were still too weak. And she wanted to follow her resolve.

Don't cry, darling. Don't let the act slip.

Lila gave the slightest nod, only for him to see.

The old strigoi were closing in, and Lila knew the moment she stabbed him and ran back to the Reinicks, they'd be off. Good, they won't wait to make sure he crumbled to ash.

As Lila positioned the stake next to Ambrose's heart, his hand warming her shaking fist, she thought one final message to him as she plunged the wood into him.

Ambrose, I love you.

He grunted in pain, his blood coating their hands, but he smiled at her, tears welling his eyes and finally breaking free, slipping down his cheek.

And I love you.

She pulled the stake from his chest, the stake he had given her, and tucked it back into the holster at her thigh.

And then he finished his performance.

Ambrose hissed in pain and crumbled to the ground, bleeding everywhere.

Quickly, Lila turned back to the Reinick brothers and demanded, before anyone stayed long enough to see that Ambrose was still very much alive, "Take me home. Take me back to the Viper Morada."

ACKNOWLEDGMENTS

I feel like I just woke up from a wild fever dream. *The Crow Lord* practically wrote itself throughout my entire writing and editing process. Lila and Ambrose encompassed my mind more so than any character ever has, and I am so beyond thrilled with how they turned out, how this book turned out, and I can't wait to write what happens to them next!

This book wouldn't have been possible without the endless support of my loved ones.

To Mike Burke, you are my sunlight. The day to my night. Thank you for always being so supportive, even if you don't really get why I'm so in love with monsters. You're the best cat-dad to Maki, and we love you!

To my mom, Lizette Lopez—specifically—thank you for loving me as much as you do, supporting me as much as you do, and nurturing my whacko brain as much as you do. I wouldn't be writing vampire smut if it weren't for you, and I think that's a lot better than being addicted to drugs or something, so I think you did a pretty great job at raising me. I love you to the moon and back.

To my parents and family (all a hundred of you), thanks for constantly supporting me in all I do and being the best hype team I could ask for. This author-dream is a lot harder than the media makes it out to be, and because of you guys, I am able to continue to persevere through the hardships.

Anto Marr once again blew me away with her amazing cover and the layout elements of this book are just to die for. I want them all tattooed on me *right now!* Thank you for keeping me (mostly) sane during this whole process and for being my go-to vampire homie. Thank you for letting me sleep over on nights when my brain became too much and thank you for literally always being there for me. I love you so much and as you know, you're stuck with me forever.

Brandi McGugan, you're also stuck with me forever. I love you so much and I thank you for helping me develop the babies, Ambrose and Lila. You are forever the best hype man and cheerleader, and I know if I am ever doubting myself or anything I create, I can go to you for a pick-me-up.

To Jessi Harpe and the writing club, thank you for always being helpful when I was stuck and letting me talk your ears off with ideas.

I'd like to say a special thank you to Elsie Alarcon, Kathleen Condy, Larissa Moyer, Ren Rice, Samantha Fabry, and Wren Blomeley for reading and giving such great feedback in such a delicate time. You all are the best and I appreciate you all for being the first readers of *The Crow Lord*.

And finally, I would like to thank you, reader. Thank you for reading this book that enthralled my heart and mind for almost a year. I hope you found it as enjoyable to read as I did to write, and I promise Lila, Ambrose, and the whole of Malvania will return soon.

ABOUT THE AUTHOR

J. M. Failde (fah-eel-deh) spent just over one hundred fortnights rigorously studying the complexities of the English language at Florida International University. While she is not conjuring up stories, she can be found searching for *el chupacabra*, befriending the ghost in her house, or dying her hair a new shade of blue. Failde currently resides in her gothic manor on the outskirts of Atlanta, Georgia, with her partner, Mike, and her familiar—the round but feisty calico cat, Maki. Follow her on Instagram @jmfailde.

WWW.JMFAILDE.COM